THE OUTSIDER

A WASTELANDER NOVEL

E.S. LUCK

Contents

For the outsiders of this world: take up space and use your voice. Your soft moments, your gentleness, and your joy, even in the darkest times, are your greatest rebellion. Remember: never underestimate even the smallest and weakest of creatures.

Content Note

The Outsider is set in a post-apocalyptic world where daily survival is a challenge, and violence and brutality are commonplace. As a result, readers should expect themes and events that may be upsetting. Your mental health is important, so please be kind to yourself and practice self-care as you read, particularly if you find some of these subjects difficult.

Readers can expect graphic violence & death, sexual violence (implied, off-page), human trafficking, family abuse & alcoholism, depictions of cult rituals related to a fictitious religion, cannibalism, grief and discussions about grief, infidelity (NOT between the MMC & FMC), discussions about infertility, mild drug and alcohol use, mild homophobia (from antagonist), explicit sexual intimacy between consenting adults, and a cliffhanger ending.

Part I: Odessa's Eye

But who hath seen her wave her hand?

  Or at the casement seen her stand?
Or is she known in all the land,
The Lady of Shalott?

-"The Lady of Shalott", Alfred Lord Tennyson

CHAPTER 1

Claire

The world was on fire, and no one could save me but him.

My Wastelander was near, but he wouldn't make it to me in time to stop the man sitting on top of me from killing me.

As I lay on the hard ground of the trailer camp that had become a battleground, I looked up into the face of my killer: a black mask emblazoned with a golden eye that obscured his entire face. Only a fine black mesh, fitted into the sclera of the golden eye, revealed the dim light of his eyes behind it. The emblem glittered in the flickering light of the flames that engulfed the wooden barricade around our camp. That eye represented everything I'd lost: my sister, my husband, my home, as well as the cultists who now hunted me for reasons I didn't understand.

The masked man's white-blond mohawk was his only defining feature, the only thing I remembered as I plunged my tiny blade into his neck.

I felt his life drain away as blood spurted out like a firehose. He clutched at his spraying throat, then collapsed on top of me, fumbling uselessly for purchase. Pinned to the ground, I was forced to stare at that hideous mask.

"Blood on your hands," he croaked, his voice a death rattle. "You live on borrowed time, girl. Time borrowed for you by a man you'll never belong to, in a world you'll never belong to. The next blood on your hands will be his."

A terrible dread gripped me then, as I somehow *felt* his grim prophecy coming true, burgeoning from his words like an angel of death spreading its wings. Only it was me—*I* was the angel of death.

The world shifted somehow, and my assailant removed his mask, only to reveal my friend Asha's face beneath. Her dead eyes bore a hole through me, and her voice came as a death rattle, a groan from the void: "Have you forgotten me, Claire?"

A strangled scream tore from my throat, a scream of nature that seemed to penetrate and shatter a deathly stillness deep inside of me. A stillness that had been there perhaps my whole life, a paralysis that had been gifted to me the moment I'd been born inside the compound, one that said *don't fight, don't resist, it's useless.* But I didn't want to be that person anymore—the one who sat in her learned helplessness and let life float gently by, trapped by chains that she'd never felt until they were gone.

"Hey, it's okay," a familiar voice soothed me, and I felt a hand on my clammy forehead. "You're alright, baby. Wake up."

My eyes fluttered open, and I became aware that I was lying on my back in my sleeping bag, inside the tent that we'd pitched in a copse of trees. John was lying beside me, propped up on his elbow and stroking my forehead, his expression concerned.

"John?" I murmured, reaching out for him.

"I'm here," he replied, then bent to kiss me.

I clung to the kiss, wrapping my arms around his neck and pulling him deeper, urgent with the need to feel him close to me. He was the only thing that made me feel safe now after the destruction of the only home I'd known in the Wasteland.

"Another dream, huh?" John said when we finally broke apart. "Come here."

He'd laid his sleeping bag next to mine. He rolled back on top of it, pulling me with him. He snuggled me in close, still wrapped up in my

sleeping bag. It was the second time he'd rescued me from a screaming night terror since we left camp.

"You on watch?" I mumbled, still sleepy as I buried my face in his
shirt.

"Just got off," he said. "Kimmy just went out when you started
screaming your head off. Scared the shit out of us."

"Sorry," I said, embarrassed. "I can't stop them."

He pressed a kiss against my hair. "Tell me about it."

I did, recounting the bit about 'borrowed time', but omitting the
appearance of Asha. Seeing her in the dream filled me with crushing
guilt that I didn't knowhow to talk about.

"I'm scared," I said before I could stop myself, and I heard the
edge in my voice. "I'm scared the cult will find me. I'm scared that
they'll hurt you and Kimmy. I'm scared it'll be all my fault. And I
still don't understand why they want me. Why they cared enough
to send people after me."

I didn't realize I was trembling until John tightened his grip
around me. I looked up at him, and his soft brown eyes were determined.

"Hush," he said as he raised a hand to stroke my cheek. "No more
about this being your fault, you understand me?"

"But—"

"No more," John said firmly. "You can't help that these people
attacked you. I'm doing everything I can to make sure it never
happens again. I'll keep you safe."

I nodded. I knew that. He'd proven it too many times for me to
doubt.

"I just don't want you to have to," I said with a sigh, relaxing
against him.

"You let me worry about that," he replied, cradling my head with
a tenderness that made me ache. I'd never been loved the way John
loved me—unreservedly and fully, without question. I wouldn't
have believed it possible had I not felt the same way about him.

John stroked my hair for a long while, soothing me back into
drowsiness. I'd almost drifted off again when he spoke, his voice
barely a whisper.

"That's what family does for each other."

"But I'm not..." I trailed off, too sleepy to finish my contradiction.

"Shh," he murmured. "Coming home with me means you're my family now. Argue, and you'll be skinning the rabbits—blood, guts, and all—all by yourself for a week. And maybe a spanking to really drive home the point."

"Don't threaten me with a good time," I mumbled, and a low chuckle reverberated in his chest. "It's been over a week."

There was an unfortunate heat between my legs at the thought. As much as I loved Kimmy, camping with her all the time meant zero privacy. I missed being in bed with John. I missed his hot, naked body and the way his touch made me arch and moan with pleasure. I missed watching his tight control snap when he came, and the way he groaned my name.

"I know," John sighed. "Trust me, I've been...painfully aware."

The bulge of his erection brushed against my belly, and I giggled. He grinned, then kissed the top of my head before readjusting, preparing to sleep. I exhaled slowly, and I could sense his smile as I fell back into a peaceful slumber in his arms.

❋

Somehow, it'd only been a week since we'd left the camp. It'd been a flurry of scavenging for supplies, covering our tracks, and foraging for food. Our tent barely slept two people, and the city outskirts were dangerous enough that one of us always had to be on watch at night anyway. We slept in shifts, which was tiring and left a weary ache in my bones that wouldn't go away. We hadn't seen any major gang activity since we avoided the city centre, but we'd spotted a few lone scavengers who were looking for supplies just like we were. We lay low, always choosing stealth over confrontation. We'd been sighted in only one instance, by a man and woman who were painfully thin and, as far as I could see, unarmed. They scurried away before we even had the chance to approach.

Nobody trusted anybody in the Wasteland. They couldn't afford to.

October was upon us as we prepared for our trip northward to the Valley, the remote homesteading community that John and Kimmy were from. In my head, it'd been built up as a kind of wilderness Eden, beautiful and safe, where they had things like running water and electricity that nobody outside the compounds had anymore. First, however, we'd need to traverse over a thousand kilometres, all on foot, through dense wilderness and inclement weather. By John's best estimate, it was going to take us at least a month of hard travel.

Seven months ago, I'd lived inside the Cave, a walled compound that had been my home my entire life. A brutal attack destroyed my home and forced me out into the Wasteland—our name for the outside world. An insurgent cult wearing mysterious masks painted with a distinct gold eye had killed everyone in the compound, including my then-husband, Neil. My dreams were still haunted by my mother and my sister, Holly, who'd revealed themselves as part of the cult that destroyed my world. Holly helped me and my friend Asha escape the compound in secret, but I hadn't seen her since.

Asha. She and I had been separated after an encounter with a pack of cannibals. I didn't know if she was even still alive. I still ached at the thought of what might have happened to her. More than that, I had a growing sense of what my father would've called survivor's guilt. It didn't seem right that I should have a future with a man I loved, in a home where I might finally be safe, when she was gone.

Despite my fear and distrust of Wastelanders and utter lack of survival skills, John and Kimmy took me in after John rescued me from the cannibals. Over time, John earned my trust and eventually, my love. He'd protected me from the moment we met, and eventually, the heart of gold beneath his gruff exterior was impossible not to love. I loved him like I'd never loved anyone, including Neil, who I'd only married because it'd been arranged for us by the shadowy leaders of the Cave. I'd never felt like I would've died for anyone until John, but it wasn't difficult when I knew he'd do the same for me in a heartbeat, and we'd been in situations where it was a real possibility.

The masked murderers had then resurfaced and attacked the camp where I'd lived with John and Kimmy until a week ago. They'd come to find me and had tried to perform some sort of cult ritual. We'd fought them off, but it was why we'd left with such haste: there were more of them, and they somehow knew I was there. It wasn't safe anymore.

"Not much here," Kimmy called from the kitchen area of a partially collapsed house we were searching.

"This lovely set of broken dishes," I volunteered, holding up a large shard of pottery that'd been on the floor. "Perfect for entertaining."

Kimmy giggled. "The only use left for that is to stab someone's eye out."

"I'm not going to ask how you came up with that," I replied, raising an eyebrow.

She laughed again. "Good, because I'm not gonna tell you."

There was a dull thump as John landed on the worn wooden floor. The staircase had collapsed, so he'd climbed up to the third floor and rappelled back down using a long length of cord he'd brought from the camp. He'd attached a grappling hook that he'd fashioned himself, and when I'd asked what we could use it for, he'd chuckled.

"Looks like someone's never had to climb," he said.

"I'm not sure—given the twenty-foot walls around the place—that climbing was a valued skill at home," I said, raising an eyebrow.

"Fair enough," he said with a nod. "I'll show you."

We'd spent an hour using it to climb various trees, until I admitted that it would've been much harder to climb without it, especially the ones without low branches.

"Anything useful?" I asked as I watched John approach through a gaping hole in the wall, rolling up the cord as he went. The fading rays of sun illuminated his tall figure, and I stopped for a moment just to admire him. His lean, strong body radiated heat that kept me warm on the colder autumn nights, and the more I stared, the more I wished we were alone...and I wouldn't complain if we were naked, either.

"Nah," he replied with a shrug, but the upturned corner of his mouth told me that he knew I'd been checking him out.

While John and Kimmy had found supplies for the trip before today, I still needed a winter coat, which would be a major problem the further north we went. John and Kimmy had winter clothes, but all I had was a rain jacket. Thankfully, I'd knitted half a dozen pairs of socks, a pair of mittens, and a hat when we lived at the camp, but the lack of a good coat was a problem. We'd found some decent winter boots for me, which were a little large, but wearing thick socks made them wearable.

"Just keep your eyes peeled for a coat," John had said to me. "We'll do the rest."

We'd hunted for ammunition and for useful materials and tools—anything from sewing needles to salt for food preservation. We'd had decent luck, but the winter coat still eluded us. Thankfully, for now, the weather hadn't turned cold enough during the day that I needed one immediately.

The sun was setting, though. It was about to get much colder, and I wanted to make camp for the night.

"Time to call it," John said with a sigh. "We head back out in the morning."

"Good, I'm starving," Kimmy grumbled, and she strode back through the hole in the wall to the outside.

John moved to follow, but I caught his elbow and backed against the wall, pulling him with me so that he trapped me against it. He made a noise of confusion but was quickly muted by my lips smothering his. I gripped the front of his jacket and pulled him in deeper, slipping my tongue past his lips to taste him, and he groaned, soft and low in his throat. It was the sexiest sound, and I wanted to hear more.

"Claire," he mumbled against my lips, attempting to pull back. "Not here."

"Yes, here," I said, my grip on his jacket tightening as I pressed my knee between his thighs and rubbed against his growing erection.

"Fuck," he grunted, and I sensed victory.

He surrendered and grabbed my face in his hands, crushing his mouth against mine and flattening me against the crumbling wall. His tongue plunged into my mouth, giving me what I craved, and a helpless moan escaped me. We came up for air a moment later, both panting.

"Not here," he repeated, and moved back with effort. "It's not safe."

"I want you," I said, kissing down his jawline as he shuddered. "I miss you."

John's expression softened. "I miss you too. It's not that I don't want you...Christ, I do. But it's not the right time or place."

I sighed, defeated. "I know."

"Hey, if you two are done ignoring our surroundings, can we make camp?" Kimmy called, evidently impatient. "And it's gonna be dark soon."

I flushed, and John grinned before planting a kiss on my forehead and leading me back outside.

We camped out in an abandoned strip mall on the edge of a derelict suburb. It was far enough from the city core that it was less likely to attract gangs, but close enough that supply trips were manageable. The buildings were crumbling, but they held their shape enough that we could camp inside, mostly sheltered from the elements. We set up our tent and got dinner started.

Kimmy built the fire and started roasting some of the meat we had from a hunt two days earlier. Meanwhile, John and I foraged for edible plants. I had my homemade logbook open, and we referenced it as we wandered through a small, wooded area beside the strip mall.

As luck would have it, John spotted a bunch of blackberry bushes. Birds had gotten to some of the berries, but there were enough there to make up a sizable harvest. We loaded them into my bag and headed back. There was a grassy patch some distance away from the campfire, and we both sat cross-legged to wash the berries.

I'd been scheming the whole way back, and as I watched John methodically washing blackberries across from me, I decided to put it into action. I let out a low, quiet sort of sigh, staring intently at the berries in my hands. Out of the corner of my eye, I saw John glance up at me, but when I didn't say anything, he returned to his work.

I sighed again a moment later, more dramatically this time, and he looked up again.

"You okay over there?" he asked.

"Yes," I answered, then chewed my lip. "I just wish we were alone."

"I know, sweetheart," he said sympathetically, stroking the back of my hand with his thumb. "Just be patient. I'll find a moment for us to slip away once we're finally out of the city. A couple more days, maybe."

A couple more days? I scoffed.

I glanced over at Kimmy, judging that she was far enough that if I kept my voice low, she wouldn't hear.

"Well, whenever it happens again," I said, making my tone huskier, "I have some plans."

John raised an eyebrow and studied me. His soft brown eyes had a hint of yellow in them that I'd only noticed after hours of gazing at them, and they shone like dark amber in the fading light. I could tell he was considering whether to ask me what exactly I had in mind. To help him decide, I lifted one of the berries to my mouth and bit into it, slowly and deliberately, not taking my eyes off him. He cleared his throat and looked away, and I knew I'd had the desired effect.

"Don't you want to hear my plans?" I asked innocently.

John seemed to fight with himself for a moment. "I know what you're up to. It won't work."

"What won't work?" I asked with a tiny shrug. "I wanted to tell you so that you'll be prepared, but if you don't want to know...I guess I'll just have to think about it by myself while you're on watch."

He scowled. "Now you're not playing fair."

"Am I not?" I said, toying with a couple of the berries between my fingers. "Maybe I'll think about our last time in the woods when you gave me a spank over your knee to make me come. All the while, you'll be outside, unaware that just ten feet away, I'm coming to the thought of you."

"Christ," John said, palpable longing in his voice. "You liked that, huh? You been thinking about it a lot?"

I exhaled sharply. "How could I not?"

He was leaning slightly forward now, and his expression was a little tortured, which made me grin.

"I want you every minute," I breathed. "I think about cornering you someplace private and kissing and touching you until you beg to take me. I think about crawling into the tent during Kimmy's watch and riding you, knowing you can't make a sound, until you can't stand it anymore. I think about teasing you with my mouth, sucking you off slowly, tormenting you."

I leaned in and pecked his lips.

"I want to push you to your limits, Wastelander," I whispered against his mouth. "I want to bring you to your knees."

I slowly backed away, watching John's reaction. His pupils slightly dilated, and his hard gaze bore a hole through me. His mouth tightened, and he clenched his jaw. For a brief moment, I worried he was somehow angry; his whole body seemed coiled tight like a spring. Then he called out.

"Kim! Keep an eye on things. Claire and I are going for a walk."

Before I knew what was happening, he'd pulled me to my feet, holding my hand in a death grip.

"What?" Kimmy called back, sounding confused.

John stopped only briefly. "I'm doing some teaching. We'll be back soon."

Without waiting for another reply, he pulled me along with him as he strode toward the edge of strip mall's former parking lot.

CHAPTER 2

John

"**Y**ou think you can play that game with me?" I growled. "I invented it."

I'd hastily bolted the metal door of a tiny outbuilding and pushed Claire against it, grabbing her face in my hands and forcing her lips against mine. My cock pulsed almost painfully at the heat of her, at the way she moaned as I forced my tongue into her mouth.

My mouth moved to her neck, sucking and nibbling, and I spotted her expression: smug as hell, with a smile that said she was very proud of herself for making me lose control.

"On your knees," I ordered. "I'm going to fuck that smile off your face."

Claire bit her lip, taking a short little breath that told me how turned on she was. That did nothing to shrink my hardened cock, which strained against my pants.

Slowly, she lowered herself to the ground. I unbuckled my belt to free my cock before giving it a couple pumps and moving to her mouth.

"For the record," Claire said, raising an eyebrow, "I think smugness is warranted, given how quickly the pants came down."

Before I could give some sarcastic answer, she'd taken my cock between her lips. I groaned as she started to suck. I moved a hand into her hair, holding her in place so I could more easily fuck her incredibly hot mouth.

"Christ," I gasped out, bracing my other hand against the door. "I've wanted to fuck that pretty mouth for days. Who knew it was so filthy?"

Claire moaned around my cock, pleased by the praise, and I already felt ready to come in her mouth.

"I should take you over my knee for breaking me like this," I said, low and husky. "Would you like that?"

A shiver went through her, and without stopping, she looked up at me and gave a little nod. Fuck.

Panting, I moved away with effort, then pulled her to her feet. I looked around the tiny shed. There was barely any standing room; most of it was taken up by a utility tank.

"Put your hands on that," I said, my voice almost a snarl as I spun her over to the tank. "Don't move."

Claire shuddered, then obeyed, which only aroused me more. I shoved her pants to her knees, baring her perfect, round ass. She squeaked as I gave it a little spank.

"Yeah? This what you wanted, princess?" I taunted. "You wanted me to fuck you anywhere I could? Take you openly? Hmm?"

I gave her ass another sharp slap, and she cried out.

"Yes," she choked out. "God, yes, I wanted that."

"Good," I said, my hand wandering between her spread thighs. "Let's see how wet you are, then."

Claire shuddered as my fingers found the hot slit of her cunt. She was soaking wet, and my fingers were instantly slick as I slid them inside her and fucked her slowly. She gasped and her grip on the metal tightened.

"Filthy girl," I murmured in her ear. "Teasing me like that. I bet you were soaked this whole time, weren't you?"

She huffed, her expression defiant.

"Teach me, then," she said, her breath uneven. "That's what you're supposed to be doing, isn't it?"

I gave her another hard spank on her ass, and she whimpered.

"Yeah," I replied, "and you'll get exactly the education you deserve."

I pushed her upper body over the tank, then moved between her soft, pretty thighs and entered her from behind. She gasped at the penetration, then moaned loudly as I took her with a hard thrust. I grunted at the feel of her. She was so hot, so wet, so...mine. I grabbed a fistful of her long hair, kissing the dark red strands.

"Fuck," I groaned as she clenched around me. "You always feel so. Goddamn. Incredible."

I gave her a couple more slow, hard thrusts, gritting my teeth against the unbelievable sensation of sliding into her slick cunt. She moaned helplessly, scrambling to rub her clit. I caught her wrist and stopped her.

"No," I growled. "You made me suffer, so now, you're not going to come until I say."

"John," she groaned, openly begging. "I need it so badly."

I pressed a hard kiss against her shoulder but didn't budge. Instead, I fucked her harder over the metal tank, pumping into her without mercy until she clapped a hand over her mouth to muffle her frustrated cries. I covered her hand with mine, pulling her toward me.

"Mine," I panted into her ear, right at the edge, kissing her hair. "Mine to protect, mine to love, mine to fuck."

I pushed into her hard and groaned as I came, my cock pulsing with each wave of intense pleasure until I felt wrung out and shaky. Claire whimpered again, stuck at the edge of her own orgasm. I pulled out of her and stepped back, watching pearly liquid seep onto her thighs.

"My come is spilling out of you," I said harshly. "That's what you wanted, isn't it?"

"Yes, God, yes," Claire gasped. "Lesson learned! For the love of God, John, I need to come."

I smirked and slapped her ass a couple more times, enjoying myself. She was going to bite through her bottom lip if she wasn't careful. Finally, I took pity and slid my fingers back inside her, pumping into her roughly, and she squeaked in relief.

"Touch yourself," I said. "Show me how hard you can come for me now that I've teased you."

Her hand shot between her legs so eagerly that I chuckled. I pumped my fingers in time with her strokes, and delivered more short, hard spanks on her ass with my free hand. She made small, helpless sounds after each impact, and got even wetter.

"So good," I growled. "Come on, beautiful, you're almost there."

It didn't take long. Another minute and she was crying out, her voice hoarse and her cunt pulsing around my fingers. When she finished, I withdrew, then reached down and pulled her panties back up.

"You're going to walk around like that for the rest of the day," I said, stroking her ass through the fabric. "Every time you move, you'll feel me, and remember that you're mine."

Claire shivered, and I hauled her against me, her back to my chest. I put my arms around her and pressed gentle kisses against her neck, letting her recover. She relaxed, covering my hands with hers.

"Was that good?" I murmured. "I wasn't too rough?"

"No," she sighed. "You were just rough enough. I liked it."

"Good."

I kissed her once she was facing me again, cradling her head in my hands.

"So," she said after a moment, "what are we going to tell Kimmy that you taught me?"

I grinned and kissed her again. "Discipline."

After we got back from our 'walk', Kimmy teased me and Claire mercilessly as we had dinner around the campfire.

"What did John teach you?" she asked, grinning at Claire's beet red face. "I'm guessing, with how long you were gone, it was pretty *hands-on*."

Claire cringed, and I laughed. I was used to Kimmy, and after eighteen months of travelling together, she couldn't have embarrassed me if she tried. Claire's shyness was cute, though, so I joined in.

"There were hands involved," I said, and Claire shot me a glare. I chuckled. "More than that, I can't say, on pain of death."

"That's right," Claire said, crossing her arms. "So quit while you're ahead."

Figuring we'd embarrassed her enough, I wrapped a blanket around Claire and me and moved in close to her.

"Tell me something about the Valley," she said as she took her sketchbook out of her pack.

I thought for a moment, trying to think of what else I could tell her. Claire never seemed to get tired of hearing about our home, and I'd answered this question a hundred different times.

"Summerhurst is a bit off by itself, because the east side of the valley used to be all farm and pasture. Closest to us is Brookside, which is the Harding homestead; Dreamspring, which is the Armstrongs'; and Greystone, which is a horse ranch owned by the McNeils. Over on the west side, there are maybe 30 families, and to the north, another 20. The south end, with the glacier lake, has the most people...I'd guess around 60 families live around the lake."

"Wow," Claire said as she flipped through the pages. "It'll be interesting to interact with people again."

"What are me and Kimmy then, chopped liver?" I asked, chuckling.

She grinned and snuggled close. "You know what I mean."

I watched as she started shading a sketch of a horse she'd started the day before. When she finished, she confided in me that she'd never seen one—only pictures or in old movies.

"We left our two with the Armstrongs," I told her. "I'll teach you to ride."

She smiled and kissed me. "I'd love that—you being the expert and all."

"Don't know about that," I said. "Even after all the training I did, they didn't give me the outrider job."

That was still a thorn in my side. Outriders were the protectors of the Valley. They guarded our borders, responded to emergencies, and enforced our laws. My grandfather had been one of them, and for a long time, I'd wanted to follow in his footsteps. So much of my survival training, along with endless drills on horseback, had been focused on that goal. But it didn't matter in the end.

I'd told Claire about that forgotten dream this past week. I mostly kept it to myself, but she'd been sweet and encouraging, wanting me to try again once we got home. *I can't think of a better protector than you,* she'd said, with a smile that made me feel all warm and fuzzy on the inside.

Love really does make you into a hopeless dumbass. I'd never thought that would be me until I met her. And worse, I somehow didn't even care. I just wanted her to smile at me like that all the time.

"That's because you left though, right?" Claire asked, returning to her drawing.

I sighed. "Yes and no. It was kind of political, I guess. I got along okay with Geoff—the chief—but...not everyone was keen."

That was putting it mildly. But I didn't want Claire to worry about any of that. She had enough on her plate without digging up history that was best left buried, and I'd just gotten her to really trust me completely. I couldn't risk that. Couldn't stand to have her look at me the way she used to—as a brutal savage. Not when she was so genuinely proud of me. Not when I'd been thinking about asking her to marry me.

I hadn't found the right moment yet. We hadn't had much time alone together other than our stolen romp in the utility shed, and she deserved better than a proposal in front of an old water tank. I'd never thought much about getting married before, but the thought of Claire being my wife made me happier than I'd ever been.

"Who wouldn't be keen on you?" Claire asked, amused. "Tall, dark, handsome. You swear like a sailor, but other than that, quite the gallant gentleman."

I laughed. *Gallant gentleman* was not how anyone would describe me, whether they liked me or not.

"What gave me away? The cyberpunk hair or the leather jacket?"

She grinned and gave me a kiss. Kimmy, on the other hand, shot me a pointed look across the campfire that said she didn't approve of me not answering Claire's question. We'd had words about this in the last few days, but my answer was the same: *too fucking bad.*

"I'm excited for the Valley," Claire murmured.

The firelight made her eyes sparkle, and her pale, perfectly smooth skin almost seemed to glow. Not for the first time, I was hit by how gorgeous she was. As a compound resident, the implant she'd had since birth had turned her from an already-attractive woman into a knockout beauty. It made her look almost uncanny—like she couldn't quite be real.

"It won't be easy," Kimmy said as she cleaned her rifle. "You need to be prepared, Claire. You won't be trusted or liked. You'll need to keep your head down and stay alert."

I sighed as Claire's face fell. We still had a long trip ahead, and we needed to focus on what was in front of us. *Or,* a voice in my head nagged, *you just don't like seeing her scared.*

"Would...I mean, do you think they'll hurt me?" Claire asked in a small voice.

I'd put a bullet in anyone who tried, I'd promised her.

"No," I answered firmly. "Of course not."

"You don't know that, John," Kimmy said impatiently. "We have no idea how they'll react because no outsiders have been allowed since we were little kids. You know that Jameson won't make it easy on her. Or on us, for that matter."

I shot Kimmy a warning look. "Jameson will do what he always does: bitch to the council about how unfair it all is, then when he's outvoted, bitch about how unfair that is. Rinse and repeat. The guy's all talk, just like Granddad said."

"Maybe," Kimmy said, but she looked frustrated. "His boys are trouble, though. They always have been."

She wasn't wrong, unfortunately.

"Who's Jameson?" Claire asked, looking back and forth between me and Kimmy.

She bit her lip in that way she did when she was anxious, and my instinct was always to protect her. I reached over and tucked her hair behind her ear.

"Nobody important," I said gently. "Old drama from our grandparents' time. Not for you to worry about."Kimmy huffed. "What happened between them—"

"—is ancient history," I cut in, irritated. "And it was when we left. We've been gone nearly two years now, so who knows what's changed since then."

"Exactly!" Kimmy burst out. "We have no idea. All I'm saying is that Claire needs to tread lightly and be aware of threats. Even if the council is understanding by some miracle, that doesn't mean there aren't those who would take things into their own hands if opportunity knocked."

I opened my mouth to argue some more, but Claire laid a hand on my arm.

"It's alright," she said softly, then gave Kimmy a brief nod. "I appreciate the warning, Kim. I know it'll be difficult; I wasn't trying to diminish that."

Kimmy crossed her arms. "Good. It's just...the more I think about it, the more worried I get. Now that we're finally headed home, shit just got real for me."

Claire smiled weakly. "I know the feeling."

It was uncomfortably quiet after that. I sensed Claire's worry and hated that there wasn't a hell of a lot I could do about it. Finally, Kimmy announced she was going to bed and crawled into the tent. Some part of me knew her warning was valid, but I still watched her go with irritation.

"You should get some sleep," Claire said, moving in to lay her head against my chest. "It's my turn to be on first watch."

I caught her chin in my hand and tipped her face up to me. Her expression was guarded.

"Don't be afraid," I said in a low voice. "I'll look after you."

"I know," she replied with a nod, then traced my bottom lip with her thumb. "But who will look after you, Wastelander? I don't want to bring misery down on you."

"You won't," I insisted. "I can take care of myself. So can Kimmy. It'll be fine."

She didn't look totally convinced, but at least she relaxed her shoulders. I kissed her goodnight and headed for the tent. Our busy days meant that Kimmy was already asleep. I crawled into my sleeping bag and stared at the ceiling.

I just wanted to keep my Claire safe. The Valley were my people and my problem. Whatever happened, I'd deal with them myself.

CHAPTER 3

Claire

The night was quiet, until it wasn't.

Keeping watch was often a dull exercise. It was pitch black and quiet, so I kept myself busy with such thrilling activities as listening to the crickets and counting the cracks in the floor in front of me. Every so often, I made slow, silent patrols of the small building we were camped in with my pistol or rabbit gun in hand. The early October air was chilly—a portent of things to come, unfortunately—and I clasped my blanket tighter around myself.

I was shading the leaves on my sketch of a tree when there was a faint scraping sound outside, like something being dragged over concrete. I frowned, listening closely, then got up and went to the broken window at the front of the building. I heard voices speaking rapidly back and forth, and then the glow of flashlights.

Before I could so much as turn to alert the other two, the night suddenly lit up with orange and yellow light. Fire. It came from an old, rusty dumpster that'd been dragged out in front of the building, thirty feet away. Three figures, all dressed in black, held torches lit from the inferno they'd set in the dumpster. The firelight revealed black masks that covered their whole faces, painted with big, shimmering gold eyes.

The cult.

I nearly tripped over my feet as I turned and ran to the tent, yanking open the flap. I violently shook John and Kimmy awake, a stream of jumbled alarm coming out of my mouth. My heart was pounding in my ears.

"Claire, you're not making sense," Kimmy said urgently. "Slow down."

I swallowed briefly, trying to slow my frantic breath.

"They're out there," was all I could manage, looking at John with a plea in my eyes. "*Them.*"

He seemed to understand, because his eyes widened in alarm, and he sprang to his feet. Kimmy followed, grabbing her pistol from under her pillow. At that instant, there was the unmistakable *bang* of a gunshot hitting the exterior concrete wall. They were firing on us.

John pulled me down onto the ground, covering me with his body. Seconds later, he and Kimmy scrambled on their knees around the tent, gathering weapons and their packs. Once armed, we crawled out of the tent, trying to get a better view of our attackers. More shots erupted, and I found myself pressed on the ground again, John on top of me. Kimmy lay next to us, her teeth gritted.

He spoke to her in a low, rapid voice.

"They can't find Claire. You and I are going to draw them away and pick them off as we can. Let's go."

Kimmy gave a short nod, and all of us rose to our knees.

"John, I can't stay here," I whispered, terrified. "Don't leave me."

He found my hand in the darkness and kissed it.

"I'll come back for you," he replied, squeezing my hand. "Keep the rabbit gun ready. Watch my back."

I tried to argue, but he dropped my hand and signaled to Kimmy. They stood, staying low, and made a break for the back door. Meanwhile, gunfire continued outside, peppering the concrete with ear-splitting bangs.

Staying low to the floor, I crept to one of the windows, peering over the edge. There were six dark figures out front, all wearing black tactical uniforms and carrying rifles. It was too dark to see anything else. The dumpster I'd seen still burned, illuminating the night with a strange amber glow. They'd stopped firing. What struck me was that they appeared perfectly at ease—not as though they were leading a charge. Rather, they were waiting for something.

Whatever they were waiting for, it didn't come. Instead, there was another loud bang, and one of the masks shattered. The woman underneath, her face a gory mess, fell forward like a sack of potatoes, hitting the ruined pavement with a sickening thud.

Chaos erupted, and all ease vanished in the assailants. John and Kimmy had taken cover behind the building, and our attackers scattered. *No, you don't.* I raised the rabbit gun, aimed, and fired out the broken window. I hit one of the cultists in the abdomen, who fell to the ground and cried out in pain.

John and Kimmy briefly emerged, dashing for the building next-door and diving behind it for cover as shots followed them. The cultists had taken cover behind nearby crumbling structures. They were ready for a fight.

A small object flew through one of the nearby windows, hitting the far wall with a dull *thunk*. Before I could react, the room began to fill with thick white smoke that made my lungs burn. I hacked a cough, pulling my shirt over my nose, but it didn't help much. I could hardly breathe; my eyes streamed. I dropped to the floor, trying to stay below it, but it didn't help much. I gasped for air, face down in the dirt.

Dazed, it took me a second to register the bang from the back of the building. A battering ram appeared where the back door had once been, followed by three black-clad figures wearing gas masks. I choked back another cough and scrambled to my knees.

"She's here," a female voice said. "Hurry. Jim J wants her whole."

They descended on me as I tried to get to my feet, and with a hard shove, I was on the ground again. They bound my hands and ankles, then tied them to a long steel pole they unfolded. The other two cultists—both men—then hoisted me up, dangling me painfully between them. A female cultist approached, the gold eye on her mask shimmering in the glow of the firelight outside.

"The Vessel," she murmured, then turned to the men carrying me. "Carry her out quickly. No mistakes this time."

They carried me toward the back door, then paused, listening. There was still a fight happening outside.

"These Wastelander scum are more trouble than they're worth," the female cultist muttered.

As they waited for an opening, I struggled against my bonds. I tried to throw my weight into it, hoping to make the men drop me. They just laughed, and a moment later, carried me out of the building.

The night was illuminated again by fire as something was thrown from the roof next-door. Whatever it was, it burst into flames that engulfed one of the masked figures, making him shriek horribly and run uselessly in circles.

I couldn't see John or Kimmy. I thought they were on the roof of the next building, judging by the gunfire, but in all the chaos, I couldn't be sure. I *was* sure, though, that they had no idea what was happening to me.

There was only one thing left to do. I summoned all the voice I could muster, taking a deep breath.

I released the loudest, most bloodcurdling scream I could muster.

"JOHN!"

CHAPTER 4

John

I flattened myself against the roof, cursing. Bullets whizzed all around us. The building was only one storey, but we still needed the higher ground. We'd scrambled up via a rusty old ladder that'd crumbled instantly behind us. There hadn't been a break since then. They pummeled the building with lead, even as we picked them off one-by-one.

We were running low on ammo when Kimmy pulled out the Molotov and let it fly. The flames engulfed one of the attackers and drove back the rest.

As Kimmy got another ready, a female scream chilled my blood. *Claire.*

"Go!" Kimmy burst out, lighting the wick on the Molotov. "Now!"

Terror-filled adrenaline hit my bloodstream. I grabbed my rifle and sprinted for the back of the roof. I scanned the ground for enemies, then dropped onto the ground, avoiding the jagged rebar left behind by the ruined ladder on the back wall. I raced in the direction of Claire's scream.

I reached the back of the building next-door. Three masked cultists struggled violently with a frantically thrashing Claire. The woman had no chance; I shot her twice before she even glanced in my direction. One of the men managed a shout before I shot him, too, which caused him to drop Claire's ankles. She yelped as she hit the ground, and there was another burst of flame nearby—probably Kimmy's second Molotov.

The last cultist reached for his weapon, but I was too close now. I tackled him, knocking him to the ground beside Claire. He swung wildly at me. I barely felt the hit as I reversed the rifle and caved his skull in with the stock. With laser-like focus, I drew my hunting knife and slashed across his throat. His hands clutched his neck uselessly as his life gurgled away.

I stood, panting, and dropped on Claire's other side. She babbled something I didn't understand. I focused on cutting through her bonds, then helped her stand. The sounds of gunfire had faded. I backed up against the wall of the building for cover, then peered around the corner. There were only two dark figures left on the battleground.

I waited patiently for them to take their shots, looking through the scope of my rifle, and took them both out at once.

"Where's Kimmy?" Claire asked, her voice breaking.

I nodded at the roof next-door. "Come on."

I took her hand and ran for the next building. When we were in sight of the back wall, there were two dead cultists on the ground, and the sounds of a struggle nearby. Kimmy was backed against the building, fighting furiously with another cultist. He threw her backward against the wall, and she made a pained, gasping cough.

"You're dead now, bitch," the guy taunted. "I—"

Kimmy buried her hidden blade underneath the cultist's ribs. He choked, splattering Kimmy's face with blood, then fell. Kimmy nodded to me with a weary expression, and Claire and I ran to her.

"Front looks clear, any more back here?" I asked.

She stayed slumped against the wall and shook her head. I left to make sure. The area was littered with bodies—some of them still burning—but it seemed like we got them all.

"John!" Claire called frantically. "Come back!"

Fuck. I rushed back to them. Kimmy stood in exactly the same spot against the wall. Claire looked up at me, wide-eyed.

"She's hurt," she whispered.

Her tone told me it was bad. Instantly, I snapped back into survival mode.

"Where?" I demanded. "Show me."

"It's not that bad, John," Kimmy said weakly, but her face was white as a sheet.

I ignored her and moved closer. Claire lifted Kimmy's shirt. Dark blood soaked through. Kimmy gave a small groan, and I saw the gruesome wound: a short, sharp piece of rebar stuck in her flesh. She'd been impaled on it. My stomach twisted, and my heart started pounding.

It was a living nightmare. She wouldn't survive.

"What do we do?" Claire asked, tearing a strip off her shirt and wrapping it around the rebar to soak up blood. "If we move her...she'll bleed."

"Have to," Kimmy said through gritted teeth. "If you don't, I'll die right here."

She was right. At that moment, I would've done anything to save her.

"Grab the medical kit from Kimmy's pack," I ordered. "Get everything ready—suture, alcohol, cotton, bandages. When I lift her off the bar, I'll set her face down on the ground. Then we have to work fast to stop the bleeding."

I didn't let myself think about what would happen if we weren't fast enough. Claire sprang into action, and I held Kimmy's hand as we waited for the kit to be ready.

"Keep squeezing my hand," I murmured, hoping to hell that she couldn't hear the raw panic clawing at my throat.

"Don't...it's...pointless," Kimmy's eyelids fluttered, a sign the adrenaline was wearing off and she was passing out. "I'm not gonna make it."

"Shut up," I said firmly, but I smoothed her black bangs out of her eyes. "You're going to be fine. Still annoying, but fine."

The corners of her mouth ticked up, but she said, coughing, "I'm a nurse, John. I know...what this means."

I couldn't stop myself from snarling a reply. "No. You don't get to give up on me."

"We're ready," Claire said to me, kneeling on the ground by the open medical kit.

I swallowed hard, then wrapped my arms around Kimmy.

"I'm sorry," I whispered in her ear. "Has to be done."

I lifted under her arms, trying desperately to pull her off the jagged metal in as straight a line as possible. Her scream was ear-splitting, and the wet, squishy sound turned my stomach. Once free, I quickly set her on the ground, and Claire pressed bandages into the deep puncture wound as it gushed with fresh blood. Kimmy screamed again.

"Keep the pressure on it," I instructed. "I'm going to disinfect, then start suturing."

Claire's face was pale with worry, but she nodded. I took a deep breath to steady my hands, then started cleaning the wound with alcohol. My heart broke at every one of my sister's hoarse screams. Claire held the wound closed as best she could while I sutured it, my stitches nowhere near as tight and neat as Kimmy's.

She was made for this, not me.

Kimmy's screams faded into hoarse groans, then to nothing as she finally passed out.

An eternity later, we'd closed the wound and stopped the bleeding. I helped Claire wrap bandages around Kimmy's torso, covering the stitches.

"We need to get out of here," I said. "I'll carry her until we can stop and make a drag litter. Take the compass and point us north."

Claire helped me hoist Kimmy into my arms, then retrieved the compass. I didn't care where we went as long as it was as far from the city as possible.

❄

We wandered for an hour northward, out of the city and into the woods. Then I built a drag litter out of branches, and we went as far as we could into the brush, eventually finding a ruined cottage in a wooded area. The back half of the house had collapsed, but the foyer and adjoined living room were intact. It'd have to do for now. Kimmy needed rest.

I set up the tent inside the dilapidated front room. Ancient, dusty furniture lined the walls, but at least there was a fireplace. Claire tended to Kimmy, washing her face with cool water and murmuring gently, like a mother to a sick kid. It would've been sweet if the situation wasn't so bleak.

She's going to die. It kept repeating in my head like a mantra, and now that we were out of immediate danger, I couldn't stop despair from setting in.

I'd seen people with wounds like that before, some of whom Kimmy herself had treated, and most of them were dead. If the initial hit didn't get her, infection would. Even our tiny supply of homemade antibiotics—the kind that Kimmy made by cultivating mould—was gone, used after the attack on our camp.

We didn't have enough medicine. We didn't have a sterile environment. We didn't even have a real bed for her.

I lit a fire in the fireplace, then started cooking some leftover meat from my last hunt. Claire crawled into the tent with Kimmy and settled her into her sleeping bag. When she finished, we sat by the fire and ate together. Neither of us said a word.

Claire stared at the floor, her red hair glowing in the firelight. Even covered in dirt, sweat, and blood...she was beautiful. And she might be all I had left now. There was a knot in my chest that wouldn't go away.

"How long do we stay here?" she finally asked in a low voice, breaking the tense silence between us. □"We can't keep going with her in this state. We may have to wait out the winter here, until she's healed."

She didn't get it. I didn't want to explain it to her.

"You haven't learned a goddamn thing out here, have you?" I said, suddenly bitter.

She frowned. "What's that supposed to mean?"

I shook my head, digging my fingernails in my palm.

"It means," I said, "that you still don't have a fucking clue, do you? You think we can just sit here, all winter long, without medicine or supplies?"

"No—"

"Do I have to spell it out for you, Claire? Again?" I interjected, and I knew I was being an asshole, but I couldn't seem to stop. "The best we can do now is make her comfortable and hope she doesn't die screaming in agony. Then we go home as planned. Without her."

I let out a heavy breath. "That clear enough for you?"

Claire looked like I'd slapped her. She bit her lip and nodded, staring back at the floor. I wanted her to hurt me back, to give me something to be mad about that wasn't the fucking black hole of despair at losing my sister. My lifelong companion.

She surprised me by wrapping her arms around me. I stiffened, but she didn't stop. If anything, she held me tighter.

"You don't have to be brave," she murmured. "Not right now."

My shoulders shook uncontrollably.

"But I do," I whispered, my chest tight. "If I don't, who will?"

"Me," she answered, then pressed a kiss against my jaw. "Lean on me. You can go back to being my unstoppable Wastelander tomorrow."

My arms trembled as I curled them around her. I buried my face in her hair and stayed there, letting her rub my back and comfort me—something I would've never let anyone else do.

"I'm sorry," I said, my voice cracking. "I didn't mean...any of it. I just can't..."

"I know," she soothed. "It's alright, darling."

It wasn't, but I let myself pretend, breathing slowly and inhaling her scent. Eventually, I stopped shaking. Claire pressed another kiss against my jaw. After a long time, she sat back, looking thoughtful.

"What if there were another way?" she said, reaching out to hold my hand.

"What do you mean?"

"What if I knew a way that we could get her medicine?"

Against my better judgment, my heart suddenly raced.

"Where? How?"

Claire hesitated. "Neil was a doctor. He saw accidents like this occasionally. Specifically, he used a drug called Regenerex. It's the same drug that's in my implant that speeds healing—just an acute dose. As far as I know, it was exclusive to the Cave...and may still be there."

Instantly, my hope vanished.

"Even if we could go there without getting killed," I said darkly, "why would our merry band of murderers leave good medicine just lying around?"

"They wouldn't," Claire conceded. "But they probably don't know about the nurse's station at the school. The drugs there were hidden and password-protected to prevent theft. Only the staff knew the password...and with the possible exception of Asha, I think I'm the only one left alive."

My eyes widened. That was a better chance than I expected.

"I know it might be a wild goose chase," Claire continued, "but...we have to try, don't we? If you can get us in there...there's medicine, and maybe even more PNCs."

"You're serious? You know where to get them?"

She nodded. "The school had a supply shed. There could be some there, at least."

The idea of saving Kimmy and heading home with more PNCs was too good to pass up. It was also probably too good to be true.

"The place is built to keep people out," I said. "How the hell would we even get in? Based on what you've told me, the walls are too high to climb and topped with razor wire. So...?"

Claire had an answer for that, too.

"There's a breach in the northwestern wall. I saw it during my escape. They blasted a hole in an area near the gate. Most likely, they couldn't get the gate to open at the time because we were in lockdown."

She bit her lip. "And I keep thinking about a throwaway comment my father made when I was a kid. I was worried about him going on patrol, what with the defences around the compound. He comforted me and said that with his implant, the guns on the wall won't fire. They can sense it somehow—a way to protect our patrols and technicians from being killed accidentally. I think...if you could carry me, maybe I could get us inside without activating the defences."

I stared at her, barely daring to hope, but I couldn't help it.

"You're sure about this?" I said.

"No," Claire replied with a shake of her head. "But if we don't go, we know Kimmy won't survive. This way, even if it's a small chance...I know it doesn't solve the problem of the cult. But we're out of options."

I swallowed hard. Even as I wanted to reject the plan for being way too risky, I knew this was Kimmy's best chance. It was her only chance.

And after everything we'd been through...I at least owed her my best shot.

"Okay," I sighed, barely daring to hope. "Show me on the map where we're going, as close as you can."

CHAPTER 5

John

We cobbled together the Cave's approximate location based where we first met at the abandoned factory and Claire's best guess on the nearby landmarks. She said it was at the fork of a river. That matched what I'd heard local people say on my way into the area, as they warned me to steer clear of it. It would have to be enough.

By the time we were done, the sun was coming up. We woke Kimmy and told her the plan.

"You can't go," Kimmy argued weakly. "It's a suicide mission, and for what? This isn't survivable."

She was lying on her front inside the tent, looking miserable. I couldn't blame her. The few painkillers we had left weren't strong. Claire carefully measured clean gauze to change the bandages.

"Too fucking bad," I said with a shrug. "I can't just sit here and watch you die. Would you do that in my place?"

Kimmy sighed and rolled her eyes. "That's different."

"Uh-huh. Sure it is. Now lie still for Claire."

Still crabby as hell, she let Claire unwrap the soiled bandages. Kimmy's wound was a nasty shade of yellow and purple around the stitches. The skin all around it was bright red—the beginnings of an infection. Claire bit her lip as our eyes met.

"It's already starting to fester," Kimmy croaked. "The fever won't be far off. Even if you find the medicine you don't know is there, you won't make it back in time."

I meant to say something, but a lump had hardened in my throat. Claire spoke up instead.

"How long do you have?" she asked.

Kimmy coughed. "If I were my own patient? A few days. A week at most."

I cleared my throat. "So, we better get moving."

I didn't want to leave Kimmy, but I couldn't find the place without Claire. Claire bravely offered to go by herself, but I'd be cold in the ground before I let her take that risk. We needed each other.

We left Kimmy almost everything we had. We needed to pack light, which meant guns, basic first aid supplies, and not much else. After packing, I steeled myself for what might be the last goodbye.

"You're still determined to do this?" Kimmy said with a groan. "Stubborn ass. Just like always."

"Takes one to know one," I answered, brushing hair out of her face. "I'll come back as soon as I can. Do me a favour and don't die between now and then."

She laughed weakly. "I'll do my best."

I kissed her cheek, then left the tent. Claire appeared a moment later and gave me a hug, her eyes red and cheeks wet.

"Sorry," she mumbled against my shoulder. "It's just...I love her too."

"I know, baby," I said gently, stroking her hair.

She wiped her eyes.

"Right. Let's go."

By my best guess, it'd take more than a full day to get to the Cave. We took a risk by following the main roads, but it was faster. Eventually, we both needed rest, but neither of us wanted to stop. The long walk gave us time to talk about the latest attack from the cult.

"How the *fuck* do they keep finding us?" I said, frustrated. "I covered our tracks. Every step of the way. I made sure of it."

Claire sighed. "I don't doubt you. They must have another way. The compound has technology that I don't fully understand."

"But even if they have you bugged, how have we not found it?" I asked. "I searched everything when we left."

I knew there was another possibility. If the implant could stop guns from firing, it wasn't a big leap that it might also be capable of tracking someone. But I wasn't ready to face that yet because I had no idea how to solve the problem, and we were already a little busy. *One thing at a time.*

"I don't even understand why they want me," Claire said softly, a slight tremor in her voice. "They called me the Vessel...whatever that is."

"Doesn't matter," I said, taking her hand. "Whatever it means in their fucked-up belief system, I guess, that made them destroy the compound."

She nodded. "It fits with Holly's behaviour before the attack, and the way she and my mother drugged me. In retrospect, I think...they were trying to recruit me. Some sort of initiation rite. But I failed the test somehow."

I squeezed her hand.

"Not surprising. You're nothing like them."

She gave a thin smile. "I hope that's true."

We were quiet for a while, but it was an easy silence between us. Just Claire's presence comforted me.

"So...the plan," I said eventually. "The only way we'll succeed is by staying hidden. That won't be easy, but I think we're fucked otherwise."

"Agreed," Claire replied. "I expect the breach to be guarded, and it won't be easy to reach—it's near the river, which acts as a natural barrier around the walls."

We kept going for the rest of the day. I enforced breaks for us to sleep and eat, even though I only slept in short bursts. The last thing

I needed was for Claire to keel over on me too. We took turns sleeping a couple of hours, we walked for a couple of hours, rinse and repeat. I focused all my energy on one thing: *don't think about Kimmy.*

Instead, I thought about Claire. Our future together. The future I still wanted, no matter how this turned out. When she woke from one of her naps, I laid out the most important part of the game plan.

"No matter what happens in there," I said firmly, "you have to promise me that you won't take any risks you don't have to. Going is enough of a risk as it is. You let me handle the risky stuff."

"But—"

"No," I interjected. "Just like our PNC trip together. If I tell you to hide, or to run, you're going to do it. No questions asked."

She sighed. "Do we have to do this every time now?"

"Yes, damn it," I said, hitting my thigh for emphasis. "Because if I'm going to lose my sister, I won't lose you, too."

Claire softened and pecked my lips.

"Alright. I promise."

A day and a half after we left, we finally saw it in the distance: massive concrete walls rising up out of the landscape. Even a kilometre away, it was intimidating. We stopped—me to marvel, Claire to feel whatever mess of emotions she must've felt. I couldn't fully see her face, but I felt her arms tighten slightly around me.

"You okay?" I asked, touching her hand.

"Yeah," she sighed. "I just never thought in a million years that I'd be back again. And in the early days at the camp, when I used to daydream about going back, I always imagined I'd be welcome."

I squeezed her hand. We started walking again, cautiously moving northeast, toward where Claire thought the breach was. It was maybe a half hour till sundown. Darkness would be our only ally here.

"We must be getting close to the patrol area," Claire said anxiously.

Sure enough, the landscape changed. Fewer trees, and rough paths worn into the ground. Another minute, and we discovered a small billboard. Unlike most billboards I'd seen, it looked in decent shape—no rust, just a little overgrown.

NO ENTRY was written across the top. Underneath that, there was a picture of a stick figure getting his head blown off. *Charming.*

"That warm compound hospitality," I muttered, rolling my eyes.

Claire nodded. "It's not going to improve."

I sighed. "Climb on, then."

I bent so that Claire could get on my back, then secured my hands behind her knees. Carrying her and both of our packs was not my idea of fun, especially because it made me slow. But it was the best way to hopefully slip past the heavy machine guns that topped the compound walls.

I made the long walk to the riverside. It was quiet—no signs of defences triggered. No sign of patrols, either. It made me uneasy.

As we got closer, I watched the heavy machine guns that topped the walls. My heart was hammering hard against my ribs.

After a moment, Claire let out a long breath. "It's working."

"How can you be sure?" I asked, giving the guns a doubtful look.

"Well, if it wasn't, we'd probably be dead."

"Awesome. This place just keeps growing on me."

We followed the river until we faced the northwest wall. The breach appeared in the distance just as the sun was setting. The concrete was smashed, and a small tunnel had been carved out. Someone had patched the outer wall with what looked like part of a chain-link fence. Easy enough to cut through, but the other side was dark, and I wasn't sure what to expect.

I looked down at the river. It probably only hip-deep, and the current wasn't strong. I touched the water—cold, but not freezing. I estimated the other side was several metres away. Crossing was doable, but risky.

"There's no other option," Claire said, voicing my concern. "This is the only way in. The main gate is heavily fortified. The side gate was only ever opened to maintenance workers. Using either of them would draw attention to us immediately."

I nodded. "We're lucky it isn't too cold. The water's still gonna be a shock, so prepare. Hold on tight and keep the bags and guns above water as best you can. We're gonna move slow and steady. Ready?"

We slowly, carefully shifted so that both packs were elevated—one on her back, and one held above her head. It took longer than I liked because we had to make sure that Claire's body was always in contact with mine, protecting me from the guns.

Finally, I lowered myself into the water, still carrying Claire on my back. The water was only hip-deep, but the cold shot through me.

Goosebumps covered my skin, and Claire gasped as the water rose to her knees.

"You alright?" I asked as I took a step.

"Y-yes," she answered, shivering.

I focused on wading through the murky water. The current pushed against us, and our progress was painfully slow. I bit back my frustration at the time we were burning through. It couldn't be helped. By the time I got to the other side, I was sure my balls had fully retreated into my body.

But we'd made it to the breach in the wall, where the wire fence sealed off the compound. I was suspicious enough of the slap-dash repair to palm a rock and toss it at the fence.

No telltale crackle of electricity. No indication that it was anything but what it looked like—a shitty fence.

"Bolt cutters," I said, holding my hand up, and Claire retrieved them from my pack and handed them to me. As darkness fell, she held a flashlight over my shoulder, letting me get to work on the fence.

"Why'd they do such a shit job patching this up, you think?"

"I don't know," Claire replied, a little anxiously. "It's possible that they don't have the resources. The wall needed regular maintenance. Killing so many of the residents might mean that the people capable of fixing it are dead."

I finished cutting through the wires and carefully removed a large patch of the fence. The small tunnel through the wall was barely big enough for me to stand up in, and the other side was dark. It took me a second to realize that it'd been blocked with a metal sheet from the other side. *Damn.*

"I'm going in first," I said in a low voice. "Wait for my signal before following. Got it?"

"Yes. Go into the tunnel first so that you're covered, then let me down."

I lifted the fence piece off and threw it aside before taking the first step into the small tunnel. Once inside, Claire slid carefully off my back. The overall structure of the wall seemed intact; I just had to hope it wouldn't collapse on top of us. I kept one hand on the hilt of my hunting knife, then used the other to push on the metal sheet, testing its weight.

It was thick and heavy. I motioned to Claire, and she moved to help me. We gave it a good, harsh push and the metal gave way...falling right on top of two men standing on the other side.

One shouted in surprise as he fell over. I leapt on top of the sheet, trapping him under it. His head stuck out under the edge, and I bashed it against the concrete path under us. The second guy let out another shout and started wriggling out from under the metal. To my surprise, Claire jumped on top of him and copied me, smashing him into the pavement. Both men went still, and we stood, panting.

We were standing in a small back alley behind a couple buildings. Storage containers lined the alley, but it was otherwise empty. Claire helped me drag and dump the two men into a nearby dumpster, where I then slit their throats to make sure they were dead. We hid behind it, listening for footsteps. It was weirdly quiet, and I was surprised that the shouts hadn't alerted anyone.

"Good work," I said to Claire in a hushed voice. She trembled a little, but she was holding it together. "But where's everyone else?"

She took a deep breath. "Only one way to find out."

"Right," I sighed. "Stay close and tell me where to go. If we see anyone, hide first, fight second."

CHAPTER 6

John

With that, we hugged the back of the building and left the alley. I peeked around the corner into the street, but it looked deserted and quiet. Small shops lined the road. The buildings were all painted a silvery grey, with only colourful signs to tell them apart. Some had obvious signs of damage, like shattered windows, but most were fully intact and looked like their owners had just gone on a lunch break and never came back.

I'd never seen a street that looked so...new. The paving sparkled as if made of tiny crystals, uncracked and whole. The paint on the buildings was fresh. It was somehow more disturbing than the hollowed-out shells of civilization that I was used to. It felt like walking over a fresh grave.

"Is this normal?" I asked Claire in a low voice.

She shook her head. "This was the market district, so it was often busy. But if a lot of the shopkeepers are dead, maybe they don't use it."

We followed the dark, empty street. I stayed on guard, but even as we walked the next couple blocks, we saw no one. We were just rounding a corner towards what Claire said was the main road when we finally heard voices drawing closer. I grabbed Claire's wrist and pulled her with me into a nearby alcove.

"Sir, it's Hanson's turn to patrol," a young male voice said, obviously impatient. "I was supposed to be relieved so that I could attend the Gathering this evening."

"Hanson has been *relieved of duty*," another man replied gruffly. His tone made me doubt that Hanson was just taking a break. "So, you'll have to make do for now. The commander says he knows you won't make the same mistakes."

Their voices were getting closer. Claire cut me a look, silently asking me what to do, and I shook my head. *Not yet.*

The younger guy cleared his throat, then spoke in a very different tone.

"Of course, sir. I understand. Can you spare Jensen to accompany me?"

"You know the answer to that. We're shorthanded as it is, Smith, what with the Gathering and all the special operations the commander keeps authorizing."

That's why the streets are so empty. They were all at whatever this Gathering was. Seemed like a security nightmare to me, but I wasn't complaining. I just hoped we didn't accidentally walk into the middle of it.

"Understood, sir."

They'd see us in a minute. I pulled Claire toward a door further down the wall, then followed her through it. We entered a back storage room of an abandoned café, then waited till they left before continuing down the road.

"I used to love that place," Claire said sadly as we crept between buildings. "They had a nice selection of coffee."

"How did you guys grow coffee?" I asked, raising an eyebrow. "In this climate?"

"Lab-grown, Wastelander," she reminded me. "Not much grows in the ground here."

I grunted. At a different time, walking through this place with her might've actually been fun.

"We should follow the main road past the central park, then take a left," Claire instructed. "Taking side streets from there, we can bypass downtown to get to the school."

I followed her lead, but as we got closer to the main road, it became obvious we weren't alone anymore. We dodged a couple of patrols, and then the sounds of a large crowd grew close, getting louder as we walked.

"We can't keep going," I said. "We're going to walk right into them if we aren't careful."

Claire nodded, thinking. "What we—"

I pulled her back into an alley just as two men rounded the corner down the street from us, clapping a hand over her mouth.

"Yes, Colonel, I was just saying—"

"Sorry," I hissed in her ear. "But we need somewhere to hide. Now."

I let her go, and she grabbed my hand. We waited a moment for the nearest voices to fade, then she led me through the back door of a medical clinic. It had a second floor, where we'd be able to look out onto the main road and plan our next move.

"Neil's old workplace," she said quietly. "Never thought I'd be here again."

We headed to the upper level, which was mostly offices, and crouched below a second-floor window. I took in the scene: a large, wide open green space was full of people, all gathered around a raised platform. Claire peered over the sill and frowned.

"They're in the central park," she whispered to me. "Must be that Gathering they mentioned. I don't think we'll be able to go that way."

I cursed. "Is there another way?"

"Yes, but it'll take longer."

We went downstairs to leave, but there were voices outside. We ducked behind a wall, out of view, but the glass door didn't open.

"Jensen, you'll be stationed here to oversee the procession," someone said just outside. "Don't leave this post until His Address has been given and the Gathering has begun."

A masked cultist parked himself outside the entrance, facing away from us. Judging by his wide stance and the lazy way he held his rifle, he wasn't going anywhere anytime soon. We tried another exit, but it was also blocked by a guard who was watching the crowd. *Goddamn it.* Every minute stuck here was a minute that Kimmy couldn't afford.

"We'll have to wait them out," I muttered. "No choice."

We went upstairs again and sat in what Claire said was Neil's old office. It was surreal, being in my girlfriend's dead husband's office, but it had a clearer view of the park. The crowd only got bigger. Most of them wore the painted eye masks. On the platform, an altar stood, draped in black with a large golden eye painted on the front.

"What do we do now?" Claire whispered.

"Lie low and wait for our chance," I answered, sounding more confident than I felt.

We sat on the floor beside a floor-to-ceiling window. The blinds were down, giving us decent cover, but I made a small opening so we could watch outside. Several minutes later, there was the rumble of drums, and it seemed like whatever was happening was about to begin.

A tall, thin, light-skinned man in his forties took to the platform, smiling down at a crowd that instantly started losing its shit. Unlike the rest of them, dressed in all black, he wore an elegant navy-blue suit. He ran a hand through his wild brown hair and long brown beard. When he spoke, his voice was amplified.

"Family," the man said, raising his hands to the crowd. "A warm welcome, as always, to our weekly Gathering. Odessa, Lady of Shadows, Mistress of Cruelty...she blesses us with this shroud of night, and with her Eye, we see through the darkness to the ultimate purpose: Dominion. For the benefit of our guests, I'll introduce myself: my name is James, but friends call me Jim J, your Prince of Pain. The Order of Odessa is delighted you're here for this joyous occasion."

Claire's eyes widened. An elegant-looking older woman, dressed in a long purple gown, had joined Jim J on the platform, her eyes glued to him. She had Claire's eyes, but her mouth was thinner and pinched, like she pursed her lips a lot. Shiny silver hair fell just past her shoulders, carefully styled. Even though she was perfect-looking like the rest of them, with just a few wrinkles here and there, she had a mean look to her. Something in her eyes, and the critical look she gave the crowd.

"My mother," Claire whispered to me, even though I knew. If I hadn't recognized the name Meredith, her reaction would've told me. I just nodded, hoping that we'd find a chance to leave soon. I wanted to spare her pain.

"We'll begin, as usual, with the Vision," Jim J announced.

A masked man carried what looked like a massive silver wine glass to Jim J on a tray. He took a long drink, paused, then drained the rest of it in about a minute.

For a minute, Jim J just stared at the crowd with a blank expression. Then his mouth twisted into a weird little smile, and he exhaled loudly.

"I see through Odessa's Eye—her gift to me," he said, and in unison, the crowd repeated it. Claire made a face that told me how uneasy she felt.

"I see the Vessel—a woman with skin pale as snow and hair red as the dawn. I see her blood on fresh sparkling snow, her heart in my hand, as I conquer death and Ascend. This is Odessa's Great Plan, her challenge for me: crush all who do not bend the knee to Her Sight, who escape and elude me. She has hidden away her power inside the Vessel—a sacrificial lamb, whose spilled blood brings the Ascension. The last of the failed Ainsley line."

The hair on the back of my neck stood up. The guy spoke with a passion that genuinely spooked me—the sound of total delusion spoken as fact. That he was obviously referring to Claire didn't help.

I glanced over at her. Her cheeks had paled, and there was real fear in her eyes. I couldn't blame her. I reached over and took her hand. Her cold, clammy fingers gripped mine tightly.

"I won't let anyone hurt you," I reminded her. "Deep breaths, baby. Stay focused."

Claire nodded and inhaled deeply. After a minute, she looked better, and her grip on my hand loosened. *I hope coming here wasn't a huge mistake.* I could be putting her in even more danger than I realized.

"What does he mean?" she asked quietly, to herself as much as me. "I'm not the last of the Ainsley line."

"You sure he even knows?" I replied doubtfully. "The guy's mind is shot."

Jim J rambled on for what felt like forever. The guy didn't know when to shut the fuck up, but I got that he and Claire's mother, Meredith, were an item. Judging by Claire's expression, that little tidbit was as big a shock to her as it was to me. Her mother wasn't just a member of this cult...she was literally in bed with its insane leader, who for some twisted reason was hellbent on killing her daughter.

Finally, Jim J introduced a group of ordinary-looking people to the crowd. They were dressed in the dirty, lived-in clothing of farmers and labourers, and none wore masks. They were separated from the crowd by a roped-off area and armed guards.

"Wastelanders!" Jim J crowed. "Welcome to our humble abode."

The masked crowd booed.

"What is he doing?" Claire whispered urgently. "Why would they want Wastelanders here?"

Jim J gave the crowd a disapproving look. "Now, now, family. You know that we require support to realize the Vision."

He cleared his throat and spoke directly to the group of normal people.

"Wastelanders, I bring you good news. From a Wasteland you have been elevated—selected for something greater. Work hard, and you will be given the opportunity to ascend into our ranks. Help us take on the sleeping giant that is Omega, and you will be rewarded. We share the spoils of Odessa's holy war with our family."

Jim J looked through the group.

"Ah, the bright-faced young man in the front," Jim J said, gesturing towards the front of a smaller crowd, separated by a roped-off area and armed guards. "Come. Seek your fate."

One of the masked guards shoved a terrified, golden-haired boy towards the platform, and I gritted my teeth. He couldn't have been more than ten years old.

"Welcome, child," Jim J said, and his grin made me feel sick.

The boy said something, but without the microphone, I didn't hear it. An attendant handed Jim J a microphone.

"Speak up, son," he said, holding it up to the boy's lips.

At first, the kid didn't say anything. I wouldn't have, either. But after Jim J insisted, the boy said,

"I just want to go home."

Jim J threw his head back and laughed.

"Precious boy, you are home," he said, putting a hand on the boy's shoulder. "I understand you're here with your sister today. Tell us your name, and where you come from."

The boy hesitated again. "My name is Clay. Live on a farm with my mom and dad and my sister. You...your friends killed my parents."

His voice trembled, and Claire looked as horrified as I felt.

"An unfortunate casualty of the cause, Clay," Jim J said softly, as if this fucking guy had a sympathetic bone in his body. "We appreciate your sacrifice. I promise that if you work hard and devote yourself to the cause, you will discover a whole new family right here within the Order, and a life that you couldn't possibly have imagined living on that little Wasteland farm."

Even from a distance, the kid looked like he was about to burst into tears, but he was hurried off the platform by an attendant. Jim J smiled again as the masked crowd applauded him—there were even a few cheers. I shook my head in disgust. Claire just looked heartbroken.

Jim J let the applause die down before speaking again.

"Dear family, I can finally show you the gift I've promised," he said, happy as a clam. "For your loyalty, you will be rewarded with the one true gift: life."

Jim J drew a jagged, jeweled dagger from his jacket pocket, and before I even knew what the hell was happening, he plunged it into his own chest. He sighed, then twisted it, groaning.

"What the actual fuck?" I breathed.

Claire's eyes were wide as saucers. "What is he—"

Before she could finish, he'd pulled the dagger out. Blood spurted everywhere, but the man had an honest-to-God smile on his face. He didn't even seem to feel pain. He held up the dagger, and an attendant came running.

"Again, Sampson," Jim J told him. "Show the people that this is no trick."

Sampson took the dagger and stabbed Jim J again in the chest, this time with even more force. He pulled it out and stabbed again, and again, and then I lost count.

A minute later, Jim J was still grinning, even as his life bled out of him onto the stage.

"So, you see, family, that Odessa's gift is true," he said to the crowd, who broke into deafening cheers. They were loving whatever the fuck just happened. "The Mistress of Cruelty rewards me with eternal life. Once we achieve the Ascension, I will be able to grant each of you this same gift. Remember this as we take all that is ours."

He took out a handkerchief and casually started to clean the dagger. I exchanged a look with Claire, who looked as shellshocked as I felt.

"What *was* that?" I asked her.

"An illusion," she replied breathlessly. "There used to be people—magicians—in the Old World who used illusion to make magic seem real. But they were just skits."

"Gotta say, that's the best damn skit I've ever seen," I said.

She bit her lip, looking unsure. But Jim J had already moved on, ushering Claire's mother onto the stage.

"Welcome our guest speaker: Meredith Ainsley. Woman of my heart. Mother of the Vessel. Odessa sent her to me, in the knowledge that I would have need of her strength and courage, and of the Vessel she once bore into this world—a Vessel for my Ascension."

I saw Claire gulp, and I squeezed her hand.

"It's alright," I soothed. "She can't hurt you. Take another breath. Slowly."

She did, in and out, just as her mother started speaking.

"Family and friends," Meredith said with a malicious little smile. "Thank you for that warm welcome. I come bearing a history that holds lessons for our glorious movement, lessons from the Eye itself."

"You may know that before I met our Jim J, I was married once," she continued, and the crowd booed. "Some of you knew Brandon, and some of you even witnessed his greatest failure: the rebellion of '83. Of course, Omega suppressed all knowledge of these events, so if you're in the dark, you aren't alone. Together, we conceived the Vessel: the key to Jim J's Ascension."

Claire's grip on my hand was now painful, and I murmured more comforting words, wishing this shitshow would just end already.

"During the Great Sickness, when we moved into what would become the Cave, Brandon had so many ideas of how the compounds would save humanity. But, as we now know, it became nothing more than power seized by those too weak to rule in the Old World: Omega."

There were jeers from the audience at that last word. I shot Claire a look, but she shook her head. She didn't know what Omega was any more than I did.

"But Brandon was a visionary. An artist."

Meredith's lips twisted into a malicious little smile that made Claire flinch. She'd clearly seen that smile too many times. Anger curled tight in my gut.

Two attendants then appeared on stage, holding a giant canvas painting of blended dark blues and greys. It was a massive door that opened onto a bunch of clouds. The silhouette of a child peered around its corner. The whole thing had a dreamy quality that reminded me of Claire's art style.

"Thirteen years after we'd sealed ourselves away inside the walls, he insisted that if we could just reintegrate, invite the Wastelanders to live among us, we could rebuild the world anew."

More jeers from the crowd. I rolled my eyes. *Yeah, couldn't have that, could we?*

"Brandon was a fool," Meredith said, clearly enjoying every word. "His pathetic rebellion died with him. He thought if he could appeal to people's better nature, he could win. Through Odessa's Eye of Truth, we know that nature understands only one thing: power. True power concedes nothing. Through our force of will, and by the grace of Odessa, we *create* the right."

Claire had shut her eyes and was breathing deeply through tremors that shook her. I rubbed her back, but the truth was that her mother's words worried me. I'd fight to my last breath to protect her, but at the end of the day...I was one guy. Getting her away from these creeps once and for all was job one.

"When we cut the beating heart of the Vessel from her body, remember that Brandon's blood runs through her veins, and that it is Jim J alone who can purify this bloodstained legacy through his Ascension."

She looked over at Jim J with obvious adoration, and I could've puked in my mouth. An attendant came back with a lit torch, and Claire gave a small, pained cry as they set fire to Brandon Ainsley's painting. I pulled Claire into my arms, and she hid her face against my chest as we waited for the end to the madness.

"War is coming," Meredith said in a hushed tone. "Play your part and remember that we have Eyes everywhere."

She raised her hand, her palm facing the crowd. A small, black version of the Eye emblem was painted on her palm, and the rest of the Order raised their hands in perfect unison, reaching to her. *Fucking creepy.*

"Enjoy the festivities."

The crowd broke apart to allow tables to be carried over, and they began serving food. They must have an afterparty for these things. I checked on the door and was relieved that the guard had left. Now was our window. I went back to Claire, who'd gotten to her feet. She stood behind the office's desk, frowning.

"What's up? We have to move."

She looked up at me, her cheeks still pale. "There's something here for me."

She held up a small, thumb-sized object. I'd barely even used a computer before, but I'd seen enough to know that it was a storage drive. Attached was a small chain and a label that read *For Claire*.

"From Neil?" I asked, confused.

"Must be," she answered. "Not sure how I'll ever open it, though."

"The tech people at the Valley can try," I replied, checking out the window. "Take it with you. Let's go."

We slipped outside. Some distance away, the door guard seemed to be busy scolding two cultists, so I pulled Claire in the opposite direction, away from the crowd. She pointed us toward a quiet side street, and thankfully, we didn't run into anyone. Finally, we reached the flat-roofed, beige school building. Even with its clean angles and relatively fresh paint, it was so bland and sterile that it was a little depressing. No wonder Claire started to like life outside the compound better.

We went through keypad-locked door on the side of the building. Inside was a narrow hallway with three closed doors.

"The administrative wing," she explained. "No students were allowed here without escort. Nurse's office was located here to prevent drug theft."

She led me to the last door. The room held a small cot, a table with medical instruments, and a desk with a terminal. Floor-to-ceiling storage units covered the far wall, and Claire began searching through them. I joined her, and a few minutes later, we came across a small, sealed case of penicillin, alongside another that had Regenerex EX stamped on the side. Inside each was a preloaded syringe.

"For extreme emergencies," she said with a nod. "It was barely used because it was rare and expensive. I learned about it when a student was impaled by a metal fencepost in a fall, so they used it to save his life. Since then, there was always one on hand."

She slipped the penicillin and Regenerex into her bag.

"I know it'll help Kimmy."

I nodded, my throat feeling a little thick at the thought of my sister, hurt and alone in that falling-down cottage. If this didn't work, I'd regret missing her last days for the rest of my life.

"The PNCs would be in the utility shed," Claire continued. "It's in the yard."

I shook my head to clear it. *Focus.*

"Alright," I replied. "Show me the way but be careful."

Claire nodded. On our way out, she stopped suddenly beside a coat rack that I hadn't noticed. A single deep blue coat hung there.

"A winter coat," she said, pleased.

The coat was made of modern materials, lightweight but warm. It'd make the cold journey ahead a little less painful for her. She folded it into her pack.

We went to the fenced-in yard behind the building. At the far end, there was a squat building that Claire confirmed was the utility shed. I stayed alert as we walked to the door. Two voices—one male, one female—came from inside. The door was open a crack.

I pressed Claire against the wall beside me, shielding her with my body.

"Stay quiet," I whispered to her. "Keep watch. I'll take them out."

She nodded.

A quick peek around the corner told me that the space was barely big enough for the two masked cultists; the room was taken up by shelves and machinery. Both faced away from the door, looking at a screen. The man was dark-haired and had a slim build. The woman's only distinct feature was her light golden hair, cropped short and sticking out at weird angles, like a bottle brush. They were arguing. Good. They were distracted.

Next to them were dozens of small boxes that said Portable Universal Nano Controller, 100ct. Holy shit. Claire's hunch had paid off, big time.

There was no time to celebrate, so Claire crept to the other side of the doorway to keep watch. I drew my hunting knife and slowly pushed on the door. *Easy does it.* I moved it maybe two inches before it creaked. Not loudly, but enough that both cultists turned instinctively. They weren't on alert yet, but they would be. I needed the element of surprise.

I threw myself into the door, slamming it into the woman as she turned. She let out a small scream of surprise before being knocked to the floor. Another step in and I slashed the man's throat. Blood sprayed across my chest. I was already turning on the woman as he collapsed to the ground gurgling. I found her clawing toward the door. Her bushy hair let me yank her head up, exposing the throat.

Her golden hair caught the light for just a second. Long enough.

"John!" Claire suddenly cried out. "Stop!"

I froze.

"What?" I asked, confused.

In an instant, Claire was in the tiny room. Her eyes were glued on the woman I had in a hold.

"It's Holly," she managed to get out. "My sister."

"Claire?" the blonde woman croaked.

Well, shit.

I relaxed my grip but didn't let her go. We couldn't afford to. I squeezed her carotid artery until she went limp, then kept her in a tight hold.

"We can't let her go," I said firmly. Claire opened her mouth to argue but I interrupted. "She's one of them, and she'll rat us out. Someone may have already heard her scream."

"You can't kill her in front of me," Claire replied, choking on a sob.

Damn. I didn't want to scar her for life. Didn't solve the problem of what the fuck we were supposed to do, though.

There were suddenly voices in the distance, coming closer.

"We have to move," I said. "You know this place. Find somewhere to hide, and we'll bring her with us. Grab the PNCs and let's get the fuck out of here."

CHAPTER 7

John

To my relief, Claire nodded like she knew where to go. She grabbed four boxes of PNCs while I gathered Holly's sidearm, which seemed to be her only weapon. Claire took off in the direction of the back door we came from. I followed, dragging Holly along with me. She was semi-conscious, mumbling nonsense, but still stunned for now.

Claire led us through the winding hallways of the school, down a flight of stairs, and into a dank basement. We headed to a heavy-looking metal door that blended in with the walls. A keypad was concealed in the wall next to it. Claire punched in a number code, and with a click, several deadbolts disengaged. She threw her weight against the door, pushing it open with effort, and gestured for me to follow.

I dragged Holly ahead of me before tossing her to the floor and drawing my pistol. Claire let the door close behind us, and the deadbolts clicked again. A brief look around told me we were inside some kind of bunker. It was small, with cement walls and floors, and a small passage that led to another room. There were shelves of boxes lining the walls, and a small desk with a computer terminal in the corner. It seemed as safe as it could be in the circumstances. I let out a breath, relieved, but it didn't last long, because in my life, nothing could ever just go smoothly.

There was the click of a gun being cocked, and I was suddenly on the business end of a pistol. A beautiful woman with smooth, coppery skin and sleek black hair stood in the doorway to the other room. Her deep brown eyes looked wild, and her jaw was hard with tension. But somehow, her beauty was strange. She didn't have a mark anywhere on her. Too perfect. Almost uncanny.

"That's far enough, Wastelander," she said, but her voice shook. "Hands where I can see them."

Wastelander. Only compound people used that word.

"A-Asha?" Claire stammered from behind me, stepping forward.

The woman's eyes went wide, looking from Claire to me, and then to Holly on the floor, who suddenly groaned and rubbed her head.

"Claire?" she replied, slowly lowering her weapon.

"Oh my God," Claire cried, and before I could object, she'd hurled herself at Asha, grabbing her in a crushing hug.

Asha didn't hug back. She looked stunned.

"I thought you were dead," she said. "How the hell did you get here?"

"It's a long story," Claire said, sighing as she set the PNC boxes on the floor. "We found Holly."

"I see that," Asha said with a snort, gesturing at the dazed woman on the floor. "What are you doing with her?"

"Haven't gotten that far yet," Claire admitted. "We were looking for something, and she was there. Didn't want her to raise the alarm. The place is crawling with cultists."

Asha suddenly remembered I was there and looked me up and down.

"Who exactly is 'we'?" she asked, raising an eyebrow. I didn't love her tone.

"This is John," Claire answered, putting a hand on my shoulder and squeezing lightly. "He's my...well, my boyfriend."

The word didn't totally fit somehow, but it made me feel a little warm inside anyway. It was the first time she'd introduced me to anyone.

Asha reacted like someone had slapped her. Her expression changed and she took a step back. I raised my gun instinctively, and we stared each other down. There was a long moment of tense silence, broken by Holly groaning again and sitting up.

I pointed my pistol at the woman on the floor.

"Don't move," I growled. "Don't scream. Don't do anything that's gonna make me kill you."

Holly looked up at me, wide-eyed. "Who the fuck are you, Wastelander? How dare you touch me! How dare you even look at me! Filthy scum, I—"

"Oh, shut up, Holly," Asha interrupted, her weapon also pointed at Holly now. "I know they've ramped up that whole cult bullshit to eleven here, but to me, you'll always be my best friend's dipshit little sister."

Holly opened and closed her mouth over and over, like she wasn't sure what to be more outraged and surprised by—me or Asha. Her weird, cropped hair looked even stupider after being mussed up. Even so, she also had that ethereal, perfect vibe that Claire and Asha both had from their implants. Seeing the three women side-by-side made the whole effect even stranger, like meeting a group of mythical elves or some shit.

Holly tensed, then sprang up and lunged for Asha, but never made it. I caught her upper arm with my free hand and threw her down onto the concrete floor, making her moan with pain.

"Try that bullshit again," I said, "and I won't be so gentle next time."

"This what you've hitched yourself to, Claire?" Holly spat, though she stayed on the floor. "A Wastelander with even worse manners than your degenerate best friend? Who'd hit your sister?"

Frankly, I was surprised she'd have the balls to say that to the guy who literally had a gun to her head, but I guessed she didn't join a cult because she was smart.

Claire looked a little lost, like she didn't know what to do.

"Claire," I said, exhaling slowly. "What is this place, and how safe is it?"

She cleared her throat. "It's the staff panic room. Only teachers knew the door code. We were told to come here in case of a Wastelander attack. Never happened, of course, but we did a few drills."

She exchanged a look with Asha, who gave a nod of acknowledgement.

"I've been hiding out here for a few days," Asha said. "It seemed like the safest spot, given that the place is fortified and locked. I snuck in on one of their supply trucks. I haven't seen any other teachers among the cult."

"So are you..." Claire said, then trailed off awkwardly. "Are you looking for a way out, too?"

"Yep," Asha replied with a sigh.

Holly gave a small, slightly hysterical-sounding giggle.

"Out?" she said, staring at Asha. "None of you are getting out. There are patrols everywhere, and the Gathering will be over soon. Everyone will be out in force. And it's only a matter of time until they notice your tracking beacons anyway."

I exchanged a glance with Claire, who looked horrified. My worst fear about this situation had been right.

"Tracking beacons?" she asked Holly, sounding breathless with fear. "How?"

Holly gave a weird little laugh again, and I rolled my eyes.

"Talk," I said, and when she laughed again at me, I hauled her to her feet. I smashed her back against the solid stone wall, and she yelped as her head smacked the concrete.

I didn't want to hurt Holly, but I wasn't going to pick her survival over ours, no matter how hard it was for Claire. I grabbed my hunting knife from my belt and held it at Holly's throat.

"Here's the deal," I said, my voice low. "Tell us what you know and how to get out of here, and I'll be a nice guy and not slit your throat on my way out like I did your friend back there."

Holly paled a little.

"Help your sister," I hissed, "since it's your goddamn fault she's in this mess to begin with."

I backed up and glanced at Claire, who looked pissed off. About damn time.

"So, they know where to find me," Claire said. "If they can track me, how do they do it?"

"Isn't it obvious?" Holly said with a shrug. "Your implant. We've all got them. How else could we have found you at your little camp in the woods, hmm?"

Claire's lip curled, and my stomach twisted. They hadn't found her by accident. They'd followed her.

What if I couldn't take her back to the Valley now? I swallowed hard.

"You sent them after me?" Claire asked, murder in her voice. "After everything that happened?"

Holly gave an ironic chuckle. "Jim J sent them after you, not me. I couldn't've cared less what happened to you after you left. I assumed you and Asha would both die off within a few days. What a surprise, then, when Mom told me that we'd finally hacked into the Cave's security systems after months of work, and who should still be alive, but you?"

At the mention of their mother, Claire flinched. I wanted to end this shitty conversation, but we needed the info too badly. Asha folded her arms over her chest, looking tense.

"Why do they care about bringing me back?" Claire demanded. "I'm not this Vessel thing they keep talking about—I'm nobody."

Holly's weird bravado suddenly faltered. When she spoke again, she sounded like a different person: serious and guarded.

"It all started a couple months ago," Holly said. "When they discovered you were alive. Jim J delivered his Message one evening and said that he'd had a Vision. A powerful one. About you."

Her eyes glazed over and took on a dreamy quality.

"He'd seen you before," Holly continued. "Just in passing, not long before the Cleansing happened."

"The Cleansing?" Asha said sharply, speaking for the first time. "I've heard them use that term here. Is that what you call the mass murder of everyone we knew?"

Holly smiled. "Not murder. It was a ritual in blood, a Cleansing of all those unworthy to join our cause, who would not follow us into freedom from our bondage here in the compound. It was a mercy."

"A mercy," Claire repeated, and her voice shook, a muscle in her jaw twitching.

"Jim J was taken with you before the Cleansing," Holly said. "Mom told him you wouldn't join, that you were your father's daughter—a lost cause. But he wanted us to try. When it failed, he was resigned to killing you."

Fuck. I remembered Claire's story about them drugging her without her knowledge. Seemed like she was right that it was some fucked up initiation ritual. It took a lot of effort not to execute Holly right then.

"But when we learned you were alive, he had a Vision that told him the reason the Cleansing hadn't worked—why he hadn't Ascended and gained his full powers. It was incomplete because you escaped him. He realized why he'd been so taken with you; you were the Vessel."

"The Vessel?"

"Yes," Holly said, and her expression was suddenly reverent. "The Vessel for his ultimate self-actualization, the true key to harnessing the power of our goddess, Odessa—she, with her Eye of Truth, that observes all things, all places, all times. You, the sole survivor, are his ultimate test."

She said all this with the enthusiasm of a true convert, and I couldn't hide my disbelief. She was fucking nuts. The apple didn't fall too far from the tree on that one. How Claire had come from this stock was beyond me.

Claire's hands shook, but she took a deep breath. "So, he just wants to kill me."

Holly shrugged. "Among other things. In his Vision, Odessa's Eye showed Jim J your ascent to the Altar of Sight."

I thought of the altar that the cult leader stood at with the golden eye emblem and wondered if it was the same one.

"At the Altar, he'd lay claim to his Vessel, for from her body, she quenches all thirst. When he is sated, his Dagger of Truth will pierce her heart, and from her, he will take the core of the rebellious spirit—the heart of the sole survivor—and eat of her flesh, absorbing her power and becoming one with her, so as to complete his most sacred Ascension. All the world will be awash in his Vision, and all words of defiance will turn to ash in the mouths of the unworthy."

Holy fucking shit. Claire's face was pale, but her mouth was hard. I couldn't even guess what she was thinking.

"Over my dead body," I spat.

Holly smiled a grim, twisted little smile. "You read my mind."

I took a deep breath to stop my thoughts racing. I was ashamed to admit it, but fear had crept in—for Claire and for myself. Luckily, Claire interrupted my train of thought before it ran away.

"How does Jim J perform that trick of stabbing himself?" she asked. "We saw him do it on stage."

Holly frowned. "He stabbed himself?"

"Yeah, during the freakshow," I cut in. "Doesn't he normally do that?"

Her lips twisted into a smirk. "He's achieved it. Odessa's gift of Immortality. A gift he'll bestow on his followers—in time."

Well, that answers exactly nothing. Asha finally chimed in.

"This is the craziest, most unsettling shit I've ever heard," she said, and I couldn't help but chuckle darkly. "But there's one problem with your little prophesy: Claire's not the sole survivor. Still alive over here."

Holly rolled her eyes. "You think they give a shit about you? You disappeared off the security system, and I doubt they've been looking out for you. You aren't a member of the Holy Family, like me, Mom, and Claire."

Disappeared?

"Hold up," I said sharply. "You mean that these trackers—they have a range?"

She clapped her hands sarcastically. "Very good, Wastelander. Gold star."

I ignored her, my thoughts racing ahead.

"How far can these things track?" I asked.

She shrugged slowly and deliberately, obviously trying to piss me off. Unfortunately, it was working.

I glanced at Claire, trying to gauge how she was doing. To my surprise, her expression was now cool and controlled. I could practically see the wheels in her head turning.

"What happened to your hair, Holly?" she asked, eyeing the odd, choppy blonde hair cropped close to her head. "I've never seen it that short before. I didn't think you liked it."

Holly bit her lip, and her eyes filled with sudden tears that she fought to hide.

"This was my punishment!" she exclaimed. "Because of you. When they found out you survived, they knew I must've helped. They cut off all my hair because they knew I loved it. Mom laughed when she saw it and told me to take it in stride. I did, along with all the other shitty jobs that suddenly, I was stuck doing. Why do you think I was in a fucking utility closet when you turned up, instead of at the Gathering?"

Holly's glare could kill.

"Before the Cleansing, I was the one they wanted. Jim J's golden girl, meant to one day lead his Sacred Army. But now, all they talk about is you."

"They want to kill me, Holly!" Claire burst out, clearly unable to stop herself. "How can you possibly be jealous of that?"

"Because you get to be part of something bigger!" she shot back. "And that's all I wanted. That's what I was, before you fucked it all up."

"By surviving," Claire said, and there were tears in her voice for the first time. "By doing what I had to do."

I'd heard enough. Time for damage control.

"As touching as this has been, sharing time is over," I said bluntly. "Holly, show me this tracking map."

I gestured at the terminal in the corner. Holly huffed but eyed the hunting knife I still held.

"Fine," she said. "Won't do you any good, but if you all want to commit suicide, be my guest."

I followed her over to the computer station. She sat down and logged in, then blew through a few different screens. Eventually, she navigated into a file named Claire Ainsley. It opened onto what looked like a bio page. I only saw it for a second, but it seemed to include every detail of Claire's life at the compound, with insane headings like Early Childhood and Adolescent Years. Shit, they were even creepier than I thought.

Holly clicked on a link that said *Track target?* It loaded up a map with a blinking red dot, showing Claire's location. She clicked on the dot, and a small menu popped up. The first option read *Tracking Distance,* and then a couple options down, *Deactivate Tracking.* Holly quickly clicked the first option.

"According to the Cave's security system," she read, "Claire can be tracked up to 300 kilometres in any direction. After that, it requires a stronger transmitter to keep tracking, which she doesn't have. They only gave those to VIPs who needed travel privileges."

Summerhurst was much farther than that. If we made it, she'd be safe. Relief flooded my chest.

"Yeah, and thankfully, that won't even be needed once I hit that *Deactivate* button I saw you try to hide," I said casually.

Holly made a face.

"It won't work," she said in defiance. "The fact is that the tracker can't be turned off...or if it can, only Cave leadership would know how, and in case you forgot, they're all dead. It can only be temporarily deactivated. It'll turn back on within a couple days."

It wasn't enough time, but it was our only shot. Holly started to protest again, but Claire slapped her smartly across the face.

"Move," she ordered, shoving Holly aside. She navigated back to the *Deactivate* button, confirmed the temporary hold, and the red dot disappeared from the map.

Should I have been proud of my girlfriend for bitch slapping someone? Because I was.

Holly's eyes had gone wide. She seemed way more scared that Claire—who she obviously still saw as the soft, sweet older sister who'd do anything she asked—had hit her. Go figure.

"Okay, time to go," I said to Claire, who nodded. "Pack the PNCs, we'll give this place a once-over for anything useful, then head out."

"Wait," Asha said as we turned away. "I want out with you guys."

I exchanged a look with Claire. She frowned, conflicted again. So was I, but only because I knew Claire wouldn't leave her friend behind...even when her friend had left her. That alone made me not trust Asha, but I didn't want to sit here arguing about it.

"Fine," I said. "But if you give us away or do something stupid, I'll kill you. Understood?"

Asha's nostrils flared, but she nodded. "Understood."

I bullied Holly through deactivating Asha's tracker too, even as Holly complained that nobody cared about Asha anyway. Maybe not, but I had no doubt Holly would be happy to let the masked maniacs know that Asha was with Claire.

"How long do we have until the 'festivities' are over?" Claire asked Holly.

"The Gathering usually ends around eight," she replied uneasily, glancing at a clock on the screen. "You have maybe thirty minutes."

Time to move. I nodded at Claire, and we did a quick search of the boxes along the walls. Asha guarded Holly. A few minutes later, we came up with a handful of survival supplies—prepackaged food, a couple new blankets that were in way better shape than ours, and packets of hygiene products like soap and shampoo.

"One last thing," I said, and I grabbed a roll of duct tape from one of the boxes.

Holly screamed as I held her down in her chair, and Claire and Asha used the tape to tie her up.

"They'll kill me, Claire!" she screamed as we finished. "They'll know I helped you!"

"Sounds like a 'you' problem," I said with a shrug.

To her credit, Claire didn't waver. Instead, she ripped off a new strip of tape, forced Holly's jaw closed, and placed it over her mouth.

"Tell them whatever story you like," she said. "Bye, Holly."

She took my hand and pulled me toward the bunker door without looking back.

After securing the bunker, we went outside and watched carefully for patrols. Asha was silent, only speaking when spoken to, and I was fine with that. We went the same way we'd come in, and because we'd kept to our thirty-minute window, the streets were still mostly empty. We moved silently and came across a couple patrols, but we hid out in buildings till they moved on. I was worried about Asha somehow giving us away, but she was surprisingly quick on her feet and seemed confident about the possibility of combat, which made me wary.

We made it back across the river and started the long hike back to Kimmy. I only hoped she was okay. With how much had happened in the span of a day, I hadn't had time to worry about her. Over the next few hours, I didn't do much else.

CHAPTER 8

Claire

The trip back to Kimmy was long and arduous, doubly so because we had what she needed now, but there was no way for us to know if she was even still alive. We'd been gone two days, and it was likely it'd take at least another day to get back to her. I hoped her estimate of living another week was accurate.

"We need to make good time," John said shortly to me. "Kimmy's counting on us."

I nodded. For the first couple hours, the three of us didn't talk much—too focused on covering as much ground as possible. John was clearly distracted by his concern for Kimmy and pressed on at a punishing pace, especially for a man who'd barely slept in two days. We were both exhausted, but we couldn't afford to make more than one stop to rest. We walked through the night with only occasional guidance from my flashlight; we didn't want to attract prying eyes. Thankfully, the moon was full.

I stayed quiet, if only because I was stunned by the last twenty-four hours. The knowledge that the cult was seeking me out, tracking me down, was terrifying. But what made my chest tight was the news about my father. I'd known there was something strange about his death, even as a teenager. I'd just never imagined that he'd led a rebellion against the tyranny we lived under at the Cave.

I touched a lock of my red hair, so like his. I somehow recalled him more clearly now than I had in years—his kind eyes, loud laugh, and sweet singing voice. My throat ached so much that I had to push thoughts of him away. I needed to stay focused.

John reached over and stroked my arm occasionally, and I knew he was trying to comfort me without words. Asha walked parallel to us, and her every step reminded me of the whole new problem I'd somehow stumbled upon.

I'd only given a brief explanation of our journey to Asha, but if she objected to the grueling pace or lack of rest, she didn't complain. The silence weighed between us over the night, heavy with all that remained unsaid. I wondered not only where she'd been all this time, but why she clearly had nowhere to go. She'd followed us on this journey without question.

Asha was much thinner than I remembered, her hands bony and her cheeks hollow. Her clothes were new—likely from the Cave—but they hung off her. However, the most obvious change was in her demeanour; she had a haunted look to her that I'd never seen. I didn't want to admit it about my oldest friend, but her presence unnerved me. I didn't blame John for not trusting her.

When John was confident that we'd finally put enough distance between us and the Cave, we stopped to rest for a few hours. The sky was beginning to lighten, and we'd set off again at the break of dawn. I laid out sleeping bags in the grass and gathered food from my pack. Asha simply sat in the grass nearby, watching John warily. She clearly didn't trust him any more than he did her.

I pulled out a couple packets of preserved food that we'd gotten from the school, then sat next to John. They'd even included utensils—tiny sporks that folded up. Asha had already torn into one of the packets she'd taken and was eating ravenously.

"Homestyle macaroni and cheese," John said, reading the packet. *"Just add water for deliciousness,* apparently."

His sardonic tone made me smile a little, despite the tense circumstances. We added water from our bottles, and I raised a spork full of macaroni to my lips. I wrinkled my nose.

"Not homestyle, then?" John asked wryly.

"Hardly," I said. "But it's not terrible."

As we ate, I noticed Asha emptied two meal packs by herself. I felt a pang of sympathy; she must be hungrier than we were. John yawned, and I noted the dark shadows under his eyes.

"You need sleep," I murmured, reaching out to touch his cheek.

"When we're back," he answered, as I knew he would.

"No, now. I won't have you keeling over on me. I'll keep watch, okay? I promise I'll wake you at dawn."

He sighed, and I could tell his resistance was waning. I moved in and kissed him. I intended it to be brief, but he held me there for a second longer. My heart skipped a beat before we broke apart. He said goodnight and headed for his sleeping bag.

I looked at Asha across the fire, and she stared back, unblinking, giving me the impression that she'd been watching us the entire time. I shifted uncomfortably. Silence descended again for several minutes, until I heard John snoring softly. I smiled absently as I glanced over my shoulder at him; he'd been out like a light.

"You love him."

I was almost startled by Asha's voice, pitched lower than usual, sounding matter-of-fact.

I wasn't sure what she wanted me to say, so I told the truth.

"I do."

Asha gave a mirthless chuckle. "Didn't think I'd ever see you with a Wastelander, much less be smitten with one. You really think that's a good idea out here?"

"What do you mean?"

"The Wasteland's a ruthless place," she said. "Every bit the hellhole we were told about. Didn't appreciate the warm bed and full belly I always had at the Cave, all because they matched me with someone I didn't want."

She shook her head. "Spent so much of my time whining about how tough we had it under tyranny, yet not a day's gone by that I don't wish I'd wake up in my bed back home. I'd marry that poor bastard a million times over again if I could just have that."

When I'd first been cast into the Wasteland, I'd have agreed with her wholeheartedly. Now...I saw the Cave as the place I'd escaped. I saw my old life as a mundane, stifling straitjacket that I didn't realize I'd been suffocating under until I had my first gasp of outside air.

"I'm sorry," I said softly. "I don't know what must've happened to make you feel that way...but I'm sure it can't have been easy."

"You're saying that you don't agree," she replied with another bitter laugh. "Come on, is Wild Man's dick that good?"

I frowned. "John saved me, that day at the factory. From the cannibals. After you left me."

There it was—the ugly thing between us. The fact that we'd been split up and as far as I could tell, she hadn't come back for me or tried to help me. Asha seemed to bristle a little at my words.

"I didn't *leave* you," she shot back. "We got split up, and by the time I got back to where I last saw you, you were gone."

I sighed. "It doesn't matter. Fact is, he saved my life, and I've been with him since."

"How noble of him, to rescue a helpless woman to rape."

Anger rose inside me. "That's not what happened."

She gave me a skeptical look. "If he had, he'd be no different to any of the other Wastelander men I've met. Kinder, in fact, if he'd had the manners to ask first. They usually just take what they want—whatever they want."

A shiver went down my spine. "Is that what happened to you, Asha?"

She shrugged and looked at the ground, which gave me my answer.

"It makes no difference what's happened to me," she said. "What gang are Wild Man and his sister part of? You're headed back to their territory, right? In the city."

"No," I replied, my eyebrows raised. "They're not part of any gang. We were headed up north before Kimmy got hurt. They have a farm there."

Asha looked surprised for the first time and considered me for a moment, as though trying to decide if I was being truthful.

"I was in a gang," she finally said. "Just two weeks ago."

The story came out then. Asha had fled the factory, certain I was a goner with the cannibals, and wandered for another day in the wilderness. She'd walked until she collapsed with exhaustion and thirst.

"I expected to die. Then he came," she said bitterly. "Angel."

I opened my mouth to ask, but she kept talking in a steady stream. Angel—the name was clearly ironic—was the leader of a large gang that held territory by the river in the old capital. His men had discovered Asha wandering on her own and brought her home with them.

"There's a rigid hierarchy," Asha said, "and I was at the bottom, with the other new members. Food was a constant problem, because these were not the sort of people who had the patience or the tenacity to live off the land."

They'd gotten food and supplies mostly through banditry—robbing people on the road and in the city itself. They were the sort of people John had warned me about since I first arrived in the Wasteland and had taken so many pains to avoid on more than one occasion. I felt sick that Asha had been mixed up with people like that.

"If you did their bidding, you ate. Otherwise, you starved. Simple as that. And I was an ideal initiate because I had no hope of surviving on my own."

Asha took a deep breath. "Angel took me as his woman. I didn't want him, but it didn't matter. I followed his orders. And every so often, he beat the shit out of me so that I knew my place."

My chest hurt. "Ash, I'm so—"

"Don't say you're sorry," she said sharply. "I don't want your pity, and there's no room for that kind of sentiment out here. I'm shocked that Wild Man hasn't clued you into that yet."

I swallowed hard. I had the impression that it didn't matter what I said; she just needed to be heard.

"Anyway, joke was on him," Asha said with a grim little smile. "I slit his throat when he was sleeping and snuck away. I'd been planning it for weeks. Just waited for him to get a little drunk, a little sloppy, and a little less careful. Then I let him fuck me, and after that, it was easy. I went to the Cave because it was the only place I knew might still have supplies I could use."

I hesitated briefly, only because something in her tone didn't ring true. But I was tired, and it'd been a very long couple of days. I practically jumped at shadows now.

So I let out a long exhale. "I'm glad."

"Glad that I'm a killer?" she asked, raising an eyebrow. "I did things that'd make your hair curl, Claire, especially considering how innocent you still seem. Have you ever even killed anyone, or have you been letting the Wastelander do the dirty work for you?"

I didn't take the bait. "I'm sorry for what you've been through, Asha. But I'm glad you got away, and that you're here now. I've missed you."

Asha stared at me doubtfully. There was a darkness, an intensity, in her eyes that I'd never seen before.

"If that's really true," she said slowly, "then you'll let me come with you to this farm you mentioned."

I swallowed hard. "I don't know."

"Really? It's not enough that you got the hunky Wastelander and the medicine and supplies from the Cave?" she said with a harsh laugh. "You don't want to share any of your windfall with your oldest friend?"

"It's not about that," I said with a frown. "The farm belongs to John and Kimmy. It's their decision. I'll speak to John once we get back and help Kimmy, but I can't promise anything."

"You and the rest of the world."

Asha turned away from me then and lay on the grass to sleep, making it clear that the conversation was over for now. Frankly, I was relieved...and then guilt seeped into my consciousness. She'd clearly suffered horribly, and meanwhile, I'd been out here falling in love with John and making friends with Kimmy, finding the family I'd never had. I didn't regret my time away from the Cave. In fact, up until Kimmy had been injured, I'd have said it was the best time of my life.

I rubbed my eyes, exhausted. I was too worn out to worry about Asha right now, on top of everything else. I needed to stay alert. I comforted myself with the sound of John's gentle snores and deep breathing, until the blood-red rays of dawn appeared on the horizon and the gradual crescendo of birdsong signaled it was time to leave again.

❈

We returned to the cottage mid-afternoon. John dashed for the door once it was in sight, and I followed, leaving Asha trailing behind us.

Kimmy was lying face down in her sleeping bag, right where we'd left her inside the tent. John tied the flaps back for easier access as I examined her. Her eyes were closed, but I was relieved to see that she was still breathing—shallowly, but still. I dropped to my knees beside her, swallowing the lump in my throat at her flushed, clammy face. She burned with fever, her skin hot to the touch, and her eyelids fluttered as I unzipped her sleeping bag.

John rummaged through my bag to retrieve the vials of medicine as I peeled away the layers of bandages from Kimmy's back. My nostrils were assailed with the putrid stench of rotting flesh, and I held my breath to stop myself from gagging.

"We're back, Kim," I said gently, pushing her fringe out of her eyes. "We got you medicine."

Her eyes opened and she muttered something unintelligible, pupils blown wide, eyes glassy. She'd clearly slipped into delirium in our absence. It tore me up inside to see her so sick and helpless; she was usually so fearless.

"I got it," John said, moving to Kimmy's opposite side, loaded syringe in hand. "This is the Regenerex."

"That one has to be injected near the wound," I said. "Antibiotics are intramuscular."

He nodded, then carefully inserted the needle into the putrid flesh around Kimmy's wound, pressing down the plunger. A pocket of greenish pus had formed under the stitches, making my stomach turn. John followed the Regenerex with a shot of penicillin in her right flank. Kimmy gasped but otherwise remained still.

"So that's her?"

I jumped at the sound of Asha's voice; we'd been so absorbed in our work that I hadn't noticed her enter the cottage. She stood in the doorway, staring at Kimmy with curiosity in her eyes.

"Yes," I replied with a sigh. "She's not doing well, but at least we made it in time."

I turned to John. "I should change her dressings."

He nodded. "I'll gather firewood. Once you're done, you should wash up and get some sleep. As soon as Kimmy is well enough to move, we're leaving."

I retrieved Kimmy's medical kit and began measuring clean bandages. John headed towards the door. Asha shuffled out of his way, looking awkward.

"What about me?" Asha asked. "What should I do?"

John shot me a questioning look, silently asking if I was alright being left alone with her. I inclined my head slightly, and he sighed.

"Nothing," he said gruffly to Asha. "Just stay with Claire."

Asha nodded curtly, then joined me at Kimmy's side. She held the bandage taut so that I could cut it into strips more easily.

"He doesn't like me," she murmured after a few minutes.

"That's not true," I said, even though it was. "He doesn't know you well enough yet."

She gave me a tight, uncanny smile that reminded me too much of my mother.

"Neither do you."

CHAPTER 9

Claire

I tried to find a moment to speak to John alone that day, but it never came. After tending to Kimmy, he insisted that I rest, so I slept a couple of hours in the tent. I didn't know if anything passed between John and Asha while I napped, but when I woke late that afternoon, they seemed largely unchanged, sitting on opposite sides of the ruined room, ignoring one another. I sighed.

Thankfully, even after just a few hours, Kimmy seemed better. Her breathing was more normal, and the angry, red-hot skin around the wound had receded. She was noticeably cooler to the touch, and I was willing to bet her fever would break before morning. She may actually survive this.

I could tell the lack of sleep was starting to wear on Asha, even as she tried to stay awake. I sensed she didn't want to sleep in John's presence; the two of them seemed to have taken an instant dislike to each other. It wasn't a promising sign that John would be open to allowing her to tag along with us to the Valley.

Can't you at least smile or something? I wondered, my frustration mounting as I watched Asha's head fall onto her shoulder before she jerked awake again. *Do anything at all to show him you're not about to slit our throats in our sleep?*

The old Asha would've charmed him with her cynical sense of humour and silver tongue. She would've told him funny stories about our younger selves, often at my expense—since she'd always perceived me as the prissy, demure one, while she'd been bolder and less careful about what others thought of her. John would've related to that and traded tales of his own troublemaking, much to her delight.

But this new woman in front of me...perhaps she was right. Perhaps I didn't know her very well at all.

"You can sleep, Asha," I finally said, pushing aside my frustration. "We'll keep watch."

Her dark eyes immediately glanced at John, who'd taken a seat next to me by the fireplace, but after a moment, she nodded. She had no sleeping bag; instead, she fetched a threadbare blanket from her backpack and rolled it into a pillow before lying right on the ruined floor. Moments later, her heavy breathing revealed she'd already dropped off.

"She doesn't trust me," John said in a low voice, the corners of his mouth quirking up.

I opened my mouth to reply, but he shook his head.

"I'm not complaining," he said. "She shouldn't."

There was something vaguely ominous behind his words. I didn't have time to dwell on it, however. John covered my hand with his and brought my fingers to his lips, gently kissing them. The firelight illuminated his hard jawline and shining eyes.

"How are you feeling?" he asked. "Now that Kimmy's not on death's door, I wanted to talk to you about what happened at the Cave."

My stomach tightened. Memories of my father suddenly swirled in my mind, making a lump harden in my throat. I didn't want to talk about it, yet the news about my father was a leaden weight on my heart that felt too heavy to carry alone.

"What about it?" I said, keeping my voice even. "That my mother and sister revealed themselves to be even more insane than I feared, or that my father..."

I swallowed, unable to even finish the thought. I stared at the floor, but John used his free hand to tilt my face toward him. His eyes were soft, somber.

"I'm sorry," he murmured. "I know what he meant to you."

I bit my bottom lip to keep it from trembling.

"Yes, well, I suppose my mother never felt the same way about him."

John stroked my hand, still holding it tightly in both of his.

"Do you believe what she said?" he asked gently. "About him leading some rebellion?"

Of this, I had little doubt. "Yes."

"Why would he have done that?"

"Because what my mother said was true," I replied with a sigh. "He never agreed with the idea that the people of the compound were special, chosen. Despite being a soldier half his life, he took no pleasure in war. He saw himself as a protector of peace, not as a warrior. Brave, but not innately a fighter."

John nodded. "Like you."

I gave a bitter chuckle. "I wish. That said, maybe if he'd been a bit less brave, he'd still be alive."

There was a pregnant pause where John's probing gaze penetrated all my defences, and I had to look at the floor.

"I don't know," he finally said with a shrug, "but going down fighting for a better future...seems like there are worse things to die for."

I sighed. "I guess you're right."

There was a brief pause where John kept stroking my hand in his.

"Do you think that Jim J's stabbing was an illusion?" I asked.

In truth, I had no idea what I believed about that bizarre bit of theatre. It'd seemed so real...yet I knew it couldn't be. Something was off.

"I don't know," John replied with a sigh. "I keep thinking it must've been, but...I've also seen enough real stabbings. And that looked real."

I swallowed hard. "I don't know what to do with that."

"I don't think there's anything we *can* do," he said. "We just put as much distance between us and them as possible."

I nodded, staring into the fire. How could so much about my world have changed in just 48 hours?

"What was the painting they showed?"

Immediately, the image of my father's painting that I hadn't seen in years came into my mind. It had once hung in his office; after his death, my mother removed it and I'd never seen it again.

"'Doorway of Night,'" I replied, my voice sounding hollow. "He painted it when I was about eight years old. I'd been having vivid dreams about books we read together, where I faced dragons or became a princess. I'd wake him in the middle of the night sometimes, to tell him about them."

I smiled in spite of myself. "He could've been forgiven for being irritated, but he never was. He loved my imagination. The door represents the entrance to dreamland."

The memory sprung into my mind, unbidden: I pointed at the dark silhouette peeking through the door, and my father smiled affectionately at me. *That's you, Claire-bear.* My eyes misted with tears that I didn't allow to fall.

"Come here, sweetheart," John said softly. "Let me hold you."

When I didn't move, he pulled me into his lap, holding me tightly against his chest, tucking my head under his chin. I shook from the effort of everything I was holding back, my body tight as a bowstring. John rubbed my shoulders, easing them down from around my ears as he murmured endearments.

The dam inside me briefly broke, and I turned and hid my face in his chest.

"It's alright," he whispered, tightening his hold on me. "I've got you."

"I've lost all of them," I said, my chest aching. "My whole family."

"I know, baby. But you have me and Kimmy now. I know it's not the same...but it's something, right?"

I stilled, swallowing hard. "Yes. It's everything."

I took deep, calming breaths as John stroked my hair, and summoned a mental picture of what I imagined Summerhurst to be like. The image soothed me; already, before I'd ever seen the place, it'd become a sanctuary for me. A place where the people I loved most lived and belonged—a place where one day, I might belong too.

"Better?" he asked a moment later.

I nodded, moving back. "I thought of Summerhurst."

John smiled, clearly touched.

"In spite of everything that happened at the Cave," I continued, clearing my throat, "there's so much to be grateful for. Kimmy's on the mend, and we're on our way to the Valley. And we found Asha."

John's eyes shadowed briefly at Asha's name, but he didn't comment on it.

"I've wanted to be alone with you all day," he murmured, pressing a kiss against my hand.

"Is that so?" I asked with a small smile. "Why's that, Wastelander?"

He paused briefly, his eyes sparkling in the firelight, and it took me a second to realize he was wrestling with some emotion. He suddenly held my hand in a tight grip.

"John," I prompted, a little concerned. "What is it?"

He gave me a tremulous smile.

"I'll never be able to thank you enough for saving my sister. You were so brave and made me so proud."

I stared at him. "I didn't do anything. All I did was—"

"Tell me exactly where to go and what to do, yeah," he cut in. "Without you, none of what we did at the Cave would've been possible."

I shifted uncomfortably and looked at the floor. "You did most of the work. And Kimmy wouldn't have needed saving if it wasn't for me, anyway."

He shook his head. "You don't know that. A million things can go wrong on a trip like this, and what happened was just one of them. If it hadn't been the cult, it could've just as easily been a gang."

"Still—"

"For Christ's sake, Claire, can't you let me give you a bit of credit?" John asked, amused. "It won't kill you."

I huffed. "Fine."

"That's better."

Before I realized it was happening, he was kissing me, and I was kissing him back. The ache of longing started in my chest at the feel of his lips on mine. His kiss was slow and sensual, his hand fitting into the nape of my neck, cradling my head. My blood heated as he slipped his tongue past my lips, and a soft moan escaped my throat. I clumsily turned in his lap to straddle him. Our kisses grew increasingly wild, clutching at each other breathlessly, until we had to surface for air. He switched to kissing my neck, and I stifled another too-loud moan.

Asha was still sleeping on the opposite side of the room.

"We sh-shouldn't," I stammered, gasping as John gave my earlobe a soft bite.

"I want you," he whispered, making me shiver. "I'm aching for you. And you don't want me to make love to you?"

I shuddered, shutting my eyes as he sucked on my pulse point. An almost-painful throb had begun between my thighs. I wanted nothing more than his touch. My clothes suddenly felt heavy and stifling, even as the chill of the evening had settled in. It felt like a long time since that stolen encounter in the shed at the strip mall.

"It's not that," I said, my voice coming out as a gasp. "God...it's just...not with Kimmy and Asha here."

I drew in a surprised breath as he slid his hands under my thighs and lifted me as he stood, my legs wrapped around him. Without missing a beat, he carried me away from the fire and out the front door of the cottage, kicking it shut behind him. He then turned and flattened me against it, crushing his lips against mine again and pressing his hard length against me.

"It's cold," he said softly by my ear, a note of apology in his voice. "But it'll have to do."

The night air was chilly, but not freezing. With John's mouth on my neck again, however, it could've been fifty below and I wouldn't have noticed. All the uncertainty of our situation—Asha, the new knowledge about my father, my implant, my mother and sister—melted away in the wake of his nearness, his touch. He awakened a need in me that only he could satisfy.

I shivered once more as he nibbled again at my earlobe, then unfastened my pants and slid a hand into my underwear. His fingers parted me, spilling the moisture that had been building there, and I sighed.

"Fuck, you're wet," he growled. "You been missing me, beautiful?"

"Yes," I answered, my voice coming out like a squeak. "Have you missed me?"

He made a sound between a chuckle and a groan.

"I'm dying here, baby."

He covered my mouth with his again, exploring my wetness with his fingers, and I gasped against his lips. I almost cried out in disappointment when he abruptly pulled his hand away and stepped back. He flashed me a wicked grin.

"I'm gonna warm you up again, real fast," he said, low and husky.

Before I could react, he grabbed the waistband of my pants and dropped to his knees, bringing the pants with him. The early October chill rose goosebumps on my skin, but the sensation was quickly replaced by the shock of John's mouth between my legs, gently raking my innermost thigh with his teeth.

"Oh, fuck," I groaned, and he laughed.

He pressed me hard against the door, spreading my thighs apart so that he could tease my clit with the tip of his tongue. His groan on contact was low and primal, sending more heat through me. I moaned helplessly as he moved in to devour me more thoroughly, holding me firmly in place. I leaned back against the wood, surrendering to his eager tongue, pleasure alive in my veins.

"That's it, gorgeous," he murmured. "Let me pleasure you."

He teased a while more before sliding two fingers inside me, making me give a soft cry as he pressed against the ridged spot on my inner wall. His fingers were demanding, almost aggressive; his tongue was gentle, almost tender. The dueling sensations drove me wild, and my knees would've buckled if John hadn't held me up. I looked up to the starry sky and shattered with a hoarse cry.

A moment later, John stood, wiping his mouth on the back of his hand with a grin. I pulled him into a kiss that tasted like me and moaned again. I stroked over the hard bulge in his pants, and he made a strangled sound against my mouth. He broke away and gazed at me with naked desire.

"I know this isn't the most romantic place," he said huskily. "Once we're home, I'll take you to bed—do it right. But for now—"

"For now, this is what I want," I replied, unfastening his belt and freeing him. I gave his shaft a couple pumps, enticing him, and he groaned as if in pain.

He sucked in a breath. "I don't think I can be gentle."

"I don't want gentle," I insisted. "I want you."

John exhaled heavily, and then it was as if a switch flipped. He hiked my leg up high on his hip, crushed me against the door, and entered me. I muffled another cry against his jacket as he thrust into me roughly, again and again, grunting with each impact against the wood.

"I love you," he ground out breathlessly, burying his face in my hair.

He came to me all at once, pinning me against the door and groaning against my hair. I held him against me, even as my leg ached from the unnatural position. He eventually came back to himself and pressed his lips to my forehead.

"I love you too," I whispered.

He gently lowered my leg.

"You're everything to me now," he murmured, his lips still against my forehead as he stroked my cheek with his thumb. "It scares me."

I stilled. "Why?"

He pulled back so I could see his expression, which was equal parts tender and grim.

"Because there's nothing I wouldn't do—nothing I wouldn't risk—for you. I'd fight, kill, die, if it kept you safe and happy."

"You say that as if it's a weakness," I said quietly.

He looked away.

"Out here, it is."

❋

"Not a chance," John said, his arms folded. "I'd have to be an idiot to say yes."

It was the morning after our midnight tryst against the door. I hadn't wanted to ruin the sweet, peaceful afterglow of our lovemaking, so I hadn't brought up Asha. I'd fallen asleep in John's arms by the fire. Now, though, the time for us to leave was imminent—especially since Kimmy had finally awoken, fever-free, just a couple of hours before. The medicine had done its job; the wound was healing, and the infection was on its way out.

I gave him a frosty glare. "She has no one, and nowhere else to go. We'd be condemning her to death by leaving her here."

"And how is that our problem?" he shot back. "Look, her situation is shitty. Nobody is denying that. But she's figured it out on her own till now. She'll adapt."

"No, she won't," I said stubbornly. "She'll just join another gang because she has no other options."

"Yeah, that's one way of adapting. Regardless, it's not our problem."

I bit my lip. "I can't leave her."

"What, like she left you?" John asked, sounding truly angry for the first time. "She didn't double back or even try to look for you. As far as she was concerned, those cannibals could've been gnawing on your bones. Now she's asking for your help. That doesn't bother you?"

He had me there. It did bother me that my only friend had abandoned me, left me for dead. But that didn't mean I could stomach doing the same thing to her, especially knowing what she'd already suffered.

"Of course it does," I replied coldly. "But everyone deserves a second chance, and I can't just let her die out here. Not when there could be a better life for her."

"That's just it, though," John said with an exaggerated shrug. "We don't know that. The Valley is not some poor saps outreach program. We can't take in every person with a sob story; we'd have to take in everyone."

The words hit me hard, like being doused in cold water. John's eyes registered my look of hurt a second later; his expression softened.

"Is that what I am? A poor sap with a sob story?"

"Claire," he said, his tone conciliatory. "I didn't—"

"No," I burst out, covering my vulnerability with a thin veneer of anger. "I don't want to be the charity case you're taking on."

"You know that isn't what I meant," John shot back, frustrated. "After everything I said to you last night, how can you believe I'm only bringing you as a charity case?"

He took a deep breath and looked at me, his amber eyes piercing mine. I backed down a little.

"I don't think that," I said quietly. "But she's my oldest friend. How can I go on to have this beautiful life in the Valley, knowing she's suffering? After all the lucky breaks I've already gotten that she never did?"

John frowned. "Is that what she's been saying to you? Filling your head with bullshit about how hard-done-by she is, while you've been coasting?"

I swallowed hard and didn't reply, but he seemed to take that as answer enough and made a noise of disapproval.

"She's manipulating you, and you want me to welcome her with open arms?"

My mouth felt dry. Whatever had happened, I still couldn't envision leaving her behind. My conscience wouldn't allow it.

"Please," I whispered. "You want me to beg? Because I will."

He shot me a look of hurt and disgust. "Of course not."

"I can't live with leaving her. *I can't.*"

John stared at the ground for a moment, then finally looked up at me, his gaze steely.

"Fine," he said, uncrossing his arms. "But let's get one thing straight: if she steps out of line, I'll shoot first and ask questions later. I won't put us at risk for her sake. That clear?"

I let out the breath I'd been holding. "Crystal."

"Good. Get your things. We're leaving."

He left me standing there without a backward glance.

Part II: The Wasteland

Willows whiten, aspens quiver,

Little breezes dusk and shiver
Thro' the wave that runs for ever
By the island in the river
Flowing down to Camelot.

- "The Lady of Shalott", Alfred Lord Tennyson

CHAPTER 10

Claire

W hen I returned to the cottage, Kimmy was awake and sitting by the fire, and to my surprise, Asha sat with her, and they were chatting back and forth amiably. Kimmy's recovery had been nothing short of a miracle; when I'd checked her, her wound had already closed and the infection had retreated.

"So, you taught science?" Kimmy was saying. "What was that like?"

"Chaos," Asha replied. "In my chemistry classes, the kids loved anything involving fire, which occasionally meant that one or two of them went home with singed eyebrows."

Kimmy giggled, and Asha smiled sweetly—like her old self. My heart warmed; my friend was in there somewhere. I just had to figure out how to help her remember who she used to be.

"You're sure you can walk, Kim?" I asked.

"I'll be fine," she said with a shrug. "If it gets to be too much, John can carry me."

"Looking forward to it," John said as he entered the room, rolling his eyes. "Let's move out. You too, Asha."

Asha's eyes widened and she looked at me. I gave her a small, sheepish smile, and she quickly averted her eyes...which was not the reaction I'd been hoping for. *She needs time*, I reminded myself. *She needs the same patience Kimmy and John showed you when you first were out on your own.*

With clothes, food, and sleeping bags packed, we officially began our journey north. I had to admit that when I'd pictured this moment, I hadn't imagined that no one except Kimmy would be speaking to me. John didn't outright ignore me, but he was quiet and tense, and I knew he was angry with me. Worse, Asha didn't even seem particularly moved by what I'd done for her. She was silent and taciturn, even as I tried to make conversation.

We set out at a brisk pace. A few days without tracking, and 24 hours were already gone. Could we make it far enough away that the cult wouldn't be able to reach us before we got out of range? It was impossible to say, and I tried not to dwell on the idea that they may already be trying to find me.

Hours ticked by as we walked, traveling parallel to the highway north, largely through wooded areas. While John and I were mostly quiet, the same couldn't be said for Kimmy and Asha. The two of them walked ahead of us, chatting away like old friends. They traded stories, and Asha talked and laughed like her old self. Just not with me.

I glanced over at John, who was watching the two of them with a jaundiced eye, his mouth flattened into a thin, hard line.

"They seem friendly," I said hesitantly, breaking the silence between us for the first time in hours.

John nodded. "Not thrilled."

I opened my mouth to answer, but Kimmy's loud giggle cut off any reply. She'd briefly doubled over with laughter at something Asha had said, her cheeks flushed, as Asha looked on, grinning.

"Keep it down, Kimmy," John called irritably. "You want to get every roaming gang's attention?"

Asha's expression darkened at the admonishment, but Kimmy looked sheepish.

"Sorry," she replied. "You're right. Got carried away with the whole super-glad-I'm-not-dead thing."

John softened a little. "Can't blame you, I guess."

Kimmy fell back between John and me, looking back and forth between us.

"You two seem like you're on a funeral march," she observed, raising her eyebrows. "What happened to the can't-keep-your-hands-to-yourselves phase? You guys have a fight or something? It's been a while since I was grossed out by your very public displays of affection."

I looked away, swallowing hard.

"It's nothing," John replied flatly. "We're both just exhausted from saving your ass."

Kimmy snorted. "Fair enough. How about Asha and I make sure both of you get a full night's sleep tonight?"

Asha and I. I knew John caught it too because his jaw tightened slightly. Kimmy seemed to sense the mood, because she lowered her voice so that Asha—still several paces ahead—couldn't hear.

"She won't be alone," Kimmy murmured. "I'll watch her."

John grunted noncommittally in response, but Kimmy smiled.

"You two deserve proper rest," she said at a normal volume. "And dare I say, some alone time?"

She gave an exaggerated wink, and heat rose to my cheeks as a new wave of shame washed over me. I doubted that John had any desire to be alone with me at the moment. I'd ruined things between us for what I thought was a good reason—saving the life of my best friend. Except that best friend, so far, seemed content to mostly pretend I didn't exist. I could only assume that she was still working through her shock. A lot had changed in the space of only a day.

We passed through a tiny village, and though it seemed deserted, we remained on alert. As we walked down the small main street, I spotted something that made me stop dead: a faded, peeling sign on the back of a small shop. The English word had chipped away, but under it, it said *Vélos*. Below it sat accordion-style garage door that looked like it hadn't been opened in years.

John followed my gaze. "Something wrong?"

"No," I answered slowly. "But I think that may be a bicycle shop. And it looks untouched."

His eyebrows rose with sudden interest, and we walked over to the shuttered garage. There was a small gap between the garage door and the ground, but it was too tight to squeeze under.

"You speak French, Claire?" Kimmy asked, intrigued.

"*Petit peu.*" (A little bit.)

"She's better than she'd say she is," Asha said with an eyeroll. "Her dad was bilingual, and I'm pretty sure he made her read a ton of dusty old books in French."

"*Made* is a strong word," I said, shrugging. "I can't really speak it, but I can read most things."

John grabbed the bottom of the door and gave it a hard pull upwards. I winced as the rusty hinges screamed as if in pain. The door moved maybe an inch.

"Little help here, ladies?"

Ultimately, it took all four of us to force the door high enough that we could duck under it. Thankfully, what awaited us on the other side was worth it. I shone my flashlight over the walls, where half a dozen bikes hung.

"Jesus, Claire," John said with a delighted chuckle. "Nice work."

I smiled weakly, and he touched my shoulder before dropping a peck on my forehead. I warmed a little; maybe he wasn't as mad at me as I thought. We examined the bikes, then used leftover tools in the bike shop to scrub away whatever rust we could, pump up tires, and replace broken chains with spare parts.

Judging by the undisturbed dust, no one had been here in a long time, and it wasn't a mystery as to why: with no food, medicine, or weapons inside, it wouldn't be a scavenger's first choice. When all was said and done, we had four working mountain bikes with cargo racks, along with extra bike supplies for the trip. Fortunately, all of us had ridden before, and as we took off down the crumbling pavement of the main street, I couldn't help but let out a giggle of exhilaration. It'd been a long time since I'd gone any faster than my legs could carry me.

The sun was setting as John rode up beside me; his face had broken into a grin at my giggle. The other two followed behind us, but he paid them no mind.

"I'll race you," he said, a teasing note to his voice, and he pointed to the end of the road ahead of us. "Whoever makes it past the edge of town first wins."

"Wins what?" I asked, amused.

"You'll just have to find out by winning, won't you?"

Without another word, he sped up, pulling ahead of me. With another laugh, I followed, determined to at least lose with dignity.

❋

We made camp as soon as we found a suitably secluded spot in the woods. I helped John put up the tent, while Kimmy and Asha built a fire. They were deep in conversation by the time we finished. John and I may as well not have existed. I was tired of Asha ignoring me, and I desperately needed to wash myself and my clothes before dark. John agreed to accompany me to a nearby creek, but his demeanour had returned to stoic and silent.

I rinsed out my spare clothes in the small stream, lathering with a hard lump of soap I'd made before we left the trailer camp. John stayed quiet, listening carefully to the woods around us as he washed his clothes alongside me. Once we'd hung them to dry on a nearby tree branch, I decided to finally break the silence.

"You're still mad at me, aren't you?" I murmured.

John gave a heavy sigh and didn't speak for a moment, staring into the water.

"More worried than mad," he eventually replied. "We have another mouth to feed now, and another person to somehow explain when we get to the Valley. I'm worried about Kimmy because she seems...very taken with Asha. And about you."

"Why?"

"Isn't it obvious?" he asked with a frustrated laugh. "Your friend that abandoned you appears in your life again, and you care about her so much that you'd deliberately push my buttons to make sure she's safe. And how does she thank you? She stays right on her mean-girl bullshit, like *you've* done something to offend *her*."

My stomach twisted. His words were both a gut punch and a validation of everything I'd been feeling that day. Still, I tried to muster a defence for Asha, as if by saying the words, it'd make them true.

"She needs time to adjust," I said, but my voice faltered. "Just like I did."

John shook his head, and I felt his irritation.

"You may have been clueless back then, but you were never cruel," he said. "You can't ask me to be okay with someone who hurts you. Never gonna happen."

A lump rose in my throat. "What about someone who hurts you? I guilted you into bringing her."

"That isn't why I let her come along."

I frowned. "It isn't?"

"No," he replied with another sigh. "I did it because just looking at you, I knew it would eat you up inside if we left her behind. With everything we learned at the Cave about your family...I didn't want to damage you more."

I swallowed hard. "You were protecting me?"

John gave an incredulous huff. "Should that really be so surprising to you at this point, Claire?"

"I suppose not," I replied. "But I still don't expect it. No one did that for me before you. Some part of me still expects that I'll say or do the wrong thing...and then you'll leave."

I smiled sadly. "Because what's between us is too good. And if life has shown me anything so far, it's that I can't hold onto anything this good."

I tried to stare at the ground, but John wouldn't let me. He caught my chin in his hand and turned my head to look at him. I couldn't avoid those amber eyes I loved, and his gaze—focused and determined—made me feel naked, laid bare, as though I could have no secrets from him, even if I wanted to.

"It is good," John murmured, his voice gentling. "Sometimes I can't believe how good, either. I know you've been let down by a lot of people who were supposed to care for you...but don't cling to people who treat you like shit because that makes them feel safer—because you feel like it'll hurt less if they leave."

His eyes were so warm and sincere, and if I'd doubted he loved me before, I couldn't have now—not with the way he looked at me. And he knew me. He saw my attempt to guilt-trip him for what it was: the desperate flailing of a person so afraid to lose what little love I'd known in my life that I'd say things to him that I'd never have uttered otherwise. He saw every crack in my façade, every flaw I had...and somehow still loved me anyway.

"Earlier, when we took off on the bikes," he said, "I heard you laugh, and it made my bad mood vanish in a heartbeat. Because the truth is, one of the best things in my life now is seeing you happy. And I know I can make you happy if you'd just let me."

He leaned in closer, so our faces were only inches apart.

"I know you're brave," he continued, almost in a whisper. "I've seen it. So be brave for me one more time and let yourself believe that I'll never leave you, because we belong together."

John pressed his lips hard against mine in a passionate kiss, his hands moving up into my hair. I returned the kiss with abandon, pushing my body against his and grabbing the front of his jacket to pull him closer.

For him, I decided then and there, I would be brave. I'd stand up for him and myself, because of all the people in the world, he deserved my trust. He'd proven himself a hundred times over, and for the first time in my life, I had someone I knew wouldn't abandon me.

When we broke apart, I rested my forehead against his, reaching up to cradle his face in my hands.

"It's you and me," I said softly. "Right?"

John smiled. "Don't you forget it."

Crickets had begun to chirp around us, and the last rays of sun had faded into twilight. John gave me another kiss before stepping back, sudden amusement colouring his expression.

"If you plan on scrubbing down, you better get naked now, compound girl," he goaded. "Come on. Clothes off."

"Why do I feel like you have an ulterior motive here?" I asked with a giggle as I unzipped my jacket.

He shot me a scandalized look, making me giggle more.

"Are you implying that I might *like* seeing you naked?"

I stripped down to my t-shirt and underwear, shivering in the cool evening air, and he pulled me against him, a wolfish grin spreading across his face.

"I'm not implying," I said, raising an eyebrow. "I'm declaring."

He laughed. "Well, let me know if you need a hand. In the meantime, I'll keep *watch*."

He stepped back, his gaze intensifying as I slowly lifted my shirt up over my head, teasing him with what was to come.

CHAPTER 11

Claire

Our days were long and tiring. We covered as much ground on the bikes as we could, through forests and fields, stopping to scavenge for supplies and food when the opportunity arose. Keeping ourselves fed while trying to move quickly wasn't easy, but so far, we'd managed. Our luck ran out, however, when Kimmy took stock of our ammunition supply.

"We're almost out of ammo," she said to John, whose brow furrowed with worry. "We can't keep going without more. We'll have to make a stop."

"Where?" Asha asked.

"Little River's closest," Kimmy answered. "Last I remember, they were still open to trading with everyone...even if it was mostly gangs."

John pulled a map and compass out of his pack. He examined the map, biting his lip in concentration.

"What's Little River?" I asked.

"We passed through a few times while we searched the area for PNCs," he replied. "Not a place I'm dying to revisit, to tell you the truth."

"Why's that?"

"Because it's a trash heap," Asha cut in coldly. "And despite what a shithole it is, the people are still the worst part of the place."

"So you've been there?" I asked, a little intimidated by her tone.

"Unfortunately," she replied, glowering.

John folded up the map and stashed it away but kept his compass out.

"Sadly, unless you can magic more ammo out of thin air, this is what we've got," he said, then turned to me and kissed my forehead. "Sorry, baby. Wouldn't take you there if I had a choice, but...we need to trade. The area is totally picked clean, and we won't find ammo for weeks otherwise."

"Can't Asha and I stay behind?" I asked, and to my surprise, John pulled me aside.

"I'm not leaving you alone with her," he said in a low voice, so only I could hear. "I don't trust her."

I swallowed. "I'm sure I—"

"No," he cut in firmly. "I told you; I won't risk you for her sake. You're coming with us."

His stern expression told me he wasn't going to budge. I nodded.

"It'll be fine," I said, sounding surer than I felt. "I can handle it."

"I know you can. But stay close to me, alright? And try not to make eye contact with people."

That didn't exactly sound promising, but I nodded. "What do we have to trade?"

"Ironically, extra ammo," John said wryly. "Just not for the guns we have.

They also always need food. We'll stop to hunt on the way."

He slung his pack over his shoulder and walked over to his bike.

"Do they not grow any food?" I asked as we set off on our bikes. Asha rode ahead of us, Kimmy on the handlebars, chatting away as had become usual for them.

John shrugged. "Sure, but how much is left after the gangs take their cut is debatable."

"This is a gang settlement?" I asked, my pulse quickening.

"Depends what you mean," he answered. "Gangs don't live there, but they control it. The villagers trade almost everything they have to gangs for protection. It's constantly changing hands, though. Last time we were there, it was held by the Skulls."

I couldn't suppress a giggle. "The Skulls? That's so cheesy."

John's lips twitched. "Yeah, well, let's just say the guys who join those groups aren't the sharpest tools in the shed. But what they lack in brains, they make up for with bullets. So, stay on your guard."

"Always do," I said with more conviction than I felt.

We stopped for the hunt, but it didn't take long. John shot a couple geese, one after the other, before turning to me and Asha with a critical eye.

"If we're doing this," he said to Kimmy, "we have to make these two stand out less."

I raised an eyebrow, exchanging a look with Asha. To my surprise, she nodded.

"What do you mean?" I asked. "What's wrong with how we look? We're dressed the same as you."

The corner of John's mouth lifted. "Yeah, but you both have that whole mystical-elf shit going on, and this isn't a place where you want to be noticed."

I didn't really know what he meant, but Asha and I did our best to disguise ourselves under John and Kimmy's instruction. I braided my hair and wore the hood of my jacket up, since John said that red hair would attract attention. Asha did the same as John arranged a scarf I'd knitted around the lower half of my face.

"Good," he said in approval, then stooped down and grabbed a handful of dirt.

"Hey!" I squeaked as he smeared some on my forehead.

He grinned at my outrage. "Sorry. Hold still, baby."

I shot him a glare but allowed him to streak more dirt across my cheeks with his thumbs. His touch was gentle, precise, and his eyes narrowed with focus. It was a bizarre moment to yearn for him, but the way he touched me with such care, even during this absurd task, lit my heart like a match.

"There," John murmured as he finished. "A regular slum dweller, grime and all."

I laughed. "Gee, thanks."

"If it helps, you're still a beautiful slum dweller."

"Always the charmer," I replied wryly.

"Just trying to live up to my reputation as a gallant gentleman," he said with a shrug, making me laugh again.

"You're good, Ash," Kimmy said decisively, backing away from Asha.

Asha's cheeks were slightly flushed under the dirt that Kimmy had applied, and her eyes lingered on Kimmy's hands. She met my eye, then instantly looked away, her expression almost bashful. I resisted the urge to smile as we mounted our bikes again.

We followed the remains of a lonely road. In contrast to earlier, John was quiet and serious, and I tried to adopt the same attitude, even if my stomach was churning with nerves. After about an hour, we coasted downhill towards a tall wooden fence, stretching around a tiny village situated at a fork in the old road. One path led into the village, while the other continued through the woods.

The fence around the settlement was rotted in places and half-haphazardly thrown together, with planks jutting out in odd directions and bullet holes dotting them. There was an opening where an exceptionally tall, hulking man stood, leaning against a post and cleaning his fingernails with a knife. I didn't know why he bothered, since his nails were black with grime and by the stench of him, he was unfamiliar with the concept of soap. He was armed with a shotgun slung over his shoulder. Despite the chilly autumn air, he wore a shirt with torn-off sleeves, baring large, muscular arms with a messy tattoo of what looked to be a feather. Most peculiar of all, he wore a black eyepatch over his left eye.

Asha's bike slowed ahead of us, and John followed suit beside me. He frowned at the man with the eye patch, and I gave him an inquiring look.

"He's new," he said in a low voice. "Let me handle this, okay? And when we get inside, stick together."

I nodded. I had no desire to talk to Eye Patch, who could've squashed me like a bug, given half the chance. Fear bubbled just under the surface, but I was determined to keep it under control.

John led the way to the entrance. Kimmy and Asha flanked me on either side, linking arms with me, and I kept my eyes trained on the ground as Eye Patch towered over me.

"Your business?" he said to John in a deep, gravelly voice.

"Trade," John replied, keeping his tone even. He held up his game bag in demonstration.

Eye Patch barely looked at him. Instead, I felt his gaze on me, Kimmy, and Asha.

"Fine," Eye Patch said after a moment. "Market's open. You trading in feathers today?"

John frowned briefly in confusion, but quickly forced his expression back to neutral. "Not today."

I felt a shudder go through Asha beside me. I glanced at her, and her eyes betrayed a deep-seated fear that I'd never seen from her before. My pulse quickened.

"Alright. Head in, then, but leave your bikes here."

John hesitated. "They'll be gone in seconds."

Eye Patch shrugged. "Yeah, probably. Not my problem, man."

"I'll stay here and keep watch," Kimmy cut in.

"You sure—?" John looked conflicted.

Kimmy nodded. "It's fine."

Reluctantly, we left our bikes with Kimmy and entered the village, but not before Eye Patch gave me an unabashed once-over, a lewd smile on his face. I tried not to shiver. John stepped between us, guiding me forward with a hand on the small of my back and shooting the doorman a death glare. Asha stuck to my other side, and we followed a dirt path from the entrance towards the centre of the village.

The village itself was nothing more than collection of crumbling Old World structures. Some of them were only cement foundations, hastily supplemented with poorly constructed wood walls, mud bricks, and straw roofs. They looked like a decent wind would blow them all over. The most intact house, at the end of the path, still sported a massive hole in the side, which had been covered over with a partially shredded plastic tarp.

Worse, though, were the apparent residents. Two children played beside a stream that ran the length of the settlement, where the water reeked so horribly of sewage that my eyes watered. A young woman with deep lines of exhaustion on her face looked on, soaking her legs in the water. To my horror, they were covered in open, bleeding sores. Meanwhile, a painfully thin older man hunched over the stream to fill a waterskin, the corpse-like pallor of his complexion slicked with sweat.

"The water is polluted," John muttered, seeing my wide eyes.

I tried to school my expression into indifference but barely managed it. Amongst the patchwork of human misery that surrounded us, there were more men like Eye Patch at the entrance—men who looked relatively healthy and fed, all sporting the same strange feather tattoo. They exuded an air of menace, shooting us unfriendly looks as we passed, and I tried not to meet their eyes.

"This is what I was told the Wasteland was like," I said in a hushed voice. "I expected it to be bad after what you said, but..."

"This is normal," Asha said sharply, keeping her voice low to avoid being overheard. "I don't know where you've been all this time, but *this* is the real world. And it's every bit as shitty as they told us."

John shot her a look of disapproval. "I don't know where you've been, but this is not normal for me. No one where I'm from lives like this, and even the nearest trading post is leagues better than this."

Asha shrugged. "I'll believe it when I see it, Farm Boy."

He rolled his eyes, but wisely didn't take the bait.

"Who are these people?" I asked, nodding at the men scattered throughout the settlement. "Gang members?"

"That's a good guess," John answered gravely. "Not the Skulls, though. Someone else has moved in since last time."

"The Guardians," Asha said, surprising me again. "The feathers are their trademark."

"How do you know?" I asked, and she glared at me.

"I heard of them when I lived in the city," she replied, looking away.

John raised an eyebrow but said, "Let's just get what we need and get out of here."

He led the way to the end of the path, where there was a small market square with a variety of stalls. The largest three booths stood in the centre and took up the majority of the space. Each was labelled with a crude drawing: one of a carrot, another of a gun, and a final picture of a circle, square, and triangle. The carrot and gun seemed self-explanatory, but I couldn't decipher the meaning of the last one.

"Everything else," John said wryly when I asked.

"Wouldn't it be clearer to just...write them?"

"Sure would," he replied. "But you're assuming anyone here can read."

"*You* can read," I pointed out.

"Surprisingly," Asha scoffed. I shot her an offended look, but John ignored her.

"Yeah, and I'm the exception, not the rule," he said to me.

Asha waited, arms folded, in the centre of the square while we walked to the gun stand.

The merchant behind the counter was a thin, bony woman who could've believably been any age from thirty to seventy. Her posture said that she was younger than she looked, but her face was deeply lined and pockmarked with scars that made her appear ancient. Her fragile-looking sandy blonde hair was thin and lifeless, and there were gaps in the smile she greeted us with.

"Come to trade, love?" she said, batting her eyes at him.

If John was surprised by her attempt at flirting, he didn't show it. He was all business, pulling the geese out of his game bag. As he did, the woman's eyes flicked over to me, and her expression changed from pleasant to fascinated. It was more than a little unnerving.

"You're beautiful, lady," she said to me. "Pretty as a picture. If I didn't know better, I'd say you weren't real."

I averted my gaze from her wide, interested eyes, deeply uncomfortable. I hoped that John's efforts to disguise me weren't moot. I wasn't used to feeling different. In the compound, everyone had implants like mine. Smooth, clear skin and shiny hair were the norm, and I hadn't stood out.

"Yes, well, thank you," I managed to say, hoping that would be the end of it.

"Such beautiful hair," the merchant mused. I jerked as I realized the end of my long braid had fallen outside my hood. The woman's trembling, skeletal hand reaching to touch the end of it. "You could sell that hair, you know. Someone'd pay a fortune for that lovely red."

I gulped, but managed to answer as politely as I could, "No, thank you."

I cringed as her fingers played with the ends of my hair, but with how tense the atmosphere was in this place, I didn't feel like I could say no. In a flash, however, John's hand had closed around my elbow, deftly moving me out of her reach.

"Don't touch her," he said sharply to the merchant, who had the gall to look offended, then turned to me. "Why don't you wait with Asha? I'll only be a few minutes. Stay in the square."

Relieved, I latched onto the out he gave me.

"I will," I promised, and he nodded before turning back to the gaunt face of the merchant woman.

I returned to Asha's side.

"Kill time with me?" I asked, and she nodded. We took a five-minute stroll amongst the stalls of the small square, trying not to meet eyes with the Guardians, who watched us like hawks.

We were about to loop back to John when I spotted something strange at the back of the square: a small platform where two brown-haired young women stood, their heads down, their gaze cast on the ground. They held their hands behind their backs, and their clothes were torn and dirty. A large, beefy man with a bushy grey moustache and a feather tattoo stood behind a stall next to them, quietly surveying the market. Unlike the other stalls, there was no signage.

Something about the strange, subservient stance of the women unnerved me. I walked slowly towards the platform.

"Claire," Asha hissed, her hand closing around my elbow.

I looked back to her, frowning. "Something isn't right."

Asha glanced toward the women with pity, but her grip on my arm tightened. I moved slightly to the left to get a better view, and my stomach dropped as I realized that the women's hands were bound behind them.

"We shouldn't intervene," Asha said, and my eyebrows shot up.

"Intervene in what?" I asked.

She didn't answer, simply tugged on my arm. I tore my gaze from the women on the platform with difficulty. Before we could go back the way we'd come, however, a terrified-looking young woman crossed our path. She wasn't as emaciated-looking as the other residents—in fact, her complexion looked downright healthy compared to most here—and her clothes were worn, but mostly clean.

She latched onto my forearm, her eyes wild. Instinctively, I tried to pull back, but she held fast.

"Please help me," she pleaded with me. "My daughter's been hurt in an accident just that way." She pointed farther down the path, away from the square. "One of the houses collapsed and buried her. We need everyone we can to help."

She tugged on my arm, trying to drag me...right towards the platform with the bound women. Desperation marked her every movement.

"I'm sorry, I—" I began.

"Fuck off," Asha cut in, her tone hard as steel.

"Please," the woman replied, never taking her eyes off me. "All I need is your help!"

"Asha—" I said, prepared to scold her.

"You heard me well enough, bitch," Asha snarled back at her. "Tell your pimp to find another mark."

The woman's demeanour changed in an instant; she drew herself up and twisted her lips into a nasty little smile.

"So, you've got it all figured out, huh?" she said harshly, finally turning her gaze to Asha as she released my arm. She frowned, studying Asha's face for a moment. Asha shifted uncomfortably and adjusted the hood of her jacket.

"Don't I know you from somewhere?" the woman asked.

"No," Asha replied curtly, turning away from her. "I just know your kind. Now, back up."

The woman suddenly laughed. "Asha, right? You were one of Angel's girls."

I balked, staring wide-eyed at Asha. The gang leader she mentioned—her tormentor—was called Angel.

Asha had said this gang called themselves the Guardians. If their leader had been named Angel, that made sense...as did the feather tattoos. She knew who they were because this was her former gang.

Panic rose inside of me. Who else might recognize her, and what would they do if they found out she was here? I needed to get back to John.

"Cade's been looking for you, you know," the woman continued with a mean-spirited grin. "He's the one in charge, since the...*incident* with Angel. Such a coincidence that you disappeared right around that time, too."

"Give Cade the same message I'm giving you," Asha said dismissively. "Go fuck yourself."

"We should go," I said, taking a step back. "Come on, Ash—"

The man with the moustache appeared at the woman's side.

"You having trouble here, Val?" he asked her. "These girls bothering you?"

"They seem to think they'll be leaving," she answered casually, and my stomach dropped.

The moustached man grinned, showing missing teeth. "That's cute, isn't it?"

My heart was hammering in my ears, and I took another step back...right into John, who had appeared silently behind me as if from nowhere. I sagged against him, relief flooding my veins.

"There a problem here?" he asked, staring down the gang members.

"These two girls yours?" Moustache replied. "How much you want for them?"

My eyes must've gone as wide as saucers. This man was...buying us?

"Not for sale," John said, his voice suddenly a menacing growl. "Now back away."

Moustache held up his hands with a laugh. "Honest mistake. Man doesn't want to lose his harem; I get it. Take your women and go."

I wanted to vomit at his words, but John didn't reply. With a final, icy glare, he led me firmly away, Asha on our heels.

As soon as we were out of earshot of the man, John pulled me close and spoke in a low, rapid voice by my ear.

"When we get to the gate, run for your bike. Ride as fast as you can. Don't wait for me, don't look back, and don't stop."

"What—?" I replied, alarmed.

"Trust me," he said, clipped. "They'll follow us."

My pulse was a low thud in my ears. He gave me no time to reply, taking me by the hand and leading me back toward the gate. I couldn't help but notice that the eyes of the entire village were on us as we went—not just the Guardians. It felt like they were waiting for us to make some fatal mistake.

As we approached the gate, the guard watched us with interest. When we passed by, he opened his mouth as if to speak, and I took that as my cue: I bolted.

Kimmy stood dutifully with the bikes at the fork in the road. At my flight, however, her expression changed from watchful to alarmed, and she sprang into action. There were shouts behind me, and it took everything I had to not look back.

I reached my bike and sped away, my thighs burning as I pumped the pedals, riding as though the mouth of hell itself had opened behind me.

CHAPTER 12

John

As I predicted, they followed.

My guess was that robbing us on the road after we'd left—lulling us into a false sense of security—was their new plan. As soon as they'd asked me about buying Claire, though, I knew we had minutes to get the hell out. Human traffickers didn't let their prey go without a fight. *I should know.*

When Claire started running, they knew the jig was up. Chaos broke out. The guard at the gate grabbed for her, but I stabbed him in the throat. Blood spattered onto my jacket, and he fell, clutching his neck. Claire and Asha were riding ahead, while Kimmy waited for me as I sprinted to her. I jumped on my bike and we took off down the old road.

There were shouts behind us, and I chanced a look over my shoulder. They chased us after us, even though they had no hope of catching up. I frowned. Something's wrong, my gut screamed at me.

I pumped hard on the pedals and pulled ahead of the others. Claire shot me a questioning look, but I didn't slow down. Was there a second ambush ahead? A trap of some kind? Whatever it was, I wasn't about to let Claire ride right into it.

I rounded a bend in the road at a stupid speed. There was a bridge ahead, over a big, roaring river. The middle had collapsed. I couldn't stop in time.

In a split-second decision, I ditched the bike and skidded across the crumbling pavement. Pain shot up my left side. The bike flew out from under me and went over the edge.

"Fuck, no," I gasped, not because of the bike, but I'd thrown my pack over the handlebars. All my gear, including the ammunition we'd just traded for, was in that bag. Our tent was in it. Without it, all I had was my knife, pistol, rifle, and the clothes on my back.

I stood with effort, wincing at the sting of road rash down my left flank. I looked over the edge of the bridge and my heart skipped a beat. The front wheel of the bike had caught on a sharp piece of rebar, a few feet down. My bag dangled from the handlebars. *Shit.*

"Kim! Stop!" I shouted as she came whipping around the bend. "Bridge is out!"

She hit the brake, calling a warning back to the other two. She rode up beside me and dropped her bike.

"Are you hurt?" she asked, looking me up and down.

I didn't answer because Claire and Asha pulled up, and I knew we only had a minute or two before the gang showed up to claim their prize.

"Kim, we're the distraction," I said. "Claire, try and pull the bike back up over the edge. We can't lose my bag."

Claire's eyes widened, but she nodded and ran over to the edge.

"Only a couple of them will have guns," Asha said in a rush. "They're grunts, not mercs."

Kimmy nodded, eyebrows raised, and Asha followed Claire onto the broken bridge.

I raised my rifle and waited behind a tree. A minute later, five guys rounded the corner: three in front, two bringing up the rear. All carried crude-looking clubs. No guns. Kimmy and I shot at the same time, taking out two in the front line, and I got in a second shot before a bullet whizzed past my ear.

On instinct, I hit the ground, right as more shots rang out. They came from somewhere in the brush—a couple of snipers. The guys on the road were a distraction from the real threat.

Kimmy, also on her knees, grabbed my arm and yanked me toward the treeline for cover. We had to move, but...

"Claire!" I called, desperate, as I whipped around to look back at the bridge.

She was on her belly at the edge, Asha at her side. They were exposed...but so were we.

Kimmy and I crawled into the cover of the brush, staying low.

"You take one, I'll take the other," she said. "I think there's one on each side of the road."

My stomach twisted. "What about Claire?"

She gave me a hard look. "If we don't take out the snipers, they won't make it."

She was right. *Focus.* I nodded and she took off running across the road to look for the other sniper.

I stayed low to the forest floor, same as on a hunt, listening carefully. A shot rang out, somewhere to the right, deeper in the brush—not quite in the same spot as the first shots. He was moving after each shot, then, not holed up in some tree. Smarter than I'd hoped.

Even as more shots sounded from the direction of Claire and Asha, I tuned out all but the sounds that meant life: scuffling, rustling, breathing. I listened hard, waiting for him to reveal his position.

The sound of another shot led me right to him. Keeping my distance, I ducked behind a shrub to stay hidden. A short, skinny guy with an eye patch was reloading an rusty-looking hunting rifle. No wonder his shots weren't that accurate; that thing could've belonged to my great grandfather. They obviously saved their decent weapons for higher-ranking gangsters.

I raised my rifle and fired. The bullet burrowed into his brain, and he fell, dead before he ever knew I was there. I turned back to the road.

A sharp scream chilled my blood. *Claire.* I started running.

When I made it to the road, Claire and Asha were still on the broken bridge. They'd managed to pull the bike and my bag up onto the ledge—thank Christ. But the last gangster was dragging Asha, while Claire desperately tried to pull her back.

"You're coming with me," the gangster spat in Asha's face. "You'll face Cade."

Asha clawed at his hands, trying to break free. Claire pulled back harder, digging her heels in. In desperation, the guy turned and punched her, knocking her down.

Seeing her fall twisted something inside me. I saw red, and my brain blocked out everything else. The next thing I knew, I was sitting on his chest, beating the ever-loving shit out of him with my bare hands. I didn't even remember how I got there.

"John," Claire said, and I suddenly felt her hand on my shoulder. "Stop. It's alright. Stop, darling."

I realized I was panting, and my hands were slick with blood. The gangster was no longer recognizable. His head was a purple, bloody mass of tissue and teeth. My knuckles burned; I'd split them on his face.

"Damn it," I muttered, blinking fast. I let Claire help me off him, settling on the ground to catch my breath before pulling her into my arms.

"You okay?" I murmured urgently. "Let me see your face."

"I think I'm fine," she replied shakily. "Don't worry."

I gently tilted her head to the side, inspecting her jaw. A purple bruise was already forming, but it didn't look any worse than that. I wanted to hold and comfort her, but we had to get out of here. Kimmy was a few feet away, checking Asha for injury. The road rash I'd gotten earlier burned like hell, but I'd take care of it once we were safe.

We gathered our stuff and took off as fast as we could, following the river until we found another bridge that was mostly intact. We rode for a couple more hours, mostly in silence, until I felt safe stopping for the night. My poor back was killing me by then.

Claire and Asha set up camp while Kimmy tsked over my road rash.

"You could've said something earlier," she scolded. I winced as she cleaned the raw flesh, picking bits of gravel out. "No need to be such a hero."

I spotted Claire watching us with concern. Her bruise had darkened, marking her beautiful face with violence, and I hated it. It'd been a rough day for everyone, and I wanted to make her smile.

So, I shrugged. "What can I say? I was trying to impress my girlfriend, and I thought that would do it."

Claire's responding laugh made me feel a little better. She swapped places with Kimmy, who went to help Asha set up the tent. I sighed and shut my eyes as she spread ointment across my back, soothing the burn. Her touch was what I needed at the end of this fucking awful day.

"You scared me," I said quietly as she massaged in gentle circles. "They could've stolen you away in half a second back in Little River."

She let out a long breath. "I know. I'm sorry I didn't realize sooner."

"Not your fault. There wasn't a slave market there the last time we went."

There was a stunned pause. "The platform with the women...that was a slave market?"

"Yeah," I sighed. "They're not uncommon in some of the gang-owned settlements. If I'd known, I wouldn't have taken you."

"Is there a lot of slavery in the Wasteland?" Claire asked, and I could tell she was trying to keep her voice level.

"Some," I answered honestly. "Not everywhere, but...I've seen enough to know that it's out there. Not all abductions, though. That's more of an opportunity thing. Some people become slaves willingly, at least at first."

"Why?"

I shrugged. "They're poor, starving, and desperate. Sure, they're abused, but slaves usually get a home and a meal every day. That's a lot to people who've been born into nothing, or who don't know how to take care of themselves."

Claire was quiet. She carefully bandaged my back, and I kissed her in thanks. Her expression was thoughtful as the four of us gathered around the fire. We had dinner, and I noticed that she kept glancing over at Asha, who remained silent throughout. Kimmy half-heartedly tried to make conversation, but none of us were in the mood.

"Ash," Claire finally said, her tone careful. "Who is Cade?"

Asha flinched as though she'd been hit. "Nobody."

I rolled my eyes. "Look, your friends nearly killed us today. Least you can do is give us a heads-up if they might come looking for you."

"John," Kimmy scolded, right as Asha snapped back, "They're not my friends."

"We know that," Claire said, giving me a disapproving glance, and it was obvious I wasn't going to win this one. I may not have been able to stand the woman, but my sister and my girlfriend clearly saw something in her that I just didn't. For now, I'd have to suck it up, even if I fantasized more and more about pushing Asha down an abandoned mineshaft.

"Fine," I said, holding up my hands. "Sorry."

Asha softened slightly, though she still glared at me.

"No one's looking for me," she said. "We happened to run into them, which isn't that unusual. The Guardians are one of the biggest gangs in the region; they control a lot of territory. I didn't know they'd taken Little River, though."

Kimmy touched her hand. Asha flinched but allowed it.

"Is Cade someone who hurt you?" Kimmy asked softly. "You're safe from him now, you know. We'll protect you."

I wasn't so sure on that front, but there was an intimacy to the promise that made me sigh. No matter how much I didn't trust Asha, it was too late. My sister had a thing for her. It was obvious in the way she looked at her.

"Thank you," Asha replied, and to my surprise, she sounded sincere.

Later, after Kimmy headed to bed, Claire and I prepared for the first watch of the night. Asha headed for the tent to turn in, and as I watched her, she met my eye. A second passed, and then she smiled at me.

It only lasted half a second, and then she turned away. She'd never smiled at me before. It should've felt like a peace offering, maybe. An olive branch. I should've taken it as a sign that things between us may not always be so heated.

So, why did it make me more uneasy than ever?

CHAPTER 13

Claire

For all the time they spent together over the next couple weeks, the animosity between Asha and John hadn't ebbed even a little. However, with me, she finally began to thaw. It began in small bits of conversation here and there, when she'd let me share a joke between her and Kimmy or ask me how I was feeling. She even offered me the rest of her food one evening, claiming she wasn't hungry and wanted me to have it.

Hungry as I was all the time now with food rationing, I couldn't refuse. John had managed to shoot a goose that day, and the fatty, smoky meat practically melted in my mouth. I polished off the rest of her dinner, and for the first time in days, I felt full.

Asha and I were on first watch that night, so John and Kimmy shared the tent. John came over to kiss me goodnight.

"Get some rest," I murmured to him, and he kissed my forehead.

"I will. Just—" He glanced at Asha. "Be careful, alright?"

Asha rolled her eyes. "Unclench, Wastelander. She's *my* friend, remember?"

"Don't fucking call me that," he retorted, then turned back to me. "Like I said...if you need me—"

"I'll be fine," I soothed, smoothing his hair.

He kissed me goodnight, then headed toward the tent. Soon, the only sound was the crackling of the campfire and the distant hooting of owls.

"Thank you," I said, breaking the silence. "For the food. I needed that."

To my surprise, she smiled. "I know. I had to look at your bony ass for most of the day."

"It's not bony!" I said with a giggle. "Besides, you look like you could use it more than I do."

She shrugged. "Honestly, going from what we had at home to mostly gamey-ass meat and gruel, I don't have much an appetite these days."

I nodded sympathetically. "Did you...I mean, did they feed you much in the gang?"

To my dismay, she visibly retreated into herself at the mention of the past, her arms tucking into her sides.

"I can't talk about it."

I blew out a breath. "I knew that. I'm sorry; I shouldn't have asked."

She shook her head but didn't reply, and the awkward silence that followed was painful. I decided to distract myself with my nightly grooming routine, also known as my feeble attempts to maintain a basic standard of hygiene in the middle of nowhere after long days of travel.

I wet my washcloth with a small dab of water from my bottle and gave myself a quick wipe down under my clothes. It wasn't enough, but it was better than nothing. I fetched my hairbrush from my pack and began to unwind my long braid. While I'd frequently worn my hair down when we lived at the camp, I'd been braiding it more often than not on the road.

"How do you do that?" Asha asked, and when I gave her a questioning look, she nodded at my braid. "I've never been able to do the more elaborate braids. I never saw you wear them before."

"Kimmy taught me," I replied as I brushed out the bends it'd left in my hair. "She's good with hair. This one's called a fishtail braid."

"It's pretty," Asha said in an almost wistful tone. "Like something someone would wear at home. Back when pretty things mattered."

The yearning in her voice for something familiar hit me hard. I knew that longing for a place where art and music and *culture* could thrive. They were a fundamental piece of our humanity that'd been lost.

"Pretty things still matter," I said gently. "If only to us."

I fished in my pack for my sketchbook, then held it out to her.

"I still draw," I said. "Often things I see, but sometimes from my own imagination, too."

She took the sketchbook with a trembling hand and flipped through it. She looked at my drawings of the forest around our old camp, and stopped at a drawing of a unicorn, tracing her finger over its horn. I smiled at the memory of John asking me if they had ever existed in the Old World. I'd giggled at his adorably confused expression and pulled him into a kiss.

Asha had stopped on a sketch of John's face, an eyebrow raised, then flipped to the next, which was a full-body portrait looking over his shoulder, and then to the next, which was a profile of his silhouette. She made a noise of amusement, and I blushed as she skipped through the next five or so pages, which were all of John—his smile, his gaze, his hands.

"We don't have photographs anymore," I said sheepishly. "I don't want to forget."

Asha bit her lip to contain her laughter, which made me happy, even if it was at my expense. She flipped through the rest of the drawings until she reached the last one, my current work-in-progress. It was a half-finished portrait of Asha herself, as I remembered her: her sleek black hair, radiant brown skin, and big, pretty eyes. She was a joy to draw—she'd always been beautiful, and far more put-together than I was.

She traced her finger over her drawing's features for a long time in silence, making me nervous.

"It's fine if you don't like it," I said. "I just...I missed you, and—"

"You're too good for this world, Claire," she cut across me, her voice tight. "It's why I was shocked that you were still alive after all this time. The Wasteland doesn't deserve you. You were meant for better than this."

I couldn't help but bristle a little. "I found more freedom out here than I ever had back home. And I'm no angel—I've done ugly things, too. I think we all have."

She shook her head. "No, you haven't. Nothing anyone would condemn you for. If you had, you would've changed more. Like me. Like your Wastelander, even."

I frowned. "What do you mean?"

She sighed, but didn't answer. We sat in silence for a long time, and I was afraid that she'd shut me out again. I tried to find something to latch onto, to keep her here with me. She'd only just started acting more like her old self.

"Want me to braid your hair?" I asked quietly.

To my surprise, she nodded and moved over to me, her back facing me. I hesitated, then ran my fingers through her hair, which had grown down her back. It was dry and a bit unruly from a lack of care, but still beautiful. She flinched at my touch but nodded at me to continue.

"You never had it this long before," I commented as I started to brush it out as gently as I could.

"I wasn't allowed to cut it," she replied. "Angel liked it longer."

I tackled the knots at the bottom with as much care as I could.

"Well, as John would say, fuck that guy."

To my surprise, she laughed—a real, deep, belly laugh—and it touched my soul. I wanted so badly to help her heal from whatever had happened to her. I just didn't know how. For now, I focused on taking care of her hair, twisting it into a lovely fishtail braid that Kimmy would've approved of.

"This is how Kimmy bonded with me at first," I said with a smile. "She'd do my hair for me. Without her, I don't know that I ever would've adapted to life out here...or felt safe enough to open up to John."

Asha didn't reply, but she'd relaxed a little under my touch, which was something at least.

"Kimmy really is something special," I said after a moment. "Don't you think?"

Asha snorted. "You're awful at subtlety, you know that?"

I giggled. "Well, I know you two have been getting along really well."

Another pause, but then Asha said, "She's not what I expected. Never met someone who could provide life-saving medicine just as easily as she could stab a guy in the throat."

I laughed again. "Yeah, that's her. I'm glad you hit it off."

"I don't know," she said as I fished in my bag for a ribbon to tie off the braid. "I'm worried about what's going to happen when we get to this place. The Valley. From what Kimmy's told me, it's not going to be good."

"John seems to think it'll be okay."

Asha made a sound of derision. "Not sure how he could possibly think that, with all that stuff about the Jamesons and the whole mess around them leaving."

Jameson. That name Kimmy had let slip weeks ago, around the campfire.

I frowned. "What?"

She turned to face me, eyebrows raised. "You don't know what I'm talking about?"

She clearly inferred my answer from the confusion in my expression.

"He hasn't told you," she said, a frown creasing her brow, and I made an impatient noise. "Fuck, he really hasn't told you?"

"Told me what, exactly?" I snapped. "What has Kimmy been telling you?"

She shrugged noncommittally. "Just what we're up against. But I guess he didn't think that was worth sharing with you. He'd rather you be grasping around in the dark. Asshole."

I took a deep breath to calm myself against the rising tide of dread that swelled in my chest. Why wouldn't John have told me something important?

"Tell me," I commanded. "Everything you know."

Asha stared at me and pursed her lips, like she was assessing my readiness.

"You sure you want to hear it?" she asked. "It doesn't paint your boyfriend in a particularly flattering light."

"I don't care."

It wasn't true and we both knew it, but she shrugged again.

"Nobody's going to want us there when we get to the Valley," she said. "But Kim told me about who's going to be leading the charge to take us out ASAP. The Jamesons."

John had shut down the conversation about them before and wouldn't budge even when I asked him later in private. *You don't need to worry about it,* he'd said firmly. *Just focus on what's in front of us right now.*

I'd taken him at his word and put it out of my mind. But if these people were going to cause trouble for me, didn't I have the right to know it?

"They're one of the oldest families there, apparently," Asha continued. "They have a lot of influence on this council that runs things. There's six of them—father, five sons, and a daughter. See, Kim's grandfather used to be council chairman before he died. He and the elder Jameson never got along. Seems like it was common knowledge that they hated one another for decades."

I hadn't known that their grandfather had been chairman. I might've dismissed that as something that just never came up...but now I questioned every bit of information I apparently hadn't been given.

"Why do they hate outsiders so much?" I asked, my mouth dry.

Asha shrugged. "Kimmy figures it's because they see outsiders as a threat to the power structure of the Valley—the one where they're on top."

She barely gave me time to mull that over before she continued, "I guess after their granddaddy kicked the bucket, there was going to be an election for a new chairman, and the elder Jameson was considered a shoo in. Until something happened."

She paused, seeming to consider her next words.

"Involving John?" I asked, but I already knew the answer.

"Yeah," she sighed. "Kim wasn't too clear on the details. But it sounds like someone in the Valley got kidnapped by a gang. The whole community rallied and was prepared to go after them...but at dawn the next day, your boyfriend turned up with the victim at his side. He went after the gang himself."

She hesitated again for long enough that I snapped.

"Spit it out, Ash."

"Sorry, it's just—" she stopped, and her face changed from hesitation to concern. "I'm afraid for you, Claire."

I was temporarily speechless.

"Afraid?" I finally repeated, frowning. "Why?"

She just stared at me, pity in her gaze, before seeming to gather her resolve.

"Because he's unstable," she said in a rush. "Kim told me that nobody knew what exactly he did to get the girl back—only that the girl later reported hearing the horrible screams of her captors. And when that gang found us on the road, and he beat that guy to a bloody pulp—"

Asha met my eyes, her mouth twisting unhappily.

"All I could think was," she said quietly, "how long until that's her that he's hitting? For not being obedient enough, for being on the wrong side of his rage that day."

Sudden outrage flooded my system.

"John has never raised a hand to me," I said furiously. "And he never would."

Asha eyed me skeptically. "You sure about that? He's a violent man. We've all seen it. And you sound just like every other battered woman that ever existed."

"I'm not a battered woman," I said through gritted teeth. "He's never hurt me. And he's not a violent man. He's sweet, and—"

"Sweet," Asha said with contempt. "Right. It was real sweet when he killed a man with his bare hands right in front of you, and you had to calm him down."

"Because that guy hurt me!" I burst out. "You can't seriously be arguing for a gang member that would've killed me in a second, given the chance."

Asha shrugged. "Gang members aren't the devil, Claire. They're people, same as everybody else, and what your boyfriend does isn't so different."

"John would never hurt innocent people," I said firmly. "I know you have trouble trusting him, and I get it, but he's a good man."

She grinned at me, but it looked more like she was baring her teeth.

"They all start out that way," she said without warmth. "Claiming they only do what they have to, just to get by, but the list of things they're willing to do to get what they want keeps growing."

She stood up from the tree stump. "But answer me this, sweetie: if he's such a great guy, why is it me telling you all this? If he's so wonderful, what's he got to hide?"

I hated that I didn't have a good answer for her. I trusted John, but to know that he hadn't told me the whole truth made me hurt in all the old ways that I couldn't forget, no matter how hard I tried. I'd been betrayed once by the people closest to me. I couldn't bear for that to happen again.

Asha tentatively reached out to me, watching her hand as though she wasn't sure that it would obey her, and laid it on my forearm.

"I'm not trying to hurt you," she said in a softer tone than I'd heard her use since before the attack on the Cave. She sounded more like her old self, and that brought a tear to my eye. "I'm just trying to let you know that you have other options, if you want them. Where we came from, you didn't have many choices, so you may not realize you have them now."

She spoke with such sincerity that I faltered. Maybe she was just trying to help. Trying to look out for me, the way she used to, even if she didn't know how anymore.

"I've missed you," I murmured, a lump in my throat.

Asha sighed. "I'm sorry. I know I'm not who you remember. I just don't know how to be that girl anymore, you know? But I'm trying—I promise. Don't give up on me yet."

I shook my head. "Of course not. Just...I need you to be my friend again, even if you're not the same. I can handle your pain. But not your indifference."

My voice trembled, and she clucked her tongue and touched my cheek.

"I've always been your friend, girl," she said. "Ever since you let me copy off your notes in homeroom. That's when I knew."

I couldn't help smiling. "Knew what?"

"That you're the go-to girl when a hot mess like me needs someone to anchor to."

"Thanks," I said with a small laugh. "I'm thrilled to be your anchor in life."

She grinned in that uncanny way she never used to before, and that familiar sense of unease stirred. I looked up at the stars, sighing.

There would be a reckoning between John and me. Soon.

CHAPTER 14

Claire

Winter arrived with a vengeance the following day. Soon after we set out, snow began to fall in thick clumps, blanketing the barren forest in shimmering white. Unfortunately, our bikes had taken us as far as they could, and we'd have to finish our journey on foot.

"I know," John said sympathetically as I gave the abandoned bikes a wistful look. He touched my shoulder, but I shrugged it off.

I was confused and angry. His refusal to share what awaited us in the Valley felt like a betrayal. At the same time, I trusted him enough to believe that he had a reason for keeping it to himself. I didn't believe everything Asha had said—she clearly had some traumatic history she wasn't sharing—but I was still frustrated by John's silence, and it showed. Without his side of the story, it's hard to know what to believe.

John raised a quizzical eyebrow at my mood, but otherwise let it go. I was glad; now wasn't a good time to discuss it. Tonight, when we made camp, I'd get answers.

We walked for hours, well into the morning, but as noon arrived, the sky swelled with thick, ominous clouds. The wind picked up, howling in my ears, and the snowfall dramatically increased. In the span of ten minutes, it went from light snow to whiteout conditions, with barely three feet of visibility in any direction.

I held my scarf over my face, but it didn't stop the wind from whipping my skin mercilessly and chilling me to the bone. I was trying to follow John, but I could hardly see him in the swirling storm.

"Head for that tree!" Kimmy shouted above the wind, but I couldn't even see the direction she was pointing.

Confused and disoriented, I put one foot in front of the other for as long as I could. Snow kept falling into my eyes, temporarily blinding me, and the voices of the others sounded farther and farther away. I was going the wrong way, but I didn't know how to get to where they were. If they left me behind, I'd never find them again.

I took a breath and tried not to panic. The wind howled so loudly that I wasn't even certain they'd hear me even if I yelled. I picked a direction and took three rapid steps...and collided with something solid.

"Ouch!"

"Claire?" John called out.

I'd walked into a wooden wall, barely visible through the storm. I touched it, feeling the outline of logs. A cabin?

"Claire! Where are you?"

"Here!" I yelled back. "I...I think I found something."

"Stay where you are; I'm coming to get you. Keep talking to me."

His voice sounded closer, so I kept calling him. A minute later, he emerged from the wall of white, his scarf pulled up over his face like mine, his jacket covered in snow.

"I think it might be a cabin," I shouted over the wind. "We should check it out. We need to get out of this weather."

John glanced around us, clearly conflicted, but we didn't have much choice. There was no putting up a tent in this storm, and ours didn't have space for four people anyway.

"Alright," he said, "but look for signs of people. If we see any, we leave. And stay behind me."

I nodded, and he raised his rifle. We felt our way along the length of the wall until it rounded a corner and spotted a set of stone steps leading up to a front door. It was open, and the door was swinging wildly in the wind. Fresh snow had accumulated on the steps, partially blocking the entrance.

We did our best to clear the stairs, and John went in first, rifle raised. Only dim light came in from the shuttered windows—which remarkably still had glass in them—but I made out the interior of the small cabin, which included an old wood stove, some kitchen cabinets, and a rotted wooden table and two metal chairs. In the far corner, there was a door that looked like it led to a small bedroom. Other than that, it was empty, and judging by the dust and the sparse contents, no one had been here in a long, long time.

John went to check the back bedroom, but it was also empty. It was as close to safe as it could be.

"Let me get the other two," he said to me. "Stay here and keep watch. If you see anyone, you scream as loud as you can, alright?"

I nodded, and he left. I tried to close the front door to stop more snow from blowing inside, but the latch was broken. I held it closed with my weight until the others returned. Kimmy and Asha soon arrived, scarlet-faced and shivering. John tied the door closed with the climbing rope, and then we were safe at last. We huddled close together for warmth as we waited for the howling wind to quiet.

It took hours for the storm to die down. Kimmy and Asha chatted quietly back and forth, playing games like I-Spy to pass the time. John tried to talk to me, but I met him with curt answers, and he eventually stopped, shooting me a hurt look. Guilt roiled in my gut, and I wanted to confront him. I just didn't want an audience.

Eventually, in the afternoon, the storm abated. We had to dig our way out of the cabin, and by the time we finished, the light had already started to fade.

"We'll stay the night," John said, and Kimmy nodded.

"Asha and I will go hunting," she replied, hooking her arm through Asha's. To my surprise, Asha gave a very small smile. "You and Claire can set things up here."

We agreed, and then John and I went to gather firewood. Sticks and branches had been scattered everywhere during the storm, so it wasn't difficult to find. Wood was the only thing we never seemed to lack.

"So," John said, attacking a branch with his hatchet a little more aggressively than was probably necessary, "who pissed in your oatmeal this morning?"

"What?" I asked, caught off guard by his directness.

"Baby, I'm not stupid," John said with a frustrated chuckle. "I know you're pissed at me. Could you maybe just tell me why?"

His acknowledgement caused the dam inside me to burst.

"I don't know," I said with venom, "maybe because the Jamesons are going to hunt me down when we get to the Valley, unbeknownst to me? Maybe because my boyfriend is keeping vital information from me for no reason I can tell? Or maybe because he has skeletons in his closet that are starting to make their way out, and I don't know what to believe anymore."

My voice shook on the last word. John stared at me impassively, but I could practically see the wheels turning in his head.

"Has Kimmy been talking?" he finally said. "I told her not to bother you with this."

"Oh, for God's sake, John," I said, crossing my arms. "Stop avoiding me. I deserve to know what I'm getting myself into! And you lied to me."

"I never lied to you," John said defensively. "I told you that you didn't need to worry about it, which was the truth."

"Why should *you* decide what *I* get to worry about? Hmm?" I shot back. "You think I'm a child? That I'm so fragile that I can't handle the truth? Do you really think so little of me?"

Each word seemed to hit him like a blow.

"Of course not," he said softly. "It's not about that."

"Then what is it about? Start talking, I mean it."

John studied my hardened expression and crossed arms, then sighed wearily.

"Let's finish this and head back," he said. "Then I'll tell you everything. I promise."

We finished gathering firewood in silence, then hauled it all back to the cabin. Once we'd built up the fire in the woodstove, John took a seat on one of the chairs beside it.

"Tell me what you know," John said at last. "I'll fill in the blanks."

I sat across from him in the other chair. "Let's start with this whole Jameson thing."

I told him what Asha had said about the family's feud and their strong opposition to outsiders. When I finished, he leaned back in his chair, considering me.

"All true," he said. "They won't accept you. Wouldn't matter who you were; you're not one of us, and the fact that it's *me* bringing you home is gonna be a major thorn in the old bastard's side. He never liked me."

"Why?" I asked, and he shrugged.

"I never did anything to them personally, but he and Granddad always hated each other, so I guess I inherited the grudge. Having a bit of a wild streak when I was a teenager didn't help."

A ghost of a smile touched my lips. I'd heard all about John's stint as a rebellious teen—the silly pranks he'd played, the trouble he'd gotten himself into. Against my will, it softened me a little, reminded me that I *did* know him...whatever Asha said.

"What happened when your grandfather died?" I asked, more gently this time. "I...heard that Jameson was supposed to become chairman, but then something happened to change people's minds."

John chuckled darkly. "You could say that. That 'something' was a bunch of human traffickers."

I blanched. "What?"

"Yeah," he said quietly, his eyes glazed with memory. "See, they got a kid to lure Allie to them when the Armstrongs visited the trading post. They get kids to talk to other kids, gain their trust, and then abduct them."

I shivered at the memory of the woman who'd tried to lure me the same way.

He cleared his throat. "They sell them at slave markets that cater to a certain...customer. The younger, the better. I don't have to tell you about the kind of people who shop there, because you met them in Little River."

Just like the man who'd asked him how much I was.

"Anyway, that's how they got Allie," John said, and pain crept into his voice. "I've known that kid since the day she was born. Held her, fed her, played with her, babysat her countless times."

I reached across the table and touched his hand. Allie was his favourite of the Armstrong kids, and through the countless stories I'd been told, John had always acted as her protective big brother.

"I wasn't going to let them have her. I couldn't."

"I know," I said softly. "So you went after her."

"And what I found will live with me till the day I die."

I hesitated, afraid of what I was about to hear, but I'd asked for the truth. I waited, and he swallowed hard before continuing.

"I tracked three men back to their camp, prepared to just find Allie and go. But...they had maybe a dozen kids there. Working. Serving them. Wearing ripped, dirty clothes, looking like hell. And while I was doing recon, a boy went into a tent with one of the men and didn't come out for a while. When he left, he was crying, shaking."

John's hand trembled in mine.

"I had to end it," he said, icy anger creeping into his voice. "I couldn't just leave them there."

I nodded numbly, squeezing his hand, and John gave a grim smile.

"They weren't expecting me, so it wasn't hard. Took out two of them but kept the third alive. Bound him up and left him there till I got the kids to safety. They were all from the Post, as we call it, so it wasn't so hard to get them home. I wanted to take Allie home, too...but she wouldn't let me. She was obviously scared, so she stuck to me like glue."

I bit my lip. "Did they...hurt her?"

John grimaced. "She was new, so from what she said, they just made her do chores around the camp. They were planning to leave soon, take the kids with them to sell."

He took a deep breath and continued. "I made Allie hide nearby while I went back to deal with the last guy. I wanted to know where they were going to take the kids, and who they planned to sell them to. Only he wasn't going to give it up so easy. So...I had to be persuasive."

The room was silent except for the crackling of the fire, and the air felt suddenly heavy. Finally, I got the nerve to speak.

"What did you do?"

John cracked a grim, unhappy smile. "What *didn't* I do to that bastard? Reduced him to a bloody, snivelling puddle on the ground. He told me what I wanted to know...eventually."

He looked as though he'd aged a decade, his voice hollow.

"I took Allie home," he said after a pause. "Then spent the next couple months tracking down more traffickers, and a few of their biggest customers. So nobody could come after her again—or any other kid."

He let out a long breath. "Obviously, word got around the Valley that I brought Allie back. And people started saying they wanted me to be chairman, that I'd shown real leadership instead of just promising it. Old Jameson didn't like that. Not one bit."

"But it wasn't your fault," I said with a frown. "You didn't know they'd react that way."

John gave a bitter chuckle. "You say that as if it mattered to him. At first, he was as relieved as everyone else, but once they started talking about the chairman seat, he started saying I'd done it just to play the hero. That I'd put everyone at risk by going after a trafficking ring that could've hunted down the Valley and retaliated. There was infighting between people who supported me and those who sided with him."

Anger surged through me, burning in my belly like hot coals.

"Why did they listen? How the hell did he have so much power?"

John shrugged. "The Jamesons have always had the biggest farm in the Valley. It'd be hard to find someone who doesn't owe them a favour or two, which is just how the old man likes it...and he has five sons just like him. Sure, our inner circle never liked his family, but not everyone feels the same way."

"Is this why you didn't become an outrider?" I asked, and his brief pause made my heart ache.

"Not directly," he said after a moment. "But the Chief was a friend of his, and...well, I trained with Danny, and we were evenly matched. The Chief took on Danny, but not me. As far as I can tell, the only difference between us was that Jameson didn't hate Danny's family."

I shook my head in disbelief. "So, what happened after the infighting?"

"That's when the PNC situation got more urgent. We'd started reducing the use of vehicles to conserve energy. So, Kimmy and I left. I'd already promised Granddad we would before he died, and things being so tense made it easier to go."

And then I'd met him on that rooftop over a year into their search. Though it'd only been about eight months since then, it felt like a lifetime ago.

"So," John continued, "because he apparently saw me as a threat, and now I'm bringing in outsiders...I'm not gonna become his favourite guy anytime soon."

We sat in silence for a moment. I knew John was waiting for me to speak, but I didn't know what to say. My emotions felt muddled.

"If there's one thing I want you to always know," he said, his voice breaking slightly, "it's that I'd never hurt you, Claire—never. No matter what I've done in the past. And if I've broken your trust and you're afraid of me again, then I...I'll try to earn it back. If you'll let me."

"Wait, what?" I said, frowning. "Why would you say that?"

"I tortured a man," he said with a shrug. "And while I didn't torture the others, I didn't give them painless deaths, either. I did it to stop them, but I also wanted revenge, and I didn't even feel bad. Still don't. So, if you're back to thinking I'm a monster, I don't like it...but I get it."

I gaped at him. I hadn't been afraid of him in a long time, but it struck me how deeply my prejudice in those days had affected him. Shame rose inside me, along with a desire to show him the truth.

"What would you do if someone took me?" I asked quietly. "The same thing?"

John met my gaze, his eyes intent.

"Far worse, baby," he said, emphasizing each word. "I'd become their shadow—the thing they're afraid of after dark. I'd hunt them down, no matter where they were, and their deaths would be as slow and painful as I could make them."

I swallowed hard. Regardless of her intentions, Asha had been every bit as wrong as I'd thought, and I felt even more ashamed for doubting him.

John was my protector. Always had been, always would be.

My silence clearly worried him, because he sighed and said, "I'm sorry. I should've told you. I see that now. It's just...before you, I never had to...discuss things before. Never had to share like this."

"But you share with Kimmy," I said gently. "Why, then—?"

"That's different," he said, with a frustrated shake of his head. "I've known Kimmy my whole life, and I'm used to her. She's not going to get under my skin. With you, I'm..."

He faltered, his jaw ticking, and he looked so uncomfortable that I felt a twinge of empathy. I wasn't exactly an expert on trust, either.

"Vulnerable?" I offered.

He swallowed hard. "Yeah."

I moved closer and touched his cheek. He leaned into my hand reflexively, and true to his word, he looked vulnerable in a way that tugged at the edges of my heart.

"Silly John," I chided gently. "You think that your incredible, bone-deep capacity for love is your weakness? When it's really your greatest strength?"

John frowned. "What I did—what I've done—"

"—is protect the ones you love with a ferocity I've never seen in anyone else," I interceded firmly. "It's why I'm alive. If you have darkness inside of you, it's no worse than anyone else's. At least you harness yours for good."

He shook his head again. "That's not the problem. I've accepted that part of me...and I didn't care about whatever darkness I had until I met you."

I stroked my thumb along his jaw, seized by the urge to soothe him.

"You think I don't know what kind of man you are?" I asked softly.

John fixed me with his amber gaze. "I never cared so much before if anyone thought I was a good man until you. Don't get me wrong, I always had a conscience, and tried to live up to what my grandparents taught me was right."

He paused, seeming to wrestle with emotion before continuing. "But...if you didn't think I was good, I don't know what I'd do, because I don't know if you've noticed, but I'm fucking crazy about you, baby."

I smiled. "I'd heard something like that, yes."

He covered my hand with his and brought it to his lips, and my heart ached anew.

"And that night a few weeks ago, when I said it was a weakness," he said, "it was because in that moment, I felt perfect, and I thought, *if anyone ever took this from me, I'd just...die.* I wouldn't want to keep surviving without it—without you. And that scares the shit out of me. I never felt like I had something so good that it would destroy me completely to lose it."

He blew out a breath. "When my grandparents died, I thought that was the worst pain I could feel. But now I know that it's not. And if

I pulled away that night, it's because I don't always know how to deal with that."

The overwhelming tenderness in my chest wouldn't let up. I moved in and kissed him—slowly, gently, like he might break at the slightest mishandling.

"I'm not going anywhere," I murmured, our lips an inch apart. "And how you could doubt that I adore you, exactly as you are, is a mystery."

The hint of a smile tugged at the corners of John's mouth, but he still held back.

"You didn't always feel that way, though. With how scared of me you used to be..."

I kissed him again, cutting him off. "I was raised on lies about Wastelanders, and I was wrong. Besides, that was before I knew how charming you could be. And the heart of gold hidden underneath that gruff, sexy Wastelander exterior."

He couldn't hold off anymore; he laughed. "And before I knew that a lion's heart lived inside that little mouse, hmm?"

I rolled my eyes. "That remains to be seen."

He chuckled but then turned serious again.

"I promise I'll be more open with you...or at least, if I have a good reason to keep something to myself, I'll tell you."

I nodded, satisfied, and he pressed his lips to my forehead and held them there. A halo of warmth surrounded me, and despite the fact that I felt weak with hunger, I was perfectly content.

"Claire," he murmured against my skin after a beat, "I wanted—"

The cabin door banged open, and Kimmy and Asha bustled in, a dead turkey and a cooking pot full of snow between them.

"Dinner," Kimmy said briskly, holding out the carcass. "Found this guy nesting near a lake."

I gasped in delight and took it, reflecting on how much I really had changed, that the sight of a dead turkey was cause for celebration rather than disgust. The thought of eating a hot meal made my empty stomach growl audibly. John sighed, shooting me a look that said he regretted ending the conversation. I shrugged and gave him a small smile. We'd said all the important things.

John and I prepared the turkey while Kimmy set up the cooking supplies. Asha set the pot of snow on the woodstove to boil. She gave me a pointed look, and I knew she wondered what had passed between me and John. I wasn't sure she'd be pleased by the happy resolution, but I resolved to give her time. We all needed to be patient with each other and work harder to trust—even when it was painful or difficult. We wouldn't survive this trip otherwise.

CHAPTER 15

Claire

Dinner was heaven, and by the time I finished, I was certain roasted turkey was my new favourite food. My mother would've been ashamed of me. I abandoned all table manners and ate like a desperate, starving vagrant...probably because I was. I sunk my teeth into a drumstick and moaned at the fatty, smoky flavour on my tongue.

"You and that turkey need a room, Claire?" Asha asked wryly, and I laughed without thinking. She was teasing me the way she used to.

"Never thought eating could feel this good," I answered with a shrug before ripping off another chunk.

John gave my knee an affectionate squeeze. When I finished the drumstick, he pushed more on me, and by the end of the meal, my stomach was full for the first time in a while.

We retired to the tiny back bedroom of the cabin, where John lit another fire in the small fireplace. I laid out our sleeping bags in front of it for warmth. Even though the wood floor was hard and battered, it was better than sleeping on the cold ground. Better still, there was a door we could close, and some semblance of privacy—something I dearly missed.

"You want a bath?" John asked, stoking the flames with an old, rusty poker that'd been left by the fireplace. "Might be the last time for a while."

"Uh, obviously," I said incredulously, and he laughed. "I feel disgusting."

"That makes two of us, then."

He refilled the cooking pot with snow and heated it over the fire until steam rose in hot, irresistible tendrils. It wouldn't be a proper bath—there was no way to do that here—but a nice sponge bath with hot water was still better than nothing, especially with how much traveling we were doing. It may also be our last thorough wash for some time, because with how cold it was, we wouldn't be able to do more than a quick wipe down under our clothes without risking hypothermia.

I fetched washcloths from our bags and handed one to John before soaking mine in the hot water. I peeled off my clothes, staying near the fireside to keep warm. John did the same, taking off his jacket and long-sleeved shirt to reveal his lean, muscular body. A little shiver went through him at the cold air, but he sighed with pleasure as he swept the hot cloth over his torso.

I couldn't help but stare, my own washcloth forgotten in my hand. Given the lack of privacy and the cold, it'd been weeks since I'd seen him fully naked, and just as long since we'd properly made love. Mostly, we had quick, stolen moments of passion here and there, with little time to savour it. The rest of the time, we were both so exhausted from travel that when neither of us were on watch at night, we fell asleep immediately.

My eyes followed the hard, beautiful lines of his body, down to the small trail of hair that led to his groin. The flickering firelight gave his skin an alluring luminosity, and I felt overwhelmed by the need to touch him. He'd unbuttoned his pants before he noticed the intensity of my gaze.

He grinned. "See something you like over there?"

I swallowed hard. "No. I was just washing and thinking about...wholesome things. Cute animals. Grandmothers. A baby's laughter."

John's bark of a laugh told me exactly what he thought about that. He shed his pants and boxers, making it even harder not to stare as I took in his naked form. A tremor that had nothing to do with the cold went through me, and heat suddenly pulsed between my thighs.

"You seem to be having trouble focusing," John said wryly, and I made a face at him before we finished scrubbing ourselves down.

When we were both done, John moved closer and took the washcloth from my hand. He skimmed my neck with it, spreading wet warmth over my body as the water trickled down my bare breasts. I sighed as he moved down, bathing me with laser-like focus, raising goosebumps on every inch of my flesh.

"Let your hair down," he murmured as he circled my nipple with the washcloth. His gaze was soft, and the request felt deeply intimate.

I unwound my braid, letting loose waves fall over my shoulders and down my back. John watched me with a new intensity, his eyes moving over the curves of my body, the locks of my hair. He circled me, not unlike a predator surveying prey, gazing at my nakedness in the glow of the firelight.

After a moment of exquisite tension, I couldn't take it anymore. I reached over and put my clammy hand on his bare chest. He inhaled sharply at my touch and gave me a look that could only be described as wolfish before covering my hand with his.

"I want—"

John cut me off with a sloppy, hungry kiss that lasted only a second before he pulled back again.

"Kneel." His voice was rough, suddenly edged with need.

It was not a request, and deep, urgent arousal coiled deep in my abdomen as I lowered myself to my knees in front of the fireplace. I wanted to take him in my mouth like this, to give him pleasure, but the floorboards creaked as he knelt directly behind me.

John kissed along the crook of my neck, twisting a hand in my hair to gently pull my head back.

"I want you," I said, almost a whine. "It's been too long."

He sighed in a helpless way that told me he agreed. Distantly, I heard Asha talking in the main room, followed by Kimmy's giggles. John nibbled at my neck, making me moan loudly, and the giggles abruptly cut off in response.

"Naughty girl," John whispered in my ear, and I shuddered. "Wouldn't want to get caught, would we?"

"No," I breathed, even as I felt wetness blooming between my thighs.

"Wouldn't want them to know the way you moan my name when you're close, hmm?"

"You'd have to get me close first for that to happen," I said dryly, pretending to be impassive. "And I'm nowhere near that point."

Meanwhile, my whole body tingled with his nearness, the way his body bracketed mine...and the way I could feel him, hard against the small of my back.

"That right, princess?" he taunted, his hand following the curve of my hip towards my centre. "So, if I touch you now, you won't be wet?"

"Dry as a bone," I replied, but the quiver in my voice betrayed me.

John suddenly grabbed my chin in his hand and pulled my head back against his shoulder, and I gasped. His hand came to rest on my throat—no pressure, no discomfort. Just holding. Possessing.

"Shame about the noise it'd make," John murmured, his teeth grazing the edge of my ear. "Because otherwise, I'd spank that beautiful, bratty ass of yours for being so mouthy. Put you over my knee, and not stop until you were squirming, begging me for release."

A pulse of arousal went through my clit at that image. I wanted him to do it. Wanted him to hold me down and spank me until my backside was red and hot to the touch. Wanted him to get off on it, to love giving it to me as much as I craved it from him. There was something intoxicating about being under a lion's paw and knowing that he would never use his strength to crush you.

"And would you give it?" I whispered, very aware of his warm breath on the back of my neck.

"If you were a very good girl," John answered, his tone deliciously low and dangerous. He used his knee to force my legs farther apart. "Taking my cock and my come like you were told."

"And if I wasn't?"

"Then I'd fuck you till I finished and leave you aching," he said silkily. "You'd go through the rest of the day wanting me, aching to come, but I wouldn't let you. Not until you begged me for relief."

His pressed his hard length against my entrance. I heard the wet sound it made and moaned too loudly again. His soft, dark chuckle tickled my ear.

"Quiet down," he whispered. "Don't get us in trouble. And keep your hands on the mantel while I fuck you, hmm? If you do as you're told, maybe I'll let you come."

I shuddered as he slipped between my thighs and pushed inside me. I moaned, quieter this time, but John covered my mouth with his free hand—his other one was still on my throat.

He gave me a forceful thrust, and I made a tiny, muffled squeak. My back was pressed to his chest, and I was as helpless as a newborn kitten in his arms. Depraved as it probably was, I loved being at his mercy and hearing all his dirtiest thoughts about me. He desired me like no one else ever had.

"Shh," John chided again, deeply amused. "I'm starting to think you want everyone to know the filthy sounds you make when I'm inside you. When I'm driving you wild with my touch."

I inhaled sharply as his hand moved from my throat to my breast. He pinched my nipple between his fingertips, and I sighed, tightening around him. He gave a low growl and pumped into me mercilessly, his control gone. The pleasure built inside me with every thrust, slow-burning and bright, and I moaned again.

A sudden, unexpected slap landed directly on my clit, stinging deliciously, and I squealed into the palm of John's hand.

"I told you to be quiet," he said, sounding strained as he slid in and out of me. "But you just can't help yourself, can you, sweetheart?"

It wasn't nearly as hard as he'd spanked my backside in the past, and the soft flesh muffled sound from the impact. The sting had already faded, leaving my clit raw and aching with the pleasure of his touch, however brief.

My knuckles were white around the mantel as he drove into me again. When I moaned, he rewarded me with another spank on my clit. Over and over, I gasped, squeaked, moaned more, and he gave me what I craved while taking me as he pleased.

"Ah, my Claire," John growled in my ear. "I want to come so deep in your cunt. I want you to take all of me, every drop, and then I want to feel you come all over my cock. Is that what you want?"

I nodded frantically against his hand, and his hips sped up. His teeth sunk into my shoulder, and he gave a muffled groan against me as he came hard, filling me with sharp surges of pleasure.

Before he'd even had time to recover, his fingers were on my clit, stroking me urgently. He rocked his hips in rhythm, giving me the stimulation I needed inside me. He didn't move his hand from my mouth; on the contrary, he clamped it more firmly in place.

He worked me expertly, swirling his fingers around my clit and whispering filthy sweet nothings in my ear. He told me how good I felt around him; how sexy I looked, naked in the firelight; and how much he loved hearing me moan into his hand. He called me his good, sweet girl, and told me how much he got off on spanking me like I needed him to.

I came like a whirlwind—suddenly and all at once. John was wise to cover my mouth, because I gave a hoarse cry as pleasure flooded my body, spreading from my aching clit outward. I kept coming until I was shaky, unsteady, and exhausted, my knees wobbling.

John lowered his hand from my mouth and turned my head to kiss me before withdrawing. I collapsed on top of his sleeping bag, breathing heavy, my eyes closed. I felt like my soul had left my body.

I heard him chuckle softly, then felt a wet, warm washcloth between my legs, wiping away the mess there. I watched him through slitted lids as he cleaned himself and then washed the cloth again in the leftover water. He lay it flat to dry in front of the fire, then laid down beside me and pulled me against him. I rested my head against his chest and snuggled him happily. The air was still frigid, but between the nearby fire and John's ever-warm bulk, I was toasty.

No matter what was in his past or our future, I'd never been so safe and loved in my whole life. John was a gift that I'd neither asked for nor deserved at the time he came into my world, but I cherished him...no matter what Asha, or anyone else from my old life, might think.

Before sleep could claim me, I looked up at John again. His expression was sweet and satisfied, a faint smile touching his lips as he looked at me. I reached out and cupped his cheek, and he sighed and shut his eyes, leaning into my touch.

I stroked him from forehead to chin, smoothing away stress and worry lines. He carried so much on his shoulders all the time, and he always had—the story he'd told me about Allie had only confirmed it.

He felt responsible for his people, and that now included me. But I wanted to take care of him, too, to be worthy of being the one person he felt truly vulnerable with.

"I love all of you, you know," I murmured. "Don't doubt that I could love you even on your darkest day. I can't stop loving you any more than I can stop myself from breathing, and with my last breath, I'd tell you so."

John put a hand under my chin and kissed me deeply, thoroughly, for a long moment before pulling back. His eyes shone with emotion in the low light, and he buried his face in my hair.

"You are everything," he whispered roughly, then cleared his throat. "Let's get some rest, sweetheart. Another long day tomorrow."

Eventually, he shifted underneath me, and I allowed him to help me into my sleeping bag. He tucked me in, kissed my forehead, and told me he loved me. Then he crawled into his sleeping bag beside me, draping an arm over my hip.

Just as I was on the edge of sleep, there was a sound from the main room of the cabin. I frowned, listening. It sounded like something moving. And then a sigh. A gasp. A moan.

God, a moan? I flushed from head to toe.

"Christ," John muttered as another, louder moan reached us. "Really, Kimmy? Couldn't even try to keep it down?"

I did my best to muffle my helpless giggles against my sleeping bag.

"You can hardly lecture her," I said, amused. "We just did the same."

"That's different," he replied, though he didn't elaborate on how, exactly.

"Don't be such a grump," I chided playfully. "She wanted someone, and she's finally happy...*very* happy, from the sounds of it."

"Gross. That's my sister."

"Your sister, *and* a grown woman. With needs."

He shot me a look of utter disgust that only made me giggle more.

"Cheer up, Wastelander," I said, snuggling him. "Sooner or later, if Asha does her job, she'll finish."

"Oh my God, Claire, stop."

His cheeks had turned bright red. I wasn't used to seeing John mortified—he was usually so unflappable—and it was so unexpected and adorable that I buried my face in his chest and silently laughed until tears sprung to my eyes.

CHAPTER 16

Claire

Days passed as we continued north. If I hadn't known it already, I quickly learned that nature was a cruel mistress, and winter was her weapon of choice. We walked endlessly, every day, with cold, hunger, and exhaustion clinging to us like the gossamer threads of a spider's web. Ensnared, we struggled against it, but some part of us sensed that the spider grew nearer every day.

More walking meant that the food rationing became significantly harder on us. My clothes started hanging looser on my body, and I was surprised one afternoon by my reflection in a stream, my cheeks hollower and paler than I remembered. The skin between my fingers cracked and bled—a product of the dry, frigid air—and my eyes stung from the light reflection off the snow. I became cold quicker than ever and never felt like I wore enough layers, to the point that John started sharing my sleeping bag to keep me warm at night. At the end of each day, I looked forward to his warm body curled around mine, his breath at my ear, his kisses in my hair. It kept me going.

Constant hunger and cold meant that everyone was irritable. Misery sharpened Asha's tongue to a razor's edge, and more than once, I swore John was about to throttle her for her complaining. Kimmy was more tolerant, but even she got testy when I innocently asked how far we had left to go one morning. The lack of privacy and alone time was one more thing that wore on all of us. Being together constantly didn't help the growing tensions between us.

To John's credit, if he was short with the other two, he was always patient with me, and tried to comfort me even when I could tell he was hanging by a thread himself. Truthfully, he was the only one I wasn't sick of after weeks of constant contact.

The air was frigid the morning I woke up with a sore throat; I could see my breath every time I exhaled. As we trudged through snow and ice, my lungs ached from the cold, dry air. I was more tired than usual, falling behind the others, my eyelids feeling heavy. A snowflake landed on my nose, melting on contact and startling me back into alertness.

"You alright, Claire?" Kimmy asked me. "You don't look good."

"I think I might be coming down with something," I answered, coughing into the crook of my arm.

"Do you need to stop?" John asked, his voice rich with sudden concern.

"No," I insisted, and Asha raised her eyebrows at me as I hacked another cough into my arm. "I don't want to stop. We've been making good time so far."

We kept going till dusk before making camp. John wrapped me in a blanket and made me sit by the fire while he cooked dinner. Meanwhile, Kimmy examined my throat, listened to my cough, and took my temperature with the thermometer in her medical kit.

"You have a fever," she informed me as she put her supplies away. "But it's low-grade. It'll probably go away on its own, but I'll keep an eye on it."

Asha had been watching me like a hawk ever since earlier, and she finally spoke.

"You think she has the flu?"

Kimmy shrugged. "I don't know. To be safe, though, maybe we should take a day off tomorrow and let Claire rest."

I shook my head vehemently. "I don't want to lose a whole day because of a stupid cold. I—"

Unfortunately, my argument was cut off by a coughing fit, which didn't help my case. John dropped next to me, rubbing my back, worry etched into his features.

"We'll see how you feel tomorrow, alright?" he said, clearly trying to pacify me. "For tonight, let's just take it easy."

After dinner, I found myself dozing off against John's shoulder by the fire. He kissed the top of my head and murmured something I didn't understand before gently lowering me onto the blanket we were sitting on, letting me lie down. He rearranged the blanket I'd been wrapped in so that it covered me, and I fell asleep.

Eventually, the sound of raised voices, sharp and angry, cut through my slumber, yet I was too sleepy to open my eyes.

"And what are you doing about it?" Asha was saying. "Hmm? She's wasting away, and now she's sick, on top of everything else."

"You think I don't know that?" John shot back. "You think I *like* seeing her sick and starving?"

"Stop deflecting. You're supposed to be taking care of her. You think I don't know how things work out here, *Wastelander*?"

The word was spit out with such malice that I flinched. It wasn't a cute nickname when Asha said it; it was closer to a slur.

"You just *happened* to come across a helpless woman in need," Asha continued. "One who literally couldn't survive without you. And then your dick just *happened* to fall into her. What a coincidence!"

"Fuck you," John said, his tone low and dangerous.

Asha laughed harshly. "You think I blame you for taking advantage of the situation? It's what all your kind do. She gives you her body to use and abuse, and you take care of her in exchange. But you can't even do that."

I slowly opened my eyes and saw Asha's hardened expression.

"That's why you're a special kind of trash, Wastelander," she said. "You don't even take care of your things."

There was a brief pause.

"What the fuck is wrong with you?" John said with disgust.

I couldn't take it anymore. I stirred, coughing, anger coiling in my gut. John automatically reached for me, putting an arm around me and helping me sit up.

"Easy," he murmured, instantly gentle. "You're not well. Let's get you to bed."

"After what she just said?" I choked out. "No."

I turned to Asha, who bit her lip, looking like she'd been caught out.

"Apologize or leave," I said, my voice hoarse but definitive.

"What?" she asked, her eyebrows shooting up. "Claire, I was just—"

"You heard me."

There was a tense pause before Kimmy appeared at the fireside. My only guess was that she'd left for a bathroom break.

"What's going on?" she asked, looking back and forth between Asha and John and me.

"Why don't you ask your new girlfriend?" John said sardonically.

Kimmy frowned and looked at Asha. "What?"

"Long story short," he continued, "she thinks I'm a piece of shit who traps helpless women and makes them fuck me for favours."

Kimmy's eyes widened, and she stared hard at Asha for a moment.

"If that's how you really feel," I said, suppressing another cough, "you can get the hell out of here, Asha. He's the love of my life."

John's expression softened slightly at my declaration, and he enclosed my gloved hand in his own.

"Yeah, I know," Asha shot back. "You 'love' him in the fucked up, Stockholm Syndrome way that people learn to love their captors. But—"

"Is that what you think?" Kimmy asked. "That we've beaten Claire down so much that she's given in?"

Asha looked cornered. "Not *you*, Kim—"

"Just my brother," she interrupted furiously. "Just the guy I was raised with, traveled with for the last two years, who comes from the same place I do. If you think I'd tolerate him if he was doing anything like that, you don't know me as well as I thought you did."

Not difficult, since she's known you for all of a few weeks, I thought bitterly. *Meanwhile, I've known her for years and I would've never predicted this.*

"I meant what I said," I said to Asha. "Decide. Now."

She studied me, deep brown eyes full of curiosity, doubt, and resentment. Then she surprised me.

"I'm sorry," she said to John in a dutiful sort of way. "I take back the things I said." Her expression changed, and for the first time, I saw hints of everything she was holding back. "I…I've seen a lot of shit in the last ten months, and none of it was good. I'm still trying to wrap my mind around it all."

Kimmy's expression was a conflicted mix of pain and anger as she glanced back and forth between Asha and John. I looked to John, wondering if her apology was enough for him. There was anger contained in the tension of his jaw, but also a look of resignation in his eyes. I knew he didn't have it in him to leave a helpless woman to die in the cold—even one that got on every nerve he had. Even one he only saved to spare me guilt.

"Fine," he bit out. "Claire needs rest, and I think you and my sister need to talk."

One look at Kimmy and no one could doubt it was true. Her gaze was cold as ice, and Asha looked cowed for once. The corner of John's mouth ticked slightly upward in amusement, but it faded as he helped me to my feet, hearing me cough all the way up.

I was grateful when, several minutes later, he crawled into my sleeping bag with me and snuggled against my back. He always slept without a shirt now to avoid overheating, and his skin radiated warmth. I could feel his collarbone against my shoulder, rising more sharply than usual; he, too, had lost weight over the last few weeks and was thinner than I'd ever seen him. It hurt me to see him suffer, but typical John just told me not to worry about him. *Too bad*, I'd answered. *Someone has to worry about you, and it's going to be me.*

He pressed a kiss against my neck, cradling me against his body, and sleep closed in on me again almost instantly. Even my worst nightmares could be soothed with the knowledge that he was near.

"How do you feel?" John murmured by my ear.

"Better," I replied, eyelids heavy.

He took a couple of slow, deep breaths. I could faintly hear Kimmy laying into Asha, her voice edged with anger and regret, and Asha's softer replies, entreating and uncomfortably tender.

"I'm sorry," he whispered. "She's right. I haven't been taking care of you like I should."

"Not true," I said, perturbed, before enduring another dry cough. "None of us are exactly thriving in this environment. We're all doing our best. You most of all."

There was a pause, but I felt his body relax, as though I'd lifted a burden from him.

"Did you mean what you said?" he asked.

"About what?"

"That...I'm the love of your life."

I hesitated briefly. He was the only person I trusted entirely, and sometimes the vulnerability of it still frightened me. So much could happen in the Wasteland—I'd learned that the hard way. But I'd promised myself I'd be brave.

"Yes," I whispered. "With all my heart."

He was quiet again, this time for long enough that his next words were the last thing I remembered before sleep claimed me.

"You're mine too, you know. My one and only."

CHAPTER 17

Claire

The next few days were hell as my illness made its way through our party. All of us ran fevers, and we had no choice but to stay at our camp for the next several days to recover. We slept in our usual pairs in the tent, rotating every few hours while the other two slept under a hastily built lean-to by the campfire. Constant hunger made the sickness even more miserable.

As John and I lay by the fire, our bodies wracked with chills from fever, I wondered seriously for the first time if this was it for us. If we'd die out here in the cold, in the middle of nowhere, and never be found, except perhaps by the crows coming to pick at our bones. The spider that had once been at the edge of the web of our survival seemed closer than ever before, and we flies barely had anything left to fight her off with.

John was asleep beside me, his face pale and still like death, and that thought frightened me more than anything ever had. I wiped the sweat from his brow and kissed the tip of his nose. He stirred, groaning softly, and mumbled, "Thanks, Granny."

I stilled, watching him dream of some time and place far more pleasant than this one. After a moment, his eyelids fluttered.

"Claire?" he murmured, somewhere between sleeping and waking.

"Shh, darling," I soothed, stroking his hot, clammy forehead with my thumb. "You were dreaming."

He closed his eyes again. "Dreamt that my grandmother was here."

"Mmm. What was she doing?"

"Taking care of me," he croaked. "Like when I was sick as a kid."

My heart.

"What would she do?" I asked softly.

"Make me hot food. Hold me. Sing songs, sometimes."

His tone was wistful and sad, and I couldn't bear his pain—not when he was already sick and suffering, out here in the cold. With a lump in my throat, I took his face in my hands and lay his head against my breast.

My mother had never held me when I was sick. She'd certainly never sung to me. They weren't things that would have ever occurred to her to do. My father would have when I was little, but as I got older, he was around less and less—busy with his high-level military job in charge of compound security, and burying himself in work to avoid my mother's wrath. I had not known the kind of love that John had often described within his close-knit family. Mine had been broken beyond repair long before I was ever even a thought, and now...well, I had little hope for a joyful family reunion.

So I didn't know how, exactly, to comfort someone I loved. It was the sort of thing that John was better at. But as he settled against me, I held him in my arms and sang a lullaby, soft and warm as the morning sun. My voice was hoarse, my lips cracked, but he sighed heavily and relaxed against me. The song was about coming home after a long day, the warmth of the hearth and the soft, sweet words of a lover.

As it ended, I pressed gentle kisses on John's face, easing him back to sleep.

"Don't leave me," I whispered. "I need you."

I rested my head against his, a tear escaping down my cheek as the cold claws of winter continued to ravage our bodies and minds.

That night, my fever broke, and mercifully, over the next day or two, everyone else's did, too. The awful sickness passed, and though we'd had to stop for nearly a week, our spirits briefly lifted as we recovered.

Of course, it didn't last long. Trudging through winter storms with perpetually empty stomachs will eventually break down almost anyone, and maintaining constant vigilance was exhausting. Soon enough, it felt like we were at each other's throats again, which meant that a number of our days were silent other than the whistle of a lonely winter wind.

By Kimmy's rough count, we'd spent well over a month on the road, and eventually, it all blended together. I felt like I was sleepwalking through life, tethered to the world only by the knowledge that my friends and my love needed me to keep going.

One afternoon, we were trudging through the snow-covered forest, mostly in silence, when I noticed something in my peripheral vision. Partially obscured by an evergreen tree, there was a wooden pole stuck in the ground, with something mounted on top. I couldn't tell what it was; it was covered by snow. But the pole looked deliberate and man-made—it stuck out in the dense wilderness I'd become accustomed to.

"John," I called. He was several paces ahead of me, walking with Kimmy, while I hung back with Asha. "What's that?"

He looked where I was pointing and stopped dead. Shooting Kimmy a look of concern, he made his way over to the pole, picked up a fallen branch, and used it to clear away the snow.

What he uncovered made me feel ill: a shrunken, dried human head, skewered on a pike, its empty eye sockets staring at nothing.

John immediately turned and ran back to me, grabbing my wrist.

"Move," he said to Kimmy, whose eyes were wide.

He strode away, pulling me along with him, while the other two followed.

"What was that thing?" I asked, fear creeping into my voice.

"It's a totem," John replied, not slowing for a minute. "Maneaters—cannibals—use them to mark their territory."

My stomach dropped, and the memory of the last time I'd encountered bloodthirsty cannibals surfaced. The stench of rotting human flesh. The pit full of discarded human bones. The teeth they wore like jewellery, and the feral way they spoke and moved.

Just as soon as I had the thought, a horrible, ear-piercing shriek split the air.

John cursed and pulled me in front of him. "Run. Now. I'll follow."

He gave me a little push, and I broke into a sprint, dashing between the trees, trying to avoid tripping over rocks and tree roots. I heard the others just behind me as we ran for our lives. More shrieks echoed through the woods, growing closer and closer. They were calling more of their brethren.

Terrified, I felt like my lungs would burst from exertion. I was weaker than I'd once been, and my endurance was shot. What little muscle I had left was screaming at me in protest, but the shrieks were multiplying and getting louder by the second. Footfalls pursued us, and it wouldn't take long for them to catch up.

My eardrums split at the boom of a rifle shot, then another. John was some way behind us and had started firing toward the cannibals. I ran until I felt on the brink of collapse, bursting out of the dense brush to find myself at the edge of a small frozen lake. I skidded to a halt, gasping for breath. There was nowhere else to go.

Asha and Kimmy joined me a half-second later, followed by John.

"There's too many," Kimmy said, and to my dismay, she sounded afraid.

John looked out onto the ice, his brow creased in a frown.

"No choice," he said, clipped. "We have to cross. The ice will slow them down enough that they may give up. I'll cover us from the rear."

"That's insane!" Asha burst out.

"If you got a better idea, Ice Queen, I'm all ears," he replied sharply, and Kimmy gave Asha a reproachful look.

"I'll cover the front," Kimmy added with a short nod.

John rapidly uncoiled the climbing rope and handed one end to Kimmy, who coiled it around her wrist. He did the same with the opposite end.

"Run ahead," he said to her, and she took off running onto the ice, skidding as she went but managing to remain upright. Asha spared me a single glance before jogging after her.

John turned to me. "Stay in the middle. The rope will keep you stable. Move as fast as you can."

I nodded and grabbed the rope before making my way onto the ice. Despite having the rope, I struggled on the slippery surface, only managing a light jog. John followed, walking backward with his rifle out.

"Here they come!"

Subhuman sounds filled the air—uncanny snarls that chilled my blood. I dared to look back towards the treeline, and my mouth fell open.

A dozen cannibals spilled out, gathering at the edge of the lake. I couldn't count how many. They roared as they saw us, clearly enraged that their prey had slipped away from them. My stomach dropped.

A sizable chunk broke away from the screaming crowd at the lakeside, pursuing us onto the ice. They were only about 40 feet behind us and would gain ground quickly if they ran at full speed.

John raised the scope of his rifle to his eye and fired. A toothless, dirty-looking man fell onto the ice, bleeding from his head. The thump of his body hitting the ice nearly made me jump out of my skin. The enraged, subhuman screams of cannibals filled the air.

"Keep going," he called to me.

I kept moving, but there were more of them pouring onto the ice, giving chase. John shot the two closest to us, keeping them at bay, but on his own, he'd struggle to keep it that way.

Clutching the rope to maintain my balance, I pulled the rabbit gun into my arms and hastened back towards John. The cannibals had scattered in response to the shots, making it harder for John to target all of them. They approached from all directions, trying to close in.

I reached John's side. He made a sound of protest at my presence, but I ignored him. Instead, I put the scope to my eye, and fired at a big, wild-eyed man brandishing a bow, managing to fell him before he had the chance to fire an arrow.

"Good shot," John muttered.

I turned my sights on the rest of them, one by one. I was no John, but my aim, though imperfect, wasn't bad. Together, we managed to clear enough of them that the ones left retreated, sensing that as prey went, chasing us was more trouble than it was worth.

When I finally lowered the rabbit gun, I was shivering, and not from the cold. Even after everything we'd been through, I still wasn't used to killing. It still felt like it went against my fundamental nature in some way, and I didn't know if that was a good thing anymore. I needed to be stronger.

"You go ahead," John said to me, nodding back in the direction Kimmy and Asha had gone. "I'll follow. Just want eyes on them."

I nodded. He leaned over and pecked my lips.

"Thank you."

Something like pride bloomed inside me, and I smiled. I started off after the other two, who had pulled ahead and were almost to the other side of the lake. Kimmy waved as she moved onto the shore, then tied her end of the rope around a tree for stability. I moved as quickly as I could, still using the rope to balance, and John followed slowly behind me. His rifle was on his back again, but he still kept watch. Thankfully, it seemed like we were in the clear.

We were within ten feet of the other side when a deep groan came from behind me. It was not a human groan—not any sound an animal could make. It came from within the earth itself.

I looked over my shoulder at John just in time to see a long, thick crack snaking across the ice, underneath his boots. I opened my mouth to call out in warning, but it was too late. With an enormous crash, the ice split, opening like a yawning mouth to swallow him up.

"John!" I screamed as he plunged into the freezing water.

He only made a small sound of alarm before disappearing under the water.

I ran toward the hole in the ice, even as I heard Kimmy yelling at me to stay back.

He'd dropped his end of the rope onto the ice when he fell. I snatched it up and wound it around my wrist a few times, hoping to God it would hold. I dropped my bag at the edge, then dove into the lake.□

The impact of the icy water hit me in an intense, painful shockwave that paradoxically seemed to scorch my skin. I took an involuntary gasp and briefly choked on water. My eyes burned as I dove deeper into the dark, murky depths of the lake.

Thankfully, John had only sunk about eight feet below the surface, struggling frantically against an errant tree branch that had gotten caught on his jacket and was pulling him deeper. Relief surged through me at the sight of him, even as the freezing water sucked the strength from my muscles. His eyes widened at the sight of me, and there was new fear there that I couldn't dwell on if I planned on saving both of us.

Quicker than I knew I was capable of, I reached him, and with more strength than I knew I had, I disentangled his jacket from the heavy branch, allowing it to fall away and sink. I grabbed his hand and kicked furiously upward, using the cord wrapped around my wrist to pull us up. I kept my gaze on the one source of light: the hole in the ice. John helped me, pushing me as he swam upward, and finally—finally—we broke the surface, both of us gasping for breath.

"Holy shit," Kimmy yelled from the shore.

Asha was bent over a hastily built fire, trying to coax it into life.

I wasn't strong enough to pull John out of the water with me. He understood, because he unraveled the cord from around my wrist with shaky fingers, looping it around his own. He wrapped his free arm around me, pulling me tight against his body.

"Now!" Kimmy called.

She and Asha heaved with all their might on the cord, putting their full weight into it and lifting us enough so that John got traction on the ice and hauled us out. The exposure to the frigid air while soaked to the skin was somehow even worse than diving in, and I hyperventilated with every full-body shiver.

From the sounds of it, John wasn't faring much better, but he grabbed my hand and began to gingerly crawl across the ice, dragging me with him as he inched toward the bank where Kimmy waited. I followed his lead, but metres felt like kilometres when we were this cold, and by the time we made it, I was dangerously close to passing out.

Kimmy sprang forward, barking orders at Asha.

"Look after Claire. Help her change into dry clothes. I'll take care of John. I'll check on you soon."

Asha rushed to my side, dry clothes in hand. It took longer than it should have with my frozen joints creaking and jerking like rusted hinges, but we managed to change my soaked clothes. Strangely, I had stopped shivering.

Kimmy was much more efficient; she'd clearly done this before. John was already changed and wrapped in a blanket by the campfire by the time I joined them. He was shivering violently, his teeth chattering, but some colour had returned to his cheeks, which I took as an encouraging sign. I sat across from him on the other side of the fire, too numb to do much except stare blankly into the flames. I was more tired than I thought I'd ever been. My eyes burned, though I couldn't tell if it was from the water or from the overwhelming urge to sleep.

Kimmy was hard at work brewing broth for us, while Asha had ventured off to gather more fuel for our fire. It seemed to take forever, and I felt my eyelids closing and my head drooping.

"Cl-Claire," John said, suddenly urgent. "Are y-you going to f-faint?"

"No," I answered, right before my eyes snapped shut and my body fell forward.

I heard John's cry of alarm before everything turned dark. My faceplant on the frozen ground startled me back into consciousness.

"For God's sake," Kimmy said critically as she dragged me onto my back. "Why didn't you say anything?"

"I'm fine," I mumbled, my eyes closing again. "Not even shivering, Kim. Just so tired."

"Shit," she muttered. "Asha! Where are you?"

Evidently, John was not prepared to wait, because I heard him groan with effort as he hauled himself up. A moment later, he shoved my bedroll into Kimmy's arms. Kimmy set my sleeping bag up by the fire, then helped me under the covers. My eyelids drifted closed again.

"No," Kimmy said urgently, tapping my windburned cheek. "Stay awake."

John sat by my head, pulling his blanket tighter around his body as Kimmy got to work erecting the tent on the other side of the campfire. I tried to keep my eyes open and stay alert, but it felt like a losing battle.

"C-Claire," John said, giving my shoulder a shake. "Hang on. P-please."

"I'm okay," I said. "Perfectly...ah..."

My voice trailed off, and I drifted again.

"N no!" he said, an undertone of panic in his voice now. "St-stay with me, b-baby."

Darkness closed in at the corners of my vision, even as I tried to fight it. A million images flashed by my mind's eye, like a fast-motion slideshow: my sister, when we were little girls together; the golden eye of the Order, following and watching me like a hawk; and the voice of my father, gently murmuring, *sleep tight, Claire-bear.*

I was too weary to fight anymore. The cold had sapped all my remaining strength. I slipped under the surface of unconsciousness with barely a ripple.

* * *

◻I didn't remember being moved into the tent, but when I woke up, I was lying inside it, practically swaddled in a tight bundle of my sleeping bag and extra blankets. And I was finally warm.

◻I was jostled by John unzipping my sleeping bag and pulling me into his arms. He wore only a t-shirt and boxer shorts and was now radiating warmth like a space heater. I instinctively snuggled close to his core, stealing as much heat as I could. The frigid air still had a bite to it.

"You're warm," I said sleepily, my eyes still closed. "That's good news."

John chuckled and kissed the top of my head.

"How are you feeling?" he asked. "Asha lay with you until I was warm enough."

"Remind me to thank her," I said with a sigh. "Well, that was scary, wasn't it?"

"Yeah."

A pregnant pause followed, where he seemed to clutch me tighter to him. I wasn't complaining.

"Thank you," he finally murmured, pressing his cheek against my hair. "I could've killed you for going in after me back there, but...you saved my life."

"What was I supposed to do, shrug my shoulders and go on without you?" I said, my voice too muffled by weariness to sound truly impatient.

He sighed. "You could've died."

I made a disgruntled noise. "You *would* have died."

"I know," he replied, idly playing with my hair. "But...I'm supposed to take care of you. Not the other way around."

"That's stupid," I said with a wide yawn. "What would I have without you, John? You're the centre of my whole world. I'd have nothing if I lost you."

John didn't say anything for a long time. When he spoke again, there was a slight tremor in his voice.

"If you died for me, I'd never forgive myself," he whispered, burying his face in my hair. "You can't ever do that for me again."

"No deal," I murmured. "I love you. And that means I have to save you, too."

He took a sharp intake of breath and squeezed me. Silence followed for a beat before his hand found my chin and tilted my head back. He pressed his lips to mine, his hand moving to cradle the back of my head and pull me deeper.

John kissed me for a long time. At first, he was slow and tender, but there was a growing urgency in him. His tongue thrust into my mouth, and his thumb stroked my cheek. I moaned softly, and his kiss took on an almost frantic quality in response, as though I'd given him tacit permission to unleash whatever emotion was coursing through him.

He broke away to breathlessly shower my face, neck, and chest with more kisses, as though unable to stop himself.

"I can't bear how much I love you," he said, pained. "If I could love you even a little less, maybe I could stand for you to take risks. But as it is, I can't. Every second you're in danger is fucking agony."

He didn't give me a chance to respond; he caught my lips in another urgent, needy kiss that made me feel weak with its intensity. His hands explored my body hungrily, rousing me with teasing caresses in all my most sensitive places. He followed with his mouth, spreading open-mouthed kisses across my skin.

John's kisses were like an opiate, and I was intoxicated. He was insatiable and frenzied. Before I knew it, his hand had wandered into my pants, and he was strumming my clit rhythmically, his fingers inside me, as I writhed with pleasure.

"That's it, beautiful," he crooned, his voice low and urgent. "Come all over my fingers. Show me again how fucking good it is between us."

I cried out against his shoulder, coming hard for him, and he made a satisfied sound in his throat. He rolled on top of me, and we struggled with our clothes. Finally, he entered me with a helpless gasp before taking my mouth with his again.

"I love you more than my own life," he said, his voice rough with emotion. "So much that it breaks my fucking heart. I can barely stand it."

He thrust into me hard, and I gasped with pleasure, tightening my grip on him.

"You don't think," I replied breathlessly, "that I feel that for you, too? That I can stand to think of a life without you?"

He groaned as I synced my hips with his, and we moved together in a sweaty, enthusiastic heap, drawing closer to mutual fulfilment. There was a bone-deep ache, a hopeless longing, to our lovemaking that seemed to say, *we who are two would be one.* We reached climax together, clutching each other with a naked vulnerability that tugged at the corners of my heart.

"If you loved me half as much," John breathed, "I'd consider myself lucky."

When he rolled off me, I curled up beside him, too weary to open my eyes. His breathing uneven, he cradled me against his body like a precious thing he was guarding. Feeling safe and satisfied, I fell asleep with my forehead pressed against the warm skin of his throat.

❄

I woke with a start some time later, from bad dreams I didn't remember. It was still dark, with only firelight dimly illuminating the tent. John must have felt me stir because he stroked my hair.

"Shh, baby," he whispered. "I'm here. You're alright."

I calmed under his touch, relaxing once more in his arms.

"It's late, my love," he murmured, and I felt a surge of affection for him. He'd never called me that before. "Go back to sleep."

"'Kay," I mumbled, nuzzling against his neck.

John pressed his lips to my forehead. I was almost asleep when he spoke again.

"Marry me, Claire," he said, his voice soft and urgent, his hands tangled in my hair.

My eyes flew open, and I looked up at his face. His expression was solemn, his eyes full of emotion.

"What?" I asked, startled. "Why?"

The corners of his mouth ticked upward. "Because I'm so out-of-my-mind in love with you that just seeing you happy makes my day. Because I'd live my life thousand times over if it meant I got to keep meeting you. Because when I look at you, I see my future, and it's so bright that it's blinding."

I blinked back sudden tears. I hadn't even thought of marrying him as a real possibility. My first marriage had been so passionless and carefully arranged—so different from what I had with John—that it hadn't occurred to me that it was an option. But immediately, I knew I wanted it.

"Is that enough reasons?" he asked, gently cupping my cheek.

I swallowed hard. "You don't have to ask me just because I went in after you."

"But I do," he said. "You'd give your life for mine. I'm used to taking care of people, but you take care of me. I don't want to waste any more time without you as my wife. I know what I want...and it's you."

My wife. The words made me tingly with joy.

"I feel the same," I whispered.

He smiled. "Say yes, then."

I arched up and kissed him.

"Yes, John," I said softly.

He kissed me hard, then held me so tight that I had to fight a little for breath, laughing.

"There's another reason," he said after a moment, hesitation in his voice. "You already know that when we get home...not everyone is gonna be happy to see us. Especially with Asha now, too."

I nodded. "I'm sorry."

"Don't apologize. But...it'll be easier for you as my wife. There'll be less doubt about my commitment, and it shows you'll stick around."

He let out a breath, as if nervous about my reaction. I stared back at him, nonplussed.

"As far as I'm concerned," I said with a shrug, "getting married is a piece of cake after jumping into a frozen lake after you."

John smiled and pressed a kiss between my eyes.

"I know it's not going to be all that official-feeling out here, but I promise we'll have a real wedding at home—whatever you want."

"I hardly have grand expectations, darling," I said. "My last 'wedding' was as sterile as could be—signed a few papers and that was it. I'll be happy so long as I get to be with you."

I kissed him, and we got lost in each other's lips for a while before John spoke again.

"I'm excited to bring you home," he said, soft and affectionate. "Show you everything, introduce you to everyone. Show you off a little."

I laughed. "Just a little, hmm? Well, I suppose if we ever make it through this godawful winter, I'll allow it."

John sighed. "I know, but we've made it this far. Just hang in there a bit longer for me."

"Alright. Just for you, Wastelander."

He pulled me into an embrace and held me close for a long time. Eventually, he made love to me again, slow and gentle this time, cherishing every moment of pleasure we gave to each other.

"Ah, my Claire," he breathed in my ear, his voice thick with tenderness.

I pressed my forehead against his as a pleasurable shudder passed through him.

"I'm always your Claire."

Part III: The Valley

She has heard a whisper say,

A curse is on her if she stay
To look down to Camelot.
She knows not what the curse may be,
And so she weaveth steadily,
And little other care hath she,
The Lady of Shalott.

\-   *"The Lady of Shalott", Alfred Lord Tennyson*

CHAPTER 18

Claire

A week after the fall through the ice, we were finally closing in on our destination. Unfortunately, even that short time wore us all down even further. We were short with each other, cold and miserable, and hunger was our constant companion. Exhaustion permeated every fibre of our frail bodies. With little food, we were all thin and gaunt, looking more like a skeleton crew with each passing day.

Even Kimmy had been relatively subdued at our engagement announcement—most unlike her usual self. She grinned and pulled me into a weak hug, saying she already thought of me as a sister. I teared up and squeezed her. Asha remained impassive, but asked me over Kimmy's shoulder, "This is what you want?"

I nodded solemnly. "It is."

John didn't comment, but the muscle in his jaw ticked, and I knew he'd bitten back a retort for my benefit. I let Kimmy go and hooked my arm in his, which seemed to pacify him.

The terrain had changed in the last couple of days, becoming rockier and more mountainous the farther north we traveled. Nothing could've prepared me for the arduous task of climbing amongst those steep hills and cliffs on meagre rations, while the land remained firmly in the suffocating grip of a northern Ontario winter.

Finally, we stood at the bottom of a mountain range, near the lowest of the mountains. As far as mountains went, I'd seen photos of much higher peaks back at the Cave...but that didn't mean much in our current state.

"Once we cross that ridge, we'll be officially in Valley territory," John said, pointing at the top of the steep incline ahead.

My heart sped up. "We're so close."

"Don't count your chickens before they hatch," he replied with a wry smile. "We still gotta hike up there, which will be most of today."

Asha groaned, and I couldn't help agreeing with the sentiment. Two months of non-stop travel had worn me down to the point that as close as we were to our destination, I was ready to collapse with exhaustion.

"I know," Kimmy said sympathetically, touching Asha's shoulder. "It's been a long trip for all of us. But just think: tonight, we could be sleeping *indoors.*"

I giggled. "Hardly remember what that's like."

John squeezed my hand, and I knew his guilt about not taking care of me hadn't abated. We'd had a few more conversations about it, where he seemed determined to blame himself for not ensuring that I was living in the lap of luxury while we traveled. I never thought I would be the one arguing on behalf of a lower standard of living, given where I came from, but I'd learned more than once that the Wasteland changed people.

Sometimes not for the better, I thought, glancing at Asha. She'd softened a little over the course of our trip, and every now and then, there were more glimmers of the friend I remembered, but the next instant, they were gone, replaced once more by icy indifference. Truthfully, I was afraid of how she would handle integrating into a community that may not welcome us.

The hike up to the ridge was treacherous, owing to the steep incline and the mountain of untouched snow that we had to wade through. John went first, fighting his way through the snow, then attached the grappling hook to the top of the ridge. The three of us could then use it to pull ourselves up. It took a long time; we were all so tired. Halfway to the top, I tripped and stumbled on my knees, but at least managed to hold onto the rope and avoid falling down the slope.

I couldn't find the strength to stand. I was cold, wet, and malnourished.

Asha started to turn back, but John slid partway down the slope toward me, holding onto the rope for balance.

"You alright?" he asked, offering me his hand. His lips were cracked and pale, the hollows of his cheeks more pronounced than ever. I must've given him a look that betrayed my utter misery, because he said softly, "I know. It's easier on horseback. Just a bit farther, baby."

He pulled me to my feet, though his arm trembled slightly. His strength had faded just like mine, and my teeth chattered as he helped me climb. When we finally reached the ridge, however, the view took my breath away.

A vast, deep valley stretched out as far as the eye could see, and though snow clung in patches to certain areas, much of it was green—unlike the landscape that surrounded it on all sides.

"How?" I asked simply, eyes wide, and the corner of John's mouth ticked up.

"It's not as cold," Kimmy answered, her brown eyes flickering with something like yearning. "You'll feel it get warmer as we head down. Part of why the crops grow so well here—a milder climate."

In the distance, a small lake, only partially frozen, stretched over the land. John had told me it was a popular fishing and swimming spot in the summer. The landscape was a patchwork quilt of empty farmland and cleared land for homesteads, each surrounded by dense forest, all connected by dirt roads. Even in winter, it was breathtaking and beautiful—little pieces of civilization dotted across a palette of wilderness. I instantly wanted to paint it.

"We're going to try to avoid outrider routes," John said with a weary sigh. "We don't need anyone to know we're here before we're ready."

"How do they communicate across this kind of distance?" I asked, eyes wide.

"Radio," he answered. "Thankfully, the mountains make the reception to the outside shit, or we'd never be able to use them and keep the place a secret."

Asha uncrossed her arms. "How much farther is this place we're going?"

Kimmy took her hand, and surprisingly, Asha allowed it. "We're heading to Dreamspring, which is the Armstrongs' farm. Summerhurst won't be ready to live in right away. It's just a bit farther, like John said."

Just a bit farther took at least another hour and a half, and it started to snow. Fat, wet snowflakes hit my frozen face, making me even more miserable. Just as I was about to resign myself to death by hypothermia, the terrain finally began to change.

The sea of snow-covered trees gave way to fields, and in the distance, a tall brown barn rose out of the landscape. Still further ahead stood a deep blue farmhouse with sunny yellow shutters, shrouded in silvery white and resembling a holiday card. A cozy glow emanated from the windows, and a thin column of smoke rose from the red bricked chimney, completing the image.

I took a breath and held it. We were really, finally here, and the people I was about to meet would change the course of my life. I wasn't entirely prepared for that prospect...or for the appearance of a large brown dog. It bounded towards us, and I tensed, preparing to run, but John merely grinned as Kimmy called out to the dog.

"Alma! Come here, girl!"

Clearly excited, the dog sped up and leaped up onto Kimmy to lick her face. I exchanged a confused look with Asha, but Kimmy merely turned her face away and laughed. There was a pure joy in her laughter that made me ache. It was the kind of joy that came from familiarity. From being home.

John must have noticed my apprehension because he took my hand.

"Ever petted a dog before?" he asked, and I shook my head.

"No pets allowed in the compound," I said. "Only the military had dogs. I never saw them close up. My first close encounter with a dog was the one that bit me on that PNC hunt we went on."

He squeezed my hand. "That dog was feral. Scared of people. Not like Alma. Unless you're a rabbit, she's the friendliest thing you'll ever meet. Come see."

I reluctantly allowed him to lead me towards the slobbery, excitable beast, which stopped playing with Kimmy and regarded me with curiosity. He guided my hand towards the dog, and I gave her head a quick, tentative stroke. To my surprise, she leaned into my hand, encouraging me to continue, and I couldn't help but smile.

"See?" John said, pleased. "She won't hurt you."

Out of the corner of my eye, I saw Asha roll her eyes.

"Can we *not* keep standing out in the cold?"

Kimmy sobered. "Right. Guess we should make our ourselves known."

We resumed walking towards the blue farmhouse.

"Ready?" John asked me.

I gulped, suddenly nervous. "No."

"You'll be fine," he said with a chuckle, and I followed him and Kimmy to the door.

I could hear voices inside the house, talking back and forth. John knocked loudly, and they went abruptly silent. There was a pause, and then the door opened.

"You back already, hon—?"

A short, blonde, heavily pregnant woman stood in the doorway, a question in her eyes. My stomach flip-flopped, but thankfully, she didn't seem to even notice me.

"Is that John Madigan standing on my doorstep?" she said in a near-whisper, seemingly speaking to herself, eyes wide with disbelief.

She didn't give him time to respond before throwing herself at him, grabbing him in a hug. She barely met his shoulder, but her grip looked bone-crushing.

"Sarah, valuable things are getting squished here," John gasped out.

"I don't care," she replied, her voice thick. "I thought I'd never see you again. And Kimmy!"

She moved to Kimmy and hugged her just as hard. Kimmy smiled warmly, her eyes misty as she returned the embrace.

"You two have a lot to answer for," Sarah said as she moved back, wiping her eyes. "You've been gone so long. We thought you were dead."

"Thanks for the vote of confidence," John said dryly.

Sarah's gaze moved to Asha and me, partially obscured by John and Kimmy, and her eyes grew wide as saucers.

"And you brought...people," she said, looking back and forth between John and Kimmy with a frantic energy.

"Yeah," John answered, his voice softening a little, and he stepped aside so that Sarah could see me better. "This is Claire. My fiancée."

"Fiancée?" Sarah looked like she could've been knocked over by a light breeze.

John took my hand in his. "Right."

There was pause where Asha gave Kimmy a pointed look. John rolled his eyes; he clearly wasn't going to be doing the introductions. Kimmy stared back, unmoved, until Asha cleared her throat loudly.

"Oh, yes," Kimmy said hurriedly, embarrassed. "And this is Asha. A friend of Claire's. And, uh, mine too."

Awkwardness hung in the air, and I resisted the urge to hide my face behind my hands. Sarah's long stare didn't help my nerves, and the silence seemed to stretch on for an eternity.

"You brought them here?" she finally said. "Why? Do you have any idea how people are going to—"

"Yeah," John interjected. "We know. We'll call a council meeting."

"A council meeting?" Sarah said incredulously, looking sharply to the right and left, as though expecting hidden informants to suddenly appear. "Get in here. Before someone sees you and rains hell down on us all."

She stepped aside and waved us into the house. I hesitated, but John tugged on my hand, and I followed him inside. Sarah pushed the door shut with a loud snap and turned three deadbolts to lock it behind her, which did nothing to reassure me.

The air inside the house was thick and warm, like a cozy blanket in the dead of winter. It smelled like cooking—smoky and savoury, with the fresh, earthy scent of herbs. Mixed in was the scent of soap, of clean laundry, and of burning wood. It smelled like a home, so wholesome that I wanted to weep.

I hadn't eaten a decent meal in weeks, and I was still chilled to the bone, but we'd made it, and this place I had heard so much about was real. The nightmare of our journey was finally over. I swallowed hard, trying not to succumb to the tight ball of emotion that ached in my chest.

We stripped off our coats and boots, and Sarah led us into a small but cozy living room. A squashy green sofa sat against the far wall, with a mismatched pink loveseat beside it. A polished oak coffee table sat in the middle of the room, but the true centrepiece was a massive stone fireplace. The gentle crackling of the fire was soothing after another long day in the frozen Wasteland.

There was a small, golden-haired boy of perhaps five on the sofa. He stared at us with open surprise and fascination, his hands frozen in mid-air around what appeared to be a toy truck and, of all things, an elephant.

"Hey, buddy," Kimmy said affectionately. "You probably don't remember me and John, huh? You're so big now."

The boy looked to his mother with creeping alarm. "Mommy, who are they?"

"They're friends," Sarah said, though her glance at Asha and me was doubtful. "It's alright, Jake. Go back to your game."

Jake still looked uncertain, but he quickly resumed what seemed to be an epic battle between the truck and the elephant and forgot us. Sarah settled onto the sofa beside him, groaning and rubbing her baby bump.

"Sit," she ordered John. "If you expect to be served, you can think again, because I'm not getting up again in this condition."

He chuckled. "Wouldn't dream of it. So, another one, huh?"

He led me over to the loveseat to sit down. Kimmy sat on the arm, while Asha contented herself with the floor. I motioned for her to squeeze in beside me, but she shook her head.

"It would seem that way," Sarah said with a sigh, then groaned again as she shifted in her seat. "We decided four wasn't enough, apparently."

Four kids? I hadn't known anyone with so many children before. Our strict population control at the compound made it unlikely that would've ever been allowed.

"Where are the others?" Kimmy asked.

"Bruce took the kids out on a hunting trip this morning," Sarah replied. "They should be back soon. He's going to flip out when he sees what you've brought with you, I'll tell you that much."

I exchanged a look with Asha, who clearly didn't appreciate being talked about as if she weren't there any more than I did. I knew better than to speak up, however. This was John and Kimmy's show now.

"So," Sarah said, her tone suddenly brusque. "Tell me where you've been, what you've been doing, and just why you thought that bringing those girls here was a good idea."

John bristled a little. "Did you not hear that she's my—"

"Fiancée, yes," Sarah said impatiently. "I don't mean it like that. She's in danger here. Her friend, too."

My pulse quickened. I'd known, in an abstract way, that coming here meant I might be in danger, but hearing it said out loud by a Valley resident made it real.

"In case you forgot, I live here," John said. "And as my wife, Claire has as much right to be here as I do."

Sarah's curt retort was cut off by Kimmy interceding.

"What John is trying to say," Kimmy said with a pointed look at him, "is that we've been away a long time, and we've made some attachments we can't break. But this is our home, and we belong here. And thankfully, we brought back something that may sweeten the pot a little for the council."

Sarah raised an expectant eyebrow. "I assume you got some PNCs, then?"

"Better than *some*," John replied. "Enough to last several lifetimes. Enough that the Linds might be able to finally make our own and end our dependency on scavenging."

"Really?" Sarah said in wonder. "That's...wow. I don't know what..."

There was a quiver of emotion in her voice, and she paused briefly to regain her composure.

"If that's true, you've saved us."

There was a quiver of emotion in her last words, and John gave a small smile.

"I know," he said, his tone gentler. "I told you before we left that we would find them, or we wouldn't come back at all. You think I could show my face here if I returned empty-handed? I meant it."

A tear cascaded down Sarah's cheek, and she wiped it away clumsily with her hand. John gave a small smile, and Kimmy went to give her another hug. Jake stopped the truck-elephant rematch and looked at his mother with alarm.

"Why is Mommy crying?"

"Mommy's just happy, baby," Sarah said over Kimmy's shoulder. "It's all okay."

Sarah pulled him against her and tickled him until he started giggling and settled in beside her to snuggle.

"My goodness," Sarah said after a moment, a brilliant smile lighting her features. "I can't believe it. I thought you were dead, but now you tell me you've saved the whole Valley all on your own. It's...a lot."

"Not all on our own," John said, and he squeezed my hand and gave me a tender look. "We couldn't have done it without Claire."

Embarrassed, I murmured, "I helped a little."

"Too modest for your own good," Kimmy said with a smile. "But it's why she's already earned her place here. She helped save a whole community of people she never met."

Sarah's gaze fell on me, and I did my best not to look away.

"In that case, where are my manners?" she said softly. "I'm sorry, Claire. We're wary of strangers in these parts. It's what's kept us safe. But if you really helped save our home, then Kimmy's right—you deserve to be here."

I flushed with pleasure. "Thank you."

Sarah gave me a once-over and groaned as she got to her feet.

"You all look like you could do with some fattening up," she said, suddenly businesslike. "Traveling in the winter can't have been a picnic. Let's get you fed."

She led us into the bright, airy farmhouse kitchen. Sage green walls, grey stone floors, and a gleaming steel refrigerator and stove greeted us. A large island with four stools took up much of the space, along with a giant wood table. Oak cabinetry lined the walls, and a large stockpot simmered on an old-fashioned wood stove, giving off a heavenly aroma. Every surface was shiny and polished. It was the cleanest place I'd been in a very long time.

I sat at the kitchen island, sandwiched between John and Kimmy, as Sarah added more stock to the pot and stirred. My empty stomach growled, and saliva pooled in my mouth. I hadn't eaten more than a few bites of food in days, and I felt positively weak with hunger. John covered my hand with his on the countertop, tracing slow, reassuring circles with his thumb.

The three of them chatted amiably back and forth, filling in the gaps since they last saw each other. The harvest had been good this year; some of the elders had retired; Danny had taken on the Lead Outrider position; a couple called Isla and Noah had had a baby boy recently.

Asha watched Sarah warily, as though waiting for retaliation of some kind, but Sarah paid her no mind, busying herself with food preparation.

"It's been nothing but doom and gloom around here lately," Sarah said with a sigh. "The last of the PNCs got installed in October, and we'd already begun to ration electricity use."

"Did Jameson and his people ever change their minds?" Kimmy asked.

Sarah shrugged. "Sure did, but by that time, it was too late, and you'd already been gone some time. He sent others out to look nearly every day, but they came back with nothing, and nobody wanted to venture farther out. Nobody's as crazy as you and John."

"Brave," I cut in, still staring at the stockpot on the stove. "I think that's the word you're looking for."

Sarah looked surprised at my interjection, but she quickly nodded without further comment. John gave my hand an appreciative squeeze. Sarah ladled soup into bowls and set a plate of hearty brown rolls on the counter. The scent of food was making me light-headed. When she set a bowl in front of me, I dug in without so much as a thank-you; I was too hungry, and afraid I might faint.

It was delicious—leeks and carrots in hot, golden chicken broth. All things I hadn't eaten in months. A bite of one of the sturdy brown rolls only bolstered my bliss; I hadn't had bread since I left the compound.

"Dr. Irons died a couple weeks ago," Sarah said. "And there's been no school since. We really do need to find someone."

"Honestly, I thought that old bastard was gonna live forever," John said, taking a bite of bread. "You know what they say—evil never dies."

"John," Sarah scolded, but Kimmy choked on her soup laughing.

"Who's Dr. Irons?" I asked.

Sarah gave John a reproving look as he opened his mouth to answer, likely predicting that he was about to speak ill of the dead again. For his part, he shrugged at her, completely unrepentant with a mouthful of bread, which made me giggle.

"The teacher I had growing up," he said to me once he'd swallowed. "He was a university professor in the Old World. He was always offended when anyone didn't call him *doctor*, and Danny and I...may have pushed his buttons on that more than once. He must've been like eighty by now, right?"

He glanced at Sarah, who nodded.

"Oh," I said, pausing. "Is that the one who got so fed up with you that he gave you the strap once?"

John grinned. "Yeah. Granny nearly killed him. Never piss off a tiny Irishwoman, I guess."

"Yes, well, speaking as your former babysitter," Sarah said, trying to look severe and failing, "you weren't always easy to reign in."

"In my defence, Danny was a horrible influence," John said, holding up his hands. "He was also a much better liar than me, so I took most of the heat."

"Didn't you release frogs in the schoolroom?" I said, eyebrow raised.

John shrugged. "No comment."

"That means yes," Kimmy said, elbowing him. "His daughter was always nice. Can't she take over? She probably has his old notes."

Sarah shook her head. "She's already working at the wood mill. Jenna started as his assistant a month ago, but she doesn't feel ready to take over. So, we're homeschooling for now."

I didn't speak up, even though Asha and I had taught teenagers before and had some student teaching experience with younger kids. However, considering I didn't even know if they'd be letting me stay, and if I was in danger here, I wasn't going to suggest I be allowed access to the Valley's children. For all I knew, they'd interpret that as a threat or an insult, coming from an outsider.

Still, I felt a surge of hope and tucked it away to revisit later. I glanced at Asha, but she was focused on her food and didn't seem interested in the conversation. I wondered what she was thinking, but as usual, her expression was unreadable.

Just then, the front door opened, and a moment later, a tall, lanky man with brown hair appeared in the kitchen doorway, rosy-cheeked from the cold. He was followed by what I could only assume were the other Armstrong children: a young man who looked just like his father; a teenage girl with brown hair and brown eyes; and a younger, preteen girl that was Sarah's spitting image, with blonde hair and grey eyes.

"We have company," Sarah said, a twinkle in her eye.

"John!" the younger girl screeched, and a second later, he grunted at the force of her small body colliding with his.

"Hey," he managed to get out. "Allie, I...can't breathe."

She released him, grinning from ear to ear. "You look terrible."

"Gee, thanks," John replied with a laugh. "Happy to see you too, kiddo. You promised not to grow too much while I was gone—what happened?"

The next few moments were a happy reunion where Asha and I might as well not have existed. The two older children—Matthew and Maisie—exchanged hugs with both John and Kimmy, while Bruce, their father, looked on with a broad smile.

I might've felt left out except that their genuine happiness was infectious, and it warmed my heart to see how much John and Kimmy were loved. They deserved it, even as a hollow pang of loss crept into my chest. I wanted what they had. I wanted to be part of something the way they were.

Of course, the moment quickly passed, and silence fell as eight pairs of eyes were suddenly fixed on me and Asha.

"Who's that?" Allie said frankly to John, pointing at me.

"Allie," Sarah scolded. "It's rude to point."

"It's alright," I said, a little shy. It was unnerving to be singled out this way, but I suspected I'd have to get used to it. Besides, I was probably the first new person that this young girl had seen in a long, long time.

John and Kimmy launched into introductions again, and though the other Armstrongs greeted us politely, the air was thick with tension. Sarah and Bruce exchanged worried looks, and the older children looked to their parents for cues on how to react to the news.

"This is...a lot to take in," Bruce said. "We need to rally support now. I'm going to notify Abby so she can call a council meeting. Matt, can you round up the Hardings? Maisie, you should go to the McNeils."

Both of the older children nodded, and all three departed.

"What's going to happen now?" I asked John in a hushed voice.

He stroked the back of my hand. "One of the chairpersons has to call the meeting. Abby's the chairwoman, and a damn sight more pleasant than Jameson, so Bruce will go to her. She was a friend of Granny's."

"It'll likely go to a vote," Sarah said. "That's why we need to rally support."

"A vote on if we can stay?" I asked. "Just like that?"

Asha blew out a disapproving breath. Sarah looked uneasy and told Allie to leave the room. Allie huffed but obeyed.

"It'll be okay," John soothed once Allie was out of earshot, giving my hand a squeeze. "I promise."

"How can you know?" I replied, panic creeping into my voice. "What if they hurt us? Or decide to kill us? We know the secret now, so even if we leave, they'll think—"

"We won't let that happen," Kimmy cut in. "People will be wary, but most of them will listen to reason. And anyway, they'd have to go through us first."

I took a deep breath to steady myself. John kissed my cheek, then stood.

"I have something to take care of before everyone gets here," he said to Sarah. "Keep an eye on these three while I'm gone."

Sarah raised an eyebrow but nodded. I followed John to the foyer.

"Where are you going?" I whispered urgently. "Don't leave me here."

He took my face in his hands and kissed me, slow and gentle. His touch calmed me, but that made me want him to stay even more. He was my anchor in this strange new place.

"I'll be back soon," he replied, tucking my hair behind my ear. "I just have to go to Summerhurst to check on things. You're safe with the Armstrongs; I wouldn't leave otherwise."

I sighed. "Alright. Just be careful...and please hurry back."

"I will."

CHAPTER 19

Claire

John was gone for most of the afternoon. We stayed in the kitchen with Sarah, who pushed more food on us, until I couldn't have eaten another bite if I tried. My stomach had probably shrunk to the size of a walnut. While Kimmy chatted amiably with Sarah, I took the opportunity to talk quietly with Asha.

"What do you think so far?" I asked.

She shrugged. "Honestly, it doesn't feel real. Probably won't till we find out whether we're getting thrown out or not."

I bit my lip, thinking. "We could offer to help them with their teacher problem."

Asha made a face. "I don't think so, Claire."

"Why not? I know they'll be suspicious, but we could offer it as a trade. Something useful that they need. They could even have someone supervise us if they want."

"Seriously?" she said in a low voice, glancing at Sarah to make sure she was busy talking to Kimmy. "First of all, if these kids are anything like average Wastelanders, they're so far behind that it'll take a minor miracle to even teach them to read. Tiring, and ultimately pointless, since they'll consider anything you teach them to be useless anyway."

Useless. The word hit me like a punch in the gut. That was how I'd felt for so long. When Sarah had said they needed a teacher, I'd finally felt like there might be a void I could fill. But maybe I was kidding myself.

"I'm not trying to make you feel bad," Asha said, softening her tone. "I just don't want you to get hurt when they don't appreciate you for your gifts."

I nodded, but I felt hurt anyway. Maybe she was right. After all, even John had thought me useless in the beginning. *Maybe I just have to keep my head down and work quietly.*

It wasn't like I hadn't had practice.

At that moment, the front door opened again, and a cacophony of voices followed. John appeared first, chuckling at something the man walking next to him said. His companion was taller, freckled, and wore a teasing grin. His mid-length strawberry blond hair matched his thick beard, and he wore a leather hunting jacket similar to John's. I knew who he must be: John's best friend, Danny.

"This your girl?" Danny said, nodding in my direction.

"Sure is," John replied, and his proud smile melted me. I instantly forgot about the conversation with Asha.

"Pleased to meet you," I said, extending my hand. "I've heard so much about you."

"Hopefully not too much," Danny replied wryly as he shook my hand. "Don't want you to rethink staying with us."

"Not much chance of that, thankfully."

He turned back to John, still holding onto my hand.

"She's so damn polite," Danny said with a grin. "Where'd you find this one, and why the hell is she with you?"

John nudged him hard enough to make him choke out a laugh, and with a warm squeeze of my hand, he let me go. I couldn't stop a smile from curving my lips. I'd heard a lot about Danny's inexhaustible sense of humour, his inability to take life too seriously, but his presence also radiated a natural friendliness that put me immediately at ease. His playful jab at John lacked any trace of malice; he was warm, earnest, and clearly overjoyed to see his old friend. I already understood why John liked him.

Danny was followed by a much younger woman with shoulder-length brown hair and soft brown eyes. She looked nineteen or twenty, with a slim build and a big, puffy winter jacket. John introduced her as Jenna, Danny's youngest sister—the one who'd been assistant teaching. I wondered if I'd get a moment to ask her about it, but the thought was quickly banished by the arrival of three more people: a pretty, petite woman with long blonde hair; a big, hulking man with dark hair and a beard; and a little blonde baby, wrapped snugly in a sling at his mother's breast.

They were introduced as Isla and Noah, along with baby Ely. I learned that Isla was the middle McNeil sister, and Noah was her husband and childhood friend. Kimmy squeaked with excitement on seeing the baby and hugged Isla, who laughed warmly.

"I'm so sorry I missed your delivery," Kimmy said in a rush, "but oh my God! He's *precious*."

She immediately started cooing over the tiny infant, utterly distracted, and I laughed. Asha gave her enthusiasm a sidelong glance but held her tongue. Bruce and the two older Armstrong children joined us, and then the kitchen was full to bursting, everyone talking at once.

"We spoke to Abby," Bruce said to me and John. "They're calling the meeting for a few days from now. Everyone will be there."

My stomach lurched, but John simply replied, "Thanks. We appreciate it."

As though sensing my nerves, he then steered me into the living room. Everyone followed us, since there was more space for socializing. Isla approached me with a brilliant smile, her husband in tow, and John pecked my forehead before going to talk with Danny, Jenna, and Sarah. Meanwhile, Kimmy had stolen Ely and was now kissing him all over, and the tiny baby wore an identical expression to his father, utterly unimpressed.

"Claire, I'm so excited to meet you," Isla said, shaking my hand. The large man next to her said nothing, his face a stoic mask.

"Don't mind Noah," Isla said breezily. "He may *look* like he wants to be anywhere else, but he's also delighted to meet you."

Noah grunted in what I assumed was assent, and I couldn't suppress a giggle.

"How old is your son?" I asked.

"Two and a half months," Noah replied, his deep voice startling me, but I couldn't miss the note of pride in his voice. "He didn't want to come out at first. He loves his mother too much. Not that I blame him."

Isla gave him a soft look, and my heart squeezed. I knew Isla had once dated John, but any possessiveness I may have felt was quelled by the way she looked at Noah; she clearly adored him.

Kimmy moved to hand Ely back to his mother, but Noah intercepted. It didn't seem like such a big man should be able to cradle a baby so gently, but he did, snuggling Ely against his massive shoulder.

"Your shoulder's bugging you," he said to Isla, who opened her mouth to protest. "I'll take him for a while. You have fun."

Without another word, he walked into the hallway with Ely, and just before we were out of earshot, I swore I heard his deep, growly voice take on a higher, gentler tone as he spoke to his infant son. Isla smiled after them, then began chattering away with me and Kimmy, asking us all about our trip and my background. In return, Kimmy demanded all the details about her pregnancy and Ely's birth, fussing over her. Isla was bubbly, funny, and sweet, and didn't seem to mind one whit that I didn't belong there. When John pulled me aside some time later, I had the distinct impression that I may have made a new friend.

John led me to the now-empty kitchen, stopping just inside the doorway. His eyes were lit with happiness and affection, and he stopped me in my tracks with a tender kiss.

"What's up?" I asked when he moved back, smiling from ear to ear.

"I got something for you," he answered as he reached into his pocket.

I shot him a quizzical look, and he withdrew a small ring box and opened it. There were two inside, both white gold. One was thin and delicate, and looked like two vines entwined together. The other was thicker, more masculine, with a simple adornment of two lines etched around its circumference.

"My parents' wedding rings," he said solemnly. "With the way they died, during the virus...my grandparents didn't get to keep most of their stuff. These are the only things I have from my parents. I wanted to show them to you before our wedding day, and have you wear my mother's at the council meeting."

He took my left hand in his and slid the ring onto my finger. It was beautiful, and I knew what a big deal it was for him to give it to me. John treasured his grandparents, their home at Summerhurst, and his family memories. Giving me the ring meant that he thought of me as part of all that.

Given that, he probably didn't expect that my reaction would be to burst into tears.

"Hey," he murmured, drawing me close, his eyes wide with concern. "What's wrong? Talk to me."

To be fair, I was as surprised as he was by my sudden outpouring of emotion. But it hit me all at once that staying here was still a massive question mark, and that I may not be able to keep all these new people that I had already begun to feel attached to. More than that, if I couldn't stay...I couldn't ask John to abandon them. This was his *family*. These were the people who had loved him his entire life.

"It's not going to work," I mumbled, swiping at my tears. "They won't accept me, and I can't...can't ask you to leave this. They love you."

John hugged me hard, and I couldn't help but cling to him. Even if the worst happened, I knew I wouldn't be able to graciously let him leave me. I was too selfish, and I loved him too much.

"Everything'll be okay, sweetheart," he said softly. "They *will* accept you. I promise."

"Don't lie. You don't know that."

I nearly jumped out of my skin at Asha's voice. She was sitting on the other side of the room at the kitchen table, looking grim. I hadn't even noticed her.

"Should've gone with the mineshaft when I had the chance," John muttered, though I didn't understand what he meant.

"Yeah, thanks for noticing I'm still here, by the way," Asha said sourly, glaring at me. "Did I suddenly become invisible to you and Kimmy?"

"Definitely not invisible," John said sardonically, then turned back to me. "Listen, okay? I know it's going to be fine. I wouldn't say that if I didn't have a good reason to think so."

Asha eyed him with suspicion. "What's this big reason, then?"

"Stop, Asha," I bit out, returning her glare. "Lay off him."

She sighed and turned away, and John rolled his eyes, then went right back to ignoring her. He lifted my chin so he could look in my eyes. "I can't tell you how I know, but I need you to trust me on this, baby."

His jaw was set, determined, and his eyes revealed no trace of nerves. I took a deep breath to steady myself, then said, "I do."

"Good," he replied, gently wiping away a tear with his thumb. "Christ, you had me worried you were getting cold feet for a minute there."

I gave a watery laugh. "Never worry about that."

"Everyone here has been drumming up support for you," John said, kissing my ring. "It won't go as badly as you think. A lot of people are ready for change."

I nodded, feeling better. "Thank you for the ring. It's beautiful. I'll wear it proudly."

He gave me that sweet, heart-stopping smile that he saved just for me, and my heart fluttered.

"Go mingle some more," I said. "I want to talk with Asha."

He shot a guarded look in her direction but nodded. "Alright. Call me if you need me."

He headed back into the living room, and I went to sit across from Asha. She sat, arms crossed, her expression unreadable again.

"I'm sorry if we forgot you," I said, "but nothing was stopping you from introducing yourself and talking to everyone. You were welcome."

She scoffed. "I'm an afterthought, Claire. But I don't have interest in mingling with a bunch of Wastelanders anyway."

"Could you at least try for once?" I shot back, frustrated. "Living here is better than living anywhere else. Can you at least try to get along with people and act as though you're happy to be here? Because I have news for you: nobody had to bring you here."

"Yeah, I know, you're already regretting it," Asha retorted, rolling her eyes. "Just so you know, they all make promises like that at first—telling you it's going to be fine, that they'll take care of everything. It's a lie they use to lull you into a false sense of security."

My patience wore thin. "Stop projecting. Look, clearly, I don't know everything you've been through, because you won't tell me. But this isn't the same thing, and if you won't let this go, then I don't know how this is going to work. It's not fair to anyone."

There was a heavy silence, and Asha sighed.

"I'm sorry," she said. "I just...I don't know what to do. It's a new place, new everything. I'm just a little overwhelmed. I wish we were home."

"I don't," I replied, standing up. "And now, I'm going to go stand with my fiancé. You can join me, or you can stay here, but either way, leave John alone. This is a happy time for him. It can be for you, too, if you'd give it a chance."

I stalked away. A few seconds later, to my surprise, Asha got to her feet and followed me out to the living room, plastering a look of neutral interest on her face. She even endured stilted small talk with Isla, who met us at the doorway.

"Everything okay?" John asked as he walked over.

I looked at Asha, who had a manic-looking grin on her face as Isla chattered away at her. *Okay, it's a little creepy, but it's better...I think.*

Kimmy appeared at her side and looped her arm through Asha's. Asha relaxed a little at her touch.

"Yes," I answered, taking John's hand. "I think it is."

CHAPTER 20

Claire

A couple of days passed in a flurry of activity, with all of John and Kimmy's friends coming and going from the Armstrong house, visiting other homesteads to get their support for the upcoming council meeting. Even though I knew they did it out of their love and gratitude toward John and Kimmy, I was still touched by their efforts. Isla visited again with Ely, and Kimmy and I enjoyed chatting with her at the fireside while John went hunting with Danny. I did everything I could to avoid thinking about the meeting, to live in the moment, but my heart was heavy at the end of each day, knowing that I was stuck in a painful limbo.

Finally, the morning of the meeting arrived, and my stomach remained in knots as I felt John stir next to me. We'd been camping out on the living room floor, lying in sleeping bags around the hearth. He yawned, stretched, then turned over to wake me, only to find my eyes already wide open.

"You're up early," he murmured, kissing my forehead.

"Didn't sleep much," I admitted. "Too nervous."

"It'll be alright, baby. I have a plan."

He pulled me into him, cradling me against his warm body.

"I hope that plan includes telling me at some point," I said, and he smiled.

"Give me time."

He pecked my lips, disentangled himself from his sleeping bag, and got up. I heard Kimmy and Asha stirring as well. I rolled onto my back, staring at the ceiling. Today, my fate would be decided, and there was nothing I could do about it. It was a powerless feeling—one I'd been used to when I lived in the compound. I now found it hard to tolerate.

"If you want a shot at breakfast before those kids devour everything in sight," John said with a small smile as he pulled on a shirt, "you should get up now."

I sighed. There was no point delaying. I shivered at the chilly morning air as I got dressed.

Breakfast was a noisy, chaotic affair, with the four Armstrong children and six adults all crowded around the big table. We sat elbow-to-elbow, constantly bumping one another as we spread thick pats of butter onto toasted homemade bread, our plates already loaded with eggs and venison bacon. Jugs of milk, a large bowl of yogurt, and a jar of strawberry jam sat in the centre of the spread. I hadn't eaten anything like this since I left the Cave, and every bite was pure heaven.

All around me, pleasant, familiar chatter ensued. Kimmy was talking animatedly to Maisie, the older Armstrong daughter, about her apparent recent interest in medicine. Sarah scolded Allie for eating her yogurt with her fingers, though her eyes shone with amusement. John spoke candidly to Bruce about repairs that might be needed at Summerhurst, with the older man offering to lend a hand wherever we might need help.

The wholesome picture of them all made my chest ache. I'd always known, in an abstract way, that this kind of home existed, but I had no frame of reference for it. I always felt on the outside looking in, green with envy and forever longing for those elusive gifts that ordinary people didn't seem to know they possessed: love, belonging, *family*. The meeting today would determine if I could finally come in from the cold, or if I'd once again be staring through the glass at something I could never have.

I swallowed hard against the lump that had risen in my throat. *Get a grip,* I told myself sternly. I couldn't afford to look weak. *Nothing's been decided yet.*

Throughout the meal, there was one person who appeared visibly uncomfortable and apart from the rest: Asha. She spoke to no one, simply stared at her plate and glanced at me every so often, as if gauging if I felt as out of place as she did. Truthfully, I did, but I desperately wanted to carve out a place for myself here. I could only hope Asha felt the same.

***

After breakfast, we made the journey to the Lodge at the centre of the Valley. John had told me it was a large town hall, and the hub of all the Valley's services. It housed the medical clinic where Kimmy worked, the schoolroom, the hall where council meetings were held, and a small command center for outriders.

When we arrived in front of what looked like a picture I'd once seen of an Old World ski lodge, there was already a crowd of vehicles and horses outside. I gulped, but John held my hand tightly in his as he led me up the steps and through an antechamber that led to a small lounge with sofas and chairs in front of a fireplace. A windowed door on the right wall was labeled *Command Centre*, but it appeared dark and silent. In contrast, loud chatter came from an open set of double doors on the left.

"The council chamber," John murmured in explanation. "That's where we're going."

We were led into the council room, which was cramped with chairs, all arranged around a space in the centre of the floor where individuals got up to speak to the group. People packed the chamber, but everyone fell silent as we entered. On the far wall were two chairs on a small dais, where an elegant, elderly woman with sea-green eyes and braided silver hair looked on, all dressed in black. Next to her sat a middle-aged man with black hair streaked with grey, an old-fashioned leather jacket, and a scowl.

There was no doubt that this had to be Ed Jameson. His eyes locked on me and Asha immediately, and his frown deepened in disapproval, and John confirmed my suspicion in a low voice. The woman was Abby Miller, the chairwoman that he'd previously mentioned.

On the opposite side of the room were two doors with signs, one of which simply said *Clinic*, while the other read *Schoolroom*. John and Kimmy sat beside each other on the edge of the empty centre. Kimmy tapped her foot impatiently; John remained impassive.

"Welcome," Abby said formally to me and Asha. "As we consider your status in the Valley, we've determined that you both may be present for arguments."

Jameson stared at us with open dislike. "Neither of you will speak unless spoken to. You aren't members of this community. Understood?"

I gulped. "I understand."

Asha gave a curt nod, her gaze laser-focused on him. We were escorted towards a small table and chairs that two men pulled into the centre of the room, then told to sit. Dozens of eyes followed our every move, some with expressions of open contempt or guardedness, others with unabashed curiosity. They thought us strange—I could feel it. I tried to keep my expression neutral.

Abby called the meeting to order, and then it was John and Kimmy's turn to speak on our behalf. They walked to the centre of the room, in front of the table Asha and I were seated at. Kimmy shot me and Asha a sympathetic look, but John didn't even glance in our direction. From his side profile, he looked intent and focused, the way he always did when he had a job to do. I wished I knew what was happening inside his head.

"Bringing outsiders into the Valley directly breaks our most important law," Jameson said, his voice cold as ice. "Explain yourselves."

My hackles immediately rose; he spoke to the two of them as though they were misbehaving children. John's jaw tightened, and I knew he didn't take kindly to the insult. Kimmy was less subtle about her feelings; she folded her arms and glared at him.

John spoke first, giving a brief overview of how he'd met me and how our relationship had blossomed. He spoke passionately about how he couldn't leave me behind, and about how he'd proposed to me on our trip here. He told them about how I'd grown from a scared, ill-equipped compound dweller into a strong, resilient woman he was proud of, and a lump rose in my throat.

"I've shown my loyalty to this community a hundred times over," John said. "Kimmy and I have risked our lives for two years on the hunt, and we brought back the thing that's going to save our way of life here. Is that not enough for you to show some leniency?"

There was a collective murmur at this, but he continued.

"Without Claire, Kimmy and I couldn't have delivered the PNCs we needed. She shared information that only she knew and led me directly to them. For that, we all owe her our thanks—and a place in our community."

More murmuring, and I was heartened to see several people in the crowd nodding in understanding.

"I'll marry her as soon as I can," John said, and for the first time, there was a sliver of emotion in his voice. "She's already my wife in everything but name."

A hard lump rose in my throat at his words. Seeing him defend me was an affirmation of all the reasons I loved him. He was strong, determined, and unflinchingly loyal. His natural charisma made it hard not to listen to him, and I could only hope that the people of this community felt the same way.

Kimmy spoke next, giving me a glowing character reference and talking about the necessity of being more open to outsiders in general.

"We all know the reality here," she said. "If we want the Valley to thrive for future generations, we need to introduce genetic diversity, and that means opening up to outsiders. It's inevitable. So why not now? This is a chance for us to trial letting carefully vetted outsiders into our community, with low risk."

Judging by the reaction from the crowd, several members of the council seemed to find this point compelling, which I took as an encouraging sign. They didn't have to accept us purely based on emotion; there was logic behind it, too.

"And what of the other woman, then?" Jameson cut in, nodding at Asha. "What value is she to us?"

Asha's hands clenched into fists on top of the table, and I took a deep breath, willing myself to remain calm. I hoped Kimmy had a solid response. Unfortunately, she faltered for a moment, pausing briefly as she saw Asha's curled fists, then seemed to regain her composure.

"Asha has shown herself to be capable," Kimmy said. "She has knowledge of gang tactics to aid in defence. She's a chemistry teacher who may be able to offer help with making medicines and other things we need. She'll be an asset to anyone who needs her."

Notably absent from her argument was any personal feelings for Asha, unlike John's appeal for me. Asha was clearly affected, because she bit her lip hard, and her knuckles whitened as she dug her fingers into her palm. I feared her reaction wasn't reflecting well on either of us; several council members eyed her cautiously.

"We will now hear arguments against," Abby announced. "Any member is free to take the floor."

John and Kimmy took their cue to sit, and John finally looked my way. He gave me a short nod of reassurance. Several people stood and made their way to the centre to speak, and my stomach dropped. Rationally, I hadn't expected unanimous approval, but John and Kimmy's impassioned pleas had given me false hope.

An elderly man spoke first, railing against the abandonment of the 'old ways,' that the Valley had survived this long due to its secrecy and exclusivity, and that letting in two women from a compound could only spell trouble for their little community.

"All this hullabaloo about the PNCs, and how many did they actually bring back?" he demanded, hitting the ground with a wooden cane. "Only enough to maintain vital systems. Without more, we'll still have to survive with less. They've only given us a temporary stay of execution, yet they act like they've saved us all."

I frowned before I remembered to force my face back into a neutral expression. I didn't understand. John had told me that we'd found far beyond what they needed. Had he been wrong? Why hadn't he told me?

Two young women went next—twin sisters with pretty copper skin and dark hair, who stared at John in a way that made me a little uncomfortable.

"I don't think it's fair," the woman on the left said, folding her arms. "This outsider is allowed to just take one of the few single men in this community? We didn't—I mean, nobody else even got the chance."

I flushed as a couple other young women nodded in agreement, and Asha rolled her eyes. Meanwhile, Kimmy covered her mouth to hold in her giggles as the corner of John's mouth quirked up in amusement.

"I'm flattered, Asra," he said wryly, "but it wouldn't have worked between us."

The twins both turned bright red and shuffled back to their seats.

A middle-aged farmwife followed the old man and talked about how unnatural—and therefore untrustworthy—we appeared.

"With their skin like glass and eyes bright as stars, they barely seem human," she said nervously. "There's a freakish look to 'em, isn't there? Who's to say what's been done to them? They don't look quite real, and I'll wager it's because they're not. Whatever chemicals have been given to them have probably addled their brains, too."

Several people nodded, and my heart dropped. Asha looked angrier than ever, and John and Kimmy's faces had hardened.

"They're just unnatural," she added, her eyes raking over me. "You really want this chit's demon spawn running around with your kids?"

I flinched, and John's jaw twitched.

A young man of perhaps twenty went next. He stared blatantly at me, gaze roving over my form, undressing me with his eyes. I swallowed uncomfortably and looked away, but he lingered for another couple seconds before speaking.

"I agree with Adelaide," he said, nodding at the farmwife. "They're something unnatural about them. Wouldn't throw either of them out of bed, but..."

There was a burst of outrage from multiple sources, and John had sprung to his feet, his expression furious.

"Order!" Abby called over the din. "Ed, call your son to order or I'll have him thrown out."

Jameson, to my surprise, appeared irate.

"Zach, sit your ass back down," he barked at the young man, then turned to John. "You too, Madigan. Lay a finger on my son and you'll have far bigger problems than the expulsion of your ladylove."

My cheeks burned.

John looked like he could've cheerfully strangled him, but I was relieved when he jerked a nod and sat back down. A couple more council members stood to argue against keeping us, but they mostly regurgitated the same points. Mercifully, none of John and Kimmy's closest family friends—the Armstrongs, McNeils, or the Hardings—spoke against us. John's faith in their loyalty hadn't been misplaced.

Finally, they called for the vote. Asha assumed a stoic expression that I couldn't mimic. I chewed the inside of my cheek, tasting blood. My stomach twisted, and I was afraid I may be sick. I took a painful swallow and waited.

"All in favour of the motion?"

A bunch of hands shot up, but not as many as I'd hoped. It looked to be about half.

"All against?"

The other half of the room raised their hands, and my heart sank. No matter the decision, it was going to be close.

"The motion is denied," Jameson announced, sounding pleased. "As discussed at the opening of the meeting, both outsiders will be escorted off Valley lands with only what they carry on their person."

"No," I whispered, frozen with shock. Asha squeezed my hand as Jameson's son and a couple other men approached the table where we sat.

John was on his feet in an instant.

"Hold it!"

The room stilled at the sound of his voice, cold as ice, and everyone turned to look at him.

"I didn't want to do this," he said, holding up his hands, a mirthless smile curving his lips. "I gave you all the chance to do the right thing. But maybe you need a nudge."

He crossed his arms. "What old Albert said is true: I gave the council enough PNCs to keep the essential functions of your homesteads running. Enough to keep the lights on and the water working, but not much more. Your mistake was assuming that was all I had."

All the air went out of the room. All eyes were now fixed on John.

"That's right," he said, almost taunting. "I've got more than enough for probably a few lifetimes. I'd never leave you out in the cold...but keep your lives as easy as they've been, with automated farming equipment, machines, and so on? Nah, I don't have to do that."

There was a brief, heavy silence.

"You're obligated to hand them over, Madigan," Jameson said, an angry tremor in his voice. "You owe it to this community."

"I've given you what I owe," John said, defiance set in his jaw. "Anything more is a favour you're asking me. I'm your only shot at getting your hands on them."

There was an outbreak of loud, frantic chatter at this. Jameson yelled over the din, calling for order, but it took several minutes for everyone to settle.

"What do you propose, John?" Abby asked once quiet had been restored, her grey eyes wide.

"Accept Claire and Asha as full members of the community," John said, "or I swear, you'll never see a single PNC from me. I'll gladly watch your equipment break down and your harvests shrink, because if you're that stubborn, you don't deserve my help anyway."

He shrugged. "Your choice."

I gaped at him. Abby's lip curled slightly, but I couldn't tell whether she was angry, impressed, or both by John's audacity.

"Very well," she said. "We'll call a vote, but I don't think the result will be in doubt. We'll then open negotiations. At this time, I think it no longer appropriate for Claire and Asha to be present. I'd ask that you ladies wait outside the council chamber until discussions have concluded."

I nodded and stood on wobbly legs, clammy with nerves. Somehow, I made it to the door with Asha. I looked back at John just before leaving, and he gave me a small, almost sheepish smile. *I have a plan.* I suppressed the urge to roll my eyes. The man never ceased to amaze me...but a little warning wouldn't have gone amiss.

Asha and I waited in the common room. I collapsed into one of the armchairs while she paced the length of the room. My heart pounded in my ears. What would I do if they didn't take the bait? What if they hurt John? I didn't think his closest friends would stand for that, but I also couldn't be sure what the rest of them were capable of.

Voices spoke animatedly back and forth in the next room, but I couldn't make out what they said. I stared at the closed council room door, willing it to open, but it was at least another twenty minutes before it finally did. I was in agony the entire time.

The door banged open, and the entire council filed out. The Armstrongs, Hardings, and McNeils flashed us sympathetic looks, while others stared at us with open hostility. I didn't care; I only wanted to see John. He exited second to last, Kimmy at his side. Abby and Jameson followed behind them.

"Remember, Madigan," Jameson said severely, "one wrong move, and they're both out. Come spring, you'll be expected to keep your end of the bargain—whether you're still interested in the redhead by then or not."

"I'm aware," John replied irritably. "And I'll thank you not to talk about my wife like that."

Jameson grunted. "We'll see."

He turned and followed the crowd out of the Lodge. Abby stared at John with raised eyebrows.

"You're certainly Oisín's grandson," she said. "I hope you've found your Aoife."

With a small smile, she left. I waited until it was just the four of us before hurrying over to John. I couldn't help but throw my arms around his neck, pulling him into a tight embrace. My pounding heart still hadn't fully recovered.

"You insane man!" I exclaimed, exhaling heavily as I hugged him hard. "What did you do that for? You didn't even warn me!"

"I couldn't," he said, gently wrapping his arms around me. "I was hoping I wouldn't have to do it. And they had to see it wasn't your idea. You had to be as surprised as everyone else."

"Did that have anything to do with where you snuck off to yesterday?"

"Yeah," he answered, kissing my hair. "I stashed the extra PNCs in the safe at Summerhurst."

"Well, don't ever scare me like that again. I was afraid they'd hurt you."

John scoffed. "When I'm their only chance at keeping their lives nice and easy? Not likely."

I slapped a kiss against his cheek and then released him. Kimmy had left John's side to meet Asha and was now murmuring something that sounded vaguely apologetic. John caught my chin in his hand and tilted my face up to him.

"The risk was worth it," he continued, smiling. "You and Asha are staying with a six-month trial period. If all goes well, we'll get married in the spring, and you'll become a full member of the council."

"That's amazing," I trilled, unable to control my excitement.

"And there's one other thing," John said, and to my surprise, he suddenly looked a little shy. "They're finally going to let me be an outrider."

I couldn't help throwing myself at him again, hugging the life out of him. He gasped at the air being knocked out of his lungs, then laughed breathlessly as he hugged me back.

"I'm so proud of you, darling," I gushed, squeezing him hard. "Saving the day as always. My handsome hero."

To my surprise, he flushed as I pulled back.

"Now you're just embarrassing me."

I laughed. "And I'm just getting started."

He gave my backside a playful swat as we headed for the door. I glanced back at Kimmy and Asha, who lagged behind us, still talking in low voices. To my relief, they looked happier now, and Kimmy even arched up and kissed Asha's cheek. It only lasted half a second, but I grinned, and when Asha saw me looking, she blushed and made a shooing motion. I'd seen the beginnings of a real smile on her face, though, and that lit me up from the inside.

There's hope yet—for all of us.

CHAPTER 21

Claire

It was decided that John and Kimmy would go to Summerhurst that day, ahead of me and Asha, to start the process of opening it up again. Danny and Jenna were on their way over to Dreamspring to pick them up and lend a hand with Summerhurst.

"I'd like to help, though," I protested, standing in the foyer with John.

"We'll need plenty of help in the coming weeks," John replied. "But everything's boarded up right now, and all the furniture's covered and packed away. I don't want that to be your first look at it. I want you to see it how it should be. I want it to feel like home for you."

Touched, I smoothed the front of his jacket. "Alright. But be careful. The last thing we need is for you to make it all the way home and then get crushed under a rogue beam or something."

He grinned. "If I am, you'll know it was Danny."

As if summoned, there was a loud knock on the front door.

"You ready there, Johnny?" Danny called. "I'm about to freeze my balls off out here."

"That'd be an improvement," John said as he opened the door, "considering how often your balls have gotten you into trouble in the past."

Framed by the doorway, Danny grinned. "Not wrong. In my defence, though, I can't help that I'm irresistible."

"Good to know that becoming Chief hasn't gone completely to your head, Danny," Kimmy retorted as she walked out of the kitchen, and John chuckled. "Now, children...there's work to do."

John kissed me goodbye, and the three of them headed for a horse-drawn wagon, where Jenna waited. I'd never seen horses in person before, and though they were intimidating, I was curious about them and wished they could've stayed. *Oh well.*

I sighed as I headed back to the living room alone; Asha had gone upstairs to catch up on sleep. Our sleeping bags and packs were still laid out around the hearth...only now, there were children playing with them. Jake was hiding in John's sleeping bag from an inquisitive little girl of perhaps four years old, who kept trying to unzip it. Every time she tried, Jack would roll over, making her giggle loudly, and the game would repeat. Allie glared at them from the sofa, a book in her hands.

"I'm *trying* to read," she said irritably.

My eyes immediately went to the book she held. *The Odyssey* by Homer. I frowned. An eleven-year-old girl was reading *The Odyssey*?

"How's your book, Allie?" I asked, moving to take a seat next to her.

She looked at me nervously, clearly unsure how to interact with me.

"It's okay, I guess," she replied, looking down at the floor. "I mean, I don't really get most of it."

"I'm not surprised," I said, and when she looked offended, I quickly clarified, "A lot of adults don't get it. It's a difficult book."

She sighed heavily as the two younger children squealed with laughter again.

"Dr. Irons was making me read it before he died, and Mom says I have to finish it. But I hate reading."

I frowned again. "It's for school?"

When she nodded, I couldn't help judging the deceased Dr. Irons. What teacher would possibly think *The Odyssey* was appropriate reading material for an eleven-year-old?

"Did he say why he wanted you to read it?" I asked, holding my hand out for the book. Allie hesitated but handed it to me.

I flipped through the dog-eared pages. No annotations, no teaching guide, and it was unabridged, which meant it was at least 400 pages. The language was dense and difficult—far beyond the expected reading level for her age group. I'd read it for the first time in a university course about Greek classics.

Allie rolled her eyes. "He said it's 'high' literature that we should all know because if we don't, it'll be lost. He said that about everything, though."

I couldn't help but smile at her tone. "What other books did he have you read?"

She rattled off a list that included texts from Shakespeare, *The Great Gatsby* by F. Scott Fitzgerald, and *Ulysses* by James Joyce. Nothing I would've given to a preteen girl. No wonder she hated reading.

"I don't blame you for not liking them," I said thoughtfully, chewing my lip. "Lots of grown-ups don't even like them. Can I make you a deal?"

She eyed me warily, but she was listening.

"If I can find you some better books, would you give them a try?" I asked. "I want to try to change your mind about reading. Some of the most fun I ever had was while reading."

John had told me that his grandparents had a small library of books, and I knew he'd be willing to help me scavenge for books if needed. If I could just find one that was appropriate for her age group and reading level...

She laughed doubtfully. "Why would you do that?"

I smiled. "Well...I used to be a teacher. Back where I came from. I taught music and history, because those were my specialty, but...I'm qualified to teach most subjects except mathematics. That was always my weakness."

"Oh. I didn't know," Allie said, fidgeting with her sweater, "I'm sorry Dr. Irons died, but school was so boring that I'm kinda glad I don't have to go."

I bit my tongue to avoid saying something I'd regret. I knew some kids may never like school, but from everything I'd heard, it sounded like the Valley children had a better reason than most. Suddenly, John's adolescent misdeeds sounded less like a deliberately wayward child and more like an incredibly bored, under-stimulated teenage boy. If school was this dull, of course he'd been far more interested in learning about shooting and horseback riding.

Sarah came in from the kitchen, unusually red-faced, a protective hand over her enormous belly.

"Sorry to ask you, Claire," she said, clearly embarrassed, "but I knocked my knife off the counter while chopping, and I can't...well, I can't bend over to get it."

I smiled. "Of course. I'd love to help."

I followed her to the kitchen, retrieved the knife, and started to help her prepare small meat pies for dinner. As I rolled out the pastry for her, I remarked, "It's quite amazing how you've been able to maintain such a high standard of living here."

Sarah looked surprised. "Probably still much lower than you're used to, I bet, coming from a compound."

I shrugged. "It's not about comparing the two. The compound had access to a lot of high-tech solutions that made living easier. But there was a steep price for all that."

"You didn't like it there?" Sarah asked cautiously.

"I didn't know any different," I replied, rolling out another ball of pastry. "But once I was outside...I saw that we'd lived very small, constrained lives, under strict control. I like being free."

She seemed to relax at my answer, and we chatted amiably for a long time after that. She seemed interested in my life inside the Cave, so I told what stories I could, and in exchange, she shared babysitting stories about John and Kimmy. Predictably, John was the wild child, while Kimmy was more laidback and studious. She'd always wanted to be a doctor, Sarah said, while John wanted to be a cowboy.

"I don't want you getting the wrong idea about John," Sarah said after we'd both stopped laughing. "He was a bit of a troublemaker, but he was never mean. Always hated bullies and got in trouble a couple times for fighting with a kid who picked on the others. He was sweet, if a little unhinged at times."

I giggled. "Sounds like the man I know and love."

Her expression softened. "Never saw him do anything like he did for you at that meeting. He wouldn't have done that for just anyone, so he must love you too." She paused, then continued, "I mean, it's not hard to see why he'd want you. You don't look like any of the girls around here, that's for sure."

My smile faltered a little. "I suppose you're right."

There was an uncomfortable silence.

"I'm sorry," Sarah said, touching my arm. "That came out wrong."

"It's okay," I replied, trying to recover the pleasant conversation we'd been having. "I'm looking forward to living here with him. I've heard so much about Summerhurst and all of you, and it's kind of a dream come true to be here finally."

Sarah stared at me for a long moment.

"You're not what I expected, coming from a compound. You're alright, Claire."

It wasn't exactly a glowing endorsement...but I'd take it.

❄

For our last night at the Armstrongs', Sarah insisted that John and I sleep in the bedroom that Maisie and Allie shared, even though we said we'd be fine in the living room again. Kimmy and Asha would share the boys' bedroom.

"They'll survive one night in the living room," she said, giving her children a pointed look. "Won't you, kids?"

"Yes, Mom," the three oldest mumbled.

That night, I took a real, honest-to-goodness shower—my first in months, and the hot water droplets raining down on my skin felt like a revelation. I may not have missed many things about the Cave...but proper showers were at the top of the list. Sarah had also volunteered to wash our clothes—threadbare and wretched as they were at this point—and so when I went to bed, I was cleaner than I'd been in almost a year.

We retired to a very pink bedroom on the second floor, with childish animals painted on the walls. Clearly, it hadn't been redecorated in some time. I stood in front of a full-length mirror, brushing my damp hair, while John stripped down to boxers for bed.

"Pretty," he murmured, watching me.

His gaze reminded me of Sarah's earlier comment and the reaction to my looks during the council meeting. It bothered me.

"I want to ask you something," I said, "and I want you to tell me the truth."

John raised an eyebrow, leaning back on his hands. "Okay."

"Am I strange?" I asked quietly, concentrating on the knots at the bottom of my hair. "Everyone in that meeting today talked about my looks."

John frowned. "And?"

"I've never had so many people comment on my appearance...other than my mother, who was never happy with it."

Understanding softened his features. "But she was wrong."

I set the hairbrush on the dresser, staring deliberately at the floor.

"They acted like I was a...a freak," I said, mortified. "I spent so long being the ugly duckling in my family...if I'm going to be that again here, I want to be prepared."

To my surprise, John gave an incredulous laugh.

"Sweetheart," he said gently, beckoning me over, "you're so beautiful that they don't know what to think. Why do you think we disguised you and Asha in Little River? Because your beauty is a dead giveaway that you're different."

I stood between his parted knees, giving him a doubtful look as he wrapped his arms around my waist.

"But I never thought you and Kimmy were...that different."

"Nice of you to say," John replied, amused, "but to the rest of us normies, it's pretty obvious that you stand out. I may not be bad to look at, but I have scars, and the odd wrinkle here and there. The sun burns me, and bugs bite me. Not like you—perfect and smooth."

I moved to straddle his lap and studied his face. His soft, affectionate smile revealed sweet, soft creases at the corners of his eyes that I'd always liked. His skin, paled by winter, was still darker than mine, and I ran my fingers along the length of his sharp jawline, admiring him. His dark amber eyes held mine, exuding warmth. It was true that he wasn't the same as the people I'd grown up around...he was better. More real. Less concerned with artifice.

"I think you're beautiful," I whispered, like it was a secret. "I told you before that I like the scars and wrinkles. They give you character, which is its own beauty."

He chuckled. "Good news for me, since there's only going to be more of both as time goes on."

I traced over the laugh lines at the corner of his mouth. "So, you think I'm going to fit in here, then?"

"Of course," John said, pecking my lips. "Your family may not have loved you like you deserve, but I promise that mine will, if you let us."

A swell of emotion rose in my chest. No one had ever accepted me so unconditionally. I thought of the earlier breakfast with the Armstrongs, and my heart ached, once again, to belong. Here I was, being offered the thing I'd wanted since I was a child, and I just had to be brave enough to take up the space I was being freely given.

I grabbed his face in my hands and pulled his lips to mine. Surprised, he froze for a second before kissing me back enthusiastically, winding his hands in my hair. I kissed him breathlessly, with abandon, until I felt the rigidness of his erection between us. I broke apart, giggling, and he gave me a sheepish grin.

"I wish we weren't in a child's bedroom right now," I said with a sigh. "I don't think that bear on the wall would be impressed if we started...*cuddling*."

John laughed. "Kinda looks like he's judging us, yeah."

Even though there were two single beds, we climbed under the covers of the left one together. We'd gotten used to sleeping close, sharing a sleeping bag in the cold winter, so we snuggled easily into the small space. The bed was warm, and so comfortable compared to the frozen ground that I wanted to cry.

"Just wait till you see Summerhurst tomorrow," John said softly against my hair. "I know these past months were tough, but you made it, baby."

I smiled at a cluster of paper stars stuck to the ceiling.

"We all did."

CHAPTER 22

Claire

The day had arrived. I was finally going to Summerhurst.

My stomach was full of butterflies. I'd heard so much about it that it'd almost achieved mythical status in my mind. *The last safe place*, John had once called it. I could only hope that in time, I'd come to feel the same safety and adoration for the homestead as he and Kimmy did.

It was cold out, but thankfully nowhere near as brutal as the Wasteland. Bruce graciously offered to drive us over in his truck, since John said that walking would've taken over an hour. He would also be making multiple trips to deliver John and Kimmy's farm animals, who had been living at Dreamspring while they were gone. Sarah had been kind enough to pack up a giant crate of food for us to take back.

"That'll get you started, anyway," she said to John and Kimmy before we left. John protested a little at the sheer amount of food she was giving away, but Kimmy just enveloped her in a huge hug. Asha stared at the basket, impassive, but exchanged a look with me that said she didn't know how to interpret Sarah's generosity.

"It's nothing," Sarah scoffed at John over Kimmy's shoulder. "The whole Valley had a great harvest last year, and without you, there wouldn't be any more of those to come. Now, go. You all have a lot to do."

It still amazed me a little to see a working vehicle parked outside, and know that John and Kimmy had one, too. I hadn't seen such a thing since I'd left the Cave. I was looking forward to the ride, but just as I was following Kimmy and Asha towards the red pick-up, John stepped in my path.

"You and I are taking a different route," he said, holding out his hand to me. "Come on."

I frowned. "You said Bruce was driving."

"He's driving them, yeah," he replied with a grin. "The way we're taking is more fun."

"Why do I feel like it's not going to be much fun for me?"

He laughed and took my hand. "Don't be such a chicken. Where's your sense of adventure, compound girl?"

I gave him a skeptical look but allowed him to lead me to a large wooden building some way from the house. I hesitated at the threshold, but he didn't let me linger, pulling me along.

Inside, the smell of hay was followed by soft clicking sounds that turned out to be horses. There were two of them boxed up in stalls, surrounded by perhaps half a dozen empty ones. The door to a paddock at the back of the building was open.

I'd only ever seen pictures of horses before, and that didn't do them justice.

The first horse was huge and mostly white, except for silvery grey patches on its snout and legs. It was the fussier of the two, making the strange clicking noises that now had an air of impatience. The second was smaller, with a coat of rich, deep brown and soulful brown eyes that seemed to watch me with curiosity.

"They're beautiful," I said, awed.

John smiled and pressed a kiss against my hand before heading over to the white horse.

"Hey," he murmured, extending a hand toward the animal's wide neck. "You remember me, girl?"

The horse blew air through her nose onto John's face as if in response, and John chuckled.

"This is Ghost," he said to me, stroking the horse's nose. Ghost leaned into his hand, seeming pleased by his attention. "She's mine. The other one is Kimmy's, and she's called Bella."

He held his free hand out to me, motioning for me to come closer. I bit my lip, a little nervous in the presence of such strong animals. All it would take was one good kick if they were feeling temperamental.

"They don't bite," John said. "Just like me, remember? Scary at first, but mostly harmless."

I snorted at that, but slowly moved forward and took his hand. He tugged me closer to Ghost, lifting my hand to touch her snout. Her coat was soft and shiny, her eyes a deep ebony, and I decided I'd never seen a more beautiful creature anywhere. She turned her head toward me, allowing me to pet her, and I let out the breath I'd been holding.

"Here," John said, and he produced a dried carrot from his pocket. "Lay your hand out flat."

I did as he instructed, and Ghost devoured the vegetable in one bite, lapping at my hand with her long, slobbery tongue. I giggled at the way it tickled my palm.

"She likes you," John said, a smile in his voice.

I beamed. "I like her, too."

"Ready to ride her home?"

"What?" I squeaked. "From here?"

He nodded. "I'll help you. Come on."

He went through the process of reining up and saddling Ghost, narrating for my benefit. Unfortunately, I was too nervous to absorb much as I watched him lead the big beast out the back door and into the paddock.

The paddock was huge, and four other horses wandered in the distance. John fetched a block from inside the stable and placed it next to Ghost, who stood waiting patiently.

"Ready?" he asked, and I gulped.

"No, but I don't think I'll ever be," I replied. "Just show me what to do."

He took over, helping me up onto the block and then coaxing me into lifting my leg over. After a few seconds' hesitation, I managed to hoist myself up. I smiled a little, thinking of what my former self, living inside concrete walls, would think if she could see me now.

"Look at that," John said, smiling too. "You're up on a horse. How do you feel?"

"Good, I think," I replied, and was surprised that it was true. "What now?"

"Sit up straight," he said, reaching up to adjust me. "Keep your shoulders back. And make sure that your feet are facing inwards. You want to be hugging the horse with your legs."

After a few more adjustments and showing me how to hold the reins, he said,

"Okay, I think we're ready to start moving."

"You sure?" I asked uncertainly. "I don't know what I'm doing."

John raised an eyebrow. "And sitting here is gonna help you learn?"

"Point taken," I said with a sigh. "Show me how this thing works, Wastelander."

He chuckled, then made a clicking noise with his tongue. Ghost started walking slowly forward. I shot him an inquisitive look.

"You can do that to make them walk," he clarified. "Or squeeze her sides with your legs."

I nodded, and he continued to instruct me, helping me turn left and right with the reins. After several minutes, I felt confident enough to start turning on my own.

"Good," John encouraged, watching me. "You're a natural, sweetheart."

I flushed with pleasure. I hadn't been a natural at anything yet in the Wasteland, but this was different. It felt easy, pleasant even, and Ghost was well-trained in picking up on my cues. I breathed in the cool Valley air and felt peace and exhilaration, all at once.

John helped me coax Ghost into a trot, and though I was initially nervous, I soon enjoyed the faster pace. What's more, he beamed with pride at my progress, which would've been enough to get me to mount even the wildest horse. After letting me get used to riding, we headed toward Summerhurst.

John took the reins and led Ghost back into the stable. He put reins on Bella and led her out to the front, letting me follow on Ghost's back. Once outside, he surprised me by hoisting himself up behind me.

"I'm just here to supervise," he said, his voice tinged with amusement. "Turns out you barely even need me."

I laughed. "Don't speak too soon; there's still the entire ride home."

John kept a hold on Bella's reins to keep her with us, and we rode at a relatively slow pace out to the woods, following a trail towards Summerhurst. Thankfully, there wasn't nearly as much snow in the Valley as outside it.

"Technically," John said, pointing ahead of us at a tree marked with a red X, "once we cross that, we'll be on Summerhurst land."

We rode for about fifteen more minutes. I'd never seen the woods on horseback, and I quite enjoyed the experience, especially because my fiancé's warm, firm body was pressed up against mine the whole time. I leaned back into him, and he kissed my hair as we began to climb the side of a slope.

"Once we reach the top of this hill," John said, "you'll see it."

My stomach jumped as we reached the summit, and the landscape that stretched out before us took my breath away.

In the distance, across several fields, there stood an enormous white farmhouse, almost blending into the snowy landscape, except for sunlight glinting off the glass windows. It was two storeys, with dark shutters on all the windows, and the biggest porch I'd ever seen, which wrapped around the whole house, supported by white columns. I could just make out a faded red front door. Off to the side, there was a large red barn and a collection of other, smaller buildings. The place was huge in comparison to any home I'd ever seen back in the compound.

I was suddenly aware that my mouth was hanging open, because John chuckled.

"You lived here?" I managed.

"You like it?" he asked a little shyly, smiling.

"It's...incredible," I said, my eyes wide, and he kissed my cheek before urging Ghost and Bella on.

We approached a series of outbuildings, which John pointed out for me as we went.

"Storage," he said, gesturing at a squat, grey building, then counted off the tall, white brick buildings near it. "Utility shed. Distillery. Workshop. The mill is on the opposite end of the property, because that's where the river is."

I felt like my eyes were bugging out of my head as we passed each of them.

"Obviously, the barn," John continued, pointing at the big red building ahead of us, then at a smaller, brown building next to it. "Stable for the horses, which is where we're headed. The chicken coop is on the other side. We'll have to spend some time getting the animals settled back in today."

I nodded as if I knew anything about what that entailed as we closed in on the stable. John hopped off Ghost's back and led both horses towards the gate of a large paddock that enclosed the back of the stable and barn. He opened it and walked us across the pasture to the back door of the stable, then gave it a hard shove.

The door squealed painfully as he pushed it open, hinges badly needing oil. Ghost walked into the stable on her own and Bella followed—they still clearly felt right at home. John took my hand and helped me dismount. He went to start unsaddling Ghost.

"Wait," I said, and he stopped, giving me a quizzical look.

"You not get enough?" he said, raising an eyebrow. "You did good today, but we have a lot to do. We can ride again tomorrow if you want."

I shook my head. "Not me. I wanted to see you ride. It's only fair...unless, of course, you're the chicken one."

It was a childish taunt, but I knew it'd work. John never backed down from a challenge, even one so juvenile.

Sure enough, he grinned and led Ghost toward the back of the stable. The back door paddock gate squealed painfully as he pushed it open, hinges badly needing oil. I followed him out into the wide-open space and watched as he mounted Ghost as easily as he climbed out of bed in the morning.

I stopped for a moment to admire John on horseback. He cut a striking figure in his leather hunting jacket, sitting up tall, all sharp angles and masculine grace. He looked completely in control, reins clasped in hand and his jaw set in concentration. A slight flush rose to my cheek; I never thought I'd be turned on by horseback riding, but there was a first for everything.

"Come on," I said, grinning. "You have to at least show me a bit of what you can do."

"I'm rusty," he protested, and maybe that would've worked on a stranger, but I knew him better than that.

"Go on, then," I said with an exaggerated shrug. "You said I was doing well, so I've set the bar. Rise to the challenge."

John laughed. "Alright, alright. Wouldn't want to be shown up by my rookie wife now, would I?"

Wife. My heart still beat faster whenever he called me that. I wanted it to be official so badly. I wanted to wear his ring and take his name and be a part of this place that he obviously loved so much. I wanted to belong here, and by extension, belong to him—always. I'd had a taste of what family and community could mean for the first time in my life, and it awakened a painful yearning. With my passionless assigned marriage and my dysfunctional family, I hadn't known what I was missing until now.

John clicked his tongue and Ghost started forwards. Gradually, he urged her into a full-on gallop around the paddock, rapidly switching directions and holding the form he had taught me earlier. It was as I suspected: he was good, but acted like it was nothing. He had a unique ability to pick things up quickly with an ease and confidence that would make anyone feel inadequate. Anything that involved active participation to learn, he was able to simply absorb, as if by osmosis. He may not have read Hemingway or known what the Eiffel Tower was, and the so-called 'guardians of culture' at the Cave would've sneered at him, but he was the smartest person I'd ever met.

Galloping around the paddock, he looked happy, like he was finally back where he belonged, and it made me feel warm inside.

"Is that supposed to impress me, Wastelander?" I called, goading him.

John made a face at me, then cast his eyes over at the gate at the far end of the paddock. He spurred Ghost into a gallop again, building speed by circling a few times. He steered towards the fence, and it took me a second to realize what he was doing. The horse jumped and I yelped, but of course, he had things well in hand. They cleared the fence easily, and John laughed with pure exhilaration.

"Now you're just showing off," I shouted to him.

"Maybe a little," he called back, laughing some more. "Do not try that yourself."

He certainly had nothing to worry about on that front...though I did wonder what jumping might be like, and how it was done, and it even looked sort of...fun. Who am I?

John returned to the stable with Ghost, then showed me each step and let me brush Ghost while he removed Bella's reins. We eventually got both horses into their stalls, which had been cleaned and filled with water and fresh hay.

"That was job one yesterday," John commented. "Until I get the truck up and running, they're going to be the main form of transportation."

The stable was far fuller than I would've expected, with hay bales, bags of feed, and various other supplies.

"Where'd you get all this stuff?" I asked, raising an eyebrow.

"Danny delivered it," he replied. "Traded him a couple PNCs for it."

"Is that your strategy? To trade them for the things you need to get back up and running?"

"Yep," he confirmed. "Thankfully, with all you found for us, we have more than we'll ever need to trade. That said, we need a lot—not just farm supplies, but basic things like clothes and food. We can't grow much till spring, and I don't think those pants are gonna survive another season."

He nodded at the pants I was wearing, and I felt unaccountably embarrassed at how frayed they were, and the patches I'd sewn in multiple places. I hadn't thought much about the fact that everything I owned could fit into a backpack while we were on the road, but now, amongst all this, it seemed like a sorry state to be in.

"My pants are fine," I said quietly, not wanting to ask him for even more when he'd already given me so much. "I don't need anything."

John bent and kissed me gently. "You don't have to do that, you know—act like you deserve less than you do. I'm marrying you, and that means that everything here is yours, too. The house, the land, and everything else—they're *ours* now. I know Kimmy agrees."

"But—" I started, but he shook his head firmly.

"You're not asking me for anything," he continued. "I'm sharing it with you because I want to, and because you deserve to have a good life as much as anyone else here. I'm not going to let my girl go without. Especially not because she thinks she doesn't deserve it."

I'm not going to cry, I told myself firmly as I swallowed hard. He'd touched the heart of what I'd struggled with for so long, being the less-favoured child. I'd so often been given less, treated less, *loved* less.

And some part of me always believed it was because there was something wrong with me. Something unknown and evil had touched me as an infant, rotted me to my core, and that was why my mother could never love me the way she did my sister, and why I couldn't hold onto anything good. Even now, that belief remained, marked indelibly on my soul as a fundamental part of me.

That belief had caused me to accept my lot in the compound as it was: marrying a man I didn't love, working a job I didn't choose, living in a home that wasn't really mine. It was why I didn't know how to react to the kind of freedom I had once I ended up in the Wasteland. I'd never thought I deserved any better than whatever I got.

But John knew me, and he healed old, broken parts of me that I'd forgotten were even still there. I couldn't help but envelop him in an embrace, burying my face in his shoulder.

"Thank you," I whispered.

John stroked my hair gently as Ghost nickered at us from her stall.

"See, even Ghost agrees," he teased, and I couldn't suppress a chuckle. "You ready for the official tour?"

I pulled back, smiling widely as I hooked my arm through his.

"Show me the way."

As we walked toward the house, John pointed out a couple more of the smaller buildings, including a greenhouse and a woodshed. Every roof was covered with solar panels, which was connected to a main power supply in the utility shed. That was where the new PNCs had been installed.

"We got the power back on yesterday," John said, guiding me past the barren woodshed. "The water system works, but it needs maintenance. We'll get that done in the next few days."

We stopped in front of the farmhouse, and I stared up at its beautiful, imposing figure. Back in the compound, I'd lived in a small, serviceable townhome—the kind assigned to most of the younger, lower-ranking residents. It had been fine for just two people...but the farmhouse was nearly triple the size.

"You're looking at the home of generations of Madigans," John said proudly. "My great, great uncle lived here before my grandparents moved back from Ireland in the '30s."

John took my hand and led me up the steps of the big wrap-around porch to the faded red front door.

"Would you guys sit out here a lot?" I asked, imagining some evening when we might sit and stargaze together.

"More on the back porch," John answered. "There's more room and it's screened in."

He led me through the door and into the foyer.

"Wow," I said, my eyes widening.

The ceiling was high, probably twenty feet, and featured a large, old-fashioned chandelier. The walls were painted an off-white, and a wood floor of rich mahogany flowed from the foyer down a long hallway that ended in a set of French doors. A wooden staircase stood off to the left, leading up to a second floor landing enclosed with dark wood railings. A small wooden bench stood by the door, next to a closet with white doors.

It was grander than I'd dared to imagine. I turned to John.

"I didn't picture this," I said, looking up at the chandelier again. "How big is this place?"

"Six bedrooms," he answered, with more nonchalance than I thought that announcement deserved. "Five bathrooms. Like I said, it's been in the family forever. Generations have lived here, often under one roof."

I took another minute to marvel. Was I really going to live here?

"Where do you want to go next?" John asked, watching me.

"You tell me, it's your house," I said, still in disbelief.

He smiled, then lifted my fingers to his lips.

"It's your house now, too."

"I might need a minute on that," I said, shaking my head.

He grinned at me, then took me down the hallway to the kitchen. Cream-coloured cabinets wrapped around the room, with lacquered wood countertops. A large island sat in the middle with a double sink and three raised chairs in front of it. A large steel fridge stood in the corner. On the opposite side of the room was a wood table, painted a deep blue, with four chairs. A set of glass doors on the far-left wall led into a dining room. Next to that, a white door stood ajar, and Kimmy stood inside a spacious pantry, putting away the food that Sarah had gifted us.

"Wondered when you'd turn up," she said casually. "I got the other animals settled with Asha's help, so I think we're okay to be in for the evening."

"Where is Asha?" I asked.

"Exploring the property," Kimmy replied, and she suddenly sounded strained. "We...had a little fight."

"Oh no, what happened?" I asked. "Is it about the council meeting?"

She sighed. "Yeah. I guess I didn't do the best job defending her yesterday, but what did she expect me to do?"

John stared at the floor, looking uncomfortable.

"You could've called her your girlfriend," I said with a shrug. "Not judging, but I can see why that might've—"

"She doesn't want me to," Kimmy interjected sharply. "And she's made it very clear that she's not my girlfriend, so I don't know what she wanted me to say."

"But...you guys are together," I replied, staring at her. "It's obvious."

Kimmy crossed her arms. "Apparently not. She's fine to travel with me for two months, to live with me, to *fuck* me—"

"Wow, this definitely doesn't sound like my business," John interjected, shifting from foot to foot. "When you two are done talking, I'll be waiting in the hall, Claire."

He left the room, and when Kimmy met my eye, we burst into giggles. For a moment, we couldn't stop, and it felt so good to laugh together after months of tedious travel.

"I'm never gonna get tired of embarrassing him," Kimmy said, wiping her eyes. "His face is fucking priceless every time."

She imitated John's brow, furrowed with discomfort, and I endured another bout of giggles.

"I'm sorry, Kim," I said once we'd calmed down. "I didn't know. I thought maybe you were just nervous about telling everyone about the two of you."

"I am," she replied. "I get it, though. It's new, between us. But that girl gives me whiplash. One moment, I think she's happy to be with me, and the next, she's giving me the cold shoulder."

I crossed my arms. "I'll talk to her."

The corners of Kimmy's mouth turned down in distress.

"Please don't," she begged. "She'll be upset that I even said anything to you. I don't really know what happened with her past, but...I think part of the problem may be that she's hung up on some ex of hers."

I frowned. "I've never known her to be hung up on anyone."

She shrugged. "Can't tell you more than that. It's just the impression I got."

A heavy silence followed.

"She's my friend," I said quietly, "but if it's not a good relationship, you don't have to settle for her."

"Be real, Claire," Kimmy said with a bitter chuckle. "How many gay women do you think live in this community? Hint: you're looking at her."

Unfortunately, she had a point, as much as I hated that for her.

"You deserve love as much as anyone," I said gently. "I want that for you."

She sighed. "Sometimes I think maybe it could become that with Asha. If she'd just get out of her own damn way."

I gave her a sympathetic smile. "I know."

We stood in silence again for a moment before I changed the subject.

"This place is amazing."

Kimmy smiled warmly. "Glad you like it. Why don't you go see the rest? Besides, I think we've mortified John enough for one day."

I laughed, then went to rejoin John. Next, he showed me the living room, where two grey sofas faced one another in the centre of the room. The back wall was all wall-to-floor windows, looking onto the back porch. The ceiling was similarly high to the hallway, and was paneled, while the rest of the room was the same off-white. A large stone fireplace was the centrepiece of the room. A fire was already crackling away. The room radiated a homey glow. A worn leather recliner stood in the corner. All of the furniture was arranged around an old-fashioned, square wooden coffee table.

The rest of the main floor held a formal dining room, a small bathroom, and the door to an enormous cellar with rows of shelves, which John said was usually full of liquor. Summerhurst had been one of only two liquor-producing homesteads in the Valley. A couple rows of dusty bottles were all that remained now.

Upstairs, John showed me the bathrooms and the unused bedrooms, which had all been retrofitted with woodstoves to keep them warm in the winter. Finally, he led me to the study, which to my surprise and delight, was lined with books. A small, antique desk stood in the centre. The big windows allowed for ample light, and it looked out onto a gated garden in the distance.

"I thought maybe you could paint in here," John said with a small smile. "We're going out tomorrow for supplies, so we can ask around for art stuff."

"I'd love that," I murmured, imagining where I'd put my easel.

He pointed at the fenced garden I'd noticed. "That's the rose garden. A gift for Granny for their fiftieth anniversary. It's where I was thinking we'd get married."

I flushed happily at that thought. "You'll have to take me there another day."

The final stop was the master bedroom. John led me to a set of double doors and paused, looking uncertain.

"This was my grandparents' room," he said. "I moved my furniture in here yesterday because I thought we could use the extra space. Haven't spent much time in here since they died."

I took his hand, rubbing reassuring circles with my thumb. "I'm sure it's lovely. Show me."

The master bedroom was old-fashioned and spacious, with antique mahogany furniture and faded green drapery. On one side stood a small desk that doubled as a vanity table with a chair, as well as the door to a walk-in closet. The opposite side was home to an ornately carved full-length mirror, two dressers, the woodstove, and the door to an ensuite bathroom. The centrepiece was a big wooden bed made up with soft grey bedding and a massive, heavy blanket of fur.

I touched the blanket in wonder.

"Bearskin," John said, amused, as he watched me. "You didn't think that bear back at our camp was my first one, did you?"

Just touching it, I knew it'd keep me toasty all winter long. I pictured sleeping in this room each night, snuggled up with John, and my entire body filled with warmth. The whole house was beautiful in a way that nothing at the Cave had been; history echoed from its every corner. I was determined to soak it in.

"You like it," John said, watching my expression.

"Duh," I replied, and he chuckled.

I peeked into the ensuite bathroom, and besides the usual shower, there was an old-fashioned copper bathtub with clawed feet.

"Don't use that so much," John said, nodding at the tub. "Wastes water."

Rationally, I understood, but it felt like a crime to never use something so beautiful.

"You've always liked taking baths with me," I said, biting my lip.

He grinned. "Nothing to do with the bath, baby."

I sat on the edge of the bed, still admiring our surroundings. As foreign as this big, old house was to me, I could see myself living here. The house already felt familiar, as if by knowing its inhabitants, I'd somehow developed a kinship with it. I wanted to make my own memories here, to join the legacy that emanated from every corner.

"I think we'll be happy here," I said.

John kissed me. "I know we will be. Now, let's get some supper and rest. Tomorrow, the real work begins."

CHAPTER 23

Claire

The next day, the four of us set out on horseback to trade for supplies from the various homesteads around the Valley. John mounted Ghost behind me after helping me up, though to my surprise, I didn't need much assistance. An unfamiliar thrill went through me at being up on a horse again. I hadn't expected to like it as much as I did, and part of me longed to ride on my own.

"With the truck, it'd be faster, but until I get it running again, this'll have to do," John said apologetically. "It'll probably take most of the day."

"Yes, and as we saw, I hated riding yesterday," I replied with a giggle.

I heard John's pride in his voice. "You did take to it very quickly."

"Can we go for a ride later?" I asked, eager to try again despite the lingering aches from yesterday's ride.

"Let's see how you feel after this. Did you remember to bring the drive from the Cave?"

I nodded solemnly, touching its outline in my coat pocket. "I'm a little nervous about what they'll find."

He squeezed my shoulder. "I know. We'll figure it out, though, no matter what happens."

Asha cursed loudly a few feet away as she tried to climb up onto Kimmy's horse, Bella. She was struggling to swing her leg up and over. Kimmy giggled, then offered her hand. Asha took it with a begrudging glance at the horse, then finally managed to mount behind Kimmy.

"That was more trouble than I suspect this is worth," Asha said with a heavy sigh.

"You'll get used to it, Ash," Kimmy said with an encouraging smile. "It definitely beats walking."

Asha scoffed. "I've done enough walking for a lifetime."

"Then you'll appreciate the break," John said pointedly, clearly annoyed. "Let's get moving. This isn't gonna be a quick trip."

We set out from Summerhurst at an easy pace, and I couldn't help but marvel again at the size and beauty of the homestead, even covered in a thick blanket of snow. It would be a sight to behold in the warmer months, when lush greenery painted the landscape. It was still hard to believe that this was my home now, too.

Soon enough, we made it out to the road, which was thankfully clear of fresh snow. John chatted easily as we rode, pointing out various landmarks and giving me a general sense of direction.

"It's going to be a lot to figure out," I said, biting my lip. "It's such a big place."

"You'll do fine," John replied. "You just have to get used to it. There's only one central road through the whole Valley, and we're on it now."

I resolved to draw new maps as soon as I could. Perhaps that could be a useful contribution that'd endear me to those less excited about my arrival.

We followed the road for what felt like a long time, then took a turn at an intersection marked by three oak trees.

"Where are we going first?"

"To the Taylors'," John answered. "The ones working on building our own PNCs. The elder Taylors—Rebecca and Scott—are a married couple who were a scientist and an engineer in the Old World. Their three kids help them now, and one of them—Jackson—is the resident machinist. We need parts to repair the truck and the water system."

I nodded. "How do they feel about me and Asha?"

"They voted for you to stay. You'll get along fine."

Cheered by that news, I leaned back into him, and he kissed the top of my head. I glanced back at Kimmy and Asha, who were riding behind us in silence. Kimmy looked a little upset, while Asha avoided eye contact. I sighed. I wanted to give Asha the benefit of the doubt, but it wasn't hard to figure out that she wasn't enjoying the ride and didn't want to be there. The longer she kicked and screamed about her circumstances, the harder it would be for her to adjust, and the more she'd suffer as a result.

After all, I'd learned the hard way that refusing to accept my lot hadn't changed it. Instead, I had to make the best of what I'd been given, and that path had led me to the man I loved and the beautiful, shining possibility of our life together in this place he clearly adored.

Maybe that was why since arriving in the Valley two days before, I'd felt little else besides excitement. I didn't expect instant acceptance from anyone, but I had hope. The weight of the ring on my left hand reminded me that John needed me to be strong.

We rode until a fork appeared in the road, and we took a right. Eventually, we came upon another large, cleared stretch of land, surrounded by a wooden fence. Unlike at Summerhurst, the house was close enough to be visible from the dirt road. It was tall and white, with blue shutters and a matching door. However, as we drew closer, I noticed that there had clearly been several additions to the house since it was built: a sprawling west wing with blue siding; an east wing that was several storeys high and dwarfed the rest of the house; and a south wing that was mostly windows, probably functioning as a greenhouse. Like all the buildings at Summerhurst, every square inch of roof was covered with solar panels.

It was the strangest house I'd ever seen.

"The additions house different equipment," Kimmy said, seeing my puzzled expression. "Because they handle most of the technical operations in the Valley, they don't do much farming themselves. They're busy keeping everything running. They have other manufacturing buildings elsewhere on the property."

We tied the horses to a nearby hitching post before John knocked on the front door. An older man of perhaps sixty answered. He was tall and thin, balding, with thick-rimmed glasses that rested precariously on the bridge of his nose. He wore a simple black shirt and pants, with a calculator tucked into his breast pocket.

"Wondered when you'd all be dropping by," he said with a kind smile, then turned to me and Asha. "Scott Taylor. Good to meet you."

"Thank you for allowing us to stay," I said earnestly. "We appreciate your faith in us."

He waved it away. "When you've lived as long as I have, you learn that those who want to keep us in the past inevitably get left behind. We've needed new blood for ages. You're welcome here." He looked back to John. "I'm itching to get my hands on some more PNCs, and I'd bet that there's no shortage of things you need to get Summerhurst up and running again. Come inside."

We followed him into the strange house, down a long hallway that led to an office. To my surprise, the room was full of computers. I hadn't seen a computer outside the Cave. They were old and had clearly been refurbished many times, but they were functional. Asha's eyes widened at the sight of them, and she took a few steps between the desks.

"Never seen Wastelanders who had anything like this before," she said.

"Glad you like it," Scott said, seeming pleased. "Our technology is old, but we do our best to keep everything running as well as it can."

He sat at a computer and typed up a list as John and Kimmy rattled off the various technical supplies we needed: parts for the truck, for the water system, and for the distillery. Scott had the parts for the water system on hand, but everything else would need to be specially made. He promised to deliver the rest when they were ready. John handed over a large number of PNCs in exchange, and Scott's eyes lit up at the sight of them.

"Rebecca will be elated," he said. "This should be enough to finish our research. Thank you."

"There's one other thing," John said, nodding at me.

I reached into my pocket and pulled out the drive.

"I found this back at the compound—where we got the PNCs," I said hesitantly, holding it out to him. "I wanted to know if you could open it."

"Certainly," Scott replied brightly, taking the drive from me. "I'll have to scan it first to ensure there's no malware, but after that, it should be no problem."

He fiddled with his computer for a few minutes, then eventually plugged in the drive. I held my breath. I'd tried many times to imagine what Neil could've left for me without success. The mystery had nagged at the back of my mind for months.

"It's encrypted," Scott said, and I exhaled slowly. "And the encryption is fairly sophisticated—certainly beyond anything I could create here with my existing tech."

"So, you can't open it?" I asked anxiously. I wasn't sure how I'd live with never knowing, but that'd always been a possibility.

"I may be able to decrypt it," he answered, looking at me over his spectacles. "But I can't say how long it'll take. If you'd be willing to leave the drive here with me, I can give it my best shot."

There was hope. "Of course. Thank you."

He gave me a warm smile. "I'm happy to do it for the people who helped save our little community here."

I flushed, and John grinned. We said a polite goodbye and departed for the next homestead on our list. Unfortunately, the next household—the Wangs—refused to allow me or Asha in. John made a fuss, but they wouldn't budge. Instead, they insisted we wait at the gate to their homestead while they dealt exclusively with John and Kimmy.

"I'm sorry," John said to me, pained. "Are you—?"

"It's fine," I replied, forcing a smile for his benefit. "Just get what you need, darling."

He gave me a kiss and reluctantly left me at the gate with Asha. Kimmy shot us both a look of apology as she followed.

It didn't end there. The next two households also refused us, leaving us waiting at their gates. I should've been prepared for it, but a wave of mortification still broke over me as I waited for John and Kimmy to return. *You're already on the outside looking in, a nagging voice in my head said. That's how you'll always be.*

A dull ache in my lower back made itself known as Asha aggressively shoved her hands in her jacket pockets and stood there with utter contempt on her face.

"They're treating us as if we're the savages," she said, and her scathing tone could've wounded even the most stoic person in the world.

"We would've treated them the same," I replied weakly, even as it hurt me to admit it. Now, more than ever, I *felt* how wrong I'd been about Wastelanders. Nobody who could build a place as beautiful as the Valley was a savage. They were the architects of the only hope this fallen world might have.

Asha sighed. "I guess. Can't wait to start scavving. Get out of this place for a while."

"We just got here," I said, nettled. "Can't you at least give it a chance?"

She fixed me with that unsettling stare of hers. "Look where we are. You think they're giving us a chance?"

"We're still here," I pointed out. "And if we play our cards right, they'll let us stay."

As the words came out, I knew I was saying them for myself as much as her...especially when we then had to visit the Jameson homestead. Predictably, they didn't want us either. The eldest son, Zach—the one who'd made the crude comment about me at the council meeting—met us at the door and sneered.

"Take your outsider trash to the gate," he said, and John told him to go do something I didn't have the gall to repeat. Kimmy's lips twitched, but she managed to maintain her scowl.

"You kiss your wife with that mouth, Madigan?" Zach replied, raising an eyebrow. "Knowing the quality of woman you've got there, she probably enjoys it. You think because you're Oisín's grandson, you get to break the rules? Nah. But you'll get her and her friend off our property, or I'll let my father know about this. Good luck getting half the Valley to trade with you then."

The irony of Zach Jameson accusing John of abusing his grandfather's former position to break the rules was not lost on me, and John looked like he could've cheerfully murdered him. I touched his arm.

"Don't," I murmured. "It's okay. I'll go wait."

John gave me a helpless look that said he didn't want to let this go. But I knew he had to. The Jamesons had the biggest farm in the Valley, and we needed seeds for planting in the spring. I also knew that with the amount of influence they apparently wielded, we couldn't afford to be on their bad side—especially now, when our presence was so new.

I turned away and walked back towards the gate with Asha.

"Good," Zach grunted behind us. "At least *this* trash takes itself out."

Kimmy made a sharp retort as we walked away. Asha and I waited again at the gate, and I tried not to be totally dejected, but it was a losing battle at the moment.

"I wouldn't worry, Claire," Asha said, putting a hand on my shoulder. "The guy's a complete waste of space. You don't need to impress him, and he doesn't deserve it anyway."

I gave a weak smile. She was trying to comfort me, the way she used to. I touched her hand, and we waited in a more companionable silence for the other two to return.

"The next one'll be better," John reassured me when we finally rode away. I winced; the ache in my back had spread to my bottom. I wasn't used riding for hours in a hard leather saddle.

"Yeah, Nimkii's lovely," Kimmy said brightly, then added, "I always thought it was too bad she was straight."

Despite my mood, I laughed as Asha raised her eyebrows. Kimmy flushed a little in response and handwaved it away: "You know what I mean."

"No, I don't," Asha said, and there was real amusement in her voice. "Pray tell, why would you wish she wasn't straight? I didn't know you were into girls."

Kimmy's only response was a snort, and my heart lightened a little. It felt good to see Asha teasing her, to know that the friend I remembered was still in there somewhere.

The next homestead apparently belonged to the Payette family, who specialized in textiles. I was finally going to get new clothes, which—whatever I'd told John before—were sorely needed. My current wardrobe had been worn so much that I worried it might disintegrate at any moment.

The Payette home wasn't visible from the road; instead, there stood a large, rectangular building with a flat roof that looked more industrial than residential. A double glass door faced the road with a sign overhead that read *Payette Textiles & Footwear.*

"That's the workshop," Kimmy explained. "They prefer people go there instead of the house for trade. That's usually where they are during the day anyway."

She led the way to the door, and a bell tinkled cheerfully as we entered a spacious room with concrete walls and floors. A desk faced the door, and a thick binder lay open on what appeared to be a page of orders from customers. Scattered throughout the space were mannequins wearing half-made outfits, tables covered in measuring tapes, sewing needles, spools of thread, scissors, and sketches of clothing. In the far corner was a bench, surrounded by discarded shoehorns, foot measuring tools, and other equipment intended for shoemaking. Rolls of various fabrics were stacked on shelves at the back of the room, next to a door that led elsewhere in the building.

But what really stood out about the place was the walls: they were covered with paintings. Some were of clothing, but others depicted the landscape of the Valley, nature and animals, and abstract colour schemes. A blend of passion and skill, they were vibrant, eclectic, and beautiful. They lit up the room, and an ache opened in my chest. It'd been so long since I'd painted anything.

The distant hum of what I assumed was machinery came through the back door, along with a slender, well-dressed woman in her early to mid thirties. She was average height, with thick black hair that she'd braided to one side, and radiant copper skin with smile lines that gave her a pleasant, cheerful appearance. She wore woven bracelets and layered necklaces, and her left earring featured a long grey goose feather. Her deep purple dress featured small, intricate beading and embroidered floral designs that I could only assume she'd done herself. It might've been the loveliest article of clothing I'd ever seen.

"Welcome," she said as she made her way over to us, and when she reached the front desk, she smiled at John and Kimmy. "So good to see you again, friends. I am glad you made it back, safe and sound. You have our gratitude for everything you've done for us in the Valley."

John gave her a polite nod, while Kimmy grinned nervously. Asha shot her a look between amusement and disapproval.

The woman turned to me and Asha, reaching her hand over the desk. "I know we haven't had the pleasure of meeting one another yet. I'm Nimkii. My family and I run this shop."

After our introductions, I said, "I was just admiring the amazing paintings in this place. Did you create them?"

Nimkii beamed. "So glad you like them. They are my passion project...when I have the time. My son is only two, you see."

I nodded enthusiastically. "I like to paint, too."

"She's an amazing artist," John interjected. "You should've seen her mural back at the camp we stayed at. It was incredible."

The obvious pride in his voice made me blush, but I continued, "I'd love to know where you get your paints."

"I make them," Nimkii said, her eyes twinkling. "Usually watercolours. I have spares that I'd be happy to trade for."

I looked to John, who scoffed. "You don't need my permission. We'll take them, along with whatever canvas you have."

"Wonderful," Nimkii replied. "Now, I assume you're here for clothes."

"I need...everything," I admitted. "So does Asha. I hope that's alright."

As if on cue, John placed a couple of PNCs onto the desk in front of Nimkii. Her attention snapped to them, and her eyes betrayed her need.

"That's generous," she said, raising her eyebrows. "We've needed more for weeks. Some of our automated equipment has stopped working. Thank you."

John nodded. "Just make sure that Claire gets everything she needs...including a wedding dress."

My flush deepened, and Nimkii's face lit up.

"It's always exciting when I get to design for a bride," she said with a charming smile. "Let's get started."

She temporarily returned to the back room, calling to someone in an unfamiliar language. A moment later, a man similar in age to Nimkii and an older woman—who she introduced as her husband and mother—joined us. While Nimkii focused on me, the other two served Asha, Kimmy, and John.

"Your work is beautiful," I said as she flipped through a sketchbook of designs. "Do you do everything by hand?"

"Oh, no," Nimkii said with a laugh. "That'd take ages. Thankfully, we have a couple of industrial looms, which makes weaving much easier and faster. But we keep a herd of sheep for wool and grow crops like flax, which we then often spin by hand. We use a mishmash of methods."

She got to work taking my measurements, then assembled designs for a functional, pragmatic assortment of t-shirts, sweaters, pants, and undergarments, all suitable for working outside in all seasons.

All the while, we chatted happily about painting, swapping techniques and tips. Nimkii had a soft, affable manner that made her easy to talk to. She told me about her young son, Makade, who had already discovered a love for fingerpainting, and her Anishinaabe heritage, which fascinated me. In return, I traded stories about the Cave and my life as a teacher.

Eventually, we finished with the everyday clothes, and I stepped down from the stool she'd had me stand on.

"We've got the boring things out of the way," Nimkii said with a wink. "Now, we'll fit you for a sweet little dress to wear on special occasions. Something pretty."

"That's probably not necessary," I replied, but my protest was weak. I wanted to see what kind of magic she could weave.

Nimkii raised an eyebrow. "Your fiancé said to get you everything you need. And I say you need a pretty dress."

I glanced over at John, who was being measured for a new pair of boots. He was watching me, and tipped his chin toward me, clearly prompting me to get back to what I was doing.

A giggle escaped. "Alright, then."

Nimkii showed me sketches of dresses she'd made in the past, offering adjustments to make mine unique. She held swatches of fabric up, made adjustments, asked me a hundred questions about my preferences.

She fussed over me in a way that nourished my soul, filling me with a bone-deep contentment that banished the sadness I'd felt earlier. It'd been so long since I'd done something as normal as shop for clothes or had the luxury of wondering if I looked pretty or not. Too much time had been taken up by bare survival. It made me feel human again.

When she'd finished with the casual dress, we discussed wedding dress ideas, and she created a beautiful sketch that incorporated my desire for a simple, elegant design. She promised to work on it in the coming months and have me back for a fitting.

When everyone had finished, we headed for the door, and I impulsively hugged Nimkii goodbye. To her credit, she gave a sweet, tinkly laugh and hugged me right back.

"Thank you," I murmured. "You made me feel so welcome today, even when others turned me away. I...I needed that."

She nodded. "You make your own path, Claire. You can make your differences your strength if you choose to."

From the Payette homestead, we visited the homes of the blacksmith (for tools), the glassblower (for glass containers), and the chemist, who restocked Kimmy's medicine supply and traded us for toiletries like soap and shampoo. She even made perfume and lotions, and offered me a small jar of rose oil, which I happily accepted.

Finally, as it was getting dark, we decided to call it a day, our saddlebags filled to bursting. I would've felt sorry for the horses, but I was too busy feeling sorry for myself: my whole body was screaming in protest as John helped me mount Ghost for the ride home.

The ride back to Summerhurst was excruciating. Every muscle in my body burned fiercely. Teeth gritted, I stiffened, which only amplified the pain.

"Nearly there," John murmured behind me, stroking my thigh.

I now understood why he hadn't promised me another ride earlier: he knew that I'd be practically begging for mercy after my first long day on horseback. My lower back and buttocks felt like they'd been through a meat grinder.

By the time we'd settled the horses in the stable and walked to the farmhouse with our saddlebags, I was ready to die. I half-heartedly offered to help put away our new things, and Kimmy chuckled at my lack of enthusiasm.

"You should go to bed," she said, then turned to Asha. "You, too. Neither of you are used to riding."

In truth, Asha looked every bit as exhausted as I did. She headed for the stairs without another word. I looked to John, who gave me a knowing half-smile.

"Go on," he said. "I'll be up soon."

Relieved, I climbed the stairs, wincing at every torturous step. I went to our room and collapsed onto the bed face first, not even bothering to take off my jacket, and passed out. I was woken an undetermined amount of time later by the sound of running water.

I rubbed my bleary eyes. The room was dark except for the low glow of the woodstove; John must have stoked it back to life. A sliver of light peeked through the cracked door of the ensuite bathroom. A moment later, the water stopped running, and light poured into the room as John appeared at my bedside. He'd shed his jacket and looked infinitely more handsome than I probably did at the moment.

"Murder me, Wastelander," I groaned, burying my face in my pillow. "Put me out of my misery."

He chuckled. "A little saddle-sore, are we?"

"A little? I'm pretty sure my backside has been worn down to nothing."

"Luckily, it's still intact," he said, a playful grin touching his lips as he gently stroked my sore bottom.

"How do you tolerate this?"

"You get used to it," he replied. "Once you've built up some strength again, and work on holding proper form, it won't hurt so much. Now, let's look after you, hmm? Wouldn't want to risk any permanent damage to that perfect ass—it might be my favourite part."

"Perv," I muttered, groaning with effort as I lifted myself up off the bed, and he laughed.

He led me to the bathroom, where a full bathtub awaited, tendrils of steam rising in the air.

"I thought you said it was wasteful?" I asked, arching a brow.

"We're making an exception tonight," he answered, steering me towards the tub. "Just don't get too used to it."

I stripped off my clothes, shuddering at the cold air, and climbed in. The hot water was an instant balm on my aching body, and I moaned in a provocative way that made John grin.

"Baby, I know you're in pain right now," he said with wicked amusement, "but don't tempt me."

He undressed and carefully climbed in behind me, letting me lean back against him.

"All I'm tempted to do is pass out again," I replied, resting my head on his shoulder. "I absolutely could get used to a hot bath and a naked you at the end of the day."

John chuckled. "I'll have to keep that in mind."

He gathered my hair in a loose ponytail, moving it away from my face and over his shoulder.

"Today was lovely," I sighed after a moment. "I liked meeting every-one."

"Yeah?"

"Uh-huh. I was surprised how many people were...receptive to me being here. I know a few households didn't want me today, but...most of them let me in."

He was quiet for a moment, idly playing with my hair.

"You've been needed here for a long time," he said finally. "Bringing in outsiders was a matter of when, not if. We just nudged them in the right direction."

"You did, you mean. I'll never be able to repay you for bringing me here, you know."

John kissed my cheek. "You don't need to. I didn't do it as a favour. It's only right that my wife should live here with me."

My heart gave a pleasurable tug.

"But Asha," I continued, and I felt him tense slightly at her name. "That was a favour to me. I know she's hard to deal with sometimes. I can thank you for that, at least."

He didn't reply directly, just kissed my temple. We relaxed in comfortable silence until I was dozing off against him, and the water had gone lukewarm. He helped me out of the bath and led me back to bed. The room had warmed considerably thanks to the woodstove, and though my body still hurt, I felt pleasantly heavy as I sunk into the mattress and closed my eyes.

John clicked open a container, and the faint scent of rose oil filled the air. A second later, his strong hands, slick with oil, turned me onto my front and kneaded gently at my lower back, loosening the knots embedded there. I gasped in half-pain, half-relief, then moaned as he continued down the base of my spine. Slowly and patiently, he massaged away tension and pain, then started on my legs—first my aching thighs, then calves, then feet.

I melted into the bed.

"Oh my God," I groaned as he pressed on the tender arch of my foot. "Where have you been hiding these skills all this time?"

He laughed. "Used to do it a lot for my grandparents, especially in the later years. Guess I got good at it."

I basked in his attention for a while longer, feeling wonderfully loose and drowsy. My pain had quieted to a dull roar, while a whole new ache had begun between my thighs. His prolonged touch made it inevitable, and his focused attention on my body was undeniably sexy.

He worked the oil into my skin, his strokes growing long and languid over my buttocks. He parted my thighs, and I moaned as he stroked me open, carefully sliding a finger inside me. I tensed a little in response.

"Relax for me," John murmured. I let out a long breath and obeyed. "Good girl."

He added another finger, stretching me, and I moaned into my pillow. Still in no hurry, he slowly, methodically pumped his fingers into me, stroking my sensitive inner wall. He tormented me for a long time like that, making my clit ache worse than ever, desperate for contact.

"Don't fight for it," John said as he moved to kneel between my legs. "Just let me give it to you, nice and easy."

I sighed heavily, releasing more tension, and he hummed his approval. "That's it, sweetheart. That's so good."

He slid his free arm underneath me, propping up my hips, and then his mouth was on my clit, teasing it with his tongue. I moaned louder, fisting my hands into the sheet as he shamelessly devoured me from behind.

"I was missing the taste of your pretty cunt," John said softly, his hot breath on my clit. "Couldn't help myself, seeing you laid out so nicely for me."

He pressed his tongue harder against me, licking irresistible circles, and I cried out into the pillow. My orgasm worked through every cell in my body, injecting pure bliss—and crushing exhaustion—into every muscle.

John laid down beside me again, pulling the bearskin blanket over both of us as he gathered me against his body. His rigid erection poked against my belly, and I reached for him, even as I felt myself slipping dangerously close to dreamland.

John shook his head.

"Sleep, baby," he said, nuzzling my hair.

"But...it's your turn," I replied drowsily, giving him a half-hearted pump with my fist.

He chuckled and took my hand in his. "I can have my turn tomorrow."

I sighed. "Now I love you even more."

He laughed again. "I know. Now, rest."

He didn't have to tell me again.

CHAPTER 24

Claire

Despite the busy flurry of activity the past week, the real work on the homestead was just beginning. John woke me at dawn the following morning with a packed to-do list. He and Kimmy sat at the kitchen table and went over the plan as I made breakfast at the woodstove.

"Kimmy and I are working on the irrigation system today," he said to me. "I'm hoping we'll replace all the parts that need it in the next couple days."

"That'll be a relief," I said, turning the omelet in the pan. "How can I help?"

"Honestly, not sure you can," Kimmy replied, a note of apology in her voice as she dug into her own omelet. "There's a lot of technical stuff that we don't have time to teach you right now. John can show you some other time, but for now, we need to be able to work as fast as possible."

A twinge of guilt nagged at me for my inadequacy. I should've been used to the experience of learning that I knew nothing useful, but it still hurt that I couldn't help as much as I wanted to.

I looked a little forlornly at my still-sizzling omelet. It smelled delicious; I'd seasoned it with dried herbs from Sarah's welcome basket. I was a decent cook and did it often, mostly because it was one of the few ways I could be of genuine assistance. But I didn't want that to always be my only contribution.

I needed to become worthy of this place and of John's faith in me.

"I want to do something useful," I said quietly, scooping an omelet onto a plate and placing it in front of John. "Even if it's not that."

John pulled me down for a kiss. "You're doing just fine. Because Kimmy and I are going to be busy, I asked Jenna to come over and keep you company. She'll show you the ropes around the farm. That sound okay?"

Jenna hadn't spoken much at the Armstrongs', but to be fair, there'd been a lot going on. Still, she'd seemed nice enough, and she'd voted for me to stay. It'd be a good chance to get to know one of our neighbours without the buffer of John or Kimmy. Even if the thought made me a little anxious.

But John couldn't keep holding my hand forever, and I didn't want him to, either. Finding my footing felt daunting...but it could also be the beginning of something new and hopeful.

"Sure," I said brightly as I started preparing my own omelet. "Is Asha going to be joining us?"

She hadn't come down to breakfast. Kimmy and John exchanged a look.

"She left before first light," Kimmy said gently, but I noted the regret in her tone. "Off on her first scav mission. She's taking it pretty seriously."

I sighed. "Yeah. I hope she's okay."

"I'm sure she's fine," John said as he carried his plate to the sink. "Seems like she can handle herself."

After breakfast, a loud knock sounded on the door. I followed Kimmy to answer it, and she greeted Jenna with a warm smile and a hug.

"Thanks for coming to help out," Kimmy said. "We appreciate it."

Jenna made a face. "Anything to escape Danny's dad jokes for the day."

She turned her gaze to me, and her chocolate brown eyes were kind. "Hi, Claire."

I forced a smile despite my twinge of nerves. "Good to see you again, Jenna. Thanks for teaching me today. I know you probably have lots of other things to do."

She scoffed. "Nah. I have more free time than I like lately. Let's get started, hmm?"

While John and Kimmy headed to the utility shed, Jenna led me to the stable, where Ghost and Bella were awake and clearly hungry. They nickered at us as we retrieved their bags of feed.

"So, you lived in a compound?" Jenna asked casually as she fed Bella. "This must be a whole new world to you."

Like her older sister, Jenna had an open demeanour that suggested she spoke her mind. Unlike most of the Valley residents the day before, she didn't treat me with reserve or suspicion, and I appreciated it.

"You could say that," I replied as I filled Ghost's food tray. "Honestly, I still feel overwhelmed sometimes by how different it is out here. But I'm glad to be here."

Jenna nodded thoughtfully, tilting her pretty face toward Bella.

"What was it like, living there? I've heard stories, from time to time. That you guys have so much more Old World stuff than we do."

I shrugged. "We had access to a lot of cultural material from the Old World, yes. Most of it was preserved digitally. We also had advanced technology that meant we didn't have to work as hard to survive on a daily basis."

"What do you miss the most?"

I hummed, thinking. "Besides not having to worry about food all the time? I really miss music. I know John said that some people have a small collection of Old World music in hard copy here, but at home, we had an unlimited virtual library. Millions of songs."

"Millions?" Jenna asked, eyebrows raised in disbelief. "How did you ever listen to it all?"

I giggled. "Well, we didn't. But we had the option. And because I was a musician, I liked having more song to learn to play."

Jenna broke into an unexpected grin. "I like to play music, too. I play violin at some of our community dances with Liam. What did you do?"

We launched into a happy conversation about music as we mucked out the horse stalls and let the horses out to pasture. I learned that Jenna had been playing violin since she was seven years old, and she seemed to share my passion for music. She played in a duo with her friend, Liam, who played piano. I told her about my singing, how the piano was my favourite instrument, and sang a few of my favourite songs. Unsurprisingly, she'd never heard most of them before, but she was nonetheless intrigued. Her large, friendly eyes sparkled with interest and intelligence, and perhaps for the first time since I'd left the Cave, I felt like I'd discovered a kindred spirit.

A spark of delight ignited in my belly. I loved John and Kimmy, but they were nothing like me. I'd come to appreciate our differences, but Jenna loved so many of the same things I did—music, books, art.

"Isla always made fun of me for it," Jenna said as we moved on to the barn, "but there are never enough books around here for me. I go through them too quickly. We only get what we can scavenge, and sometimes, they come back with nothing. I'm so jealous of how many books you guys had."

I smiled. "I do miss it. I never realized how much of a privilege it was until I lost it."

We repeated the feeding and cleaning process in the barn, chatting amiably about what other things I'd had access to in the Cave. Jenna was fascinated by the idea of TV and movies, so I spent a lot of time telling her about the ones I'd seen. I told her about modern art, and my paintings, and the artists I'd admired. Inevitably, it led me to recounting my second teaching subject: history, and that fascinated her more. She asked me all sorts of questions about the past, with a thirst for knowledge that rivaled my own. It made the hours pass at a lightning pace.

For her part, Jenna was patient and kind as she showed me how to do various tasks around the farm. On top of basic animal care, she taught me how to milk the cows, helped me gather eggs from the chickens, and instructed me on how to check the animals for signs of disease. She told stories about life on her family farm, growing up with

Danny and Isla and their grandparents. Their parents had died when Jenna was only a year old, so they were the only family she'd known.

"And you were a teaching assistant to Dr. Irons?" I asked as we headed back toward the farmhouse.

She nodded. "I loved the job, especially working with the little kids. Dealing with Dr. Irons, though…"

"Seems like he had a reputation," I remarked, and she chuckled.

"He wasn't a bad guy," she answered. "Just old-fashioned. Stuck in his ways. Liked to do things by the book. He was a better teacher when I was a kid. The years had started to catch up to him by the time he finally admitted he needed an assistant."

"Why didn't the council find a replacement sooner?"

Jenna sighed. "Politics, mostly. When Oisín was chairman, he tried to find someone, but nobody wanted the job. On top of that, Dr. Irons found the search for a replacement insulting somehow, like we were saying he was old and washed up."

I didn't point out that it sounded like he had been old and washed up, but Jenna seemed to read my thoughts, because she chuckled.

"Anyway, after Jameson took over, suddenly it wasn't a priority anymore," she said. "He was always tight with Dr. Irons, and much more conservative. So, the process stalled until I got the assistant job. He planned to train me to eventually be his replacement, but—" she shrugged, "—then he had a heart attack."

We walked to the greenhouse, where Kimmy had told me they grew medicinal herbs for the clinic, as well as a small number of crops in the winter. Of course, at the moment, it was desolate, but I could at least begin the process of restoring it to its former glory.

The greenhouse was small and mercifully warm, a welcome change from outside. Jenna helped me haul bags of soil and fill plant pots, remarking that she was impressed with how much I already knew about planting. That, at least, made me feel a small spark of pride. The many hours I'd spent in the garden at our camp hadn't been for nothing.

"What did you do, back at the compound? Did you guys have jobs?" Jenna asked as she scooped dark soil into an empty pot.

"Yes," I said, keeping my voice casual. "I was a music and history teacher for several years before the attack happened."

Her eyes flew open, wide as saucers, and I avoided her gaze.

"Why didn't you tell me?!" she exclaimed. "Here I am, commiserating about how we don't know what the hell's next as far as school goes, and you've been a teacher all this time? You can literally solve all my problems."

She said the last part with such certainty that I couldn't suppress a giggle. Nevertheless, I said, "I'm an outsider who was barely allowed to stay. I don't think anyone would really want me teaching their kids."

"That's just not true," she replied, patting down dirt a little more aggressively than was needed. "You're more qualified than anyone we could possibly find. And I'd help you—I know all the kids and their parents. I know what's going on, lesson-wise. I can fill you in."

I hesitated. "I don't know. I don't want to make waves."

Jenna clucked her tongue. "That's the only way you'll make a difference, though. And you're smart and resourceful and lovely; you'll change their minds."

"You just met me," I said, bemused.

She fixed me with a serious stare, but her eyes twinkled. "Yes, and I'm an excellent judge of character."

Her complete confidence made me laugh—it reminded me of Kimmy—but I was still unsure as we walked back toward the farmhouse, our duties done for the day.

"Please, Claire," Jenna begged. "I need a mentor. Together, we could get the education here back on track. Please at least say you'll think about it."

I bit my lip. "Alright. I'll give it some thought."

"And come to music practice with me and Liam," she said with a grin. "We meet twice a week to play together."

The thought of playing music again made excitement rise inside me, and despite our age difference, I was eager to hang out with Jenna again. It just felt so good to have shared interests with someone again.

"I will," I said happily. "Thanks for helping me today. It made everything much less overwhelming."

Jenna scoffed as she followed me into the house.

"What are friends for?

CHAPTER 25

Claire

The last few weeks of January passed by in a blur of activity.

Summerhurst's revival began to take shape. John and Kimmy successfully repaired the irrigation system and the truck. We finished planting in the greenhouse, and we got the distillery up and running again so that it'd be ready for spring. John started hunting and trapping again to supplement our food supply, and Kimmy and I got up early every morning to feed and care for the animals together. John busied himself working on the tractor, which needed major repairs to be ready for the spring.

Restoring the truck meant that I had my first car ride in over a year—and the only car ride in which a person was driving. The compound only had self-driving vehicles, which were a public utility that anyone could use.

"I promise not to leave us in a ditch," John said with a playful grin as he palmed the steering wheel to make a U-turn.

I was nervous at first, but the truck was clearly built for offroad driving, and he quickly put me at ease. He navigated Summerhurst effortlessly, the way he did most things, and just like when I first saw him ride Ghost, watching him drive was strangely sexy. His strong hands on the wheel made me picture all the times they'd been on my naked body, and I had to distract myself by gazing out the window.

Spending mornings one-on-one with Kimmy made the work go by quickly. Her easy sense of humour and friendly nature reminded me of why she'd become one of my best friends. We laughed together and chatted easily as we worked, and I looked forward to it every day. Unfortunately, however, one of our most frequent topics of conversation was Kimmy's frustrations with Asha, who remained, if anything, more distant than ever. After she'd left on her first scav mission, she hadn't looked back and was gone for days at a time.

"I hate that she goes off on her own," Kimmy complained one morning as we were collecting eggs from the chicken coop. "It's against the rules. We scav in pairs for a reason."

I sighed. "Why do they let her, then?"

Kimmy hesitated. "Because she's an outsider, and they don't want to go with her. They don't trust her."

"But they're still willing to take anything she brings back," I noted, unable to keep a note of bitterness out of my tone.

"Yeah, it's fucked; I know. Worse, she's good at it, even on her own. All the more reason she shouldn't do it, but apparently being here with us—with me—is so fucking unbearable that she just has to escape."

"I don't think it's that, Kim," I replied, touching her arm. "She cares for you. She just doesn't know how to do that the right way anymore. I'd bet anything that she's realizing that now, and her response is to run away. It's easier than admitting that she cares about staying here and fitting in."

We fed the hens, then began the walk back to the farmhouse with our basket of eggs.

"I should talk to her about it," she said, resigned. "She's just...super sensitive about it, and sometimes will pull away even more if I come across too confrontational."

"All you can do is your best. If she needs space to figure out what her place is here, then it's okay to give it to her. But you don't have to wait around for her, either."

Kimmy sighed. "I guess. I'm glad to be going back to work soon. I need the distraction."

A few days after that, Kimmy went back to the clinic to treat patients, while John was to begin his new outrider duties, which mostly involved patrolling and responding to complaints and emergencies. He also briefed to Danny about the Order, detailing our experiences with them, and I drew a sketch of their masks for reference.

"I doubt we'll have problems with them this far away," John said as I handed Danny the sketch. "But they're a real threat, and they seem hungry for power, so...you never know, I guess."

Danny nodded thoughtfully. "Best to keep our eyes open, in any case."

The morning after that, I went with John to the small outrider office in the Lodge that they used as a central command center. The outriders on patrol communicated by radio with Danny, who, as Chief, was usually the one manning the desk.

They held a small oath-taking ceremony in the office, where John pledged to follow and enforce council law, guard their borders, render aid when needed, and to protect the Valley and everyone in it to the best of his abilities. He gave me a pointed look when he said the last part, and I smiled. John wasn't one to express pride in himself, but he was practically glowing. His happiness was infectious.

"Congrats, man," Danny said, shaking John's hand. "You're finally in. Don't think you're off the hook, though. Your initiation just started."

John grinned. "Got it."

Danny handed him his new handheld radio, then sent us on our way. John would have his first patrol shift the next day.

"Command to Ghost," the radio buzzed as we walked out to the truck. "Do you copy?"

As if he'd been doing it his whole life, John lifted the radio to his lips and replied, "Ghost to command. I copy."

"Good," came Danny's reply. "No escape now, rookie. You're stuck with us."

I chuckled, then asked, "Why does he call you Ghost?"

"Precaution," John replied, caging me against the truck door with his arms. "It's unlikely anyone could hear the calls outside the Valley—the mountains block out everything—but just in case, we use our horses' names."

Happiness lit up his handsome features, and I couldn't help touching his cheek. The roughness of his stubble under my palm contrasted the tender look he gave me.

"Look at you, achieving your dreams," I said, touching his cheek. "We should celebrate you tonight."

He grinned and turned his head to kiss my wrist. "I know what kind of celebration I'd like. It involves a certain someone getting naked and waiting for me, bent over the bed."

"Well, I hope that someone is me, or else I have a lot of questions."

He laughed and kissed me. "Luckily, it is you. The first few months of duty tend to be rough, from what I've heard, so I have to give you a night to remember. Something to keep you warm on those nights I'm on patrol."

John wasn't wrong; his new schedule was brutal. New recruits had to take the overnight shifts that nobody wanted as a kind of initiation, plus they had to work more hours than the more senior outriders. Suddenly, he was gone almost every night and slept during the days, which meant that I saw him less and less as we headed into February.

I was proud, but I missed him, especially as I was trying to find my place here. Any free time we did have together, however, he took me on horseback rides, showing me more of the Valley and teaching me how to ride. It was always my favourite part of any given day—pressed against John's warm, hard body on Ghost's back, learning the many things he simply knew, as if by instinct.

I still hadn't chosen a community job, and no one seemed in a hurry to give me one. The idea of teaching was still there, hovering in the back of my mind, but I hesitated. I'd broached the subject with Asha again one evening, when John was patrolling, and Kimmy had gone to visit Isla.

"It might make our case stronger if we offer together," I said as we sat together at the kitchen table. "And Jenna is eager to learn. It'd be good for her to see different teaching styles, and you have a better grasp on teaching science and math than I do."

Asha was quiet. This was the first night she'd been home in several days. She always had a restlessness about her now, as if staying in one place was unbearable. I wondered if the trip here had conditioned her to always want to be on the move.

"I don't want to be a teacher," she finally said after several minutes. "I never loved it like you did, and I don't want to deal with the Wastelanders here more than I have to."

I frowned. "Including Kimmy? Because it sounds like you've been ghosting her a lot lately."

Her mouth thinned into a hard line.

"That's none of your business."

"Isn't it?" I said, folding my arms over my chest. "She's my future sister-in-law, and she deserves better than to be strung along. She cares about you, but if you're not into her, why not just tell her? Save her the pain of worrying about you all the time."

"Butt the hell out, Claire," Asha shot back, her hands clenching into fists on the tabletop. "You have no idea what you're talking about. Not everyone can moon over mediocre men and suck Wastelander dick every five minutes like you can. Some of us have self-respect."

The words hit like a blow, and I stood up abruptly from the table. I took a deep breath, trying to remember that Asha tended to lash out when she felt attacked. *It's not personal*, I told myself.

"I'm trying to help you," I said, and I hated the tremor in my voice.

She shrugged. "So am I. How do you think the people here are gonna react when they realize your uterus is useless to them? That's what they want, by the way. They need to keep their population up, and there's no way to do it anymore without new blood. If they let you stay after six months, it'll be because they think you're going to pop out a few babies for Farmer Boy."

"It's not up to them," I replied, but I didn't sound certain even to my ears.

"Have you even talked to him about it?" Asha asked, raising an eyebrow. "Surely, he knows that you'll never be able to give him kids. That kind of thing creates resentment over time."

Truthfully, with everything that'd been going on lately, my fertility was the last thing on my mind. Asha was right, however. My implant effectively made me unable to get pregnant, and only the Cave leaders—whoever they'd been—knew how to deactivate it.

"He loves me," I said simply. "And I think if you would let her, Kimmy would love you, too. But if you keep pushing her away, or if you're still hung up on someone else, you'll ruin any chance you have with her. I want you to be happy."

She deflated a little, her shoulders dropping.

"I know," she said, in a much milder tone. "I want that for you, too. Sometimes I think about how much better it'd be if we could just go home. Leave the Wasteland behind. Maybe I could finally feel safe again. Be more like myself."

"You don't need walls to feel safe," I answered softly. "And without freedom, you can never really have safety."

Asha sighed. "I wish I believed that. I'm sorry for what I said to you before. It was rude and uncalled for."

"I know." I forced my face into an understanding expression.

"But," she continued, "I still don't want to be a teacher. If you say I have freedom here, then I want to be free to choose a different path than the one I was assigned at home. I like scavenging. I'm good at finding things, and I don't mind being alone. That's the only time I feel even somewhat normal nowadays."

I nodded slowly. "Okay. I can accept that."

Asha went to bed shortly after, leaving me alone with my worries. The following morning, I was surprised when she joined me and Kimmy for morning chores. Unfortunately, John had been called in again that morning to pull a double patrol shift because one of the other outriders had fallen ill. I worried about him getting enough sleep, but he reassured me, as always, that he'd be fine. The dark shadows under his eyes didn't make me feel better, though.

"You can't burn the candle at both ends forever, Wastelander," I'd said at the door.

John pecked my lips. "It's alright, baby. Just part of the initiation process. It won't always be like this."

He headed back out into the frigid morning with Ghost. I sighed, still worried. I hadn't seen him for more than an hour at a time the past several days. He kept pushing himself, doing more, trying to prove himself—as though he hadn't done it a thousand times over already.

"Stubborn man," I muttered, then went to bundle up before heading out to the barn with Kimmy and Asha.

It was a freezing, blustery February day. I enlisted Asha's help in feeding the cattle, while Kimmy went to the stable to take care of Bella. The cows needed milking, which apparently disgusted Asha.

She did her best to help, but after seeing her shudder, I said, "It's alright, Ash. I'll do it."

She gave me a grateful look. "Thank you. I don't know why it bothers me so much."

"How about you skim it after I'm done?" I replied, taking a large ladle from the tools hanging on the wall. "Separate the milk and the cream."

She flashed a rare smile. "Deal."

I started on the first cow, slipping a metal bucket underneath the udder and adjusting my stool. The cows were well-trained, so my first time hadn't been as difficult as I'd feared. It was almost meditative now, and I narrowed my focus to the task at hand. When I finished, I handed the bucket to Asha and started on the next cow.

The second bucket was nearly full when the barn door burst open and the howling wind blew in. I jumped up, startled, and the bucket clanged as it toppled over. Milk spilt all over my boots and the concrete floor, and the cow gave a very unhappy moo.

"Great job," a young male voice jeered from the door. "That'll definitely convince everyone you belong here. Idiot."

Zach Jameson stood in the open doorway of the barn, a cocky smirk spread across his face. I had no idea why he was there; we hadn't been expecting anyone. At the sight of the spilled milk spreading across the barn floor, I cursed, and Zach laughed.

"You sure scare easy," he continued. "Can't imagine what Madigan is thinking, bringing you here. You think you won't face far worse than a little spilled milk before we kick your ass out?"

He was confident, arms folded over his chest, and he leaned against the doorframe like he owned the place.

"I know you're not threatening me right now," I said, sounding braver than I felt.

His lip curled. "Not a threat, sweetie. A promise."

Asha sneered at him. "Go home, Wastelander."

Zach snorted. "That cute nickname supposed to scare me, cupcake? All it does is remind everyone that you're an outsider. You fucking Madigan to earn your keep, just like Red over there? I gotta hand it to him, you compound chicks are good-looking, if totally useless in any position except on your knees."

Asha's displeasure deepened the lines on her face, and she opened her mouth to reply, but Kimmy appeared behind Zach.

"Is there a reason you're in my barn, Jameson?" Kimmy said acerbically, stepping past him. "Don't you have your regular appointment to jerk off and cry somewhere?"

She retrieved a rag from a pile of barn tools and handed it to me. I dropped to my knees to clean up the mess, biting my lip to stifle my humiliation.

Zach laughed. "The viper herself, in the flesh? Hate to break it to you, babe, but dykes aren't my type. Red, on the other hand, looks awful pretty kneeling like that."

My cheeks burned, and Kimmy looked ready to murder him, her hands curling into fists at her sides.

"What do you want?" she demanded. "If you just came here to harass my family, you can fuck right off."

Zach rolled his eyes, unfazed. "I'm here to trade, unfortunately. I went up to the house first. Anyway, we need more PNCs. My father is willing to make a generous offer."

Kimmy shrugged. "John's the one who's been keeping track of the PNC trade. You'll have to come back when he's home."

It was the wrong thing to say. Zach's lips twisted into a nasty smile.

"He's not here, watching over his women?" he said, his eyes scanning over me. "Interesting."

I stood, sodden rag in hand, my chest tight. I didn't like the way he looked at me, leering, like I was a piece of meat. He looked at Asha the same way, and it made me want to crawl out of my skin.

"Get off my land," Kimmy ordered, her eyes like steel. "Now."

Zach huffed but backed up a couple steps. "Fine. I'm going."

He turned on his heel and left, not bothering to shut the barn door behind him. We waited for a moment, listening to his footsteps crunching in the snow.

"I'll follow him to the gate," Asha said, her expression hard. "Make sure he leaves."

Kimmy nodded, then gathered another bucket and milking stool to help me finish my work. Thankfully, there was only one cow left that needed milking. After Asha left, we worked in silence until the job was done and the cows were safely back in their stalls.

By the time we'd finished, Asha still hadn't returned. I had a peculiar feeling in the pit of my stomach as we left the barn to search for her.

He wouldn't do anything to her on Summerhurst property...right?

Kimmy's expression told me she was having similar thoughts. As we approached the front gate, however, Asha appeared, walking back in our direction.

"What happened to you?" Kimmy asked. "We were starting to worry."

Asha gave a small, cavalier laugh that sounded unlike herself.

"It was fine," she said. "He cussed me out, and we went our separate ways at the gate. Nothing else happened."

"He didn't threaten you, did he?" Kimmy said skeptically.

"Not directly, but there's always a threatening undercurrent with men like him. Not used to being told 'no.' Fortunately, he's also stupid and not very calculated."

When we got back to the house, Kimmy and I made dinner. John was supposed to be home to eat, but we finally admitted defeat after a half hour of waiting for him and dug in. After dinner, I wandered aimlessly on the first floor before deciding to go to bed.

Upstairs in our room, I walked into the closet to put my clothes away. Unsurprisingly, my side of the closet was somewhat chaotic, with clothing folded haphazardly and partially hanging off of hangers. Meanwhile, John's side was neat as a pin, each item folded with care and sorted into precise, sensible piles by type, colour, and season.

I was seized by a sudden sadness and yearning that I didn't completely understand as I stared at a stack of his t-shirts. Other than today, I'd barely spent any time with John in the last couple weeks. It wasn't his fault, of course. He'd been working so hard to make this place livable again, along with hunting to feed us through the winter and his patrol duties.

And Kimmy was busy right alongside him, both with the restoration of Summerhurst and with the return to her nursing duties. So far, Asha had tried to be home as little as possible, heading out on scavenging missions daily, and even if she'd been around, I knew she'd take any complaint from me as further confirmation that we didn't belong here. And I wanted to belong here. I *needed* to belong here.

I pressed my fingers to my eyes. *Surrounded by people, and I'm still lonely somehow.*

Without giving it too much thought, I grabbed one of John's more well-loved t-shirts from a shelf. I took a shower in the ensuite bathroom, washing my hair for the first time in a week and luxuriating once more in the miracle of indoor plumbing. When I got out, I pulled the grey t-shirt over my head. The hem skimmed my thighs, and the soft, well-worn material smelled of laundry soap and the indefinable scent of John's skin.

I crawled into bed, hair still damp, and turned out the lights. The bed was cold without my human space heater, and loneliness closed in again like a vice. I rolled onto his side of the bed, then pulled the t-shirt collar over my nose and inhaled deeply.

I must've fallen asleep that way, because the next thing I knew, the fabric was being gently lifted off my face and a warm, familiar hand was smoothing my hair. I stirred but felt too groggy to open my eyes.

"Didn't mean to wake you," John whispered.

"Where were you...?" I trailed off, too sleepy to continue.

"I'm sorry," he replied regretfully. "There was an emergency at work, right at the end of my shift. Alan Wheeler fell off his roof and injured his back. It took us a while to safely move him to the clinic."

I sighed and rolled over, eager to go back to sleep. I heard him undress, then felt his weight as he climbed into bed on my usual side.

"There a reason we're playing musical sleeping spots tonight?"

I made a noncommittal sound and buried my face in his pillow.

"Why are you wearing my shirt?"

"Smells like you," I mumbled.

There was a pause, and then I found myself enveloped by his body as he hauled my back against his chest and enclosed me in his arms.

"I'm sorry, baby," he whispered, pained. "I haven't been there for you lately, have I?"

"You have," I replied. "Just busy. Not your fault."

He covered every inch of me he could reach with kisses, and I squirmed.

"I'm trying to sleep!" I squeaked, and he chuckled as he settled in, spooning me.

"I have a day off tomorrow," he murmured, tucking my hair behind my ear. "We could go to that trading post I told you about. It's a couple hours' ride."

"Now you have my attention," I teased.

"Figures," he said, amused. "You got the horse-riding bug. Anyway, I thought maybe after, I could make you dinner."

"And ravish me by moonlight?" I asked, batting my eyelashes before realizing he couldn't see them. It didn't seem to matter, though, because he snorted.

"I mean, if that's what you want, I'm not gonna say no," he replied, and I could hear his smile in his voice. "I'm sure I can power through."

"Power through? There are other ways for a lady to get off these days, you know, if it's such a hardship for you."

I squeaked with laughter as he pounced, playfully pinning me against the mattress.

"True," John said, "but *my* lady's pleasure is never a hardship. It's the whole damn point."

And he kissed me until I was breathless—until all loneliness was banished by the simple pleasure of his lips on mine.

CHAPTER 26

John

The next day, after morning chores, Claire and I mounted Ghost and rode toward the McNeils', where I'd already let Danny know we'd be coming.

"I thought we were going to the Post?"

"We are," I answered, stroking her thigh. "Just have to make a stop first."

Danny met us at the gate to Whitewater, the McNeil ranch.

"I got her saddled up," he said, with a nod toward Claire, who gave him a confused look.

He led us toward the massive stables on the ranch, where a couple dozen horses lived.

"They're the horse breeders in the Valley," I explained to Claire. "I thought you might like to ride on your own, and since Kimmy needs Bella today, I asked Danny if we could borrow you a mount."

Claire's expression instantly changed from confusion to excitement. "Really? You think I'm ready?"

"Sure you are," Danny answered for me, winking. "If even I can manage to keep myself upright on a horse after a drink or two, so can you, Claire."

"'A *drink or two*,'" I sneered. "Try four. It was also two o'clock in the morning, and *someone* had to follow him to make sure he didn't fall and break his fucking neck."

"Hey, in my defence, my girlfriend just dumped me," Danny replied, holding up his hands with a grin.

"Girlfriend? You saw her twice at the Post, and you didn't even kiss her."

Claire giggled, and Danny retorted, "The heart wants what it wants, Johnny. Maybe I should tell Claire some of *your* stories."

"I already told her everything," I said, shooting him a look. "Now shut up."

"Once, John got high smoking the hemp his granny grew for medicine, and he ate an entire blueberry patch. When she asked him what happened to the hemp, he puked blueberry vomit all over her."

Claire burst into laughter. "When was that?"

"I was only sixteen," I cut in, but I couldn't help but smile at the sound of her laugh. "And I got extra chores for a month."

"We've spent so much time wondering if our people will accept Claire," Danny said with a chuckle, "yet we've never asked the most important question: can *she* accept *us*?"

We reached the stable, where a beautiful, red Clydesdale horse waited.

"This is Poppy," Danny said to Claire. "She's a younger horse, but fully trained. Real sweet temperament—good for a beginner. I think you two will get along."

I helped Claire mount Poppy, but she otherwise needed no assistance. We let her ride a little around the paddock, getting a feel for the horse, and for riding by herself. She looked fucking giddy, which warmed my heart.

We left for the Post, and Claire handled Poppy incredibly well for a beginner rider. She steered and maintained control easily, and her form had really improved. I was proud of her.

After a couple hours on horseback, we spotted the ruins of the city in the distance, along with the fenced-in portion that made up the Post.

"It's in the city?" Claire asked with a frown.

"Kind of," I answered. "It's only a few streets at the very edge, and they're fenced-off from the rest of the city. That's called the Red Zone, because the only people who live there aren't people you'd want to meet. It's mostly abandoned, though, and there's enough security at the Post to keep those few at bay."

"How many people live there?"

"Not that many," I replied as I turned Ghost towards the stable, which was a short walk from the Post. "Maybe a hundred full-time residents. Everyone else either lives nearby, or—more likely—is nomadic, and they come and go whenever they like."

The stable was large and run by a short old man who everyone called Corny, and a few of his kids. He'd always been an odd guy who collected weird Old World artifacts just for the hell of it. Once, I traded him a mint condition pocket watch, which apparently, he still wore, tucked into the breast pocket of his jacket.

"Didn't think to see you again, young man!" he exclaimed as we rode up. "It's been a very long time...and you brought a lady friend! This why you haven't been visiting us?"

"Yep," I replied, flashing a grin toward Claire. "She's got all my attention lately."

Claire smiled shyly back. We both dismounted our horses, and I traded a small flask of beer for their stay. I'd made the first new batch of beer with barley I'd traded for back in the Valley and brought several of the small bottles today. Quality alcohol was always in demand.

We walked back toward one of the gates, and I gave Claire the rundown.

"Act like everyone is armed, because they are," I said. "Don't be scared by any aggressive sellers. They're pushy, but they can't do anything else. The residents shut down trouble pretty quickly, but still, not everyone who passes through here is someone you want to know."

Claire chewed her lip. "Will there be a slave market?"

"No," I answered firmly. "Not allowed. The standard of living here is a lot higher than Little River. That doesn't mean there aren't any traffickers here, though, so stay close and alert."

After checking in with the guards, we were allowed through, and Claire's eyes widened. The trading part of the Post was mostly one street that people called the main strip, and it was lined with market stalls and small caravans. There were a few more permanent shops set up in the ruins of Old World houses. Holes in the walls were filled in with mud bricks and wood planks, and retrofitted fire pits kept the shops warm. It wasn't as busy along the main strip as during the warmer months, but there were still a bunch of vendors, and visiting shoppers strolled casually down the street. A few guards patrolled the main strip at all times, and it kept things quiet on most days.

Compared to Little River, it was night and day, and surprise was written on Claire's face as she took it in.

"It's so...cute," she said, glancing at me. "Like a little Christmas village."

"It's definitely better than most settlements," I replied. "Mostly because it's remote, and the residents here take out the trash when needed."

I took her hand and walked with her down the strip, pointing out the things I recognized. We went into one of the more permanent shops which billed itself as a general store, and I traded for ammunition and a small pair of jade earrings that I caught Claire admiring.

"You didn't have to do that," she protested.

"I know. I wanted to. Get used to it."

She huffed, then laughed and hooked her arm through mine. As we got to the end of the strip, she pointed to the last house, which had a bunch of people milling around outside.

"What's that? Lots of people."

"Tavern called *Longfellow's*," I answered. "Been here forever. Beer tastes like piss, though. Wouldn't recommend it."

She laughed. "Sounds like they could use some of your stock."

"Maybe in the spring, yeah," I said. "They have seasonal festivals here, and the spring one is the busiest. They have music sometimes. We could come back in June, if you like, for your birthday."

"I'd love that," Claire replied with a smile.

We made a few more rounds among the stalls, which sold a totally random assortment of crap, including bath products, hammers, and old radios.

"Why radios?" Claire asked, raising an eyebrow.

I shrugged. "Probably the only form of long-distance communication that still exists. When you have no phone lines and no internet, radio is what's left. Who knows if any of them still work, though. At home, we're able to maintain ours, whereas I doubt any of those still work."

The next stall sold a mishmash of books, and predictably, Claire jumped on it. We traded to get a geography book and a couple novels for teenagers.

"Allie will love these," Claire gushed, holding up something called *Help! My Boyfriend is a Vampire*, with a faded drawing of a teen girl next to a teen boy wearing a ridiculous-looking cape on the front.

I raised an eyebrow at the cover, and she laughed. "I promised her that I'd find her a book she'd like to read, remember? She needs something more appropriate for her age. She says she doesn't like to read, but it's because she's bored."

"I didn't think reading was something fun till I met you," I admitted. "I just thought it was something you did because you had to, to learn things."

"Learning can be fun," Claire countered, and I smirked.

"I think you might be a little biased."

Finally, we decided to call it a day and walked back to the stable.

"Thank you for bringing me," Claire said, her voice full of sincerity, as we directed the horses toward home.

"Of course, baby. It's our first real date; we had to do something special."

Her smile was like pure sunshine. *Christ, I'm turning into such a sap.*

"And for getting Danny to lend me Poppy," she continued. "I might have gotten a little attached. I'll have to visit her."

"You rode very well today," I said. "And if you like her, she's yours."

Her eyes got wide, and I chuckled.

"What?"

"You heard me. I told you we were borrowing her so that you could decide if you liked her without any pressure. But since you do...she's yours."

Her eyes lit up with a joy that made the whole thing that much more worth it.

"You got me a horse? Jesus, John."

"What?" I asked playfully. "We have more PNCs than we can use in a lifetime. I might as well spoil my wife once in a while. Call it a wedding present, if you want."

It took a while to get home, since I always left a false trail to avoid anyone following us. After we'd finally made it back and returned the horses to the stable, Claire pulled me into a kiss. She smelled fresh, like the outdoors, and I never got tired of her silky hair under my hands. I sighed as she slipped her tongue in my mouth, and the kiss got needy, hungry. With my stupid schedule, it'd been a while since I took her to bed.

I missed her soft thighs wrapped around my hips, cushioning me as I drove into her. Missed her sweet little moans, the way she tasted on my tongue. How she said my name when she came.

I backed her against the wall, and kissed her harder, deeper. I didn't care that we were in a stable that smelled like hay and animals. I ground my hardening cock against her, and she moaned. I broke away to frantically spread kisses down her neck.

"John," Claire murmured, "we're not going to make it to dinner."

I grinned against her throat. "Definitely not."

"Take me home to bed, then. I don't want to have sex while my new horse watches."

I laughed. "Fair enough."

We only just made it back inside the house. I pinned her against the closed front door, nibbling her earlobe the way I knew she liked.

"Wait," she gasped, "what about Kimmy...and Asha?"

"Asha's scavving, and I asked Kimmy to stay over at Isla's. We're alone."

She smiled coyly. "Oh. You came prepared."

"Always do, baby."

I caught her mouth with mine again, and she sighed. After a moment, she reached for my belt...and a sudden buzz came from my jacket pocket, where I'd stashed my outrider radio.

"Command to Ghost," Danny's voice said. "Sorry, man, but we need coverage of the west side tonight. Sadie's kid got the flu, and she can't make it. But we only need a few hours, tops. I got Will to cover the rest."

I groaned. "Fuck me."

"I was going to," Claire quipped. "But it seems like they need you."

"I'm sorry," I said, gathering her face in my hands. "I promise it won't be like this forever—"

"But it's your job," she replied gently. "I get it. What you do is important, and you care about it. I'll be here when you get back."

I pressed a hard kiss against her lips.

"I promise to make it up to you later," I said with a suggestive smile. "Whatever you want when I get home."

Claire grinned. "Whatever I want? I'll have to get creative."

CHAPTER 27

John

Having a boner on horseback in the freezing cold wasn't my idea of a good time.

And a few hours in the saddle hadn't cooled my passion. If anything, thinking about Claire at home without me made it worse, since I started daydreaming about what I'd do to her when I got back.

I got home after midnight, and the house was dark and quiet. I went upstairs to our room, hoping to find Claire ready for action.

She'd left the door open a crack, and there was a candle burning on her bedside table...but she was fast asleep. Lying on her stomach, red hair fanned across her back, tucked under the bearskin blanket. She'd obviously tried to wait up for me and failed. I couldn't help smiling a little.

I kissed the top of her head and snuffed out the candle, then headed for the shower. I washed up quickly before climbing into bed. I'd told myself I wouldn't wake my sleeping fiancée, but as soon as I felt her warm body near mine and realized she was naked under the covers, all bets were off.

I was firmly in thinking-with-my-dick territory, and there was no turning back.

I positioned myself over her on my hands and knees, then started kissing her neck. She stirred, and I gently blew into her ear and nibbled her earlobe.

"John," she mumbled. "What time is it?"

"Late," I answered, kissing along her jaw. "But you and I have unfinished business."

Her eyelids fluttered, and she let out a sleepy groan as I slipped a hand underneath her and cupped her breast. I teased her nipple, grinding my palm against it. Her back arched, and she rose automatically to my touch, making my cock harden. I slid my other hand under her and teased her other nipple, too, until she was writhing under me.

"Thought about you all night," I said as I peeled the blanket off her, exposing her beautiful body.

Claire sighed. "I thought of you, too. Wanted you."

I pressed myself against her back as I slid my hands back under her tits. She squirmed and moaned, and eventually, I couldn't help myself. I slipped one hand lower and found her cunt.

"Oh, fuck," I breathed in her ear, my cock pulsing against her bare ass. "You're wetter than I thought you'd be."

"I...took care of myself," Claire said, breathing heavy. "Before I fell asleep."

Fuck, that's hot.

I pictured her, hand between her thighs, stroking herself to thoughts of me, of us. Getting hotter, getting closer, until she tipped over the edge with my name on her lips. It was enough to make me ache with the need to fuck her wet little cunt until she begged me to let her come again.

"Is that right?" I murmured, and she gasped as I bit her neck. "Couldn't help yourself, sweetheart? Needed to come so bad that you couldn't wait for me?"

"Uh-huh," she whimpered as I licked away the sting from my bite. "But I need to come again now. Please."

She knew that begging was my weakness. I loved hearing her plead with me for more, and it was hard to resist. But I was distracted.

"Tell me what you thought of while you were stroking that pretty clit, hmm?" I said. "What made you come. Then maybe I'll consider making you come again."

Claire took a shuddering breath. "Thought of you coming home and taking me roughly. Fantasized about you using me for your pleasure. Knowing I could make you so wild for me that you'd just take me."

She had no idea.

"Baby," I huffed in her ear, "you want me to make your fantasy come true?"

She shivered, then said, "Yes, please. I need you to touch me."

"Hmm," I hummed against her throat, pleased. "I would, but...since you started without me, you'll have to wait till I get my fill."

She groaned in frustration, then yelped when I bit her neck again, harder this time.

"I know my girl wants to please me," I said in her ear, rubbing her hard nipples with my thumbs. "I know she wants me to use her however I want, until I'm satisfied. Doesn't she?"

Claire whimpered again, then said in a small voice, "Yes, John."

Her submission made me fucking feral. My hands moved to her hips, and I hauled her onto her knees. Even in the dark bedroom, where I could only see her outline, she looked damn good on all fours for me.

I slipped two fingers into her throbbing cunt, and she gasped as I gave her a couple slow pumps. I made sure both fingers were coated with her wetness, her come, before pulling them out. She didn't groan this time, just made a small sound of disappointment that made me grin. I enjoyed making her wait almost as much as pleasing her.

Kneeling behind her, I leaned over her and pushed my wet fingertips against her lips.

"Open for me, beautiful," I ordered. "Taste yourself. Show me how good you can suck."

She hesitated for a second, but then obeyed. At first, she took them up to the second knuckle, sucking her wetness off my fingers. I pushed in gently, urging her to take more, and she moaned. She let me work them all the way into her mouth and started sucking hard, squeezing her thighs together.

"Such a good girl," I said. "You like tasting yourself? You see why I'm addicted to you and your pretty cunt?"

She gave another muffled moan around my fingers in reply, and I couldn't wait anymore. Keeping my fingers firmly in her mouth, I used my other hand to line my cock up at her entrance.

"I say you're a good girl," I said, "but you did start without me. So, tonight, I'm going to fuck you the way a bad girl deserves to be fucked. To remind you who you belong to."

She squealed as I shoved my cock into her. Her slick cunt squeezed me, pulling me deeper, and I couldn't help but groan. As soon as I bottomed out, I started to fuck her the way I needed to—hard and fast, like a goddamn punishment.

Claire's cries around my fingers turned me on like nothing else. I could feel her pulsing around me, and I knew her clit must be aching.

"You liking this, gorgeous?" I panted. "You like being used for my pleasure?"

"Yeah," came her garbled reply. "Oh, God, yeah."

"You want me to spank you like you deserve?"

Her response was muffled, more a sigh than a word. "Please."

I drew my hand back and delivered a hard spank across her ass, and she cried out. It only made me want to keep going. I spanked her raw, until her skin was bright red and hot to the touch. Until my hand ached. She never wanted me to stop—my sweet, dirty girl. Instead, she made more helpless, high-pitched sounds as I rutted into her like I owned her...because in that moment, with my fingers practically down her throat and my handprint across her ass, I fucking did.

"Gonna come, baby," I gritted out, right at the edge. "Gonna mark you as mine."

She whimpered in response. I abruptly pulled out of her, grinding my cock against the soft flesh of her ass, and groaned uncontrollably as milky-white come sprayed across her pretty skin.

Panting hard, I withdrew my fingers and kissed her shoulder, then sat back on my knees. In the dim light from the woodstove, I could see my come marking her, and it satisfied me on some lizard-brain level.

"You look so fucking good wearing nothing but my come," I said, and she sighed as I easily slid two fingers inside her. "Do you like being marked, baby? Knowing you're mine?"

"So much," she replied softly, her voice edged with need. "Please make me come now. I want to come like this, on my knees."

The desperate note in her voice was irresistible. I pumped slow and deep, the way I knew she liked, and she moaned loudly. I savoured the sounds she made, the way she felt around my fingers. She gasped as I used my other hand to stroke her clit, then leaned into my touch. "Lay your head on the bed, sweetheart. Good. Stay just like that. Let me admire you, covered in my come, while I give you pleasure."

Claire arched her back and pumped her hips, fucking herself on my fingers. I added a third finger, and her breath caught before she let out another primal moan. With her red hair in her face and her pale, perfect ass in the air, she was the sexiest sight. After denying her, I craved her pleasure.

I let her keep moving her hips while I stroked her clit and listened to her moans get rougher, more guttural. She wasn't quiet—she took what she wanted, and I loved every second. Watching my reserved, somewhat shy Claire let go of control and give herself over to pleasure was hot as hell.

"I'm so close," she whimpered, shaking her head restlessly against the bed. "Harder."

I thrust my fingers into her more forcefully, enjoying the wet sounds they made.

"You're my beautiful, brazen little fucktoy, hmm? Eager to be used whenever I need release?"

"Oh fuck, John," Claire panted. "Yes. I need it so bad."

"Dirty girl," I growled. "Come for me. Now."

I pressed hard against the tender, ridged spot inside her, and she finally came apart. She buried her face in the bed and cried out, riding the wave on my fingers, her hands curled into fists around the bedsheet. Sweaty, unrestrained, and gorgeous.

I got up to grab a damp washcloth, then cleaned the mess I'd left on her ass. She collapsed onto the bed, weak and rosy-cheeked, eyes still glazed from orgasm. I got into bed and pulled her into my arms.

"Was that what you wanted?" I asked. I stroked her ass gently, soothing her skin, which was still warm to the touch.

Claire sighed, resting her head against my chest. "Yes. I missed you."

"I missed you, too."

We lay there quietly, recovering.

"I'm going to hate myself in the morning," Claire eventually said with a groan, hiding her face in my shoulder.

I kissed the top of her head. "Get up and feed the chickens, then take a nap. I'll do the rest with Kimmy."

"You were just patrolling," she replied, accusatory. "And you have another night shift tomorrow. You need your sleep."

"Isn't that what death is for?" I asked with a grin, and she nudged me.

"Don't joke about that. I'm serious. You need to take care of yourself. You're too important to risk."

In a world that was always demanding more of me, Claire was the only one who really stopped to look after me, who worried about me.

"Okay," I said, snuggling closer to her. "But don't work too hard."

I fell asleep holding her close.

Part IV: Lanternlight

A nd moving thro' a mirror clear

That hangs before her all the year,
Shadows of the world appear.

- "The Lady of Shalott", Alfred Lord Tennyson

CHAPTER 28

Claire

March arrived with a winter storm that blanketed Summer-hurst with a fresh layer of snow. No signs of spring yet emerged, but I didn't mind. I had a newfound appreciation for the coziness of sitting by a warm hearth, wrapped in blankets, reading my way through the Madigans' small collection of books. I started painting again, and my first work was of the farmhouse itself, set against the vibrant white of snow.

I was pleased and a little embarrassed when John insisted on hanging it in the front entryway, so it was the first thing people saw when visiting. Each time I finished a painting, he found a new place in the house to hang it.

With a horse of my own, I could visit people more often. Nimkii invited me for tea, and I met her rambunctious toddler as we discussed painting. I took Jenna up on her offer and joined her and her friend, Liam, for music practice. Jenna was delighted, and even more so when I sang for them.

"You sound great!" she trilled. "This is so exciting! You'll have to sing with us at the next community dance."

"Oh, I don't know—" I stammered.

"You want people to fall in love with you or what, compound girl?" Jenna demanded.

I couldn't help laughing. "Not sure a dance will do that, but I suppose I should try."

Later in the week, I visited the Armstrongs and gave Allie her new books, which she showed a surprising amount of enthusiasm over. Along with the vampire book, there was another called Help! My Boyfriend is a Werewolf, and Allie giggled at the faded illustration of a wolf-boy and a teen girl on the cover.

"What's a werewolf, Claire?" she asked. "Do you know?"

I launched into a brief explanation of werewolf mythology, along with a simplified history of how it'd been around for thousands of years.

"So, they accused real people of being werewolves?" she said, mouth hanging open. "That's so stupid."

I smiled. "Yes, but people back then believed all sorts of things that we might think of as silly now."

"What kind of things?"

"The Fountain of Youth," I answered with a giggle. "Just a small sip was enough to keep you young forever. Or eternal life, like with vampires."

By the time Sarah checked on us in the living room, the afternoon was nearly over, and I'd spent the better part of two hours answering Allie's endless stream of questions. It felt good, like slipping into an old pair of shoes that fit just right. For her part, Allie was intelligent, funny, and a good listener. I thought she could be a good student, if she had a teacher who bothered to engage her in the learning process.

"Sarah," I said, pulling her aside into the kitchen, "I'd like to ask you something. I know school still isn't running yet, and...well, I'd really like to tutor Allie in the meantime, with your permission. I used to be a teacher, and I think I could help her—and Jake, if you like—stay up with their studies. I'd hate to see them slide backwards."

Sarah gave me a surprised look. "You'd do that? For what?"

"Oh, nothing," I hurried to say. "I don't want anything. I just...I'd like to feel useful, and I think your daughter is bright; she just hasn't been given the right opportunities."

She still looked mildly baffled, but she smiled.

"That's kind of you," she replied. "But I'll have to give you something for your trouble. I'll send you home with dinner every day that you come teach them."

I beamed. "That'll be plenty."

On a blustery winter afternoon a couple weeks later, I returned from visiting Isla and Noah to find the house empty. John wasn't working till that night, and the chores were done, so I'd expected he'd be home. When afternoon turned to evening, I started to worry and went to look for him on the property.

Even as dusk fell over Summerhurst, I headed out into the snow. The night was clear but as cruelly cold as ever, my windswept cheeks stinging. Flashlight in hand, I ventured around the barn, the chicken coop, and the stable, but John was nowhere in sight. I walked across the length of the homestead, searching, but didn't find him. Just as the shadows lengthened and I was beginning to worry, I spotted a faint light in the distance, nearly concealed by a copse of trees at the very edge of the homestead, near the woods.

My boots crunched through the thick blanket of fresh sparkling snow as I followed the light. The trees were strangely arranged in a nearly circular shape, which seemed deliberate. Only a sliver of light was visible through them, but as I approached, John's voice, soft and sweet, reached me.

"We did it, old man," he said with a mirthless chuckle. "Brought the PNCs back. We got even more than you wanted. That's what you'd call rising to the occasion, huh?"

I peered around a tree. John was on his knees in front of a polished slab of stone, a large shovel beside him. A nearby pile of snow indicated that he'd had to dig it out.

Next to him sat a lantern, illuminating the text on the gravestone and casting long shadows in all directions.

Oisín Madigan. 2014-2095. Father, grandfather, soldier.

Aoife Madigan. 2012-2095. Mother, grandmother, healer.

He knelt on the grave of the only parents he'd ever known.

"I kept my promise," John continued, his voice rougher. "Didn't know, at the time, that you wouldn't be here to see it, but..."

He paused briefly. "But we saved our people. Our home. I like to think you'd be proud."

My throat constricted, and I was frozen in place. It felt like I was witnessing something deeply private, but I was unable to look away. This sweet, vulnerable John that so few people knew had always held my heart captive.

John gave another chuckle. "And while I was gone, I met a girl. Finally, right? I can practically hear Granny's relief. I'm going to marry her in the spring." Another pause, and then his voice broke as he said, "You'd have loved her."

I couldn't stay hidden anymore; my heart would burst. I walked toward John and dropped beside him in the snow. He didn't seem surprised by my sudden appearance as I put my arm around him and lay my head against his shoulder.

We didn't speak for a long moment. The flickering lantern light and the whistle of a winter breeze over the snow were our only companions.

Finally, I said, "I'd like to sing a song for them—taught to me by my father, long ago. Would you like to hear it?"

Swallowing hard, John nodded, never looking away from the headstone. I felt his fragility in the rigidness of his body, in the way he didn't return my touch. I recalled the words of the song from a deeply painful place inside of me that I rarely visited. A place where my father still lived, as vivid and real as he'd ever been, yet remained forever out of reach.

I am the sun that shines

The blue sky and shady pines

I am the deepest valley and highest peak

The glistening raindrop hitting your cheek

I am the wind that sings
In the sails of your ship
I am where your dreams go
The goodbye on your lips

Search for me in the snow as it falls
In the light of the meadow
My love, I am everywhere
And nowhere at all

Listen for me when you hear
The bluebirds sing, the raven's call
The lush symphony of spring
There, I'll wait for you
At the end of everything

My voice was soft but strengthened with each verse, and I remembered my father singing those same words to me. I couldn't have known how prophetic they'd be.

The dead we love never leave us, Claire, he'd murmured to thirteen-year-old me. *Take it from a man who survived the end of the world. They become one with all things.*

"Beautiful," John murmured, and when I lifted my head from his shoulder, his cheek was wet, sparkling in the dim lantern light. "He wrote that?"

"Not long before he died. Knowing what I know now, I wonder if he wasn't preparing me for a life without him."

I followed the tracks of his pain with my lips, gently kissing them away.

"They'd be so proud of you," I said softly. "Like I am. Like we all are."

He nodded tightly, jaw clenched. There was something he still held back. I waited quietly.

"How is it possible," he said after a moment, "that after we do everything we set out to do, and everyone is safe, that I still feel...pain?"

He let out a long, ragged-sounding breath. "Don't get me wrong; I'm so happy to be home. Even more happy you're here with me. But today, it was like it hit me: none of it brought them back. I'm home now, but they're still gone."

"Oh, my love," I murmured, wrapping my arms around him. "I know."

"And now," he continued, his voice barely a whisper, "home is different to when they were here—to when I was here. Since I've been gone, people have died, babies have been born, things have changed. I wanted the home I had with them back, but that's gone forever. And some part of me still feels homesick."

My heart felt like it would break, but I only squeezed him hard.

"Hiraeth," I said. "It's a Welsh word that refers to a feeling of deep longing for a time or place that no longer exists. A kind of homesickness tinged with grief. I read it in a poem once."

To my surprise, that got a small smile from him.

"Should've known that my smart fiancée would have just the word for my particular flavour of feeling sorry for myself."

I kissed his cheek. "You're allowed to grieve, John. Remember what I said about your bone-deep capacity for love? Your grief is just all that love with nowhere to go."

He sighed shakily and kissed the top of my head, finally returning my embrace. He reached for the lantern and held it up to me, showing me the flickering candle inside.

"I light it every time I come here," he said. "For them. Wherever they are."

I nodded and kissed him. He clung to me, his hand coming up to cup my cheek, and kissed me back in a way that likely wasn't entirely appropriate for a gravesite...but I felt the desperation and need in that kiss. He needed to know that he wasn't alone, that we were in this together now.

"I'm not afraid of your pain, love," I said when we broke apart, smoothing his hair away from his face.

He gave a small shudder, then pulled me against him again, resting his head on top of mine. Snow began to fall softly in small, intricate flakes, nesting in my hair and eyelashes—a cold kiss from winter itself.

We sat quietly, watching it float down to earth, until John finally said, "Want to get warm, baby? I'm ready."

I nodded again, lifting my head. I pressed a kiss against my gloved fingers, then pressed them to the cold headstone. John's expression faltered at the gesture, but then he took my hand, and we stood together. I carried the lantern as we headed back towards the house, making a brief stop at the woodshed for firewood.

John loaded my arms full of firewood before bending to pick up his own share. I was forced to awkwardly set down the lantern, blowing harshly to extinguish the candle inside, before heading out into the darkness of night.

"Sorry," John said as we left. "I forgot the sledge up at the house last time I did this."

"It's alright," I replied with a small smile. "I get to watch my handsome man hauling stuff, so it's not all bad."

That got a chuckle out of him. Only the light coming from the farmhouse windows was visible through the darkness, so we followed it like a north star to home and safety. The darkness held within it the fathomless depth of both love and loss, of endings and new beginnings, of the thousand tomorrows we'd create together.

CHAPTER 29

John

Hours after my graveside visit, I was near the end of a midnight patrol. Ghost didn't seem to mind the late-night shifts, but I was fucking wiped. I knew it was a standard test for new recruits, to push us a little and see if we could cope, but I'd be damn glad when it was over.

I rode towards the Lodge, where we normally did our shift change. Danny was supposed to relieve me. I had a feeling that he'd scheduled himself on more night shifts just to see me. It was like old times. We sometimes had a quick bite to eat together before he relieved me. Other than that, the only other person on patrol tonight was Sadie, a tall, sharp woman who had four kids and took zero shit from anyone.

I spotted him standing outside the Lodge with his horse, Bolt, geared up to go. He waved me over. As Ghost and I pulled up beside them, both our radios came to life at once.

"Star to Command, reporting suspicious smoke in Summerhurst area. Investigating."

My heart leapt, and Danny frowned.

"Received," he said into his radio. "You smell smoke?"

The reply took a minute, but eventually, Sadie said, "That's a yes, Command. Will update when I know more."

I turned Ghost around, then galloped towards home. I heard Danny call after me, but I didn't stop. Might've been insubordination, but I couldn't make myself care. My fiancée and my sister were at home, asleep, and I wasn't going to wait for permission to help them.

Hooves beat the ground behind me, and I knew that Danny was following. We raced toward Summerhurst, and as we got closer, a column of smoke appeared, rising into the night sky. It was hard to see in the dark, but Sadie had a keen eye. Sure enough, my radio crackled to life again at my hip.

"Command, smoke is confirmed to be a fire. Looks like an outbuilding at Summerhurst. Alerting residents now."

"Shit," I muttered, urging Ghost to go faster, even though she was already galloping at full speed. I lifted my radio to my lips. "Star, this is Ghost. Confirm resident safety. Please."

The silence that followed was torture, even though it was unlikely Claire or Kimmy would be near an outbuilding at this time of night. Ten minutes later, I was on the homestead. The air smelled like a bonfire, which wasn't a good sign, and as I got closer to the house, orange flames lit up the night.

The woodshed was ablaze. By the look of it, we'd missed the worst of the fire; the shed was already black and partly collapsed.

A second later, the radio buzzed again. "Resident safety confirmed, Ghost. No fire near the farmhouse. Awaiting orders from command."

I let out a long breath. *At least they're okay.*

"Stay with the residents, Star," Danny answered, and when I looked over my shoulder, he was coming up behind me. "Ghost, go home for now. I'll investigate further."

Good. I needed to see my family, orders or not. There was no saving the woodshed, no point in risking our lives for a pile of ashes. Letting the fire burn itself out was probably safest; the shed wasn't close enough to the other buildings to spread. *Thank fuck for that.*

I rode to the farmhouse, where the lights were on, and Star waited outside. I slowed Ghost to a trot, then left her beside Star before running up the porch steps and bursting through the front door.

Sadie was in the foyer with Claire and Kimmy. Kimmy had her winter jacket on over her linen pyjamas and winter boots on her feet. Claire stood beside her in her nightgown, wide-eyed, a wool blanket from our bed wrapped around her shoulders. To my surprise, Asha was also there, fully dressed. I hadn't seen her in a few days.

"John," Kimmy said on seeing me. "What's going on?"

I crossed the room to reach Claire before answering. "The woodshed's on fire. We don't know how it happened yet. Doesn't seem like anything else is burning, though."

I took Claire's hand in mine, and she squeezed it. She looked afraid.

Sadie lifted her radio and said, "Star to command. Do you need help out there?"

"Star and Ghost, head to the woodshed," came Danny's reply. "Bring residents with you. There's something you should see."

That couldn't mean anything good. Claire shot me a worried look, and I kissed the top of her head before releasing her hand.

"Bundle up," I told her, keeping my voice calm. "Ghost is outside. Sadie and I can take you all there."

A few minutes later, we were on horseback again, heading towards the charred remains of the woodshed. When we got there, Danny was standing beside Bolt, holding a misshapen object, blackened by fire. The fire had mostly died out on its own, with only a few hot spots left.

I dismounted, then helped Claire down. Behind us, Sadie, Kimmy, and Asha did the same.

"Think I found the source of the fire," Danny said, holding up what looked like a partly melted lantern. "Any of you leave a lantern in the woodshed?"

Oh, fuck. I glanced at Claire, who'd turned as white as the snow around us. It was only a quick look, but I knew Kimmy had noticed it, because she frowned.

"I did," Claire said, in the smallest voice I'd ever heard her use. "But I blew it out first."

"You sure?" Danny said skeptically, but not unkindly. "I know I've forgotten a candle or two in the past myself. It's easy for that to slip your mind sometimes, especially if you're just going through the motions."

"I—" Claire started, but she faltered. "I don't know."

"You could've burned down the whole Valley," Sadie snapped, accusatory, and that got my back up immediately.

"Hey—" I started, but Asha interjected, "We don't use candles in the compound. We never used anything with an open flame like that. It's understandable that Claire would forget. It's not her fault."

I wracked my brain, but I couldn't remember if Claire had extinguished the lantern earlier. I should've paid better attention, but I'd been preoccupied.

"So, the compound robs you of common fucking sense?" Sadie shot back, throwing up her hands, then turned back on Claire. "You're supposed to be convincing us that you won't pose a threat here. This is not a good look."

Claire put on a brave face, but I saw the slightest tremor in her hands.

"I don't know what happened," she said quietly, "but I know I blew that lantern out."

"Look, Claire," Kimmy said, "it's okay if you just forgot. People make mistakes."

"But I didn't!" Claire insisted, wringing her hands.

Sadie moved toward Claire, and she instinctively took a step back.

"So, the woodshed just burnt *itself* down—"

"That's enough," I cut in, stepping between them. "It's my lantern. So, if it was left out, blame me."

"You just gonna let this stand, Danny?" Sadie asked, whipping around to face him.

I looked at Danny, who'd been watching the whole thing carefully. He met my eye, frowning. For once, I couldn't tell what he was thinking.

"The woodshed is Summerhurst property," he said after a beat. "And it looks like this was just an accident—"

"But—"

"—*regardless* of how exactly it happened," he continued loudly, talking over Sadie. "Since it's Summerhurst property, and they don't have a complaint to report, there's nothing else for us to do here. So, move out."

Sadie looked like she wanted to argue some more, but Danny gave her an icy look that screamed *insubordination*, and she clammed up.

She mounted Star, and with one last irritated look in Claire's direction, took off into the night.

Danny let out a long breath. "Damn. I need a drink."

"Me too," Kimmy said, rubbing her eyes.

Between Danny and me, we got everyone back up to the house. Right as Danny was about to leave, he turned back to Claire.

"Just so you know, it's okay," he said warmly. "Shit happens. No one was hurt. Try not to take it too hard; just be more careful in future."

Claire opened her mouth as if to reply, but then her shoulders slumped in defeat, and she nodded. He left, closing the door behind him, and the four of us stood in the foyer for a minute, staring after him.

I didn't know what to think. On the one hand, I still couldn't remember if Claire extinguished the lantern...and a few nights ago, she *had* left a candle lit when she fell asleep. That wasn't the kind of thing she did a lot, but...was it that much of a stretch that she'd just forgotten about the lantern?

On the other hand, something felt off to me in a way I couldn't put my finger on. If it really was the lantern, why hadn't it caught sooner? In theory, it'd already been burning for hours by the time I left for patrol that night. And why hadn't I noticed the light when I left? By that time, it was totally dark, and even a small light from the woodshed should've been obvious.

"Well, I'm going to bed," Asha said, arms folded over her chest. "Thrilled that the whole place is gonna think Claire and I tried to burn it down now. I'm sure that'll endear them to us, especially since they were already so happy to have us here."

She turned on her heel and went upstairs. Kimmy hesitated, but with a parting look at Claire, followed her.

As soon as they were out of earshot, Claire said, "John, I didn't forget to put out the lantern. I *know* I didn't."

I rubbed my temples. "Are you completely sure?"

The hurt in her eyes caught me off guard. "Yes, I'm sure. I've gone through it a hundred times in my head, and I know what I did. I'm not that stupid. Please."

That nagging sense that something wasn't right was still there, and I sighed.

"I believe you, baby," I replied, and I meant it. I gathered her against me, feeling her relax at my touch. "I just...I'm not sure what it means. Maybe Danny was wrong, and something else caused it, but..."

"It has to have been the Jamesons," Claire said anxiously. "Especially Zach. They're the ones leading the charge against me."

I hesitated. I hated the bastard for that night at the dance, but we had no proof of anything. I may've not cared about bullshit Valley politics—which Jameson and his sons reveled in—but I wasn't stupid enough to accuse one of the most powerful families without anything to back it up. We technically weren't even sure it was arson.

"We don't know that," I said gently, stroking her hair. "It could still be an accident that happened some other way. We can't just accuse them without proof, especially since you're on probation."

The corners of Claire's mouth turned down.

"So, what do we do, then?" she asked. "Just...let this go? Do nothing?"

I didn't like it, either, but what else *could* we do at this point? I held her at arm's length, cupping her cheek.

"We do what we always do," I said. "We stay on our guard, watch for threats, and do our best with what we have. You'll stay close to home; I won't let anything happen to you."

She nodded, but she looked so dejected that I hugged her tight.

"What about the woodshed?" she asked sadly against my shoulder.

"We'll rebuild in the spring," I answered, stroking her hair. "It's not a big deal. Don't worry."

I'd do whatever it took to keep her safe. I'd even leave the Valley if I had to. But it was hard to deny that this *was* the safest place for her when compared to anywhere else. Even if she was right about Zach, my woodshed seemed like a small price to pay compared to living in the wilderness again on a trip that nearly killed us. Even if we had to take extra precautions.

Even if the sinking feeling in my gut wouldn't go away.

❋

Word spread faster than the fire around the Valley, and the more the story was told, the worse it got. Danny got a dozen complaints over the next week, all angrily demanding that he *do something* about the compound girl who was so clueless about real life that she didn't even know not to leave a lantern burning overnight. At the next council meeting, Jameson was smug as fuck, explaining to everyone that this was why he'd been so cautious about allowing the compound women to stay, and now he was vindicated, because who knew what she'd burn down next?

It took every bit of my control not to pound that slimy mother-fucker into the ground. But I knew it'd just make things worse for Claire. Even if the accusation came from me, they'd blame her, and the last thing she needed was more venom aimed at her.

Worse, though, was Danny. Although he didn't have any animosity toward Claire, it was clear he hadn't believed her, and that made even our friends give us sideways looks.

"Look, man, it's not a big deal," Danny had said, sitting behind his desk in the small command center at the Lodge. He leaned back in his chair, crossing his arms. "She made a mistake. We don't have to crucify her for it, but ignoring it isn't gonna help either."

I paced the room. "*We* may not crucify her. That doesn't mean there aren't others here that would, given the chance. You know Jameson has it out for her."

Danny frowned. "If she's gotten direct threats, now's the time to tell me. You know I won't put up with that. Even if it's from Jameson."

My sigh obviously told him the truth: we had no proof of anything.

"I can't force anyone to like her, Johnny," Danny said quietly, staring at the floor. "And it's not a crime to gossip or spread rumours. I know it's shitty, and I'm sorry, but there's nothing for us to do here. Nobody's crossed any lines."

"I know," I conceded. "But I still maintain she didn't do this. Not even by accident."

He gave me a sympathetic look that made me want to flip the table over.

"She comes from a different place," he said, with an annoying level of patience in his voice. "A different time, you could even argue. I don't blame her for needing to adjust. Maybe you need to accept that she's having more trouble than you thought."

"Skip the patronizing bullshit," I shot back, and before he could reply, "I need some air."

I walked out and went on patrol early. Not only did my best friend not believe me, but the Chief Outrider didn't believe me. That wasn't a good look for Claire, no matter how I tried to spin it. Later, when I got home, even Kimmy guiltily confided to me that a couple of patients at the clinic had asked her if there was anything she could do about Claire. The rumour mill just kept turning, and I didn't know how to stop it.

"Don't you think it's possible," Sarah said gently to me one afternoon, "that she just—"

I could hear Claire's voice in the next room, patiently instructing Jake on how to write his name. She gave a little clap and cooed at him for finishing the first letter.

"No, I don't," I replied stubbornly. "She's not stupid."

Sarah huffed. "I know *that*. She's doing so well teaching Allie and Jake. But she's had a whole different upbringing than us. Isn't it possible she just made a mistake? Nobody would blame her."

I blew out a breath. "You're not listening. Yes, they would. Don't talk to me about this again."

"But—"

"I mean it. If you want her to keep teaching your kids, you need to keep your opinion on this to yourself."

Sarah looked hurt but gave a short nod. I didn't care. It was bad enough that Claire had to deal with everyone else's suspicion; she didn't need our friends turning on her, too. The only one who seemed completely unbothered by it was Jenna.

"She's smart," Jenna said when I asked, shrugging. "And I don't think she'd lie if she really didn't know she'd put out the lantern. I've already yelled at Danny about this, and for what it's worth, Isla agrees with me. We're trying to talk to the people who'll listen."

I couldn't help but smile. "You're a good kid, Jen."

She rolled her eyes. "When are you gonna stop calling me a kid?"

"Never," I answered with a grin, and she clucked her tongue. "Because even when I'm eighty, you'll still be my best friend's kid sister. Some things don't change."

For her part, Claire was doing her best to keep her chin up, not showing how it affected her...but I knew it did. She kept herself busy around the homestead by tending the greenhouse and taking care of the animals every day, especially Poppy. One morning, after the chores were done, I went looking for her and found her in the stable, brushing Poppy's coat and talking to her. Her back was turned, so I leaned against a wood beam, just watching her.

"I'm scared that I'm doing this all wrong," Claire murmured, brushing Poppy's neck. "I don't know what to do. How I should be. Where I belong. I want them to like me. I want to be more than my survival, to contribute something. But if they never trust me, how can I?"

She sighed heavily, stroking Poppy's mane.

"I suppose you never have to worry about things like this, spoiled girl," she said with humour. "You're just worried about where your next carrot is coming from."

She yelped as Poppy's long tongue licked her cheek, then dissolved into laughter that warmed my insides. Poppy looked over at me, and Clare followed her gaze. On seeing me, she looked a little embarrassed.

"How long have you been standing there?"

"Long enough," I said with a smile. "And it's true; horses are pretty single-minded. But they're good listeners. They don't judge."

She smiled sheepishly. "I guess I need that right now."

I went over and took her in my arms, kissing the top of her head. She leaned into me, and I felt the tension in her body. Poppy nickered quietly at me, and I patted her snout.

"Wanna go for a ride?" I asked.

She looked up at me and smiled. "You know I do."

I kissed her forehead. "Get saddled up. I've got something to show you."

CHAPTER 30

Claire

Outside, the world was white again, covered in a thin blanket of fresh, sparkling snow. The horses' hooves made satisfying crunching sounds as we followed the western trail from Summerhurst into the woods.

"Overgrown now," John remarked as he ducked out of the way of a tree branch on Ghost's back. "Usually every spring, I'd go through and clear it. Two years has caught up with it."

Poppy was quiet under me, following Ghost's lead, but she was responsive to my every move and touch. It was easy to see why Danny said she was good for a beginner; she knew exactly what to do and was highly responsive to direction.

We rode for a long time through the forest, our path obscured by the overgrown brush. Eventually, though, John dismounted and began to lead Ghost off the trail.

"It's off the main path," he explained. "Not much farther."

I copied him, leading Poppy through the trees until we reached a wide-open meadow. Tall, brown grass swayed in the winter wind, giving way to a flat area with a large, partially frozen pond that was fed by a small spring falling from a rock wall beside it. A willow tree, naked of its leaves, curved over the water.

The meadow was beautiful even in winter. Peaceful and secluded, it felt hidden away from the world—a place where one could go to escape. We led the horses to the pond for a drink, and John spread out a thick blanket underneath the barren willow tree, then motioned for me to sit with him. I settled beside him, watching the spring trickle water into the pond.

"This was always my favourite spot," John said. "Sometimes for hunting or fishing, but also just to get away from everything. I never brought anyone before."

I gave him a skeptical look. "Even Kimmy?"

He gave me a small, affectionate smile.

"Nope. Just you, compound girl."

"You haven't called me that in a while," I said with a laugh.

"Maybe because you aren't one anymore."

I sighed. "Wish everyone else felt that way."

"They will," John replied. "But I want you to know that your life isn't about making everyone else happy at your own expense anymore. You're free now."

Touched, I reached out and took his hand. "I'm just afraid of what might come. Especially once they figure out..."

I trailed off, biting my lip. Asha's words about my fertility had been hitting me harder since the fire. The Valley needed people—babies. Being able to provide that might've been my one saving grace in a community that distrusted me. Worse, maybe Asha was right; maybe John would come to resent me for it.

"Figure out what?"

The look he gave me was so tender, so kind, that I wanted to weep. Instead, I managed to clear the stone of emotion lodged in my throat and said, "You know about my implant, and...it's why we've never had to be careful, right? I can't get pregnant, and I don't know if I'll ever be able to. Theoretically, my implant's functions can be deactivated remotely, but...it seems unlikely that we'll find an opportunity to do that."

I took a breath. "I may never be able to give you children. I didn't want to talk about it when you proposed, because I was just so happy, but...it seems unfair not to bring it up. Especially since people will wonder eventually."

"That's between us," John said curtly. "Not their business."

"Maybe. But what about you?" I asked, fidgeting. "I don't want to take something from you that you really want. If...if you had second thoughts about—"

"Second thoughts?" he interjected sharply, a crease forming between his brows. "You think I didn't consider this before I asked you to marry me?"

"I don't know," I conceded. "But we never discussed it at length before because...well, when we first started sleeping together, we weren't sure where it was going."

John huffed, amused.

"Maybe you weren't," he said, leaning back on his hands. "After our first time together, I knew I wanted more. My hang-up was that *you* didn't seem so keen on *me*."

I smiled in spite of myself. "I was. I just didn't want to think about what that might mean at the time."

We were quiet for another moment before John put an arm around my shoulders and pulled my bulk against his, laying his head on top of mine.

"What if I couldn't give you children? It's possible. I haven't tested it out, have I?"

A reluctant giggle escaped me. "I guess not."

There was a keen whistle of wind through the woods, and I shivered.

"Would you not want me anymore, Claire?" John asked quietly. "Not love me anymore?"

A painful lump rose in my throat at the thought.

"Of course I'd still want you," I whispered.

"Then you already know how I feel."

He tilted my head back and kissed me, slowly and sweetly. My heart felt all aflutter when we broke apart, and he rested his forehead against mine, closing his eyes and breathing deeply—the way he did during moments he wanted to savour. I allowed my own eyes to flutter closed. I imagined coming back here in the spring, with the wildflowers abloom, the willow tree thick with leaves, and the sun shining. A new place for us to share, to mark our new beginning.

"So, you haven't dreamed of a family?" I asked after a moment.

John shrugged. "I didn't have high hopes I'd even get married before you. There was nobody I wanted to do that with. Becoming an outrider was my dream before."

"And now?"

He kissed my forehead. "Now, my dream is you."

I sighed as he ran a hand through my hair.

"What do you want?" John asked, reminding me that for the first time, what I wanted actually mattered.

I bit my lip. At the Cave, I'd known that I'd have to apply to have a child one day, and that it was expected of me. I also knew that a group of faceless bureaucrats would be the ones who'd decide for me either way. I'd resigned myself to motherhood the way that one resigns oneself to household chores: necessary, inevitable, unavoidable.

"I don't know," I answered honestly. "I always just assumed I'd have to. But...I think for now, I want to have a life that's just about us and the people we love. I want to enjoy our time together, now that we're not as focused on bare survival."

He nodded thoughtfully. "Well...if one day, you had our baby, I'd be happy. I'd work hard to be a good husband and father to both of you. But if all I get is to watch you get stronger, sweeter, more beautiful as the years pass...to grow old with you, and know that we spent our lives happy together? That's more than enough for me. *You* are enough for me. You're everything."

Happiness swelled inside of me. He was more than I deserved, this man I was marrying. He was more than I'd ever have dared to ask for. My throat ached.

"Damn it, John," I choked out. "Do you have to be so wonderful?"

He laughed and kissed the top of my head. "You bring it out in me."

"Smooth," I teased, and he chuckled again and gave me an affectionate squeeze.

"Before we know it, this trial period will be over," he said after a moment. "I know it's hard right now, with the way everyone's been. They're just scared. I know they'll come around; they're family."

I nodded hesitantly. "I just...I've always been looking for my place, I suppose. Even back at the Cave, I felt like I was searching for it."

"I know. But sometimes, you have to make a place for yourself. Find a space where something's missing and fill it."

I shot him an accusatory look. "You've been talking to Jenna."

"Yep," he replied without an ounce of regret, his eyes serious. "There's a place for you here, Claire. But if you're hoping for someone to give you permission, they won't. You've gotta claim it, and not give a shit what a few bad apples say about it, because you fucking belong here. Prove it to them."

He's right. I recalled the conversation we'd had when I first started to live at the camp with him and Kimmy. He'd called me out on my arrogance about learning to survive...and he'd been right then, too. I could always count on him to tell me what I needed to hear, to jolt me out of my fear response.

"Alright," I sighed. "I need some paper, a pen, and Jenna. And maybe a ride to the Lodge."

John grinned. "You got it."

❀

The schoolroom was at least orderly...even if I wasn't sure how it had housed all the school-aged children in the Valley. The room wasn't small, but with 40 desks crammed into it, it felt a little claustrophobic. I sat behind the teacher's desk at the front, flipping through the documents that Dr. Irons had left behind, making notes with a pen.

"It was cramped," Jenna admitted as she helped sort through the paperwork. "We traded off days between the older and younger kids. I mentioned to Dr. Irons that the council should build a schoolhouse, but...I don't think he took it seriously. I was only his assistant for a couple months."

I nodded absently. There'd been a whole file cabinet full of his lesson plans, as well as files on each of the students. Useful, but as I expected, his curriculum was lacking. Much of it was too advanced for the age groups he was teaching, and his lesson plans involved no aspects of experiential learning. Worse, the younger children's education was clearly being neglected in favour of the older kids.

The schoolroom had books—all stacked in piles on a forlorn-looking bookshelf at the back of the room—but clearly lacked the space to store them. As a result, its selection remained relatively limited, and the books present were mostly classics and Old World science textbooks.

"How bad is it?" John asked, reading my expression.

I tapped my pen against the desk. "Define 'bad.'"

He chuckled. "How much work is it?"

I took a deep breath before replying.

"I'll need to create a new curriculum," I said. "Some of the professor's lesson plans can be repurposed, but...everything is in dire need of an update. It won't be easy. We'll need materials, and I agree with Jenna that a schoolhouse will be needed eventually. We can make do with switching between age groups for now, but going to school two days a week just isn't enough. Which means we'll also eventually need more teachers."

Jenna blew out a breath. "That's a lot."

"It's almost like leaving a crusty old bastard in charge of education for like thirty years was a bad idea," John quipped. "Whatever you need, let me know. If we can't make it here in the Valley, I'll add it to the scav list."

"Books are the main thing," I said, massaging my temples. "As many books as possible, on every subject. Fiction and nonfiction."

"We have books," Jenna supplied. "There are boxes and boxes of them in storage in the Lodge cellar. Some were used for school in the past. But the others are unsorted. Oisín wanted to get them all catalogued, but..."

John's expression briefly darkened, but I pressed on.

"Good, thank you," I said, encouraged. "Well, any time anyone finds a new book from now on, they should deliver it to me. I'll come up with a filing system for all of them. Finding storage will be another problem, but..."

"We can keep them in the cellar for now," John supplied. "But it sounds like we'll be adding a library to that schoolhouse."

I buried my face in my hands. "This is a huge project. They'll never go for this."

"Claire, this is why you have to do this," Jenna insisted. "You're the only one who knows what we're missing. You know so much that nobody else does, and it's not their fault, but they don't know what they don't know. You can help us rebuild some of what's been lost to time."

"I don't want to be the rowdy outsider that comes in and tells them they've been doing it wrong for decades," I replied with a sigh.

"You don't have to do that," Jenna said. "You just have to show them what you can do."

The certainty in her voice gave me strength. I'd only known Jenna a short time, but she believed in me. And even if I never had children, I could make a difference in the lives of dozens of kids just by doing the job I'd been trained to do.

"Alright," I said, standing. "Let's get started."

CHAPTER 31

Claire

For the next week, I planned the new curriculum in the study at Summerhurst, Jenna at my side. John and Kimmy took over my chores, and I worked day and night—not even because I had to, but because I wanted to. A new passion had ignited in my veins. I was good at this, and for someone who'd felt useless for so much of her time in the Wasteland, I cherished that new sense of purpose.

Jenna was, predictably, a good student, and a capable assistant. She read over the material, made suggestions, and asked insightful questions. She told me about the children, their habits, and the learning styles she'd observed. Together, we took on the mammoth task of cataloguing what turned out to be hundreds of books in the Lodge cellar. Noah and Isla were kind enough to get Noah's mother to babysit Ely so that they could help us, and that made the work go faster. We divided the books into school books and general interest books, in the hope that one day, we could convince the council of the need for a public library.

I decided that I'd mostly help the older kids, since that was my area of expertise. Jenna preferred working with the younger children anyway, so I assigned them to her with the assumption that I'd be training and mentoring her as we went. Ideally, we'd have more teachers eventually, but that would require a proper schoolhouse.

After that, we tackled the various subjects, planning experiential learning lessons and field trips, such as visiting the Valley's lumber mill. I updated each subject as best I could, and to my surprise, Asha was even willing to consult on the science curriculum, removing outdated information and making helpful additions.

"They don't deserve you, Claire," she said as she made a note in the margins. "But you've done a great job."

"Thanks," I said wearily, rubbing my eyes. "It's been good for me."

John supported me by adding books and supplies to the community scav list, as well as trading for things we needed. By the end of the week, he'd brought me a couple boxes of books that he'd bought from other Valley residents.

I chewed my lip as I sorted through them. Next week was when I planned to begin classes.

"But what if I go to the council and they say no?" I'd asked John, back in the schoolroom.

"So, don't go to them," he'd replied with a shrug. "Easier to ask for forgiveness than permission. I'll put a notice up on the community board that you're holding lessons, and anyone who wants to can attend. That way, you're not forcing anything on anybody; you're just using an unoccupied community space to offer free, voluntary classes."

"Won't they just drag me out of there?"

He huffed. "They'd have to go through me first. Look, school's been out for a long time now, and the parents are getting antsy homeschooling. It's already been brought up a bunch of times in meetings, but nothing's getting done. So, you offer their kids an education, and they'll show up...and once they do, it'll be hard for the rest of them to complain about it."

The following Monday morning, I drummed my fingers anxiously on the teacher's desk in the schoolroom. Jenna and I had set everything up with John's help, and in a few minutes, we'd wait outside for people to show up.

John covered my anxious fingers with his hand. "It'll be okay, baby. You'll see."

To my surprise, when I went to open the door, there was a small crowd in front of the schoolroom. Perhaps a dozen children waited with their parents. Sarah was there with Jake, and Isla waited beside her with Ely, who was dozing in his baby wrap. Jenna had approached and was chatting with one of the other parents, who at least looked receptive to what she was saying.

"You're all here for class?" I asked Sarah, who nodded, rubbing her pregnant belly.

"Jake is very excited," she said, and as if in demonstration, the small boy next to her grinned.

"And I know Ely's a little young for school," Isla said with a smile, stroking her son's small head, "but we wanted to show our support for Claire and Aunt Jenna, didn't we, buddy?"

The baby groaned sleepily and hid his face in his mother's breast, which made me chuckle.

"Thank you," I said sincerely, then turned to the crowd. "Everyone's welcome, including parents, if they'd like to stay and see our new program."

We filed into the room, and once everyone was seated, I stood at the head of the class, while Jenna stood at the back. We'd decided that since she liked working with the youngest children, she'd walk among the desks during the lesson and help them with anything that might be a bit advanced for their age group. Each desk had a worksheet that John had gotten printed for me at the lumber mill, which had a small press.

Suddenly, two dozen pairs of eyes were glued to me. But I had done this before. I took a deep breath, and some part of me reawakened. I launched into the lesson with ease, quelling my nerves by glancing at John, who stood at the back of the room, watching me with a small smile of encouragement.

We started with an exercise to learn everyone's names, which involved spelling and writing. After that, the first lesson was a trial of some more interactive learning, which had been sorely lacking before. I'd asked John to be present not just for support, but for a class about outriders, and more broadly, the Valley itself.

I'd drawn a map of the Valley on the blackboard in chalk. I'd consulted with John beforehand about where all the homesteads in the Valley were in relation to each other.

"Do any of you know where you live inside the Valley?"

The children's puzzled looks didn't worry me. They were too young to know; I just needed their best guess.

"Mama says we live in the south," a girl called Melanie offered.

"Great," I answered, and I marked her homestead on the map. "More specifically, Melanie, you live *here*. Right near the lake—I'm jealous."

She giggled, and her father sitting next to her gave a shy smile. We went through everyone's place on the map, introduced the concept of *geography*, and why it was important to know where things were.

I introduced John as an outrider, and we went over what he did and why before letting the kids ask questions.

"Is it ever boring, riding around all the time?" a little boy called Omar asked, looking skeptical. "I'd be bored."

John grinned. "Sometimes. I play a lot of I-Spy with myself. Other times, I think about my family, who I'm protecting by doing my job. That usually helps."

He gave me a warm glance, and a few of the kids, particularly the girls, smiled. Better yet, their parents looked a lot less wary and more engaged. It's working.

Noon came faster than I could've ever predicted, and class ended. I waited by the door as everyone filed out, and to my delight, several of the parents stopped to speak with me, praising the lesson and promising that their kids would return tomorrow. At the end of the line was a dark-haired woman with a young son, who she sent ahead of her, out of the room, before turning to speak to me.

My stomach flipped.

"Excuse me, we haven't formally met," she said, extending her hand. Tentatively, I shook it. "I'm Alice Wang."

Wang. That was one of the families that wouldn't let Asha and me through their gate and forced us to wait outside. My guard immediately rose.

"I just wanted to apologize," she said, making a face. "For treating you so coldly when you first arrived. The class you just taught was great; you're a gifted teacher. I hope you'll consider staying on, and if the council gives you trouble...well, just know I'll be supporting you. I haven't seen Jace that engaged in school before."

"Oh," I replied, a little taken aback. "Well, I appreciate your support. I hope you'll tell the other parents about the class, so more will come."

"I certainly will. Have a good day."

She left me standing in surprised silence, and John walked over with a proud smile. He'd been just outside, talking to some of the parents.

"Told you," he said in a low voice. "You're a superstar."

I laughed. "I don't know about that, but at least it seems to have softened my image a bit."

"You are," he insisted. "Finally seeing you up there? I get it. You're sweet, and knowledgeable, and kind. You hold the room, but not in a commanding way; your authority comes from how well you come across. Like you've been doing it forever."

I shrugged. "I mean, before a year ago, this was what I did every day for four years. It's like muscle memory. I just know what to do."

He nodded. "Not gonna lie, it was kind of sexy, too."

I endured another full-blown belly laugh. "Now you're just being silly."

"Nothing silly about a woman in charge," John replied with a flirtatious smile. "Can't wait to see you do it all again."

✳

Weeks passed, and every day, more kids showed up for class, even from families who'd been more than a little reluctant to accept me. Their desire for their children to be educated—and realistically, safely out of the house for a few hours every day—overrode their suspicion and dislike in the end, especially because they usually stayed for the first lesson.

More and more, the children opened up and enjoyed learning. Without regular school, they'd been criminally understimulated and ultimately, bored. They ate up the lessons I planned and asked for more, and I was happy to oblige. They were intelligent, and sweet, and unusually well-behaved compared to compound kids, likely because they'd been doing disciplined farm work almost since birth. Over a few weeks, I'd grown fond of all of them, and perhaps the most surprising thing of all was that the feeling seemed mutual.

I painted a mural on the back wall of the schoolroom, recreating a more elaborate version of the map of the Valley that I'd drawn on the chalkboard. I kept it cartoonish and fun, with little pictures of the farmhouse at each homestead in its place on the map. I let the kids write their family names beneath each house, adding a personal touch to it, which they loved.

There were a few naysayers who showed up to essentially heckle us, but Jenna insisted on dealing with them. Firecracker that she was, she told them quite plainly where they could stick their complaints. Nevertheless, I knew a reckoning must be coming, and on one morning in early April, the elder Jameson was waiting in front of the schoolroom door when I opened it to invite the class inside. Heedless of the crowd of children and parents behind him, he started talking before I'd even greeted him.

"You've been running an unauthorized school program, never approved by the council," he said firmly. "You are not a qualified teacher, and this is not a real class. You've appropriated our schoolroom for illegal purposes. You'll stop now, or you'll jeopardize your probationary status in this community."

I could've heard a pin drop with how quiet it got.

"If it's illegal, where's Danny?" Jenna asked, crossing her arms. "Have him arrest us. Me, too, since I've been just as much a part of this as Claire has."

"This is not your concern, child," Jameson spit back. "You are not an outsider."

"He's not here," Jenna continued, growing louder, "because there is nothing illegal about what we're doing. We've never claimed to be an official school program; this is a voluntary program that anyone is *free* to attend or not. And I didn't realize that things only became illegal when outsiders did them. I can't say I remember my brother ever telling me that."

Jameson stared at her coldly. "It may not be illegal, but it violates the spirit of having a council to decide how *our* children should be educated."

I found my voice. "With all due respect, your decision so far has been to *not* educate them. So, you'll forgive me for finding a solution to a problem that so far, your council has been unwilling or unable to solve."

He looked like I'd hit him. "You clearly don't know your place, outsider."

"She does," Alice Wang said from the crowd, looking stern. "It's right here, where she's earned the trust of our kids. If you have a problem with that, you can call a council meeting, like anybody else. But I think everyone here will vote against you."

There was a murmur of assent from the crowd, and my heart felt fit to burst. I'd earned their respect at last. I was being accepted, trusted, and finally, *useful*. I could've cried with joy and relief, but I managed to hold it together as Jameson shot me a venomous look and stalked away, muttering to himself.

"Okay, *that* was awesome," Jenna murmured to me as we filed into the classroom. "Claire, you have balls! I was wondering when I'd see you stick up for yourself at last."

I smiled. "Turns out that I have something to fight for after all."

CHAPTER 32

Claire

M id-April, just as we were starting to get seeds in the ground, Jenna convinced me to attend the next community dance, where she and Liam planned to play music as usual. It had all happened so quickly—one moment, I was helping her tune her violin, the next I heard myself reluctantly agreeing to sing a few songs with them.

"You'll be a hit," Jenna gushed. "And we've been practicing for a while now."

"O-kay," I said, my stomach churning. "I'll...see you there, I guess."

A few days later, I found myself sitting in front of the vanity table in my bedroom, filled with equal parts dread and a strange sense of excitement. It'd been a long time since I'd sung publicly. The music practices with Jenna and Liam had restored the musical part of me that'd withered from disuse, so I had to hope this would be good for something, at least.

I put on the one and only dress that Nimkii had made for me: a light green frock that brought out my eyes. I hadn't yet had an occasion to wear it.

"I'm nervous," I said to John as I fixed my hair at the vanity in our room. I pinned it half-up, then smoothed the front of my dress.

Fresh out of the shower, John pulled a clean shirt over his head as he answered, "You have a beautiful voice, baby. It'd be a shame not to use it. Besides, Jenna's gonna be up there too, and Liam."

"Yeah, Jenna talks an awful lot about him," I said with a small smile. "He's so quiet, though. Hardly talks during music practice, but she acts like he walks on water. Who's he related to again?"

John grinned. "Didn't know she was into him. Guess it makes sense. He's one of Noah's little brothers. Quiet like Noah, but not as socially awkward. Always thought he had the hots for Asra, though."

"The one who's in love with you?" I teased with a smirk.

John rolled his eyes. "Still can't believe she said that at the council meeting. We never even went out. I helped her fix their truck *one time*."

I giggled, couldn't help it. Realizing that John was the reluctant hottie of the Valley cracked me up. It shouldn't have been surprising, given how attractive he was, but his utter indifference to the female attention he received was undeniably funny.

I didn't feel worried or threatened by it, and my heart squeezed as I realized that it was mark of the trust I had in him—trust that I'd worked so hard to cultivate.

I'm not perfect, but I've come a long way.

"I'm just glad Asha's coming," I said absently as I fiddled with my hair again. "For Kimmy's sake. She's been gone so often lately; Kimmy's been a little depressed about it."

John put his hands on my shoulders and bent to kiss my cheek, watching my face in the mirror.

"Well, no one's going to look as good as you tonight," he said in a low, intimate tone.

"Will you dance with me?" I asked with a playful smile.

He chuckled. "I never dance."

"You did once with me," I reminded him.

"That was different. I had a crush on you, and it was a chance to hold you close without telling you."

My smile broadened. "You can hold me close now all you like. And, if you're lucky, maybe more."

John turned my face towards his and kissed me full on the lips—hungry, needy, wanting more. It'd been over a week since we'd last had sex. Between school, work, and the farm, we'd both been exhausted every night.

Tonight was our first leisurely evening together since our date, and my body ached to make love to him, especially when he thrust his tongue into my mouth. I let out a muffled gasp, and he seized my face in his hands, forcing his mouth harder against mine. We kissed frantically for another moment before resurfacing for breath, and he moved his lips to my throat, making me gasp again.

"Forget the dance," John murmured against my skin. "We'll say you're sick. Let's stay in for the night. Alone."

I groaned. "I can't no-show on Jenna. And you said we'd be there. It won't look good if it seems like I'm avoiding seeing people."

The tip of his tongue caressed my earlobe, and I shuddered.

"Then go get your coat," he whispered in my ear. "Or I'll be on my knees with my tongue inside you in the next sixty seconds."

Pleasure shot straight to my groin at that image, but I took a deep breath and stood. I tore myself away from his hungry gaze and went downstairs to fetch my coat.

❉

The hall inside the Lodge was already bustling with people by the time we arrived. Chairs lined the walls, and two tables at the head of the room held food and drink. Sarah and her husband, Bruce, were in the corner, chatting with Danny and their oldest son, Matthew. Nearby, Isla and Noah sat with Ely, who was nursing quietly in Isla's arms. As soon as he finished, Noah scooped him up in his arms and started walking with him, patting his back.

Kimmy and Asha went to sit with Isla, who looked pleased with their company. They'd both dressed up. It felt nice to see Asha looking more the way I remembered her—wearing nice clothes, her hair braided and shiny, her warm brown skin clear and bright. She also stuck close to Kimmy, linking arms with her, which warmed my heart, especially because Kimmy looked so happy about it.

Jenna and Liam had already started playing on the small platform where the council chairs normally sat, and there were a few people dancing. Jenna smiled and nodded at me to come over.

When the song finished, I went up on the platform, nervously surveying the room. People looked over at me with curiosity, and I recognized many of the parents of my students. My heart leapt into my throat, however, when I realized that Zach Jameson was standing near the back of the hall, drink in hand, with what I assumed were his brothers. He pretended to ignore me, but I caught his occasional, razor-sharp glances.

I tried to forget about him as Jenna signaled the start of the next song. Instead, I focused my gaze on John. He'd gone to stand beside Danny, but he was watching me, a small smile on his face and a drink in his hand.

I took a deep breath and started to sing. It was the same song I'd once performed for John and Kimmy by the campfire, the first time they'd heard me sing, over a year ago. *It was the first time I knew I wanted you,* John told me later. *When I couldn't get your voice out of my head.*

I kept my eyes on him, avoiding the stares of everyone else, and my voice grew stronger. When the song ended, the sudden burst of applause almost startled me. Most everyone looked pleased by my performance, other than those I already knew didn't like me, and I sagged a little with relief. Danny whistled, which made me flush, and John's smile widened. He raised his glass to me as I started into the next song.

Altogether, I played three songs with Jenna and Liam, and each seemed to be a hit. When I finally joined the party again, Kimmy and Asha were there to meet me.

"Your voice is beautiful as always," Kimmy said fondly. "It made me nostalgic, hearing you again. Feels like so much longer than a year that you've been with us."

"She's always had it," Asha added, far more warmly than usual. "I always tried to get her to sing at bars back home, but she never would. Glad that you finally did it."

"Guess I just needed to feel like I belonged," I answered, and something dark flitted across Asha's face. A half-second later, however, she'd assumed a pleasant expression again, making me question if I'd imagined it.

"I'd like to borrow my girl," John's voice said behind me, and then he turned me toward him. "If that's alright with you two."

Kimmy smiled and nodded, pulling Asha toward the dance floor. To my surprise, John did the same with me.

"What are you doing?" I asked.

"I thought you wanted a dance."

"You said you wouldn't," I replied as he placed a hand on my back. Jenna and Liam had started playing a slow ballad.

He drew me closer, lacing his fingers with mine. "I changed my mind."

A lot of couples were on the dance floor now. John oscillated us slowly, but his movements were still unnatural and out of rhythm, which made me giggle.

"You're still a hopeless dancer, I see," I teased.

John grinned. "Did you really expect anything else?"

I recalled again the night we'd danced—or more like swayed together, really—by the campfire. At the time, we hadn't even kissed yet, and every touch between us felt electric. Although I was used to his touch now, feeling his hand shift lower on my back still sent a small spark of pleasure through me.

"I suppose not. But I like you anyway."

"So kind of you," he said, amused.

We were quiet for a moment, listening to the music as we swayed gently. John's eyes never left my face, shining with sweet contentment, and the corners of his mouth curved upward. He was perfectly at ease—a rare thing in the last few months—and was only more handsome for it.

"You look beautiful," he said in a low, husky tone. "I haven't seen you in a dress since the day we met."

"Hardly a dress by that point, was it?" I replied wryly. "Just a tatter of dirty fabric."

The corners of his mouth ticked upward. "True. At least this time, it won't be a group of maneaters ripping it off you."

I gave him a scandalized look.

"You're not ripping anything! This is the only dress I own, and it's staying fully intact."

"We'll get you another," John said, his gaze moving to my lips. "As many as you want. I like seeing you like this."

"Like what?"

"Like you feel pretty," he said with a warm smile. "You carry yourself differently. More confident, less shy."

Of course, that made my cheeks redden, and he chuckled. I moved my hand from his shoulder to caress along his jaw with my fingertips. His grip on my other hand loosened, and we stopped swaying.

"Kiss me," I said softly.

John lowered his lips to mine. The pressure was gentle, the kiss initially chaste, but it quickly turned hungrier as his hand moved from my lower back into my hair. He nipped my bottom lip playfully, teasing me, and I remembered we were in public just in time to suppress a quiet moan. The whole world seemed to fall away when he kissed me like this—sweet, but with an undercurrent of desire and a promise of more that made me feel weak-kneed.

I only realized that the song had ended when we broke apart, a little breathless.

"Hey Johnny, you too busy swapping saliva to hang out with your buddies?" Danny called, and I cringed a little, embarrassed. He stood over in a distant corner of the hall, drink in hand, next to Jonah and the oldest Armstrong son, Matthew.

John flashed me a sheepish grin.

"I better go mingle, or he'll never shut up," he said apologetically. "He's even more...Danny when he's a bit drunk."

A new, livelier tune started playing, and Danny mimed a ridiculous dance move, swaying precariously.

I giggled. "That's alright. I need the bathroom anyway."

"Do you want me to walk you out?" he asked, glancing at the back exit. "It's dark."

I shook my head and pecked his lips.

"I'll be fine, darling. Go have fun with your friends."

As John made his way over to a clearly inebriated Danny, I went to gather my coat for the trek to the outhouse. I spotted Kimmy chatting away with Jenna in the opposite corner, standing next to Asha. Asha was tight-lipped as usual, but for once, she was actually smiling. It didn't take me long to understand why: Kimmy was holding her hand in a loose grip and stroked her arm absently while talking. Where everyone could see.

Well, that's new.

Heading out the back exit, a rush of frigid air stole the breath from my lungs. I hugged my coat more tightly around me and trudged toward the somewhat forlorn-looking outhouse. A single small lamp hung from a hook next to the door, illuminating the way. Perhaps unsurprisingly, it was a good fifty feet from the back door. The snow drifts and biting cold made it feel like a thousand.

To my surprise, inside was relatively clean and had an electric light. The composting toilet was not as horrible as I'd expected. Someone had left a bottle of homemade hand sanitizer on a tiny shelf, which made it feel a little less pioneer-esque. Still, I would continue to treasure the return of indoor plumbing to my life.

I pushed open the heavy wooden door to return to the Lodge. Suddenly, it swung open, pulled from the other side.

"John, I'm f—"

I froze. Zach Jameson stood in the doorway, his frame outlined by the light of the lamp. His mouth was twisted into a malicious little smile.

"Sorry to disappoint," he said, amused.

I didn't know what he wanted, but it wasn't anything good.

"He'll be looking for me," I said, forcing calm into my voice. "I should head back."

He snickered. "Don't think so. Last I saw, he was on his way to being in the same condition as that idiot McNeil. Useless, in other words."

I swallowed reflexively, assessing my options. I was unarmed and in a tiny space where he blocked the only exit. My odds of fighting him off without a weapon would've been low to begin with, but in this scenario, it would be nearly impossible.

"Don't look so scared, Red," he goaded. "I just wanted a little alone time."

"I'll scream," I said, sounding braver than I felt. "Like a banshee."

He frowned. "The fuck's a banshee?"

Oh, right. Not a reference a Wastelander would get. I had the absurd urge to laugh but choked it down.

"Doesn't matter," I replied forcefully. "All you need to know is that if you touch me, I'll raise hell."

Zach narrowed his eyes, but his stance remained casual as he leaned against the doorframe.

"You really think screaming would stop me? I'd have you on your back before you could make a sound."

He nodded toward the outhouse door, held open by his bulk.

"Door's heavy," he said. "Pretty soundproof. They wouldn't hear you. 'Course, you wouldn't be doing much screaming with my hand around your throat."

A shiver went down my spine. He spoke with the confidence of someone who'd planned this. My palms felt clammy inside my gloves.

"Lucky for you, Red, that's not why I'm here. Not tonight, anyway."

Startled, I shot him a disbelieving glance. "Then what do you want?"

Zach paused briefly, his eyes doing an active scan of my body. Uneasy, I shifted from foot to foot.

"You went out here all by yourself, huh?" he mused. "You're too comfortable. The fact that you can waltz into the Valley and not even have to look over your shoulder? Not even sleep with one eye open? Don't sit right with me."

I hated to admit it, but he was right. I'd let my guard down; I didn't even have my knife. Out in the Wasteland, I wouldn't have been caught dead without it, but I'd grown used to the easier pace of life in the Valley.

He smiled without warmth. "And even Madigan thinks you're safe enough to leave alone now? Nah. Let me make one thing clear: my family owns this place, and I'll be cold in the ground before I let an outsider whore warp the minds of kids. You'll never be safe here, so long as I have anything to do with it. So, this is your last warning: get the fuck out while you still can, or my next visit won't be so friendly."

I tried to take another step, but his arm shot out in front of me.

"Let me go," I said through gritted teeth. I had a horrible feeling at the pit of my stomach. My heart pounded out a hideous staccato rhythm against my ribs.

He chortled. "That's the spirit, Red. Pretend you're walking away tonight because I was so scared of your big bad boyfriend...and not because I let you. And that's why you'll keep this our little secret, huh? Because if he lays a hand on me, you'll both be facing a firing squad. My father would see to it."

He reached out to touch me. I recoiled away from his hand, but in the small space, there was nowhere to go.

"Touch her and it'll be the last thing you do."

John's threat was a low growl, followed by the click of a gun being cocked. Zach whirled around and came face to face with the end of John's pistol. He raised his hands in a pacifying gesture.

"No need to get bent out of shape, man," he said casually, but there was a note of fear in his voice. "Just chatting with the lady."

"Cut the bullshit," John gritted out. "Move away. Slowly. Reach for your gun and I'll kill you."

Zach did as he was told, inching away from the outhouse. The heavy door shut behind him, and I was shrouded in darkness. Snow crunched under his feet as he walked away from the door.

"She doesn't belong here, and you know it."

"Didn't ask for your opinion, asshole," John snarled. "Keep walking."

Silence followed, and I let out a breath as I slumped against the wall, equal parts relieved and terrified. Another minute passed before the old door swung open again, the hinges squealing in protest. John stood in the doorway, his pistol back in its holster at his hip. His expression was still hard and focused, the way it always was in the wake of a crisis.

"You hurt?" John asked. "Did he touch you?"

I shook my head, feeling mute with shock. He gave me a once-over, clearly looking for signs of injury that I wasn't reporting. Satisfied that I was in one piece, he offered me his hand.

"Come on," he said gruffly. "Let's go home."

I slid my hand into his and he led me back towards the Lodge.

"How did you know I was in trouble?" I asked, staring at Zach's footprints in the fresh, shimmering snow.

"I saw him leave and had a hunch," he answered, cold fury in his voice. "Thought he was being slick. Stupid motherfucker."

Back inside the Lodge, everything seemed normal: music was still playing, and people were dancing, laughing, chatting amongst themselves. Kimmy and Asha were dancing together in the centre of the floor, looking happier than I'd seen them look together. Tonight seemed like a big night for them, and it was about to be ruined.

I pulled back on John's hand, and he stopped, giving me a quizzical look. I leaned in close so he could hear over the music.

"Don't tell them," I said. "Just say I got sick or something. I don't want to spoil things for them."

"No," John said firmly. "They can do what they want, but I'm not keeping this secret."

He went to tap Kimmy on the shoulder. He spoke rapidly in her ear. She looked over in my direction with concern but nodded at whatever John said. She immediately leaned over to talk to Asha, who was still on her arm. John returned to me and took my hand again, leading me through the lounge and back outside to the truck.

"They'll be okay getting home without us?"

"Yeah," he said. "They'll get a ride with Danny and Jenna."

"Hey, Red!"

Zach was standing ten feet away under a tree, but he wasn't alone this time. The other four Jameson brothers were with him, smoking what I could only assume were hand-rolled cigarettes. My heartbeat resumed its frantic rhythm.

"The carpet match the drapes?"

A barrage of male laughter assaulted my ears.

"Hey Madigan, anyone ever tell you that sharing is caring?" one of the other brothers called. "Pass your compound whore around and let us all get a taste."

I flushed with humiliation and turned away. In an instant, John had stepped between me and them, partially shielding me from view.

"Ignore them," he muttered, glaring at the men as he held the passenger door open for me. They continued to shout what I assumed were more crude comments, but at least I couldn't make them out once the truck door was closed. John said something in reply, low and menacing, before getting in the truck.

The ride back to Summerhurst was silent, and though John appeared calm, I knew better. His hands were tight on the steering wheel, and tension emanated from him in waves.

I leaned back against the worn leather seat, staring out the window blankly. I felt as though something precious inside of me had been shattered. I'd been adapting to Valley life so well until tonight, and although I knew that full acceptance was still some way off, it seemed like I was making significant progress...enough that I'd allowed myself to feel secure. Remembering what I'd told John just a few nights ago brought tears of shame to my eyes.

I'd been so unbelievably naïve. Still, even now, more than a year after leaving the Cave, I was too stupid to understand the reality that being in the Wasteland meant I'd never be safe. Between the Order and the Jamesons, even the safest place in the Wasteland wasn't safe for *me*. I'd been so foolish to ever let my guard down for even a moment.

I swallowed against the bitter taste in my mouth. In some strange way, it was probably karmic justice that I was getting a taste of my own medicine from the Wastelanders I'd once feared and scorned. I was now the outsider in a world I wasn't built to survive in.

Once we were home, things were a blur. John told me he was going to lock up, and I nodded absently, feeling numb, before heading to our room. I felt oddly itchy, as though I wanted to crawl out of my own skin. I headed into the ensuite bathroom.

I turned on the shower and waited until the water was almost scalding. The heat was a relief. I scrubbed away the mysterious itch until my skin was red and angry-looking. I dried and changed into a heavy nightgown before getting into bed. I huddled under the covers, feeling chilled somehow despite nearly cooking myself.

John came in a few minutes later, stopping next to the bed with a glass of amber liquid in each hand.

"Here," he said softly, holding one out to me. "Thought you could use a drink."

I sat up slowly and took it. He lowered himself onto the bedside next to me and took a slow sip from his glass. I copied him, the whiskey burning my throat all the way down and igniting warmth in my belly.

We sat there for what seemed like a long time, silently sipping. Despite how wretched I felt, it was nice. Comfortable, the way it always was with John. His presence alone was always a balm on whatever ailed me.

When our glasses were empty, I lay back against the pillow. Drinking often made me sleepy, but right now, I felt like I may never sleep again.

"I know it's hard," John finally said, breaking the silence, "but I need to know if Zach made any specific threats. We need to be pre-pared."

I sighed. My tongue felt fuzzy, and it took me a moment to reply.

"He alluded to raping and strangling me. Then he promised that I'll never be safe here and told me to get out while I still can."

I let out a long breath. "I think he was just trying to scare me. This time, anyway."

"*This* time?" John repeated, his brow crinkling. "There won't be a next time. I won't allow it."

I snorted. "And just how do you plan to do that? You can't be there 24/7, Wastelander."

"Watch me," he said defiantly. "From now on, you won't be leaving my sight."

"How is that going to work?" I asked, pinching the bridge of my nose. "You have outrider duties, and I have a class full of students to go to four days a week."

He frowned. "You can't seriously plan to go back to school after this?"

"Of course I am," I replied, anger rising in my chest. "Those kids need an education, and it's my job. I'm not going to let a petty rich boy with a powerful father ruin this for me, or for the kids that need me."

John paced the room. "This isn't about some stupid grudge any-more. This is about your *safety*, for fuck's sake. I can't let you—"

"You're not 'letting' me do anything," I shot back. "I'm *telling* you my decision. This is the first thing that's made me feel like I really belong here, John. I feel useful for the first time since I left the Cave. I feel *wanted*. How can you want to take that away from me?"

He stopped pacing and crossed his arms. "I'm trying to keep you safe. It's either that, or I shoot him."

"We both know that's not an option," I said wearily. "Look, this is what he wants! He wants me to hide away and be marginalized, like I was before. You were the one who told me I had to not care about a few bad apples. Being a teacher isn't just good for me; it's making everyone else change their minds about outsiders. Why else would he threaten me now? It's because it's working, and he sees it as a threat, just like you said."

John stared at me, amber eyes burning. "You don't get it. I don't give a shit if you're finding the cure for all disease if it means I have to bury you, Claire. The world could be on fire, and I'd let it burn if it meant saving you. I know it's selfish...and I don't care."

His voice broke on the last word, and it stripped away the anger and frustration to reveal the truth: he was terrified. His posture was tense and rigid, but there was intense vulnerability in his eyes. *Every second you're in danger is agony.*

I took a deep breath to calm myself, then moved to take his face in my hands. He flinched at my touch, but then sighed and leaned into it. It seemed to soothe him, the way his touch did for me in times of distress, and I was glad.

"I understand," I said gently. "It's scary. But there has to be a way to keep me safe and not lose the progress we've made. Can't we at least try to come up with a plan?"

John followed my lead and took a deep breath before replying. I could practically see the wheels in his head begin to turn. He reached up and took my hands in his, then rattled off a list of security measures: he'd keep driving me to and from every class; I shouldn't answer the door for anyone but him, Kimmy, or Asha; I had to carry my pistol at all times.

He shifted, as if knowing I wouldn't like what he had to say next.

"And finally, in the morning, I'm going to officially report this to Danny."

Memories from the woodshed fire came rushing back. Reporting it hadn't helped; if anything, it'd made everyone more suspicious and more convinced of my incompetence. I didn't want to make an accusation that would just backfire and make me look like a troublemaker.

"But—"

"It's not just about you," John interjected. "He made a direct threat, and I'm an outrider. Just like it's your job to go into a classroom and teach even when some asshole might kill you, it's my job to report threats to my Chief."

I sighed. "Okay. I get it."

"Good. Let's get some rest."

CHAPTER 33

John

"Well, he's dumb as shit," Danny said the next evening, sitting behind his desk at the outrider station. "Denied everything, but then when I told Claire's side of the story, he flipped his lid and said she deserved it. So."

"Piece of shit," I spat. "He's lucky I didn't kill him on the spot."

"Yeah, I'm sure that would've gone over well with old Jameson," Danny replied doubtfully. "After all, what's a little homicide between old friends?"

I blew out a breath of frustration. If he'd been outside the Valley, he'd already be dead. I'd gotten too used to handling everything myself, being away from home so long.

"Anyway, he's got a formal warning to stay away from her now," he continued.

"What if he doesn't?"

Danny drummed his fingers on the desk. "Kind of uncharted territory. Not like we have to order people to stay away from each other that often. But even if we did, Claire's an outsider. I don't honestly know if the same rules apply."

"You can bet Jameson will say they don't, just to save his loser son."

I paced the room, unable to stand still.

"Buddy, you're gonna wear a track into my floor," Danny said. "Look, whatever the rules say, I'm gonna do what I can to protect your girl. If he comes around her again, I'll handle it. The thing I'm most worried about is that you can't go and kill this kid. You've been an outside cat for too long. Don't do something stupid."

I exhaled slowly, reining in my anger. "I won't. Even if he fucking deserves it."

"Glad to hear it. Go get ready for the night shift. It'll be you, me, and Will, and he doesn't laugh at my jokes, so I'll be fighting for my life over the radio tonight."

Despite my mood, I laughed. "Noted."

I briefly visited Kimmy at the clinic before my evening shift. She was showing Asha around the place, telling her about the job, and to my surprise, Asha actually seemed interested.

"But you're heading off on another scav trip tomorrow morning," Kimmy said, her tone teasing, "abandoning me again."

Asha kissed her, and I just about fell over. Of course, I knew something had been going on between them, but I'd never seen Asha show affection in front of anyone before. Kimmy actually blushed, and I hated how much harder that made it to dislike Asha.

I think I've seen Kimmy blush a grand total of twice in my entire life, I thought as I walked through the lounge for the front door of the Lodge. *Fuck me, I'm gonna have to start calling her my sister-in-law eventually, aren't I?*

There were a few people hanging out in the lounge area, including—for fuck's sake—Zach Jameson. He was sitting by the fireplace with his brother, and he gave me a death glare as I walked out. It took real effort not to react, but I ignored him, and thankfully, he didn't stir the pot.

I wanted to take it as a good sign, but I just felt uneasy.

Another night, another patrol.

As Danny said, it was just me, him, and a younger guy called Will who'd only started a couple months before I did. It was two in the morning, and it'd been an uneventful night. After hours of boredom, Danny decided to entertain us—or realistically, *himself*—by telling lame jokes over the radio every so often.

"Command to Ghost and Copper," my radio buzzed for what felt like the hundredth time. "I'm great for protection. You use your fingers to get me off. What am I?"

I led Ghost in a canter towards the outer edge of the Valley. The night was calm, and though the air was still cool, spring was finally here. Soon enough, we'd start planting some of the bigger crops.

Meanwhile, I rolled my eyes and lifted my radio to my lips. "Seriously, man, how old are you?"

He didn't reply right away, so I finished my perimeter check, then steered Ghost back towards the interior. I rode for a few minutes in silence.

"Ghost to Command," I said into the radio. "Everything okay?"

No response. I frowned. It wasn't like Danny to not reply right away, but maybe he'd spotted something. I kept riding farther into the Valley, but when another ten minutes had passed without a response, I knew something was wrong.

Will's voice came over the radio. "Copper to Ghost: you heard from Command? Haven't heard anything since last transmission."

"No," I replied. "Starting search. Stay on your route and wait for my call."

He agreed, and I took off in the opposite direction to follow Danny's patrol. He'd been on the northern route while I'd taken the eastern perimeter. It'd take some time to get there.

On the way, I kept trying to reach Danny, but he never responded. The silence of the night felt suddenly eerie. My chest was tight with worry. Danny was a jokester, but not about things that really mattered. He wouldn't do this just for a laugh.

The northern route had the toughest terrain because there were only a few homesteads on this end of the Valley. The brush was thick, and the patrol path was narrow. The ground was rocky and uneven, which meant Ghost had to tread carefully.

The radio buzzed, and for a minute, only static came through. Then came Danny's voice, weak and rough-sounding.

"Command to..."

He trailed off, and more static came through.

"Command, this is Ghost," I replied, trying to keep my voice level. "What's your position?"

No reply. My grip on the reins tightened. I continued along the patrol route, but I was slower than I needed to be. Static came through a couple more times.

"Danny," I said into the radio, ditching protocol. My tone sounded more frantic than I liked. "If you can hear me, please tell me where you're at. Come on, man."

Nothing. *God fucking damn it.*

We reached a stretch of flatter ground, and I urged Ghost to go faster. The darkness deepened as we headed farther into the woods, and I had no choice but to use my flashlight. Almost as soon I clicked the light on, Danny called out, "Hey! Over here!"

I followed the direction of his voice, and just off the path up ahead, I came on the gruesome scene. Danny was lying on his back on top of some bushes, groaning with pain. He couldn't move because from the knee down, his left leg was pinned underneath his horse, which was very dead. The horse's head was bloody; he'd been shot.

"Fuck," I muttered as I dismounted, rifle in hand, and grabbed my medical kit from my saddlebag. I waded through the brush to reach him. "What the hell happened?"

"Don't know," Danny replied through gritted teeth. "Heard a shot, then Bolt tumbled. Tried to call you, but...blacked out, I think."

I ran my flashlight through the trees all around us, searching for anyone nearby, but it was dark and quiet now. Owls hooted in the distance. Could someone be watching through a scope? I didn't know, but I also didn't have a lot of options. Danny needed emergency care.

"You hurt anywhere else?" I asked, dropping beside him.

"Don't think so," he answered, wincing.

I did a quick exam to make sure, but other than some gnarly bruising, the rest of him seemed fine. I made a radio call to Will, telling him our location and calling for reinforcements. Kimmy was working at the clinic, so she'd be the one treating him. For now, I had to figure out how to move Bolt's corpse off his leg as carefully as possible.

My medical kit had a small bottle of morphine for emergencies like this one. I loaded the syringe and injected Danny. I led Ghost over to the scene and unhooked a spool of rope from her saddle. Over the next few minutes, I tied Bolt's legs together, then tied the loose ends around Ghost's shoulders, building a makeshift harness.

I hoped she'd be able to drag the dead horse far enough that Danny could slide his leg out.

"A few inches is all we need," I said.

"That's what she said," Danny replied, but whatever effect he wanted was ruined by his laboured breathing.

"Danny, now is not the time," I growled. I knelt beside the horse corpse, shoving my arms underneath it. I clicked my tongue to signal Ghost, and as she pulled, I lifted the dead horse upward, off Danny's leg.

"Now!" I said, and with a horrible scream, Danny slid his leg out. I let the horse fall back to the ground.

There was no way to soften the blow: his leg was gory as shit. Crushed below the knee, and his ankle was turned at an unnatural angle. Blood oozed from the site of a clean break, where his shin bone protruded from the skin.

Danny's skin was ashen and pale, and his breathing was fast and shallow. His eyes were glazed, but he'd relaxed some, which I hoped meant that the morphine was working.

"Johnny," he gritted out. "Don't leave me here."

I reached out and took his hand. "I'm not going anywhere, buddy."

I waited for what felt like an eternity for a radio call. Danny passed out, which was probably for the best, and I wrapped up his leg as best I could. Finally, more outriders arrived. Someone had driven their truck as close to our location as possible so they could drive him to the clinic. With effort, we managed to get Danny over the rocky terrain and down to the vehicle without fucking up his leg even worse. Some of the others stayed behind to investigate the scene.

When we finally made it to the clinic, relief surged through me at Kimmy's presence. She set to work immediately, barking orders at us like a drill sergeant as she prepared for surgery. Granny would've been proud.

I stayed by Danny's side while the others went to round up his family.

"John," Danny croaked as Kimmy prepared anesthetic to put him under. "Gloves."

I frowned. "What?"

"Gloves," he repeated, like it was super important. "The answer was gloves."

I stared at him. "To your stupid joke?"

He grinned like he was the funniest guy in the world, then immediately passed out again. I sighed. *Trust Danny to give me the punchline even on death's fucking door.*

❊

The days after Danny was attacked were grim.

Kimmy managed to set his leg—a minor miracle—but she predicted permanent nerve damage. He may also walk with a limp. His ankle was broken in several places, and she'd done her best to set it and put it back together, but it'd likely never be the same. She kept him there overnight, and his poor grandparents looked like they'd keel over with worry. They depended on him more than ever, and he'd struggle to support them with the coming harvest.

Jenna was beside herself when she arrived at the Lodge. She'd always thought of her big brother as invincible. With Danny's sense of bravado, maybe we all had. Isla joined her in the grand hall, where they sat and cried together.

I was exhausted, and the only relief came when Claire arrived. Seeing her beautiful face, even when she looked so worried, instantly made things a little better. She didn't speak, just pulled me into her arms and held me close. I buried my face in her hair and inhaled the comforting scent of her.

An attack on the Chief Outrider had never happened before, and that scared the shit out of everybody at the council meeting the next day. Worse, it'd been totally unprovoked. The investigation of the scene turned up nothing, other than that whoever had done this had been careful to cover their tracks...and that Danny's radio was missing. They combed the area searching for it, but it was gone.

I tried, over and over, to remember if I'd seen it when I found him, but I hadn't. That suggested his attacker took it. They'd also killed the horse but left Danny alive. How had they found their way into the Valley? And what were the odds that some random outsider had just happened to cross paths with Danny?

Nothing made sense, and at the council meeting, everyone seemed to feel either anxious or suspicious. I was in the second category.

I watched Jameson carefully as he led the meeting, Abby by his side. To his credit, he seemed as shocked as the rest of us. Unlike his father, though, Zach seemed agitated. After his threats toward Claire, he seemed like the obvious suspect. The problem was that he had no clear motive for hurting Danny or stealing from him. He saw outsiders—and me, I guessed—as a threat to his family's power, but Danny wasn't. That said, having access to the radio would give him insight into where all the outriders were at any given time, including me.

I clenched my jaw, watching Zach fidget in his seat.

The meeting ended with no real resolution other than we'd keep investigating. None of us knew what to do, or who to trust. Violence was rare in our small community. In my few months as an outrider, the most I'd ever had to do was break up a drunken brawl or mediate a heated argument between neighbours. This was way beyond anything we normally dealt with.

The morning after that, I drove Claire to school, along with a hefty pile of books she wanted to bring into the classroom. Books stacked in my arms, I pushed open the schoolroom door...and stopped dead.

Claire's mural, painted on the back wall of the room, had been defaced. Long, dried streaks of what looked like blood spelled out *GO HOME, WHORE.*

My blood ran cold as Claire followed behind me.

"You can just leave the books on the desk, darling," she was saying as I turned to block the door.

It was too late. Her eyes got huge. "What the hell is that?"

Her voice came out high-pitched and terrified, and I rushed to do damage control.

"Turn around and walk out to the lounge," I ordered. "This is a crime scene."

She did as I said, but I couldn't erase the heartbroken look she gave me. I closed the door to the schoolroom and made my way across the building to the command center.

All we could be sure about was that this wasn't over.

CHAPTER 34

Claire

If John had been wary after Zach Jameson's threat at the dance, he was downright paranoid in the week after Danny's attack and the vandalism in the schoolroom. He stuck to me like glue at any moment that I wasn't teaching. Now that planting season had started in earnest, he had Kimmy run the tractor so that he could be at my side every morning for chores. He drove me to and from school on teaching days. When he had to work on the farm or in the distillery, he took me with him, and when he had to patrol, he left me with Kimmy, the only person besides himself that he trusted to protect me. No matter where we were, he was alert, on guard, watching our surroundings like a hawk.

The only time I was ever alone was in the house, though even there, he tended to hover over me, as though worried I might spontaneously burst into flames. Even still, I felt his fear, because every single night since the vandalism, he'd made love to me—sometimes tender and sweet, other times rough and urgent and anxious, like he couldn't get enough of me before I disappeared forever.

"I'm alright, love," I murmured after one such session, stroking his hair. He'd laid his head against my naked chest, every part of his body touching mine, his arms firmly around my middle.

"I know," he sighed, and he stayed there like that, quiet and still, until I fell asleep.

The parents of my students were shaken, too. I saw it in their eyes when they dropped their kids off. Even so, several of them pulled me aside and expressed their support for me, and how much they wanted me to stay on. If that hadn't convinced me, the continued development of my students would have; they remained as bright and engaged as ever, even with the massive sheet I'd had to hang on the back wall to conceal the writing. I'd have to find time, eventually, to paint over the offensive message.

Under a microscope, the Valley's medical team had determined that the blood used on the wall wasn't human, which was the only good news about the incident. There were few viable suspects, since school had been cancelled the day after Danny's attack. The vandalism could've happened anytime between the night of his attack and the next school day, a whole day later. In that time, dozens of people had passed through the Lodge, and nobody claimed to have seen anything suspicious.

There didn't seem to be any movement on finding the culprit behind Danny's attack, either. One thing seemed certain, at least in John's mind: it hadn't been done by an outsider. Indeed, there was no evidence in the weeks to come that anyone had breached the Valley's security. John naturally suspected Zach, but there was no proof, despite continued investigation.

I hated that he never felt at ease anymore, but in the end, I was grateful for his constant vigilance, even when it was inconvenient. It made me feel safer at a time when everything seemed unstable and uncertain.

A week after the vandalism, I sat in the living room with Kimmy and Asha while John was on patrol. It was late evening, and fire crackled in the fireplace as Kimmy sat in the recliner with her knitting. Wrapped in a blanket on the sofa, I consulted a farmer's almanac for useful information on the upcoming growing season. Asha simply sat on the other end of the couch, a hot mug of tea in her hand.

Kimmy set down her knitting with a yawn. "I think I'll head to bed, if it's alright with you."

She looked over at Asha, who nodded and replied, "Wait for me. I'll be up in a few minutes."

I raised my eyebrows. They usually didn't openly go to bed together and had separate rooms. I couldn't miss the spark in Kimmy's eyes as she bid me goodnight and headed upstairs.

"That's new," I said, nudging Asha with my foot. "Look at you, playing house with your girlfriend."

She grinned, but it didn't reach her eyes. For several minutes, the silence between us was deafening, yet she looked as though she wanted to speak.

"What are you thinking, Asha?" I finally asked. "You have that silent, brooding thing happening again."

She sighed again. "I'm thinking about the message on the schoolroom wall. The way the Wastelanders here will never accept us, no matter how kind you are to them. No matter what you do."

I frowned. "I don't think that's true."

"Then why do you live like a prisoner now?" she asked, her mouth pressed into a thin line. "You can't go anywhere without him. You have to stay inside, tucked away, so no one can hurt you. It's wrong."

"John is protecting me," I replied steadily. "It won't be forever, but it's a difficult time right now. When things calm down—"

"Things will never calm down," Asha cut in. "It's been months, Claire. Months that you pledge your loyalty and serve a community of people who have such disdain for you that they deface the very place that you teach their children."

"It wasn't everyone," I retorted. "The parents of my students wouldn't do that."

"How long are you going to keep defending these Wastelanders?" Asha demanded, springing to her feet. "How long are you and I going to try hopelessly to fit in with these Wastelanders who scorn us, who never wanted us? Next time Zach Jameson comes around, what if he hurts you? You could be killed."

"That was always a risk," I said wearily. "I knew that long before we got here."

"And you were willing to settle, because you had no choice."

I felt a prickle of irritation. "I did have a choice. I chose to stay with John and Kimmy."

"When the alternative is going it alone or being dumped in some other nowhere town with Wastelanders you didn't know, is it really a choice? Even Farm Boy is preferable to that."

She sat back in her chair, folding her arms across her chest and eyeing me with an air of superiority that rankled me to my core.

"You care for Kimmy," I said coldly. "She's just as much a Wastelander as John or anyone else here, by Cave standards."

For the first time, Asha hesitated. "Kimmy's different."

"In what way?" I asked, annoyed. "Because she immediately reached out to you and tried to bridge the gap between how you lived before and how you have to live now? She did that for me, too. It's who she is. She's a wonderful person...as are many of the people who live here, if you'd bother to notice."

Asha clucked her tongue impatiently. "There were plenty of them willing to toss us out. Only reason they didn't is because John held their feet to the fire."

"Yeah, which somehow didn't warm you to him at all," I shot back. "He saved you from that."

"You think he gives a damn what happens to me?" she replied huffily. "He did that for you. I was the spare."

She shook her head. "You're doing what you always do, making excuses for these Wastelanders who act exactly like Wastelanders do: they're willing to do anything to keep even the tiny bit of power they've carved out for themselves."

"Our compound was no better," I argued. "We killed not only Wastelanders, but our own people, ostensibly to keep the peace."

"But at least we lived in safety!" Asha burst out, folding her arms. "Safety and comfort. Here, we make do with what we've got, but this'll never stop being a backwater bit of nowhere, Claire, and you know it."

I clenched my jaw. "Summerhurst isn't nowhere. It's our home."

"Yeah, sure, it's you and John's home. It'll never be mine."

The words landed like a blow. After months of trying to fit in, I'd finally found my place in the Valley...but Asha hadn't. Asha, who was gone as often as she could be. Who'd made no real friends and seemed to have no desire to.

"If that's how you feel," I said, rubbing my eyes, "then how do you expect to stay here?"

Asha bit her lip. "What if there was a way to go home? And that we could go—you and me."

I balked. "What do you mean? Home is gone."

"Just answer. What would you do if you had a real choice—if you and I could leave, go back to something like our old lives?"

I tensed at the suggestion. For the first time, I felt true disgust toward Asha. She would throw away what we had for the half-life we'd once lived?

"How could you ask me that?" I said, unable to keep the indignation out of my voice.

"Before you get upset, think about it," Asha replied, holding up her hands defensively. "You'd finally be safe again. No more looking over your shoulder for the Order, or for backward Wastelanders who feel threatened just by your presence. Imagine walking down the street without worry. And having all the things you miss—libraries, stores, proper school supplies for your students. Imagine going grocery shopping again instead of slaving away in a field, for God's sake."

As she spoke, my old life came alive again in my mind's eye, filled with all the modern conveniences I couldn't deny I sometimes missed. In many ways, daily life was certainly easier in the compound. But it came at a steep price of freedom and autonomy, and of the kind of love that I had with John.

Even if I had to look over my shoulder for the rest of my life, I wanted to be with him. He was part of me now, and he made me stronger. He was the one who taught me what it meant to be brave.

"I love John," I said softly, leaning back against my pillow. "And I love the Valley."

"But—"

"I'll always choose them, Asha. You were right that you're not the friend I remember, but here's something you missed: I'm not, either."

Asha stared at me with genuine hurt in her eyes, but I held fast. I wouldn't entertain any more fantasies about a place that was gone, and a time that was dead and buried. More than that, I'd found my true family outside the Walls. With them, I was finally free, and maybe that also meant it was time to let go of the person I kept wishing Asha would become again. That person had died along with the Cave.

"I'm sorry you haven't found your place here," I continued as I stood to leave, "but I have nothing left to give you."

❋

It was evening on the first day of May, and there was a knock on the front door. Kimmy and I sat in the living room again, this time alone. John was once again on patrol, and for whatever reason, tonight I felt his absence more keenly. I wished he was there to cuddle with me on the sofa and make me laugh. Since the conversation with Asha days before, a gloom had settled over me that I couldn't shake. She hadn't spoken to me since, and she'd left us behind again on a scav mission.

Kimmy frowned as someone knocked for a second time; we hadn't been expecting anyone. Shooting me a look that told me to stay put, she left. A moment later, I heard the door open.

"Scott! What a surprise," Kimmy said, her voice floating down the hall. "What brings you here?"

"I wanted to let Claire know that I finally managed to decrypt the drive she brought me months ago. Is she home?"

My heart leapt. Neil's drive, addressed to me. In truth, I'd forgotten all about it. I jumped up from the sofa and padded down the hall to the entryway.

"Hello, Scott," I said brightly. "I heard what you said. Did you manage to open the drive?"

He smiled pleasantly at me, his glasses on his nose.

"I did," he replied. "There was only one file on it. It's a document. A letter, I think. Addressed to you. I didn't read it."

"Oh," I said, surprised. "Alright."

"I can show it to you, but you'll have to come back with me," he said.

I paused, looking at Kimmy. "Do you think—"

"I'll come with you," she interjected. "We'd be happy to."

Scott drove Kimmy and I back to his family's strange house in his truck. I followed him the same way as before, down winding halls, until we reached the computer lab. He led me to one of the machines, where the screen was open on what indeed appeared to be a letter.

I took a deep breath and sat in the chair, Kimmy at my side. Both she and Scott hovered around me, and suddenly I couldn't read my dead husband's words with an audience. I had no idea what he'd needed to tell me, but whatever it was, it felt like it deserved privacy.

"Sorry, but...do you two mind waiting outside the door?" I asked meekly. "I just...I want to read his last words...in private."

They exchanged an awkward glance but then nodded.

"Of course," Kimmy said, squeezing my shoulder. "I'll be right out there if you need me."

She and Scott went to stand outside the open doorway, and with another breath, I began to read Neil's last letter.

Dear Claire,

If you're reading this, it means my work here has been discovered. I'm sorry.

For some time, I've been researching the circumstances of your father's death. I know how important he was to you, and I haven't been able to get your suspicions out of my mind.

As a physician, I gained access to his medical records, which provided me with two key findings: 1) his death certificate records his death as undetermined, not homicide, and is marked with an unusual, stylized 'X' symbol, and 2) you are his only biological child.

I tracked down dozens more death certificates marked with this 'X' symbol, with no explanation. All these deaths were marked undetermined, or in some cases, 'disappeared', with no further detail. Unfor-

tunately, I haven't uncovered the symbol's meaning. Given the little I know about our compound's leadership, I can only speculate that they stepped out of line in some way and perhaps paid the ultimate price.

There are few clues to Holly's true paternity. Your father's name is on her birth certificate. He may not have known she wasn't his. I hope you may remember something that can help solve the mystery. I don't know if this is connected to your father's death, but I thought you deserved to know.

Alongside this, there are rumours of an insurgent movement within our compound. I hear whispers from patients and colleagues. Be wary and trust no one, including your sister.

No matter what happens, I wish you well. We may not have chosen one another, but you've been a friend to me in our short time together. You, and everyone else, deserve the truth.

Yours,

Neil Lockhart, M.D.

February 28, 2097

⁕

Whatever I might have expected from Neil's last letter, it wasn't this. It was dated the day before the attack on the compound. I knew he'd had his suspicions about something dangerous happening at the Cave, but he'd clearly known far more than he'd ever had the chance to tell me. My heart ached for him. He may not have been the great love of my life, but he deserved so much better than what he got.

I took a moment to silently remember Neil and thank him for his efforts. Then I scanned the words over and over, as though that would make it easier to understand the incomprehensible. I examined Neil's first finding; I couldn't even wrap my mind around the second one.

He confirmed what I'd always feared and suspected: my father was not killed by Wastelanders while on patrol. But that answer, as much as I'd craved it, only opened up new and harder questions, especially knowing that his records were marked in the same strange way as other mysterious deaths in the compound.

*How did he really die? Did they kill him because of his failed re-
bellion, like my mother claimed? Who were the real leaders of our
compound, and what did they have to hide?*

The worst part was that I had no way to find out now. I couldn't
return to the Cave, and it seemed unlikely that there'd ever be an
opportunity to interrogate the leadership, given that they may have
perished in the attack...and I didn't even know who they were.

I couldn't have prepared myself for the revelation about Holly. I'd
never had a hint from either of my parents that she wasn't my father's.

But the more I thought about it, the more it made sense. My
parents' collapsing marriage. My mother's posthumous hatred of my
father, and her animosity towards me: his only child. The way my
mother had always favoured Holly...the daughter of her lover, who she
really wanted. How she'd inducted Holly into her cult first, without
giving me a second thought. My mother would've happily allowed
me to die in the slaughter at the Cave because my very existence had
become offensive to her. I was a constant reminder of a person she
deeply resented, and of a past she'd rather forget.

As painful as it was to acknowledge, I also knew that as much as my
mother favoured Holly, my father had also favoured me. I was the one
he told stories to, taught music to, shared his passions with. Because,
from my red hair to my love of painting, I was like him. Because I was
his daughter.

I had no proof, but that led me to believe that he knew. The leaders
of our compound didn't tolerate unsanctioned pregnancies between
unapproved parties. My mother must've applied to have a child with
my father and gotten pregnant with another man instead. My father
was the sort of man who'd have given Holly his name to protect
her. He wouldn't have wanted her to suffer whatever consequences
may have come. But that didn't mean he wouldn't have resented my
mother forever for it. Stuck in a compound that didn't allow divorce,
their unhappiness had many years to fester.

I turned over more memories, of the months prior to the attack.
Holly had pulled away from me suddenly, and frozen me out, despite
our once-close relationship. I'd never known her to be so cold and
distant before.

She knew. That was the only conclusion that made sense. She
must've found out, or else my mother had told her the truth. I could

only imagine the inner turmoil that would've caused her, to have her sense of self and place in the world suddenly stripped away from her. Vulnerable, hurt, and seeking something to replace that sense of identity, she'd have been an ideal target for a cult.

Unfortunately, my memories revealed no candidates for Holly's biological father. Holly and I were only four years apart, which meant that I was a small child whenever the affair initially happened, and my mother never brought men around the house after my father died. It was one of the many reasons that seeing her with Jim J, that night at the Cave, had shocked me.

A horrible sensation—as though I was falling—jolted in the pit of my stomach. I suddenly couldn't bear the thought of staying one more minute in this small computer lab. I shot to my feet and made for the door, where Scott and Kimmy were waiting.

"Get everything you need?" Scott's face was friendly and open, and totally inappropriate for everything I felt at the moment.

"Yes, thanks," I replied hurriedly. I was going to vomit; I was sure of it.

"Claire?" Kimmy said, concerned.

I swallowed back bile and rushed down the hallway, determined to get outside before it happened.

"Wait! Do you not want your drive back?" Scott called after me, sounding puzzled.

"No. Burn it."

The last thing I remembered was his befuddled expression as I made it outside and promptly emptied my stomach on his lawn.

CHAPTER 35

John

As usual, it was late when I got home that night. The first thing I noticed was light pouring into the hallway from the living room. I frowned. Typically, everybody was asleep by now.

Claire was curled up on the recliner by the fireplace, a glass of wine in her hand. The lamp was on beside her, and the fire burned low, in need of another log or two. A half-empty bottle of wine from the cellar stood on the side table to her left. I'd never known her to drink much, never mind by herself.

If that hadn't tipped me off, her face would've. She looked lost, and her eyes were a little red, like she'd been crying.

"What's wrong, beautiful? Why are you up?"

Her bottom lip trembled, and she drained her glass. "Sit with me."

She moved to make room for me on the recliner. I sat and pulled her half onto my lap, enclosing her in my arms. It was a tight fit, but I didn't care. She needed me. In my world, that overrode everything else.

Claire rested her head against the hollow of my collarbone and took a deep breath. As I stroked her hair, she told me about Neil's last letter and the bombshells he'd dropped from beyond the grave. I listened quietly, letting her unload.

"And now I don't know what to feel," she finished. "I'll still never know what happened to my father. And I'll never be able to reconcile with Holly."

She trembled a little in my arms. I held her tighter because it was all I could do. Grief was a wound you lived with forever, as much as I wished I could heal it for her.

"But the worst part is...about Holly's father..."

Claire trailed off, like it was too hard to even get the sentence out. Somehow, though, I sensed her thoughts.

"You think it's Jim J," I finally said after a minute.

"Do you think I'm wrong?" she asked, her voice a squeak. The thought clearly scared her, and some part of her probably wanted me to disagree.

I sighed. "No. But I also don't think it changes anything, baby."

Her shoulder dropped and she sagged against me, defeated. I swallowed hard. I understood why this would haunt her, but I also knew that there was no way to get what she wanted: the truth.

"You're right," she said softly, and to my regret, she started to pull away. "I should head to bed. I have school in the morning."

She was shutting down, keeping me at arm's length. A sinking feeling took over me.

"Claire, baby, I didn't mean to—"

"You didn't," she cut in, disentangling herself from me. "You're right: there's nothing I can do. My life is here now. I...need to be strong."

"You don't," I murmured, sitting up as she stood. "Even if we can't change anything...you're allowed to grieve. You told me that, and you were right. I just...don't want you to torture yourself forever with questions we can't answer. Especially with everything we're dealing with right now."

She gave me what looked like a painful smile.

"Come to bed with me?" she asked, and I nodded. In bed, I held her close again, but she stayed rigid and quiet. I had only one thing left to offer her.

"Claire?"

"Yes?"

"I love you," I murmured. "I know it doesn't make anything better...but I do."

At last, I felt the angles of her body soften against me.

"I love you too," she whispered back, laying her head in the pocket of my shoulder. "It doesn't make it better...but it makes it bearable."

Part V: Bluebird

O ut flew the web and floated wide;
     The mirror crack'd from side to side;
"The curse is come upon me," cried
     The Lady of Shalott.

\-   "The Lady of Shalott", Alfred Lord Tennyson

CHAPTER 36

John

Over the next month, the growing season kicked into full swing. We were planting like crazy, tending to crops, and brewing liquor. I taught Claire how to drive the tractor, how to brew whiskey, and how to fuck against the back wall of the barn. She seemed especially keen on the last lesson, and I wasn't complaining.

Like she had at our camp, Claire thrived on learning, and it was a welcome distraction from the shit show we'd been dealing with recently. She seemed to put Neil's letter out of her mind, and I was thankful for her. She really was embracing her new life here, and it was beautiful to watch her grow.

I still visited my grandparents' grave every week, but at the start of May, I noticed a small bouquet of flowers left on their grave. The next week, they'd been replaced with fresh ones, and the week after that, the same.

"It's nice that you left flowers," I said to Kimmy one afternoon. "I always forget."

She chuckled. "That wasn't me. Claire does it, every week now that we have flowers again."

An unexpected lump formed in my throat. She loved this place like I did, and she honoured people she'd never met because they mattered to me. And she didn't even tell me, because she didn't do it for praise. She did it because she cared, and that was the core of who Claire was. Kind, and good, and more than her piece-of-shit family ever deserved.

Christ, I'm so fucking gone for her. This wedding cannot come quickly enough.

That evening, I showed Claire the rose garden, where our wedding would be at the beginning of July. Guarded by a white fence, the garden was neglected, but she immediately loved it, and we got to work restoring it. She dug into the dirt to plant tulips, happy as a clam, and I couldn't help chuckling at how far she'd come from that day on the rooftop.

Her birthday was at the start of June, and I was going to make good on my promise to take her to the spring festival. It was already a beautiful spring morning when I got home. Since it was her birthday, I'd let Claire sleep in while I went to visit Nimkii at Whitefeather. I dropped off my bag at the door, carrying a brown paper package into the kitchen. Asha sat at the table eating breakfast, which surprised me, since she was so rarely home. Not that I was complaining.

"Morning," she said to me, and I raised an eyebrow.

She never talked to me unless she had to. *What's the occasion?*

"Morning," I answered, a little wary as I set the package on the countertop. "You just get back from scavving?"

She nodded. "I decided to stick around for today."

"Why's that?"

"It's Claire's birthday," she said, like I was stupid. "Her twenty-eighth, in case you didn't know."

I rolled my eyes. "I know when my wife's birthday is. I just don't know why you care, since you barely show up at the best of times."

Asha dismissed me with a wave of her hand. "I don't have to explain why I'm here for my best friend's birthday."

"Best friend?" I repeated with a dark chuckle. "Is that what we're calling it?"

She turned her nose up at me, her mouth forming a thin line. I didn't actually want to fight with Asha today, so instead of saying something else that might push her buttons, I asked, "Speaking of Claire, is she still asleep?"

"Nope," Asha replied. "She's out there."

She gestured towards outside. On a one-hundred-acre homestead. Helpful.

Thankfully, I heard the back door open in the hallway, and Claire entered with a basket full of eggs. It was still chilly in the mornings, so her cheeks were pink, and her pretty red hair was windswept. She looked, as usual, like a painting—too soft and ethereal to be real. She gave me a sweet smile, green eyes bright, as I approached.

"Hey, beautiful," I said, dropping a kiss on her lips. "Happy birthday."

She smiled wider, then set down her basket and wrapped her arms around my neck, pulling me down for another, longer kiss. She slipped her tongue past my lips, making me groan softly and hold her closer.

"Thank you," Claire replied after we broke apart. "But I'm more excited about the wedding next month."

"Why not both?" I asked, touching her cheek. "We've got lots to celebrate. You still want to go to the spring festival today?"

She nodded emphatically. "I've never been to a Wastelander festival before."

"Pretty sure it's like any other festival."

She giggled. "I know that. It's just different for me, because I'm the outsider here."

I kissed her again. "Not anymore. I think I've totally corrupted you into a Valley girl now."

"You mean converted?"

"That's what I said," I teased, grinning at her. "Time for your present."

Claire frowned. "Present? You already got me a horse."

"That was a wedding present," I insisted. "This is a birthday gift. Totally different thing."

"John," she scolded, eyebrows raised, but it was half-hearted. "You've already gotten me plenty."

"I'll be the judge of that."

I led her into the kitchen, where Asha had vacated the table and gone off I-didn't-give-a-fuck-where. So much for needing to be there for her best friend's birthday.

I picked up the small package I'd left on the counter and held it out to Claire. She took it, shooting me a curious look before unwrapping the brown paper.

A blue hooded cloak spilled out of the package. Made from velvet using a wool-linen blend, I special ordered it from Nimkii months ago. I went with blue since it was Claire's favourite colour, and Claire had told me everyone always put redheads in green. It was probably the softest fabric I'd ever felt.

"Oh," Claire gasped, holding it up to examine the adjustable ribbons at the neck. "How did you—why did you—"

She looked up at me with watery eyes. The next thing I knew, the air was pushed out of me by one of Claire's signature bone-crushing hugs. I gasped, then chuckled weakly, stroking her hair.

"You like it, then?" I managed to get out.

She let me go, pressing a hard kiss against my lips.

"It's beautiful," she said in a near-whisper. "I love it. Thank you."

My heart squeezed at the sincerity in her voice.

"But it must've cost a small fortune," she continued, a little guiltily. "With the wedding clothes, too..."

She wasn't wrong; it hadn't come cheap. But I also had more PNCs than I'd use in a lifetime, so it evened out in my mind. I'd also never had anyone I wanted to spoil before her. It didn't help that she was so obviously delighted every time I did.

"Don't worry," I said, kissing her forehead. "We're doing fine. But if it makes you feel better, I can crack the whip extra hard come harvest season—make you really work for it."

She laughed. "Alright. Do your worst."

❄

The spring festival that afternoon was like I remembered, other than a few new vendors. The Post was decked out with more stalls and tents than usual, selling everything from essentials like food and weapons to random Old World trinkets that were good for nothing but satisfying people's curiosity.

"Ride with me today, Ash," Claire had said happily to Asha before we left, offering her a hand from Poppy's back.

With her blue velvet cloak, her red hair half-up, and her skin shining in the sunlight, she looked like a faerie, as my grandmother would've said. On horseback, she was even more striking than usual, and something about it pulled on my heartstrings. She looked *right*. Confident. Like she belonged there.

Asha had hesitated, staring at her hand for a minute before slowly taking it. To my surprise, she actually smiled a little at Claire as she climbed onto Poppy's back. It didn't make me like her any more than before, but for Claire's sake, I was glad. I wanted her to have her old friend back...even if that friend still hated my guts.

It seemed like everything had burst into bloom overnight. The grass was green; flowers had popped up everywhere; and sunshine beamed down on us as we left Ghost, Bella, and Poppy at the stable. I walked around with Claire, letting her explore. I'd brought some strawberries to trade in my bag, since they'd just ripened.

"Such a nice day," Claire said as the four of us walked down the busy street. "Look, John. A bluebird."

She pointed at the streak of blue that flew by and landed on a nearby tree. I couldn't help smiling. I touched the small bluebird charm at my belt.

"I always think of you when I see one," I replied, putting my arm around her shoulders as we walked. "Granny said that they were a symbol of hope. Seems fitting."

Claire flushed a little, and I kissed the top of her head.

"Get a room," Kimmy said from just behind us, and Claire laughed. "I don't like this side of my brother you've brought out, Claire. It's harder to mock him when he's sweet to you."

"I'm sure you'll find a way," I replied, rolling my eyes.

As usual, Asha was quiet and unimpressed.

We stopped at a flower stand, where Kimmy admired the azaleas and traded for seeds to plant in the flower garden. Claire stopped by one of the Old World trinket stalls because they had a tiny selection of books. I traded for a couple, to add to our ever-growing stacks in the storage shed at Summerhurst.

Further down the street, a three-piece band was playing music, and a small crowd of people were gathered, listening and dancing. Claire's eyes lit up.

"Come dance with me," she said, tugging on my hand, and I chuckled.

"Not a chance. Too many people."

"You'll be fine," she insisted. "Please?"

I kissed her. "I'd rather watch you, baby."□

She pretended to pout, but then smiled and went to dance in the centre of the crowd.

"It's been a long time since I danced," Asha said to Kimmy, holding out her hand. "Let's do it."

I stared at her in total surprise. Kimmy obviously felt the same, but she brushed past it quickly, giving her a sweet look that even I felt. "Thanks, Ash."

She took Asha's hand and they went to the centre of the crowd where Claire was, the three of them dancing together to a bouncy jig. I tapped my foot to the music, watching them dance and laugh together. It was a nice image. I liked seeing Kimmy happy; she'd been a bit mopey lately with Asha gone so much.

A large group passed in front of me to join the dancing crowd, and as they meshed with the others, I lost sight of my family. A minute later, Claire and Kimmy were still there, but Asha was gone. They didn't seem to have noticed because the crowd now took up most of the street. I looked around, trying to spot her, but it was hard to see past the mass of bodies. After a minute or two, I weaved towards Kimmy to tap her on the shoulder.

"Where's Asha?" I said loudly.

Alarm flashed across her face. "I don't know."

At that exact moment, she was violently bumped by a guy obviously having too much fun, since he reeked of booze. I steered her out of his way, annoyed.

"Stay with Claire." I squeezed her shoulder. "I'll look for her."

She nodded, frowning. Claire looked to me, concerned, but I gave her a look that said later, and she nodded. It was easier for me, being at least twice their size, to push my way through the crowd towards the opposite side of the street. When I got there, though, I still didn't see Asha anywhere.

I marched down the street. Vendors shouted out their wares as I passed, but still no Asha. The festival only stretched to the end of the Post's main strip. Beyond that area, there were only a few people outside, all residents. I frowned.

Where the hell could she have gone? Maybe she'd slipped out the opposite side of the crowd and gone back towards the stables? I didn't know why she'd do that, but she definitely wasn't here.

As I started to go back, there was movement at the corner of my eye. I turned to see Zach Jameson, of all people, walking quickly from a nearby alley—almost running. Just seeing the guy again after what he'd done made my blood boil, but curiosity got the better of me. I ducked behind one of the nearby buildings to watch him.

He headed toward the woods, in a real hurry for a guy on his own. My instincts told me to follow him. I'd stay out of sight, and if it turned out to be nothing, no harm done. Otherwise...it was my job to investigate suspicious shit, and this fit the bill.

I resolved to pass the search for Asha onto Kimmy, then track Zach. But just as I was about to leave, a beautiful figure greeted him at the treeline. I could barely make out the woman from this distance, but she had long black hair and flawless brown skin.

Asha.

She grabbed Zach's hand in an annoyed sort of way—a move that made me frown—and they disappeared into the trees together.

My gut screamed that something was wrong. Why would Asha be talking to this fucking creep? Holding his hand? Going into the woods with him alone?

I gave them a head start to make sure they wouldn't see me, then followed out of the Post and into the forest. Moving silently, I took my rifle into my arms and followed their voices, though I couldn't make out what they said.

They walked for a good ten minutes before stopping in a small clearing beside a big hollow tree. The brush was thick here, with long grass that gave me a good hiding spot to listen without being found. I crouched in the grass and listened hard.

"...utterly fucking *botched* this," Asha was saying furiously. "You had one fucking job, Zach. And you couldn't even do that right!"

"It was your stupid idea in the first place. I told you that your little stunts wouldn't be enough to scare that bitch off. She'll never hop off

Madigan's dick long enough to leave. I don't know why you care so much; we don't need her."

My breath caught.

"C'mon, sugar," he said in a way that made me want to barf. "You already said that sweet compound of yours will trade us for what we already got. Even a Wastelander like me can live the high life."

Asha laughed bitterly, chilling my blood. "If you can manage not to fuck that up, too. No second thoughts, no mistakes. If you do this, everyone you know is dead. They will go to the Valley, and they will take everything, kill everyone. You get what that means? Because I do. I lost everyone, and if you're not prepared to face that, I'm gonna leave you here."

I tracked their movements, listening carefully to figure out their positions.

Zach scoffed. "The fuck do I care about who's left there? I just wish I was there to see them kill McNeil and Madigan."

I'd heard enough.

In one quick motion, I stood, aimed, and fired. Zach Jameson's head snapped back, spraying blood on the grass, a bullet through his brain. Asha screamed and jumped back, but she didn't have time to recover. I walked towards her, rifle trained on her, and she gave me a look of genuine fear. Good.

"Drop your gun," I said, nodding towards Zach bleeding out on the ground. "Now explain to me why I shouldn't do the same to you."

Asha backed up a step, but I came closer, until the barrel of my rifle was inches from her chest. She reluctantly unclipped her pistol and tossed it on the grass.

"He threatened me," she said in her best impression of damsel-in-distress, only she wasn't a very good actress anymore. Not with a gun in her face. "I didn't know what to do."

"Cut the bullshit," I said. "Explain. Or I'll kill you, too."

"You wouldn't," Asha replied, in an entirely different voice—full of the venom I was used to from her. "Claire and Kimmy would hate you."

"If they'd heard what I just did? Doubtful. But sure, test me."

She stared at me, and whatever she saw in my face obviously convinced her, because she sighed like she was resigned. Somehow, that only pissed me off more.

"Was selling us out your plan all along?" I asked through gritted teeth. "Lying to Claire? Playing with my sister's heart? That all part of it?"

Asha huffed. "No. I didn't believe Claire when she told me about the Valley. I assumed *you* were lying to her—dangling a carrot. She's always been such a doe-eyed innocent that I knew she'd fall for that kind of thing from the first guy to sweet-talk her a little."

"Do they know about the Valley?" I gritted out, giving her a sharp jab with the rifle. "The people you were going to sell us to."

"They never responded to my radio calls," Asha replied bitterly, and I relaxed a little.

"Radio calls?"

"Yeah," she said. "There's a compound a few hundred kilometres from here. The Delta. I tried calling them. I intended to trade the information about the Valley to them in exchange for residency."

I frowned. "Why would they care?"

"Don't be stupid. You know that there's nobody else in the Wasteland like you guys. Sure, you live like a bunch of hick farmers, but you think they want you to have electricity? Technology? That's not the kind of thing Wastelanders can be trusted with. So, they'd take it."

She gave a grim smile. "Also, I think they'd have been very interested to know that the PNCs you have were acquired less than honourably, from another compound. I'd say they'd see them as stolen property, and not something Wastelanders should have."

"But they were from another compound," I said, carefully controlling my voice, "so why would it matter?"

Asha gave me that familiar look that said she thought I was dumb as a box of rocks.

"They're connected," she said slowly, as if speaking to a very stupid child. "All the compounds are. They're all owned by the same people."

I stared at her. "Which is...who?"

She shrugged. "Nobody really knows except at the highest levels. Very hush-hush."

"Why wouldn't Claire have told me?" I said, half to myself.

"She doesn't know," Asha replied. "Few do. My mother was an ambassador to the other compounds, though she kept her work secret. I only learned about it when I went back to the Cave. When I visited my childhood home, there was plenty there. It made sense in retrospect;

she told me shortly before the attack that she feared something bad was happening...and she was right."

"The Order," I said, and she nodded before I remembered the detail that had bothered me. "You said you used a radio. How...?"

She just stared at me. And reality hit me like a bucket of cold water.

"You attacked Danny that night and took his radio."

"Zach did," Asha replied. "I told him we needed a working radio, and he knew where to get one."

"You couldn't call from inside the Valley, though. The reception to the outside is shit."

Asha shrugged again. "Why do you think I've spent so much time on scav missions? The Post was the only place I could get a decent signal. Anywhere north of that is too remote."

I thought about what Zach had said. "He did all that just to live in that stupid compound with you?"

To my surprise, Asha laughed with real humour.

"You met the guy, right?" she said, nodding towards his corpse a few feet away. "He was an arrogant piece of shit looking to get his dick wet, just like every Wastelander I ever met. Manipulating him was too fucking easy. He believed everything I told him after a few blowjobs. Thought we'd run away to the compound together, that I was as in love with him as he was with himself. Fucking idiot."

She spat in the direction of his body, and I winced. Fuck her for making me feel kind of sorry for that scumbag, even for half a second.

"If you hadn't killed him, I would've," she continued.

My stomach was in knots. This woman had lived in my house. She'd dated my sister. Met everyone I cared about. I may not have liked her, but I never thought that she'd be this...cold. Calculated. Brutal.

Asha shrugged, oblivious to my disgust. "I wanted Claire to come with me. I thought if she saw the truth—that the Valley was no better than anywhere else in the Wasteland—she'd come around. But you brainwashed her."

I would've laughed at the irony there, but I was busy coming to another horrible realization. *The woodshed burning down. The bloody message on the classroom wall.*

"Fucking hell," I muttered, mopping my face with my hand. "You terrorized her? For months? And all so you could go back to living in a fantasy world?"

Asha huffed. "I wouldn't expect a Wastelander to grasp what it's like to go from being *chosen* to live the elevated life we had in the Cave...to this. Before I lived in the Wasteland, I was skeptical. After, I knew they'd told us that the 'people' who lived out here were lesser because it was true."

"Even Kimmy?" I asked. "Because she welcomed you when nobody else would've."

Asha bowed her head, surprising me. "Kimmy's...different."

"But not enough to not completely fuck her over, I guess," I said, unable to keep the anger out of my voice.

"In the Wasteland, sacrifices have to be made," Asha replied coldly. "Don't condescend to me about morality when you'd do exactly the same to save your precious Valley if it came down to it."

"Not gonna dignify that with all the ways you're wrong."

I didn't know what to do now. I knew what I should do: kill her the same way I had Zach. Leaving her alive was too much of a risk. But she'd wormed her way into the hearts of my sister and my fiancée, and I wondered if they'd ever forgive me. I could tell them that she was a massive traitor that'd been plotting against us for months, but hearing it second-hand left room for doubt.

I made up my mind. "You're coming back with me. You're going to tell your story to the council. I'll let them decide what to do with you."

I didn't say that they'd put her in front of a firing squad, but she seemed to know, because she tensed and shot me a look of pure hatred.

"Move," I said, nudging her with the barrel of my rifle. "Back toward The Post."

Asha gritted her teeth and started walking. We'd only been walking for a couple minutes, though, when I stopped again.

A column of thick, black smoke rose above the trees, back the way I came. That was when the screams started, followed by the sound of an amplified man's voice. I couldn't make out words, but my blood ran cold.

"What the hell did you do?" I demanded.

"Nothing!" she replied, her tone fearful. "Except...I only ever got one reply to my radio calls. But it wasn't the Delta."

"Christ," I muttered, pinching the bridge of my nose. "And what, you just invited the Order? Have you lost your goddam mind?"

"No!" she cried. It was the first time I'd heard Asha sound genuinely rattled. "I didn't tell them anything. I didn't think...I didn't know they could track the signal."

"Idiot," I answered sharply. "Get on the ground."

She whipped around, slashing upward with a tiny blade. I leapt back and avoided the worst of it but gasped at the slice of pain across my chest. Asha started running. Fuck.

Panting, I turned and shot from the hip. She'd made it to a sea of tall grass nearby, but she jerked as the bullet blew through her shoulder. She collapsed.

I automatically touched the thin cut across my chest. I was bleeding, but not badly. *Claire*, my thoughts screamed at me. I had to find her before they did.

I sprinted towards the smoke.

CHAPTER 37

Claire

I t started with the low hum of engines.

Barely audible over the music, they eventually grew louder, until they couldn't be ignored. The musicians stopped playing, and there was confused murmuring in the crowd. It hit me that most of the residents had probably never heard a combustion engine before. Even in the compound, only the military had non-electric engines for a few of their larger vehicles; access to biodiesel was limited and precious.

Whoever it was, it meant nothing good. I tugged on Kimmy's hand, pulling her small frame through the crowd. She followed, a frown creasing between her brows, one hand on her holstered pistol. We both looked in all directions, but John and Asha were nowhere to be found. My heart was in my throat; a sour, frantic feeling had settled in my stomach. The feeling a rabbit might have just before its leg was crushed in a trap.

We made it out of the crowd to the other side of the dirt road.

"We need—" Kimmy began, but someone near us yelled out a warning and pointed.

On the horizon, an enormous convoy truck had appeared, approaching fast, followed by several smaller, armoured passenger trucks that I recognized as being military-issued Cave vehicles. The only difference was that they were black—a hasty painting job, from the look of it, since bits of green still peeked out in various places. And emblazoned on the side of each was a shining gold eye. Odessa's Eye.

They'd come.

Kimmy saw it the same moment I did, and I found myself being sharply turned to face her. She wore her all-business face—the expression she always adopted in emergencies.

"Listen carefully," she said. "Go down the street and find an alley to escape through. Stay out of sight, make your way into the Red Zone, and find somewhere to hide. Talk to no one. Wait for me or John. We'll find you."

"I can't—" I started, but she shook her head.

"Go," she said firmly, then pulled up the hood of my cloak. "Keep your hair covered. It's too easy to identify you."

I nodded. Fear gripping hold of my senses, I hastened down the street towards the nearest alley between two crumbling buildings. Once out of sight of the main strip, I ran towards the street beyond. I'd only just made it there when the rumble of the trucks crescendoed, signaling their arrival in the street.

A brief pause followed as I kept walking. The residential streets were mostly empty, but a couple people were outside their homes. Their looks of confusion and alarm hurt me.

"Citizens of...what is this place again, exactly?"

Jim J's voice was unmistakable and magnified a hundred times by what must've been a megaphone. I quickened my pace, weaving between houses, trying to stay as hidden as I could.

"Right, the Post," Jim J continued, and I could almost hear the eyeroll in his voice. "I'd love to give you all an introduction to my family, but I've come to offer you a reward. You see, I've lost a family member: her name is Claire Ainsley."

My heart skipped a beat. I ducked into another alley as a couple of teenagers ran past me towards the main strip, looking frightened. I heard Jim J provide a detailed description of me, apparently along with a photo. He then offered a year's supply of food, plus weapons, to anyone who handed me over.

My mouth went dry. To a compound dweller, that would've been generous but not outlandish. To Wastelanders, that was like winning the lottery. In an instant, no one could be trusted, and staying hidden became paramount.

There were screams, and the echo of gunshots. I could only assume that Jim J had ordered his followers into the crowd. I knew they'd fight back, but the cult was better armed and prepared. It would be ugly.

"Bring me Claire Ainsley, and my family will harm no one," Jim J continued, his voice echoing off empty buildings. "Deliver her to me, and we'll go in peace. Conceal her from me, however, and I will raze this settlement to the ground. You have until sundown. Choose wisely."

I took a deep breath, trying hard not to panic. Sunset was hours away; how could I stay hidden that long? I had only my pistol, holstered at my hip, and the knife I kept concealed in my boot. John had the bag with the emergency supplies in it, including ammunition. I bit my lip, wishing desperately he were with me, but I imagined what he'd tell me to do next.

Focus, his voice said in my head. *One step at a time.*

I peered out from the alley, checking that no one was nearby before running across the street. I repeated the process a couple of times, running from alley to alley, heading towards the Red Zone. Finally, I spotted the faded red flags blowing in the breeze above the rickety wooden barricade that John had shown me. Unsurprisingly, the sentries were gone; they had bigger fish to fry.

As soon as I'd crossed the barricade, the sound of engines filled the air again. They were on the move, and I had only minutes until they might be on top of me. I ran down the remains of an abandoned street, scanning the crumbling Old World buildings for somewhere decent to hide. Rats scattered at my approach, squeaking wildly, and I took random turns onto side streets, trying to make it harder to follow me.

I finally ended up on a lonely side road, where a stout, red-brick building stood—an old community theatre. It was the only structure nearby that was mostly intact, and the engine sounds were growing closer. They may have already entered the Red Zone.

I entered through a back door that was forced open. Inside was a sparsely furnished storeroom, mostly filled with columns of heavy plastic totes. I pushed a couple against the outside door to barricade it, then shoved more totes against the door that led to the rest of the building. I couldn't do anything about the windows except stay away from them, but luckily, they were darkened by years of grime.

Sweating from the effort, I stacked more totes around a corner of the room, creating a small, boxed-in hiding spot. Then I crouched down behind them, pistol in hand, to wait. I knew I'd done my best, but a sinking feeling in my stomach told me that it wouldn't be enough. They'd hunted me this long.

Some part of me knew I was delaying the inevitable.

CHAPTER 38

John

The Post was chaos.

They'd set one of the market stalls on fire—the source of the smoke I'd seen. Firefights were happening between residents and Order members. The residents were putting up a good fight, but they were outnumbered. At the same time, people—mostly kids—were being abducted right from their homes, dragged out screaming and loaded into the huge convoy truck that was parked at the end of the main strip.

I had to find Claire and Kimmy, but with people running in random directions, it was impossible to know where they were. I needed to thin out the crowd.

I ducked behind a house on the corner and fired off a few rounds, taking out the cultists closest to me. The Order returned fire, and I got pinned down behind that house for way longer than I planned, playing a deadly game of cat and mouse. Someone was up on the roof, and whoever it was, they were a damn good shot. With their help, I managed to take down the three guys who were gunning for me.

My back against the wall, I waited for the right moment to run back out into the chaos. Then the person on the roof dropped down, right next to me, and I damn near jumped out of my skin.

"Should've known it was you," I said to Kimmy. "Where's Claire?"

She grabbed my shoulder, her expression frantic. "I don't know. I sent her away to hide. I didn't know what else to do."

Fresh adrenaline flooded my system. "Which way did she go?"

Kimmy pointed towards the Red Zone. "Go. I'll stay and help. I don't know how long she has before they find her, or someone gives her up. They offered a reward for her."

"Fuck," I muttered, looking around the corner for an opening.

"Where's Asha?" Kimmy asked, as if afraid of the answer.

This wasn't the time for the truth. "I didn't find her."

Kimmy nodded, obviously worried, and my stomach twisted.

One problem at a time.

CHAPTER 39

Claire

I lost track of time. It could've been minutes or hours that I stayed there, crouched uncomfortably behind the totes. I worried about John and Asha, not knowing where they were, and about Kimmy, stuck in the Post. I could only hold myself together and hope they were alright.

But I could hear people outside now. Talking, moving, searching. They gradually grew closer, and I didn't know what to do. I couldn't leave without being discovered. I could only hope they moved on, and if not...be prepared to fight for my life.

I jumped at a loud bang sounding at the outside door. I chanced a peek from a small gap between the totes concealing me. The totes I'd used to barricade the door hadn't budged. My heart pounded in my ears as another bang sounded, and then another. There were male voices right outside, angry and impatient. I breathed a sigh of relief when they receded after a moment, seeming to give up on the door.

For a while, all was quiet again except for the distant sounds of the search that continued outside. Then I heard the same male voices again, coming from the hallway outside the theatre door.

"...the last room," one of them said. "We've searched everywhere else."

I swallowed hard and tried not to panic. *Think like John.*

I peered through the gap in the totes, but I didn't have a good view of the theatre door. I shut my eyes and held my breath as a colossal bang echoed through the room—then another, and another, so much louder than the first attempt. It sounded like were using something as a battering ram.

They're going to get in. It was a matter of when, not if. I steeled myself and looked through the gap again, trying to gauge where they'd come into range of my pistol. I raised the gun to the gap, preparing myself.

Boom. The totes stacked by the theatre door went flying, scattering piles of old clothing, props, and ancient lighting equipment every-where. I listened carefully as two men entered the room.

"Nothing here but more Old World shit," one of them said dismissively, and for a brief moment, I let myself hope that they'd move on.

"Who barricaded both doors, then?" the other man replied. "I swear, Emerson, you're the laziest motherfucker alive. Help me move this shit."

I froze as one man's legs appeared in the small gap between the totes. Without another thought, I fired off a round. The bullet bit deep into the soft flesh of his thigh, and he collapsed with a scream. Blood sprayed from the wound like a firehose. I'd hit an artery.

"What the fuck!" the other man cried, and I instinctively flattened myself to the ground, covering my head. Shots rang out, blowing holes in the totes above me, and I was showered with plastic debris.

Ears ringing, I held my breath. Heavy footfalls told me that the second man took off running, leaving the first groaning on the floor. Even through the small gap, I could see that the floor was becoming rapidly soaked with blood.

I had to move—he could be back any second—but getting out from behind this tower of totes wouldn't be easy or graceful. I threw myself against them, once and then again, and they toppled over with an enormous crash.

The floor was covered with plastic totes, random debris, and hot, sticky blood, making it hard to navigate. I stumbled my way toward the outside door, scrambling. I'd cleared the totes in front of it and closed my fist around the handle when I heard that cold, mocking voice behind me.

"Claire Ainsley. Where could you be going?"

My heart in my throat, I spun around on my heel, raised my pistol, and spotted Jim J standing in the doorway, flanked by the masked man who must've fled and called him here. I fired—once, twice—at Jim J's centre mass, the way John had taught me.

Jim J's body jerked violently, and blood instantly began to soak through the front of his white shirt. I turned back toward the exit, prepared to make a run for it, and nearly jumped out of my skin as a blade slammed into the door, inches from my head.

"I wouldn't run, if I were you. My family is waiting outside," Jim J said, his voice only slightly roughened. "Even if you could escape, my dear...do you think I won't still hunt you? Still crave you? I'll never stop."

Horror was choking me as I stared at the blade embedded in the door. It was a meat cleaver...and it already had blood on it.

I turned, trembling all over, to face the man I'd been running from for months. His face was twisted into a rapturous grin that didn't touch his wild eyes. His gaze was hard, yet he also appraised me with something like desire. The masked man beside him merely stood silently, the gold eye on his mask a horrible reminder of all I'd suffered at the hands of these people. Hot bile threatened to spill from the back of my throat.

As he'd been at the Gathering, he was dressed in a three-piece suit. Blood was still soaking through his shirt, but he paid it no mind, as if being shot twice at close range was no more significant an event than his morning bagel.

Jim J took a step forward, and I instinctively flattened my back against the outside door, aiming my gun at him.

"By all means, shoot me again," he said with a shrug. "You'll find the results to be disappointing, however. I am the Chosen—an immortal."

I didn't care that flight was futile. I grabbed the door handle, pushed the door open, and ran outside...right into the arms of another masked man. Huge and imposing, he grabbed my shoulders and forced me back inside with a hard push. I tripped over the totes scattered across the floor and fell on top of a pile of old, discarded clothing. It was a soft landing, but the wind was knocked out of my lungs. I lay there, defeated.

"Smith, please escort the Vessel down to the stage," Jim J said to the larger masked man behind me. "We have preparations to make."

Smith lumbered over to me, narrowly avoiding the debris. I put up a token resistance as he manhandled me to my feet; I knew it was over. Whatever was going to happen, I couldn't stop it now. My only hope was to look for an opening, to wait for them to make a mistake.

I was led to the doorway where Jim J waited. He raised his left hand to my left cheek, and I flinched. He caressed my skin the way a lover would, and it sent chills down my spine.

"You are lovely," he said. "I'll drink deep from my Vessel tonight."

"You're sick," I whispered.

Jim J flashed me his awful, demented smile, then leaned in close enough that I could feel his hot breath on my face.

"Don't worry," he murmured. "This won't hurt."

Before I could react, he'd withdrawn a syringe from his jacket pocket, and in one fluid motion, he stabbed the long, thin needle into my neck and pressed down on the plunger.

I only remembered the twisted pleasure in his wild eyes before the world went dark.

❄

"Claire."

Someone was tapping my cheek. I was in my bed at Summerhurst, but I was too tired to open my eyes. I groaned and tried to roll over, but I couldn't.

"Claire," the voice insisted. "Come on."

"John?" I murmured sleepily. "I'm so tired."

"I know. But you have to wake up before they get back."

I cracked open one eye, and to my disappointment, my bed was nowhere in sight. Instead, I was lying on top of a steel table, my hands and feet tightly bound with rope. Overhead, there were dusty red curtains, broken light bulbs, a stage bridge...and a halo of golden hair that I instantly recognized.

"Holly," I croaked, my throat parched. "Where am I?"

Her hair had grown out since I'd last seen her. The ends touched her jaw now, and her blue eyes were the same as ever...but she looked unwell. Her cheeks were hollow and gaunt, and her gaze was haunted.

"Still in the theatre," she replied. "On the stage. Jim J stepped out to try to reach Mom over the radio before the ritual. She's still back at our camp."

I was trying to come back to reality, but whatever drug they'd given me pulled back hard on the edges of my consciousness. I blinked rapidly, trying to clarify my blurred vision.

As it cleared, I realized we were on the old theatre stage, and the audience seats were empty. Candles surrounded us. The stage backdrop depicted a faded mural of under the sea, its paint chipping and peeling. Wood cutouts of coral, seashells, and fish cluttered the back half of the stage, along with half a dozen tridents and pirate swords. A rusty, authentic-looking anchor hung on the backdrop, the tips of its hook glinting in the light.

Holly took out a knife. I flinched, but she started sawing at my bonds.

Is she trying to free me?

"We don't have much time," she said, determined. "We'll hide you somewhere until I can get you out."

"What?" I mumbled. My consciousness was a wet match that simply wouldn't ignite. "I can't...can't move, Holly. I won't make it."

If she responded, I didn't hear it, pulled under by a wave of fatigue.

"Claire!" she said my name with a frantic edge now, tapping my cheek harder. "Come on. Wake up."

In my current state, I couldn't make myself react appropriately. It was only the vague sense that I was in danger that kept my head above the waves long enough for me to whisper, "Find John."

"Where is he?" Holly demanded. "Please, Claire."

"Outside," was all I could manage. "He'll...come for me. But why...help me?"

There was a brief pause, and even through my drug-induced stupor, I was surprised to hear a sliver of emotion in my sister's voice.

"I don't want you to die."

"Oh," I sighed, blinking rapidly, trying to rouse myself. "That's...good?"

Holly choked back a laugh of disbelief but continued sawing at the ropes around my ankles. She managed to free them, then started on my wrists.

"What changed?" I murmured, working to stay lucid. Thankfully, it seemed like the sedative effects might be beginning to wane. "I thought you hated me."

"I didn't," she replied softly, and her eyes betrayed regret. "I was stupid and brainwashed. I couldn't...handle the truth. I thought that joining them would give me a sense of purpose..."

"But what?"

Her blue eyes darkened. "But then he started raping me."

"What?" I whispered. "Oh, Holly..."

She paused briefly at her work, his fingers trembling, but quickly started again.

"Does Mom know?" I asked, but I knew the answer.

"Of course," Holly replied curtly. "We all knew that Jim J took women from our 'family' as consorts. It's a great honour to be chosen by him. I guess I was naïve and thought they all wanted it."

"But you're his—" I cut off the thought.

She sneered. "You think he gives a fuck? If anything, I'm more attractive to him because of my connection to our mother. He sleeps around, but his heart is hers. He's utterly obsessed with her."

My queasiness reemerged, and I swallowed hard. "Is that the real reason he wants to kill me? Because I'm a reminder that Mom had a child with someone else?"

She blew out a breath. "Maybe. But from what I've seen, he's a true believer. He really believes you're the 'Vessel' for Odessa on Earth, that he has to destroy to be granted his ultimate powers."

I thought again about the shots I'd fired, right into Jim J's chest.

"But he does have powers," I said slowly. "Doesn't he? His immortality seems...real."

"Yeah," Holly sighed. "I don't know how, but it is. I've seen it. He won't tell anyone how he gained his power. He just keeps promising to give it to us, too, if we help him in his ultimate goal."

She freed my wrists, and I flexed them, my head throbbing.

"Which is?"

"I—"

A door opened and shut somewhere nearby, and Holly immediately sheathed her knife, tucked the shredded rope under me, and backed away from the table. A moment later, Jim J's awful smile greeted me as he walked out from behind one of the old theatre curtains. He was wheeling a small cart of terrifying-looking tools alongside him, including a cleaver and a bone saw.

Jim J's expression faltered on seeing Holly. My heart pounded hideously in my chest, and I tried to lie perfectly still, hiding my free hands beneath me.

"How odd to see you here," he said in a low, dangerous tone. "Since I specifically asked for you to wait outside with the others until called."

Holly backed up a step, her complexion wan, a sheen of sweat forming on her brow. Her fear of this man and the things he had done radiated off her; I'd never seen her so clearly terrified. My palms felt clammy as I tried to form a plan.

"I was only checking on the Vessel," Holly answered, her voice shockingly calm. "Doxtator said that she was showing signs of waking. He was right, so I wanted to be sure she couldn't escape."

Jim J scanned her face for a moment, and I held my breath.

"Fine," he replied tersely. "Just get out."

Holly nodded and left without looking back at me. I didn't know if I could trust her to help me, even if she really *had* had a change of heart. It could be a trap.

Jim J turned to me, and his sadistic smile returned. "You'll soon be ready for my family to join us. Just one more step; we'll have to get you out of those clothes."

He turned to pick up a knife from the cart he'd brought in, and a surge of panic flooded my system. Before he could turn around, I sprang up off the table, my knees wobbling dangerously. I tackled him, fastening my legs around his torso as I jumped on his back. I had no weapons, no plan, and absolutely no chance, but I didn't care. The only thought in my head was that I wasn't going to lie down and surrender.

I pummeled his head with my fists, each blow harder than the last. This man had ruined my family and stolen my home and desecrated my father's memory. If I was about to die, I'd make him suffer for it.

Jim J let out a shout of surprise and grappled with me. I clung to him, clawing at his eyes, but he caught my wrist in a vicelike grip. With a growl, he flipped me over his head and tossed me like a ragdoll. I skidded along the hard stage floor for several feet, pain shooting through my body. Jim J turned to me, his face bloodied by my assault, his jaw hardened with sudden rage.

CHAPTER 40

John

The Red Zone was crawling with cultists. I was forced to move slowly, silently taking out lone men, but I had to hide anytime a group of them got too close. I searched as I went, but I turned up nothing to lead me to Claire. I ground my teeth in frustration.

I was looking for a needle in a nest of hornets. Every second I wasted was a second that my girl could be fighting for her life—without me. It was a special kind of torture.

I ducked into an alley, behind a dumpster, as two masked cultists turned a corner behind me.

As they passed, one said to the other, "The Vessel's been recovered. Jim J's prepping for the ritual now."

"Bet she'll bleed real pretty for Him."

Shit. I took a deep breath against the panic rising inside my chest. The loss I'd been so afraid of was right there, about to sink its claws into me. But it wasn't over yet. She was alive. For now.

As I watched them walk away, I debated killing one of them and torturing the other for Claire's location. Not something I wanted, but I was fucking desperate. I'd die before I let them touch her.

Instead, I followed them. If Claire was captured, they'd probably go wherever she was. Just based on the one time I'd seen Jim J, I got the feeling he was a guy who needed an audience to take a shit.

They led me down a bunch of side streets, then eventually to a main road that was obviously the place to be. Masked men and women were crowded in front of a large, dilapidated building. A faded sign above the door read *College Theatre*. Across the street, a massive, hollowed-out shell of a building stood—a *College for Performing Arts*, crumbling into dust like everything else around it.

The cultists were waiting for something, because there was a buzz of impatient chatter. A couple of guys shouted orders back and forth. They weren't allowed inside yet. That gave me hope—the ritual hadn't started.

Daylight was starting to fade, and I stayed hidden in shadowy alleyways as I made my way around the block. I needed to scope out other possible entry points.

I settled into an alley half a block away and looked through the scope of my rifle. The back exit of the building had only three guards. Even though it was better odds, I wasn't sure how to take them out without alerting everyone. Stealth was the only way to get in there, but it might just be impossible.

Out of the corner of my eye, I spotted movement from the old college building across the street from the theatre. Looking through my scope, I realized that a woman, dressed in black and wearing an Order mask, was leaving the hollowed-out shell—on the side facing away from the theatre. The way she moved and kept looking over her shoulder said that she was trying to avoid the attention of the other cultists.

I frowned. *Why?*

I watched her for another minute. She came in my direction, weaving in and out of alcoves and alleyways, as if she was looking for something. As she got closer, a flash of golden hair caught the fading light.

If that's Holly, I'm going to fucking kill her.

Even if it wasn't, she may have info that could help me get in. I flattened my back against the brick wall, right at the mouth of the alley. I listened to her footsteps get closer. Right as she walked past, I grabbed her. My hand clapped over her mouth to smother her scream as I hauled her into the alley. I crushed her against the wall, face first, twisting her arm behind her back.

The ties on her mask sprang free on impact. The mask clattered to the ground, and I was again looking at the too-perfect face of my fiancée's sister.

"Scream and I'll wring your neck," I growled.

Holly groaned in pain, but managed to get out, "I came to find you."

It took a lot to make me speechless, but I definitely wasn't expecting that.

"I'll help you get inside," she continued. "The basement levels of the old college and the theatre are connected. I found it when I was trying to plan an escape route for Claire. But we ran out of time."

I was pretty sure my eyebrows were as high as they could go. What the hell had happened? The last time we met, she was as fucked as the rest of them. It had to be a trap.

"You're a liar," I snarled.

Holly struggled restlessly in my hold.

"Please, we're wasting time," she pleaded, and to my surprise, I heard tears in her voice. "He's going to kill her. Please."

My heart sped up, but I held my ground. "You were fine with that before."

"I wasn't fine," she replied, her voice breaking. "I was fucked up and desperate. But we don't have time for this. You won't get in without me. Please, let's go."

I hesitated, but she wasn't wrong. I didn't have many options, and as much as I hated to admit it, there was something in her tone that rang true. She sounded devastated...a side of her I hadn't seen before, even when she thought I might kill her. She'd been all attitude and bravado then.

I didn't know what had changed, but I also didn't have time to find out.

"Drop all your weapons," I ordered. "Don't try anything. I'll snap your arm like a twig."

"I can't go unarmed," Holly answered, a note of hysteria in her voice. "What if—"

"That's the deal. Otherwise, I kill you now and find my own way."

She was shaking like a leaf, but she tossed the holstered gun at her hip onto the ground. Having learned my lesson with Asha, I gave her a quick pat down for hidden weapons. *Nothing.*

"If you give me away, you die," I said with a heavy sigh. "Let's go."

CHAPTER 41

Claire

My assault didn't damage Jim J; on the contrary, I'd just made him angry.

I scrambled to my feet and dashed for the direction Holly had left in. He charged after me, into the cluttered mess of wood cutouts, and I nearly tripped over one shaped like a starfish. I threw it in his path, stalling him for a few precious seconds as I fled. He was quick, however, and caught up to me.

I snatched one of the tridents lying on the floor and turned, smashing it down over his head. It instantly snapped in two; it was a wooden prop. I used the end I still held as a improvised stake, stabbing him in the gut.

Jim J doubled over briefly but then began laughing. He wrapped his fist around the impaled end of the broken prop and pulled it out, spraying blood. I dropped the prop and tried to run again, but he lunged and slammed me against the painted backdrop. The rusty anchor attached to it clattered to the floor with a loud, metallic *thunk*.

I shrieked, but that only inspired more cruel laughter.

"I enjoy your screams very much, my Vessel," he murmured. "You'll scream much more for me by the time we're through."

Fear was alive inside my body, but I wasn't ready to surrender yet. I struggled in his hold, kicking and clawing at him. As he attempted to shield himself from my arms, I landed a knee in his groin.

Not even an immortal man could totally withstand that, it seemed, because he groaned and briefly released me. I twisted free and gained a few seconds of escape, but I heard him lumbering after me once more.

The loud bang of a gunshot rang out, and Jim J staggered. I glanced over my shoulder to see blood spurt out from a new wound in his chest. He toppled like a chess piece. I stumbled away from him, tripping over myself in my shock.

John stood at the back of the theatre, rifle raised. Relief surged through me at the sight of him, along with a new wave of terror as Jim J rose from the floor like a reanimated corpse, disoriented but surprisingly spry.

John shot him again. This time, Jim J managed to remain upright, and with an angry roar, he chased after me again. I changed course and ran for the edge of the stage, toward John, trying to navigate around the long table. He caught up to me, and I screamed as he pushed me hard. Midair, I tried to twist away to avoid hitting the table, but the back of my head smacked the back of my head on the edge.

Agony burst inside my skull, and I cried out. Wet warmth began to saturate my hair. Jim J grabbed a handful and yanked me to my feet, and I screamed again, the pain too intense to mask. John was nowhere to be seen now, undoubtedly having hidden himself among the aisles of the deserted theatre.

To my horror, Jim J leaned in close and licked across my cheek. I squeaked in outrage and disgust, but he just laughed and held me in front of him—a human shield. He didn't need it for himself; I was bait.

"The joke, my dear man, is on you," Jim J called out, amusement in his voice. "I love hide and seek."

I tried to stomp on his foot, but I was too slow. He evaded me easily, then punished me with another hard pull on my hair. With his opposite hand, he withdrew a long knife, then teased the skin of my throat with the warm steel.

"I've never liked guns," Jim J announced to the empty theatre, his voice echoing eerily in the stillness. "Too quick. Too efficient. The kill is something that the Prince of Pain *savours*. Death is a gift we give to our enemies; they should anticipate its arrival."

My stomach dropped, but I didn't dare move an inch with the edge of the knife pressed to my skin. Tension hung thickly in the air. At least the blood seeping from my scalp had slowed.

Jim J waited, but John didn't reappear, and no sound announced his movements. I knew better than to think he wasn't still there; he could be quiet as the grave when necessary. The best thing I could do was distract Jim J, in the hope that it'd give John the chance to make a move.

"James," I managed to get out, my breath shallow. "You're—"

He pulled the knife away from my throat and threw me onto the floor, knocking the wind out of me. I gasped, trying to catch my breath.

"You dare to address me, Vessel?" Jim J demanded. "Lower than dirt."

He kicked me hard, making me cry out and curl into a ball. Half a second later, hot, sticky liquid hit my cheek; he spat on me.

"Now, you'll see—"

Whatever grand announcement Jim J was about to make, it never came, because he was suddenly crushed underneath the falling weight of a bigger, heavier man. John had jumped from the rafters above and decked him. I scrambled on my knees to get out of the way.

John drew his knife, and as Jim J took in a huge gasp of air, he stabbed him in the back, angling the knife up under his ribcage. Blows that would've killed anyone else, but Jim J barely flinched. With a demented giggle that chilled my blood, he ignored the vicious stabbing that ensued; he barely seemed to feel pain. New terror flooded my system.

He's not human—he can't be.

He waited so casually, as though waiting patiently for John to tire. *That's exactly what he's doing,* I realized.

As though he'd had a sudden burst of adrenaline, Jim J rolled, violently knocking John off him. He sprang to his feet and kicked John—once, twice, and a third time for good measure. John curled into himself, stunned, and didn't move.

A shriek of pure agony, not quite human, clawed my throat as I saw him lying there. Jim J dove for me, tackling me onto the stage, and his tongue was back in my face. I sputtered and spat at him, but out of the corner of my eye, I spotted John on his feet again. The next second, the old, rusty anchor came down on Jim J, knocking him off me.

Before Jim J could react, John bludgeoned him again with the anchor. As he lay there, stunned, John raised the anchor one last time, grunting with the effort, and speared its sharp hooks into Jim J's body with all his strength.

He hopped back, panting. Jim J's manic grin returned, but as he tried to stand...he couldn't. John had skewered him to the floor, and despite how he squirmed, the anchor was too heavy for him to move.

Still breathing heavily, John dropped to his knees beside me.

"Claire," he exhaled, grabbing my face in his hands and examining me frantically. "Your head—"

"I think I'm okay," I whispered. I had no idea if that was true, but now was not the time to worry. "What do we do now?"

John let me go and stood up again, setting his pack on the floor. He withdrew a matchbox from it, and struck one to ignite it.

"I'll follow you, you know," Jim J croaked, staring at me. "Wherever you go. You can't escape your fate."

"Neither can you," John retorted, and before I understood what he was doing, he tossed the lit match into the cluster of wood cutouts and piled curtains.

Old and dry, they went up like a tinderbox, and the wood floor beneath them quickly caught, too. He struck another match and lit another pile of dusty theatre curtains. As the fire began to spread rapidly, Jim J called out.

"Help! Family! Please!"

His pitiful cries incited a new wave of loathing within me, and I was grateful when John clutched my clammy hand and pulled me toward an exit. A flaming curtain fell just as we left, covering Jim J, and his screams as he burned would haunt my dreams.

"It's okay now," John said, turning my face to look at him. His amber eyes were sharp and focused. "I'm going to get us home."

I nodded, and he led through a series of hallways, then to a door that read Basement. At the bottom of the staircase, Holly waited, fidgeting nervously.

"Wondered when you'd show up again," John said with disgust. "Thanks so much for helping us with Jim J, by the way."

"I can't let him know the truth; he'd kill me," she said sharply to John, then turned to me, her face stricken.

"Your head," she said, gesturing at me. "Are you—"

"I'll take care of her," John replied firmly, linking his arm with mine.

"You better," Holly said, but her voice shook. "Take her and get as far away as you can. I'll stall as long as I can, but the others will hunt you when they find out. Hide yourself in the woods at least until tomorrow."

John gave a brief nod to Holly and pulled me toward an exit.

"Wait," I said, looking back at my sister. "We can't—"

"We can," John said sternly. "And we are."

"No," I whimpered. "I can't leave her again, not when—"

My protest was silenced by the sad, resigned look that Holly gave me.

"You need to go, Claire," she said quietly. "I've made my bed, and my place is here."

"But—" Tears streamed down my cheeks, and a sob escaped me.

If I'd been thinking rationally, I would've known we had to leave her. But I was exhausted, injured, and seized by frantic emotions I didn't understand. Knowing she'd turned a corner made it feel like I was losing her all over again.

"You need to go," she repeated. "I want you to."

I stared at her, torn. My insides felt frozen.

"Claire," John barked, snapping me out of it. "Come on."

I swallowed reflexively and let him to pull me away. The basement held a tunnel that led to the college on the opposite side of the road. Crumbling and partially flooded with several inches of water, it wasn't an easy trek, but it was better than the alternative. With wet feet and my scalp still slowly oozing blood, we emerged into a warm June evening—into a world that appeared unchanged yet would never be the same.

The night was quickly illuminated by the burning theatre, engulfed in flames. Shouts came from the cultists, desperate to save their dear leader, even as it was futile. I did my best to put them out of my mind as we fled.

John navigated through the Red Zone, leading me through alleyways and backstreets, not slowing for a moment. I was breathless and exhausted, but I allowed him to pull me along until he found our way back to the vast forest that surrounded the ruined city. Even once we'd reached the cover of the woods, we walked for a long time, going deeper into the wilderness. Moonlight was our only guide, but at least the darkness and rough terrain would make it difficult for the cult to follow us.

Finally, when I felt as though I was about to collapse, John stopped. He pushed through overgrown brush until we came into a small clearing. It was as concealed as could be. John clicked on his flashlight and set his pack on the ground. He pulled out a blanket and spread it across the ground.

"Sit," he ordered before rummaging in his pack again with the light.

My knees gave out as I lowered myself onto the blanket, and I gasped at the surge of pain in my wounded scalp. My hair was caked with blood and felt disgusting. Despite the warm evening, my skin was cool and clammy. I hugged my velvet cloak around myself, shivering. Battered and bruised, my grip on myself was slowly slipping away, as surely as my sister had in those final moments in the theatre.

"You're still in shock," John said, surprisingly calm. He'd trained for this, I supposed. "Take a couple deep breaths for me."

I tried my best as he retrieved his outrider medical kit from his bag and knelt in front of me. Flashlight in hand, he shone it directly into my eyes, and I flinched.

"Sorry," he murmured. "Checking for concussion."

I let him examine my pupils and answered his questions. He determined that concussion was unlikely; I'd been lucky, apparently, even though I felt anything but. He scooted behind me and parted my hair to inspect the laceration on my scalp. His touch was gentle, but I winced anyway.

"It's not as bad as it seems," he said, reaching into his kit. "Head wounds bleed a lot, even when they're not deep. It'll be okay with a few stitches."

I nodded numbly, and he started cleaning the cut with a cloth he dampened with his water bottle.

"What'll we do about the horses?" I asked, my voice sounding foreign to me.

"We'll get them tomorrow," he replied. "Assuming it's safe."

I was shaking like a leaf. I didn't know how I'd ever stop.

"How can we assume that ever again? The Order can obviously track me somehow, even if I'm out of range. Holly was wrong."

John's hands in my hair suddenly froze.

"She wasn't," he said after a beat. "They found you by accident."

"What?" I asked, whirling around to look at him. "What do you mean?"

To my confusion, he bit his lip, seeming hesitant.

"There's something I need to tell you," he finally said with a sigh. "But I want to patch you up first. Just sit tight."

Still trembling, I gave a small cry behind my hand as he sanitized the wound with alcohol. He murmured words of reassurance, but I felt no comfort. I only felt confused as to why this was happening, why I'd left my sister behind for a third time, and guilty because in the end, I hadn't saved her, and I'd left her to be victimized again by that monster.

I bit down on my tongue as John started suturing. Each stitch delivered a breathtaking sting that made my eyes water, but the pain helped ground me. I focused on each stitch until he'd finished, taking deep breaths to steady myself.

"Are you hurt anywhere else?" John asked.

I shook my head, then remembered the harsh slash across the front of his shirt, where dried blood had glued the edges of the fabric to his body.

"What happened to you?"

He moved to sit across from me and clicked off the flashlight. "Sorry. Don't want to draw attention."

Darkness engulfed us, and his warm hands found my clammy ones and clasped them tight.

"Baby," John murmured, "what I'm about to tell you is really hard. But I need you to stay as calm as you can until we get home. We're not out of the woods yet."

I took a shallow breath. "John, you're scaring me. Please just tell me."

He squeezed my hands, then launched into the story of what'd happened with Asha in the woods. He spoke in a low, comforting tone about her utter betrayal. Her lies. The way she'd manipulated Zach Jameson, and me, and Kimmy, and how we'd all been fooled. How she'd all but delivered me to the cult with her radio calls, and that Holly had confirmed it when she met John to rescue me. How she'd attacked him, and he'd shot her in response. How she'd never been my friend to begin with, and that all my hopes for her building a new life after all that'd happened to her were as dead as she was, lying in some meadow alongside Zach Jameson's stone-cold corpse.

How the woodshed burning down, and the attack on Danny, and the schoolroom vandalism...all had been part of a plan to convince me to go with her to this mythical new compound. How the guilt trips she'd sent me on, and the attempts to turn me against John, weren't simply side-effects from the trauma she'd endured, but part of a calculated plot. And her romance with Kimmy was nothing but a way to prevent herself from being excised like the malignant tumour she was.

John told me all of this slowly, bit by bit, as though gently easing me into a boiling-hot cauldron of water in the hope that it'd hurt less. I could tell he was worried about me. He gripped my hands tightly in his, like he never wanted to let me go ever again.

Yet I felt nothing. A yawning abyss had opened underneath me, and I was falling, but I couldn't scream. Somewhere, underneath the numbness, I knew there was pain—tremendous, all-consuming, world-ending pain—but I couldn't access it. Detachment was my only defence against the whirlwind that had whipped through my life and destroyed my sense of security.

Silence descended when he finished talking, and for a long time, I said nothing. Time didn't seem real; it felt like all I could do was sit and wait. I didn't know what for. I only knew that I couldn't move, and that even on this June evening, I couldn't get warm.

I couldn't see John's face in the dark, but I knew when he spoke again that I'd waited too long to answer.

"Please say something," he said, his voice breaking for the first time. "I'm sorry I had to hurt your friend. I would never—"

"You did nothing wrong," I cut in. At least of that, I was certain. "You saved me. I'm grateful."

Even to me, my voice sounded oddly foreign, robotic, unlike myself.

"You don't have to be grateful, baby," John replied, sounding hurt for reasons I didn't understand. "If you're mad at me, I get it. You can be mad. Just talk to me."

"Not mad at you," I said with an exhausted sigh. "I'm tired."

My eyelids fluttered against my will. The adrenaline that'd pushed me forward was wearing off, leaving me drained.

"Lie down and rest," John said, reverting to his professional, first-responder voice. "You've been through a lot. Too much."

I followed his instructions on autopilot, lying back on the blanket on the ground, wrapping my stained cloak around myself. He lay beside me and drew my still-trembling body close. I couldn't help clinging to his warmth as my teeth chattered.

"I w-won't sleep," I said. "Not safe."

"It's okay," he murmured, brushing my cheek with his callused fingertips. "I'll keep watch. No one will hurt you."

I leaned my forehead against his chest. Even when I had every reason to doubt my safety, I believed him. A deep sigh escaped me, and he rubbed the base of my neck, soothing me.

"Just close your eyes," John whispered, and I did. Tension left my body; I had nothing left to give, and he knew it. So quietly I almost didn't hear it, he continued: "Morning will come, sweetheart."

CHAPTER 42

John

At first light, we left to get the horses from the stable outside the Post. We made a loop around the abandoned city through the forest to avoiding run-ins with gangs or the Order. I made sure Claire was hidden in the hollow of a tree before I went to scope out the Post. If the Order was still there, it wouldn't be safe for her.

Luckily, the stable was still standing, and the horses were still there. Corny told me that the 'small Asian lady' had traded with him to keep them overnight. I could only assume he meant Kimmy, so I went back to the Post to find her.

It didn't take long; she was busy treating the wounded in the street. The main strip was devastated. Stalls and caravans were overturned, and there were bodies everywhere. I was grateful that most of them seemed to be cultists, but I spotted a few familiar faces in the wreckage. No one I'd known well, but people I'd seen in passing. It hurt to see people grieving in the street around their dead loved ones.

Kimmy had dark shadows under her eyes. She'd been up all night, giving medical care to those who needed it. That was who my sister was, and Asha had never deserved her for even one second. I had to tell her the truth now, and I felt sick.

"How're they holding up here?" I asked Kimmy after she'd finished with her last patient.

"As best they can," Kimmy answered. "We drove back the Order, though they abducted a few of the children. All things considered, though, it could've been worse. Not much comfort to the families, though."

"Yeah," I said with a sigh. "I'm sorry, Kim. You shouldn't have had to handle this alone. Are you ready to head home?"

She frowned. "What about Asha? We have to find her."

The worry in her voice hurt. I was going to break her heart.

I sighed. "I already did. We need to talk."

We sat on the crumbling curb, and I told her everything about the day before. It was somehow worse the second time. When I explained Asha's plan, Kimmy didn't believe it.

"There has to be a mistake," she said, an edge to her voice. "She was...troubled, but she wouldn't do that. Not to us. To me."

I shook my head. "I'm sorry."

"You never liked her," she said, shooting to her feet, her arms crossed. "Why would you—I mean, she—"

We locked eyes.

"Have I ever lied to you, Kimmy?" I asked gently.

All at once, her denial suddenly crumbled. She let out a wild sob and dropped to her knees. I wrapped my arms around her and took a steadying breath. I'd only seen Kimmy cry a handful of times as an adult, and it tore my guts out.

"I should've seen it coming," she said into my shoulder, choking back another sob. "I could've stopped her."

"You didn't know," I replied, squeezing her.

"How could I be so stupid?" she whispered.

"You weren't," I murmured. "You were kind."

"Same difference," she said, and I couldn't help but chuckle in spite of myself.

"You trusted the wrong person. But believing someone can get better isn't a crime. It's why you have such a talent for healing people."

She moved back, swiping at her eyes. She gulped down deep breaths, and after another minute, she seemed better.

"I want to go home," she said, and I nodded. "Where's Claire?"

"Waiting for us. Let's get the horses."

❅

The weeks after the attack on the Post were rough as fuck.

When we got home, Kimmy went straight to bed, and I couldn't blame her. I lifted Claire into my arms and carried her upstairs to our ensuite bathroom. She didn't even protest.

"Let's get cleaned up," I said, and pulled my ruined t-shirt over my head.

Claire didn't react as I started the shower. She just nodded with a blank look on her face, like she wasn't sure where she was, before stripping down.

I needed to take care of her.

The hot water was a goddamn revelation. We were both sticky with sweat and dried blood. I had Claire sit on the small bench inside the shower. She looked so small and so broken that my chest hurt. Her beautiful red hair was caked with blood and dirt, and her pale body was covered with cuts and purple bruises. Each one felt like a punch to the gut. *I promised to protect her.*

I grabbed a shampoo bar and the detachable showerhead. I rinsed her head, carefully avoiding her stitches, and she sighed and relaxed into my touch. I gently washed her hair, watching bloody water circle the drain. When it finally ran clear, I offered her a bar of soap, and she scrubbed herself down while I washed up.

Once we were clean, I knelt in front of her and kissed every bruise on her trembling body, telling her things that couldn't be said with words. For the first time, her eyes showed emotion, and she touched my cheek.

After, she got into a nightgown and sat on the edge of the bed. I braided her wet hair, if only because my touch seemed to be the only thing that calmed her. We didn't speak again until I tucked her into our bed.

"Thank you," she whispered, and I gave her one more kiss.

Despite how fucking wrecked I was, I went straight to the Lodge to find Danny. Predictably, he was in the command center, sitting behind his desk with his crutches leaning against the wall behind him. When he saw my face, his expression changed to alarm, and he tried to stand up. He fell back into his chair on his ass.

"Damn leg," he blew out in frustration. "I'm losing my mind with no time in the saddle." He looked back at me, his blue eyes searching my face. "What's wrong?"

I glanced over my shoulder into the lounge. Nobody was around this early, but I closed the office door anyway. The last thing I needed was to be overheard.

I took a seat in the chair on the opposite side of the desk and sighed, rubbing my tired eyes. Danny raised an eyebrow.

"You look like hell," he observed, and I gave a bitter chuckle. "Who died?"

I winced at his choice of words, and he leaned forward, eyes widening. Finally, for the third time, I went through what'd happened at the Post with Asha and Zach. I told him everything, feeling a weight slowly lifting from me. For the first time, I was telling someone I didn't have to comfort, who didn't depend on me. The closest thing I had to a brother.

Danny listened in silence, frowning and rubbing his beard. I didn't know what to make of his reaction.

"He attacked you that night," I said with a sigh. "Asha confessed, and from what I overheard him saying, I think it's true."

At that, Danny's eyes widened. He glanced at his medical boot. Frustration and anger snuck into the crease between his brows.

"So, what happened to Asha?" he asked, still staring at his boot.

"I shot her," I answered.

"And Zach?" His name came out as a growl.

I swallowed hard. "I shot him, too."

Danny met my eye, and for a long moment, we just stared at each other. He finally broke the silence with a single, clipped syllable.

"Good."

Relief flooded my limbs, and I leaned forward and buried my face in my hands.

"I know I'll have to go in front of everyone and tell them, but—"

To my surprise, Danny snorted. "Why the hell would we do that?"

I looked up at him. "I'm an outrider...and I killed a Valley resident."

"You killed a traitor who attacked your Chief and was going to sell all of us out to a dangerous outsider," he replied with a shrug. "You kept your oath, which is to the Valley, not to its chairman. You did your job."

He leaned back in his chair. "But have some sense, Johnny. I believe you were justified, but you've been my best friend practically since birth. Hard to predict what the rest of them might do. I'm *not* giving them a reason to toss you out, especially because if what you say about this cult is true, we can't afford to lose you."

I blew out a breath. "So, what now?"

"Simple," Danny replied, looking toward his crutches. "It's your word against no one's. Can you help me with these fucking things? I can't seem to get the hang of them."

※

In the following days, outriders were sent to recover Zach and Asha's bodies based on the directions I gave. When they got back, Danny called me into the command center. He sat behind the desk, his crutches leaning against the wall behind him, and I'd never seen him look so grim. Immediately, I worried someone else had fucking died.

"We found Zach's body," he said, leaning back in his chair. "Not Asha's, though."

I just about fell over.

"What? How the hell is that possible?"

He shrugged. "You said she fell in some long grass. They reported that there was a lot of blood, and they followed a trail from there, but when it ended, they didn't find her. They tracked down a campsite in the area that looked recently abandoned, but based on what you said, she wasn't in any condition to be camping."

"Definitely not," I answered, frustrated. "So, she might've gotten help?"

Danny shrugged. "I can't see how else she got away, losing that much blood."

I lowered my face to my palm.

"Fuck. What now? Do we try to track her down?"

He shook his head. "The trail went cold after the campsite. But based on how much blood they said there was, I don't think she'll live long even if she had help. All we can do is ramp up security around here and hope Asha's shit with directions. Prepare for the worst, hope for the best."

Danny had outriders go to tell Jameson his son was dead. He then called another emergency council meeting, which happened a day after the body recovery. I sat at the centre of the meeting, Claire and Kimmy on either side of me, while everyone else stared a hole through us.

I told the story: I'd left the festival to find Asha, only to discover her and Zach. When he refused to keep going with her scheme, she'd killed him, and I shot her in self-defence. Kimmy added details where she could, backing up my story, and Claire nodded along, her eyes on the floor.

Old Jameson was surprisingly quiet as I talked, his eyes red, and for the first time, I actually felt sorry for him. He may have been a stubborn old ass, but he didn't deserve to lose his son. My lie about Zach refusing to go along with Asha wasn't planned. It was a small mercy I gave him—the belief that his son saw the light in the end and wouldn't have sold out his own people.

My pity vanished in an instant when he turned on Claire.

"You, outsider," he said, pointing at her. "How can we know that you weren't in on this? That you didn't know that...*harpy* was going to kill my son?"

His voice trembled on the last word. Claire flinched as if he'd hit her.

"She has a name," I shot back. "And Claire wouldn't do that. She was the victim of Asha's attacks."

Jameson gave me a cold look. "I didn't ask you, Madigan. We deserve answers. If she wants to stay, she can submit to questioning."

I opened my mouth to reply, but Claire's hand landed on my arm.

"It's okay," she said quietly to me, before facing Jameson. "Ask your questions."

For the next hour, he and several other members grilled Claire on what she knew and when, where she was during any given event, and where her loyalties lay. Kimmy and I spoke up where we could to verify her answers, and to my surprise, so did a lot of others. It was a mark of how much Claire had won them over that so many people came to her defence, including Nimkii, Jenna, Scott, and parents of her students.

To her credit, Claire didn't waver during the questioning. She gave short, clear answers, and she didn't take any of their anti-outsider bullshit. She told them how she'd grown to love the Valley and its people, and that she'd been as hurt by Asha's betrayal as anyone. She was just herself: soft, well-spoken, and genuine. To my relief, as she talked, the temperature in the room slowly cooled. People were scared, but not too afraid to listen to her.

"All I want," Claire said, her voice quivering slightly for the first time, "is to marry the man I love and live in peace. I want to keep building on my work here, teaching your children and creating a better education system for all. I'll do whatever it takes to keep proving my loyalty to all of you, every day."

She swiped at a single tear, and I squeezed her hand before she continued: "I think of you all like an extra-large, extended family now. I never had that before, and nothing would be worth losing it."

There was a long silence. Looking around the room, most people looked sympathetic, even moved by her words. The quiet was broken by Abby Miller simply saying, "Thank you for your testimony, Claire. I'd like us to move onto how to deal with this security situation."

I let out a long breath. She'd won them over, and all I could feel when I looked at her beautiful face was fierce pride. I put my arm around her and kissed the top of her head, and she gave me a token smile. Even Jameson seemed appeased...for now, anyway.

The rest of the meeting dealt with increasing security. The Order was an active threat, especially now that we knew they were in the area. The only thing that saved our asses was that they didn't know about the Valley, and that they weren't able to track Claire here.

We decided that nobody would be allowed to leave the Valley without getting permission. Scavvers had to sign in and out with Danny at the command center before coming or going. Outriders would pull double patrol shifts until further notice so that there were more of us on duty at a time.

It was necessary, but it meant that I went from patrolling four days a week to patrolling almost every day for up to twelve hours at a time, effective immediately. For the next couple weeks, Claire and Kimmy had to pick up my slack around the farm, especially because it was planting season. I hated it, but it couldn't be helped.

The real problem that ate away at me during that time, though, was that Claire was obviously not handling things well. After the meeting, where she'd been so strong, she'd become lifeless. She got up and worked the farm every day like she was on autopilot, then went to teach. Kimmy told me she'd stopped eating enough. The most obvious sign, though, was that her nightmares—which had slowly gone away after we reached the Valley—came back with a vengeance.

I was startled awake by her fist in my ribs, her hoarse scream splitting the night.

"Claire!" I tried to bear-hug her to stop her thrashing, but that instantly made her fight me.

"Let me go," she sobbed, flopping like a fish.

"It's me, baby!" I said firmly, and she suddenly went limp in my arms, panting and shaking. "It's just me."

"I'm sorry," she whispered after a long silence, but she didn't shed a tear when she was awake. She got quiet and detached again, and didn't sleep a wink.

Every time I saw her, it was like someone had snuffed out her spark. She was so distant, and nothing seemed to reach her. Even our upcoming wedding didn't seem important to her anymore. It scared the hell out of me.

Tears, I could handle. Anger, even. But not her freezing me out. The thing was, I knew Claire; when she was hurt or afraid, she hid. It was what she'd done when we first met. It was why it took an attack that nearly killed her to tell me she loved me. Back then, I'd tried to respect her need for space, not realizing it only made the problem worse. I'd learned that while space may be what she wanted, it was almost never what she actually needed.

Three weeks after the attack on the Post, I called in a favour so I could have the day off. Even besides my worry for her, I missed my girl. The days on horseback were long and lonely, and I missed her voice, her laughter. Sharing about our days and holding her until she fell asleep. Going on rides with her. Making love to her. She made my days better just by being in them.

It was another warm, sunny June day, though clouds threatened in the distance. After morning chores were done on the farm, it was nearly noon, and I asked Claire to come with me to Glacier Lake at the centre of the Valley for a picnic.

"It's a date, then," I said, pecking her lips. "Wear something that makes you feel pretty."

She didn't have much of a reaction to my request, but she at least got ready to leave and waited patiently on the porch for me to bring the truck around. She wore a pretty yellow gingham sundress that I'd never seen before, and she'd twisted her hair into a half-up style with a white ribbon.

"This new?" I asked, nodding at the dress.

She nodded a little shyly. "I asked Nimkii to make a few things for the summer. Traded her a few months of language lessons for her son."

"Could've just taken a PNC from the safe if you wanted."

She shook her head. "I wanted to do it. Do you like it?

"I love it," I murmured, giving her a kiss before I led her to the truck.

Claire gave me a look of surprise at the canoe strapped to the truck bed.

"Where was that all this time?"

"In storage," I replied with a small smile. "Granddad and I built it when I was a teenager. I use it to fish sometimes in the summer. Thought you might like to go out on the lake after lunch, since it's a nice day."

"Alright." Her reaction was muted, lifeless, and that only made me more determined to shake her out of her numbness.

Claire was quiet as I drove. When we reached the small lake, we were lucky to have it to ourselves. I parked by the lakeside, then spread out the blanket while Claire unpacked the picnic basket. We sat and ate in near-silence. Her face was still closed off, and she picked at her food.

After lunch, we pushed the canoe into the water and climbed in. The sun was warm, and Claire tipped her face up, which was the first time I'd seen her actively enjoy anything in a couple of weeks. I paddled out to the middle of the lake, where the water was clear, and the view was best. More importantly, we were totally alone and wouldn't be overheard.

That'd always been when she and I had talked the most back at the camp: out in the woods, where we might as well have been the last two people on Earth. She seemed to feel freer out in the wilderness—freer to speak her mind, to be herself.

I watched Claire carefully, but she didn't glance in my direction. I got the feeling she was trying not to make eye contact.

"Claire," I said cautiously, "we should talk."

"Oh?" she answered, her voice flat and emotionless.

She stared out at the water, and despite promising myself I'd be patient with her, that fucking frustrated me. It was more of her avoidance bullshit, trying to shut me out. I took a deep breath.

"I know things have been...hard. Since the attack. Since Holly, and Asha."

Claire's face didn't show any change, but her hands trembled slightly in her lap.

"I'm alright," she said, in a way that sounded rehearsed—like something she'd repeated to herself more than once.

"You're not."

She finally looked at me, her whole body rigid. Her expression barely changed. She looked vaguely lost, like she'd somehow taken a wrong turn and couldn't figure out how to get back.

"Cut the bullshit," I said sharply. "Right now. Save us both some time, and *talk to me*, for fuck's sake."

I wasn't angry with her. Not really. But I'd learned that when tragedy struck, Claire retreated into herself like a turtle into its shell. Sometimes, you had to poke at her to get her to come out again. Only then would she let you get close enough to help her.

"I have nothing to say," Claire said, staring at the floor of the canoe. "Even if I did, what good would it do?"

"We'll never know until you try," I replied. "Look, princess, you don't get to check out just because things have gotten hard."

It was the word *princess*, said in that disparaging tone I used to use with her when we first met, that set her off. I hadn't done that in a long time. Claire's face fell, and I felt instantly guilty for causing her more pain, but I'd already tried everything else.

"Hard?" Claire shot back, full of hurt and outrage. She shot to her feet and just about capsized the canoe. I grabbed the sides to steady it, and luckily, it stayed up.

"Is that the word you'd use, John? To describe the way I'm being hunted by a group of fanatics, including my own mother, to be fed to their immortal leader? Or to talk about how my once-best friend not only used me, but gave me away to the same people who want to chain me to an altar and cut my heart out?"

My plan had worked, and I stayed quiet. She needed this.

"Or maybe," she continued, "the fact that I've had to work and fight so hard for the tiniest bit of acceptance in the Valley? That I've never been able to have even a single moment of weakness, because the sharks were constantly circling, waiting for me to make a mistake? That I've had to be so strong, all the time, for everyone, especially you?"

"I never asked you for that." I kept my voice neutral.

"You didn't have to," Claire answered, her voice finally breaking. "How could I be anything less, knowing that it'd drive a wedge between you and the people you love? That it'd just make everything harder for you, and I'd be a burden on you all over again?"

"A burden?" I repeated, dumbstruck. "Baby, you're everything to me. Seeing how much you've grown—how much you've accomplished, with your teaching and your work around Summerhurst—made me fall even harder for you. All I ever tell people these days is how proud I am of you."

Claire's eyes shone with tears.

"*You* are the person I love," I continued, more fiercely. "Before all others. You think I give a shit about the rest of them if it means you suffer? I'd gladly burn it all down for you. I'd leave everything behind if you needed me to."

"But I don't want you to do that. You deserve to have the people who love you around you."

"So do you," I said gently. "So please, just...let me take care of you the way we both need me to. Let me hold you."

There was longing in her expression as she stared at me, but she still hesitated. Bit her lip and said, "I'm scared if I do, I'll just break apart."

"I'm not afraid of your pain."

Her shoulders slumped, her face twisted with everything she'd been holding back. She carefully lowered herself on the bench next to me. Slowly, I opened my arms to her, and something suddenly snapped. She lay her head against my shoulder and gave in. Sobbed loudly, uncontrollably, in a way that made my chest ache. She sounded so heartbroken and defeated.

"Oh my God," I muttered, wrapping my arms around her, cradling the back of her head in my hand.

"Whatever I've done here," Claire sobbed, "she's gone because I failed her. I should've seen it coming, tried to help her more."

I didn't know if she meant Holly or Asha or both. I sighed and just held her, let her cry.

"And even after everything I've learned and all I've done...I'm still so afraid. Of the Order. Of the future. I'm still so weak."

"Hey," I cut in. "You are *not* weak. Being traumatized by all this shit isn't weakness; it's basic humanness."

"But the problem is, Asha was sort of right," Claire said miserably. "I'm not built like you and Kimmy. I'll never be a hunter or a fighter. I'd never be able to last in the real Wasteland on my own."

"Uh, you forgetting the two-month trip here? Besides, you have your own talents."

She scoffed. "You can't eat a painting or a song. I just...I wish I was better for you."

Is that really what she thinks? The ache in my chest grew.

"You think I don't know that you're my sweet, soft girl?" I murmured, kissing her hair. "You think I would change you? Never. I need your softness to remind me that there's still good in this fucked up world. More than that, every day, I see you and I know that my purpose is to protect the goodness that's left in it."

She took a long, shuddering breath, leaning harder into me, and I cradled her.

"What you did for the kids of this community is more than I could do," I continued. "Sure, maybe you won't find the key to basic survival in a painting or a song. But you might find hope. Without that, there's no point to the survival part anyway."

There was a pause. "I guess that's true."

I huffed a laugh. "Sweetheart, you're talking about rebuilding civilization like it's nothing. Your part is *not* nothing—you're passing on knowledge from hundreds of generations. And you don't have to be strong in the way that you're talking about, because *I'm* your strength. And you're my heart. That's why we need each other."

I didn't know how long we sat there together, but by the time Claire looked up at me again, the sun was hidden behind the clouds, and the sky had darkened. Her eyes were still wet, but she looked relieved. Like a weight had been lifted.

"Better?" I asked softly.

"Y-yes," she hiccoughed. "I didn't know how much I needed that. I'm sorry I've been so distant these last few weeks. I was just...surviving."

"I know, baby," I said, kissing her forehead. "Listen, okay? It's going to take time for us to heal. But everything that's happened in the last few months...that's all over now. It's you and me, okay? Forget about everything else for a moment. We're getting married in two weeks, and this is our new beginning. Nothing else matters."

To my relief, she nodded. "You're right. I want to...start over. Put all this behind us. It'll be hard, but...I want to try."

"I'm glad," I replied, taking her face in my hands. "Lean on me when you need help, beautiful. I won't think less of you. We're in this together."

Right as I finished, the sky opened up and we were assaulted by rain. The downpour was instant and intense. I was soaked in seconds, and Claire looked much the same, her red hair sticking to her wet skin.

But to my delight, she started laughing. Real, deep, happy laughter. And when she met my eye, she kissed me fiercely, hanging her arms around my neck.

My whole world was in that kiss. All the moments we'd had together, and all the ones to come. Our marriage. Our life together. Everything I'd ever wanted, given to me in just one moment. The connection between us couldn't be broken. What we had was stronger than what we'd been through.

When we broke apart, Claire giggled again and smoothed sopping wet hair out of my face.

"You look a bit like a drowned rat, darling," she said, and I chuckled.

"I'm taking you somewhere special," I said. "After the wedding. A little honeymoon. A chance to get away from everything."

She lit up in a way that made me happier than I'd been in two weeks. "Where are we going?"

I smiled. "You'll just have to wait and see."

The rain continued all around us as I paddled toward the shore. The surface of the lake was nothing but ripples, and thunder rumbled in the distance. I was soaked to the bone—we both were—but I didn't care.

I never wanted to stop being this happy together, even in the middle of a storm.

CHAPTER 43

John

"You nervous, man?" Danny asked, standing by the mirror in my old bedroom as I straightened my collar.

I couldn't remember the last time I'd worn a button-down shirt, and my wedding day was probably the last time I ever would.

"If I was, would it matter?" I replied. "You'd be no help anyway."

He laughed. "If it helps, once they see Claire, nobody's going to look twice at you. She's a knockout, and you're just...well, you."

I gave his shoulder a half-hearted shove but couldn't help smiling. I hadn't seen Claire or her dress, and the anticipation was killing me. She'd insisted that I sleep in my old room last night, saying that I couldn't see my bride before the wedding. According to her, it was bad luck.

Considering how shitty our luck had been lately, I wasn't gonna jinx us. But that was all over now. This was the real beginning of our life together. A fresh start, where we'd make a million new memories together. Build a future worth fighting for. Grow old together. Leave this world a little better than we found it.

Claire was my north star. She filled me with hope so bright and brilliant that it took my breath away. My little bluebird appearing after a long winter.

"On a more serious note," Danny began, and I snorted.

"You capable of that, you think?"

"Sure. I haven't had a drink yet. Later is a different story."

He paused, then put a hand on my shoulder as we both stared at our reflection in the long mirror, leaning on his left crutch for support.

"I'm happy for you, Johnny," he said, and I could swear I heard something like pride in his voice. I softened a bit. "You finally found a girl crazy enough to marry you."

I rolled my eyes as he laughed like it was the funniest thing he'd ever said. But for Danny, that was pretty much the equivalent of *I love you*, so I'd take it.

There was a knock on the bedroom door, and a second later, Kimmy poked her head in.

"You nearly ready?" she asked, and when I turned to face her, she came in and closed the door behind her. She wore one of the few dresses she owned; I'd only seen her wear it to our community dances.

"You look great," she said, her voice trembling, before covering her mouth with her hand. "So handsome."

"This seems like my cue," Danny said, and he hobbled out of the room on his crutches.

For a moment, Kimmy and I just looked at each other, smiling. It didn't feel like we needed to say anything; I knew what she felt just by meeting her eye. She'd always been my right hand, always had my back. My best friend and my constant companion. She may not have been my blood, but she was my sister in every sense of the word.

"Granny and Granddad would be so proud," she said, swiping at her eyes. "I wish they could see you, all dressed up like a gentleman. I think Granny would cry, but Granddad would laugh his ass off."

I chuckled. "Can practically hear him making fun of the cyberpunk haircut with the button-down shirt."

Kimmy giggled through tears, then said, "Everyone's ready downstairs. We should head to the garden."

"Lead the way."

It was a perfect, sunny spring day, and the rose garden was bursting with colour.

Between Kimmy, Claire, and me, we'd transformed it into a beautiful space again. We'd cut back the overgrowth and planted new flowers. I'd built a simple wedding arch at the end of the path, in front of the bench, and Claire had decorated it with vines and white flowers. We'd placed torches strategically throughout for when it got dark.

Kimmy and I had set up rows of foldable chairs last night, and damn near everyone in the Valley was there now. Families I knew well, as well as those I didn't. Some of the kids from Claire's classes were there. Danny sat with Jenna and their grandparents. Noah and Isla were farther down the aisle, with little Ely napping in a baby sling at Isla's breast. The Armstrongs sat in the front row; Sarah had already started crying, while Bruce gave me a sheepish smile as he held newborn Ben in his arms. Kimmy took her seat next to them, and I walked to the end of the aisle, where Abby waited to officiate.

This was my family. And my future was about to walk down that aisle.

Finally, Claire appeared at the garden gate, looking like an ethereal princess. Her long ivory dress was simple, but it accentuated her curves and had tiny, translucent beads that caught the light. Her red hair was down in soft waves down her back, braided half-up, with pale pink roses were threaded through it.

I smiled so wide that my jaw ached as she walked to me—a vision.

"Claire," I whispered, a lump rising in my throat. "You're so beautiful."

She grinned. "You clean up nicely yourself."

I couldn't help myself; I kissed her. Laughter broke out.

"Supposed to wait for the end, man!" Danny called.

"Like I give a fuck," I said wryly, and Claire giggled.

"Behave," she ordered, and I straightened.

Abby looked amused and irritated in equal measure.

"If you're quite finished," she said to me with a severe look, "we can get on with it, hmm?"

She went through the usual ceremony, and then we exchanged vows to love and care for each other always. I beamed as I slipped my mother's wedding ring on Claire's finger, and then, as soon as it'd started, it was over.

"You're now husband and wife, for as long as you both shall live. You may kiss the bride."

"Finally," I muttered.

I grabbed Claire around the waist, and she squeaked in surprise as I dipped her low and kissed her like it was our last. She kissed me back through giggles, and the cheers and applause were deafening.

I lowered my lips to her ear, murmuring words meant only for her.

"I could live a thousand lifetimes, baby, and it wouldn't be enough with you."

CHAPTER 44

Claire

The wedding was everything I'd hoped for and more.

After the ceremony, we moved away all the chairs to create a makeshift dance floor. Jenna and Liam played songs all evening long, and to my surprise, John's dancing had actually improved—something that hadn't happened since I'd met him.

"I practiced," he admitted sheepishly when I asked. "With Kimmy. Just a little bit."

I laughed. "She probably loved that."

"Yeah, I'm pretty sure I'm never hearing the end of that one," he replied with a grin.

Sarah had been kind enough to cook a generous buffet for everyone, and John made sure that the drink was well-stocked. I danced with most everyone, including Danny, who pretended to step on my feet as Allie watched and laughed. Sarah gave me an enormous hug before taking the baby home to bed, and it seemed like everyone stopped to tell me how pretty I looked, which made me flush. Kimmy and Danny ribbed John relentlessly, and he responded with his usual wry humour, which made for a lot of laughter throughout the evening.

It felt like being home—at long last.

A part of me had worried about this day. Despite my excitement, I'd still felt a sense of loss leading up to it. My father wouldn't walk me down the aisle. My mother wouldn't cry in the front row, and my sister wouldn't watch my first dance. Asha wouldn't be there to tease me about my nerves. As deeply as I felt their betrayal, those had been the important people in my life, and they were all—in one way or another—lost to me forever.

But seeing John, and Kimmy, and the people of the Valley...I knew that whatever I'd lost, I'd also gained so much. I'd married a good man that I loved more than anything. I'd become part of a community I'd grown to adore over these past months. Young Claire, trapped inside that compound, mourning her father's death and enduring her mother's wrath, could never have imagined such a moment.

I hoped she'd be proud.

We ate, drank, and danced all night long, until fireflies glowed in the darkness, and the party had begun to wind down.

"I love you," I said softly to John as he held me, gently turning us to a slow song. Only a couple others remained on the dance floor. "Thank you for saving me off that rooftop last year."

He chuckled and tightened his hold around my waist.

"Love you too, Claire Madigan," he murmured, and my heart tugged at my new name. "And for what it's worth, rescuing a pretty girl off a factory roof turned out to be the most important thing I ever did."

I kissed him thoroughly, a symphony of crickets serenading us.

❄

After most people had left, John led me back to the farmhouse. The light had been left on in the foyer, and he opened the front door, gesturing for me to go ahead of him.

I stayed where I was.

"Technically," I said with a smile, "the groom is supposed to carry the bride over the threshold."

John grinned. "That can be arranged."

He scooped me up into his arms, then kissed me before heading inside and up the stairs.

"Don't drop me, Wastelander," I teased.

He chuckled. "Never."

He carried me down the hall to our room, kicking the door shut behind him before setting me on our bed. I caught his chin in my hand and pulled him down to kiss me. He sighed and sunk into it, cradling my head.

"How was today?" I asked when we broke apart.

John smiled sweetly at me. "Just the happiest day I can remember."

One look at him said it was the truth, and my heart melted.

"Me too," I whispered, feeling almost shy. "It felt like...I'm part of things now. Part of the Valley, of the family. Part of you."

"Ah, Claire," John sighed, and he sat on the bed so he could pull me into his arms. "You are. Always have been."

I nodded, a lump of emotion forming in my throat, and he kissed my forehead.

"You're the most gorgeous bride there ever was," he said, sounding a little wistful. "Everyone thought so."

I giggled. "How could you know?"

"Because I know," he answered, his voice gruffer, betraying an undercurrent of desire that heated my blood. "Listen to your husband."

"Or what?" I said, raising an eyebrow.

"Or we'll have another talk like we had in that shed at the strip mall," John said with a wolfish grin.

"I don't seem to remember that one," I said, innocently cocking my head to one side.

"Let me refresh your memory then, wife," John growled, and I squealed as he grabbed me and hefted me up over his shoulder.

He stood, gave my backside a light swat, and laughed when I squeaked again.

"I don't think this is what you're supposed to do on your wedding night," I said disapprovingly from my upside-down position as he walked us into the ensuite bathroom.

"No?" he replied, chuckling as he turned on the light. "In that case, why don't you show me how it's done?"

John lowered me to the floor, and I gave him my best scowl.

"Yes, I think that'd be best," I said in an imperious tone.

I faced the vanity mirror and reached for the straps of my dress, lifting them over my shoulders. I reached back to unbutton it, and managed the first one, but the others were more difficult.

"Let me do that," John murmured, his voice suddenly low and husky.

I closed my eyes as he breathed into my ear and traced down my neck with his open mouth, enjoying the goosebumps it raised on my arms and the feel of his fingers carefully unfastening the remaining buttons. The dress fell to the floor, and I sighed as John slid a finger inside the waistband of my panties, stroking my skin.

"There are so many things I want right now," he said as he stared at us in the mirror, kissing the shell of my ear and making me shiver.

"Like what?" I whispered, the air thick with tension.

He slowly ran his free hand down the length of my back, caressing my sensitive skin, raising more goosebumps.

"To get on my knees and worship you," he breathed in my ear, and a pulsing heat began between my thighs. "To give you more pleasure than you can bear. And at the same time, I want to own you. I want to use you in the filthiest ways I can think of and leave you dripping my come so you'll never forget who you belong to...and that no one will ever need you, want you, love you, like I do."

My breath caught as he palmed my breasts hungrily. I wanted everything he did, wanted to possess and be possessed by him, to feel cherished and dirty in equal measure. With a shiver, I dropped my panties, making him sigh, then moved out of his grasp toward the shower. I turned on the showerhead and stepped under it, arching my back to allow the water to flow over my breasts and down my front in a way that was shamelessly erotic.

"Fuck," John muttered, watching me, and I grinned.

I wet my hair and washed up, massaging my hands in slow, circular motions over my body. I lingered at my breasts, sighing with pleasure as I gently caressed my nipples. The cleft between my thighs grew slick at my own attention and ached with need.

John clearly had enough because he stripped at a speed that made me giggle. He stepped into the shower behind me and pulled me back against him, letting me feel his rigid hardness against the small of my back as he sucked on the sensitive spot in the crook of my neck.

"Are you trying to tempt me into taking you right now, against this wall?" he said in my ear. "Because it's working."

I smiled, pleased, and surprised again at the effect I had on him. This strong, brave, surprisingly gentle man adored me, would lay down his life for me. He was the best of us—good and kind and hard-working—and through some tangled twist of fate, he was mine.

I turned to face John and kissed him, throwing my arms around his neck and pushing my tongue into his mouth. He exhaled sharply and pressed me into him, our wet, naked skin sliding together.

"I'm so lucky," I whispered against his neck, massaging his taut body. "You're better than anything I ever dared to dream."

"The feeling's mutual," he replied, his gaze tender.

I made a show of soaping him up under the water and he didn't object, but he groaned a little as I caressed him, obviously pent-up. His skin, browned by the sun, glistened under my attention, and my arousal only increased as I watched sparkling waterdrops drip over his lean, muscular form.

"You're beautiful," I sighed, and he grinned.

"Not half so pretty as my blushing bride," he teased, and predictably, heat rose to my face. I wanted him, and my arousal only increased as I watched him rinse under the showerhead.

I knelt on the tiled floor, and before John had time to react, I wrapped my hand around his shaft. He gasped softly, and I stroked him for a moment before taking him into my mouth. He made a small, strangled sound as I worked him with my tongue and began to suck.

"Your mouth is goddamn perfect," John groaned. "Christ, Claire."

The tiled floor was hard against my knees, and my jaw ached a little after a few minutes, but I didn't care. Nothing mattered more to me at that moment than pleasing him. I took him deeper, sucking harder, and he cursed, fisting his hands into my wet hair.

"My filthy girl," he murmured, and the way he said it made it sound like the sweetest endearment. "This making you wet? Tasting my cock on your knees like this?"

I moaned around him and met his eye before giving a short nod. The ache between my thighs was almost unbearable now.

"Good," he grunted, panting now. "I want to paint your pretty tits with my come. Make me come, beautiful."

I coaxed him closer and closer to the edge. His grip on my hair tightened, his groans growing deeper and longer, his hips undulating into my mouth. I wrapped my hand around the base of his shaft and pumped in time with each suck, and I knew he was done for, because he moved to pull out of my mouth with another choked noise.

He gasped my name, then came with a breathless, guttural cry as I stroked him through climax, spilling his seed onto my breasts. I gave a little moan watching him, ever fascinated by the way he lost control. He let out a long breath and relaxed his grip on my hair, softly stroking it.

After a beat, John pulled me to my feet and kissed me. When we broke apart, I quickly rinsed, then turned off the shower.

"Take me to bed, husband," I said with a smile.

We did a quick, sloppy drying job with a towel before he led me back into our room, clearly growing impatient. A gentle push, and I lay on my back at the edge of the bed, my legs hanging over the edge.

John lowered himself over me, and I wrapped my legs around his hips. He breathed in my ear, and I moaned. More wetness bloomed between my legs, leaking onto my innermost thighs. He fitted his hand to the nape of my neck, lifting my head back to spread slow, open-mouthed kisses down the soft, vulnerable flesh of my throat. His other hand cupped my breast, lightly pinching my nipple and rolling it between his fingertips.

"Please," I pleaded, grinding up against him. "John."

"Shh," he soothed, his mouth still on my skin. "I'll give you everything you want, baby. I promise. But it's our wedding night. Let me love you for a while."

I gasped as he flicked his tongue over my nipple, then licked in slow, torturous circles until he drew it into his mouth. He sucked hard, then gently bit down, teasing me with his teeth while his fingers worked my other nipple. I made high-pitched, desperate noises, beyond self-consciousness. His eyes roved over my nakedness, from my lips to my breasts, and down to where I was already spread wide for him.

"Please don't tell me you're going to spank me now," I said breath-lessly. "I can't handle more teasing."

John grinned and shook his head.

"Tonight will be nothing but pleasure for you," he murmured as he knelt on the floor beside the bed. "You'll come for me, again and again, until you can't stand it. I know you like it when I say you're mine...but tonight, I want to be yours."

I shuddered as he lifted my legs over his shoulders. His tongue on my clit was like velvet, soft and gentle, coaxing me to open wider, further. I gasped, then complied, opening my body as a flower opens to sunlight, then moaned as he licked in slow, methodical circles. Warmth flooded my limbs, and I tightened in response.

"So good," he said, exhaling sharply. "Just let yourself feel it."

I released my muscles, allowing my body to float on a cloud of rising sensation. I gasped as he slipped his fingers inside me, hearing the wet sounds they made as he curled them against me. A deep sigh escaped me as he pressed on it, bringing forth a new rush of pleasure.

John swirled his tongue in tighter circles, pairing it with urgent massaging of my inner wall. I whimpered at the intensity. He soothed me with love words, urging me to let go, to give myself to him. I surrendered with a helpless, high-pitched cry. I came harder than I expected, and my whole body curved to ride a wave of euphoria that crashed over me relentlessly.

When I finally lay there, limp and sated, John kissed my inner thighs and then stood. The floorboards creaked as he walked to the far corner of the room, and I frowned in confusion. He started dragging the antique full-length mirror towards the bed.

"What are you doing?"

"You'll see," he answered.

He maneuvered the mirror so that it faced the bed, then sat in front of it. He opened his legs wide, then patted the mattress in front of him. I hesitated, eyeing the mirror, but settled between his legs and let him pull me back against him.

"Spread your legs," he said against my hair, his gaze meeting mine in the mirror. "Let me see you."

I swallowed, suddenly nervous. Even though he'd seen me hun-dreds of times, it felt vulnerable to watch myself do it.

Clearly sensing my hesitation, John kissed my temple.

"It's alright," he said softly. "If this is too much, we can stop. But I want to watch you, see your beautiful face as I touch you."

I giggled nervously. "It feels...dirty."

A wolfish smile spread across John's features in the mirror.

"Isn't that at least part of the appeal?" he asked, nipping my ear. "I want to see my cock buried deep inside you, and I want to watch while I make you mine again for the hundredth time. I want to see how sweetly you come for me again."

Biting my lip, I slowly spread my legs apart, baring myself to him in the mirror. It was obvious that I was very wet. I flushed self-consciously as John brazenly stared at me, his eyes following the curves of my body in the mirror, drinking me in. When he spoke, his voice was a low growl.

"You're the most beautiful woman I've ever seen, Claire. Truly."

My flush deepened, this time with pleasure. He combed his fingers through my hair and gently inhaled the scent. In the candlelight, the locks reflected red and gold, creating a halo effect.

I gave a soft shudder as his other hand migrated south, settling between my legs. He covered my clit with his palm before sliding two fingers inside me. He pumped his fingers methodically and made a gentle grinding motion against my clit at the same time. I gasped.

"Look at yourself," John breathed in my ear, his free hand coming up to tilt my chin, so I was forced to look at our reflection. "How breathtaking you are."

The woman in the mirror was heavily flushed, her eyes bright with anticipation and pleasure, her red hair flowing wild down her chest and back. She looked love-drunk and wanton, and somehow, that only stoked the flame of my arousal higher. I shook with pleasure, my entire body rigid as I chased the tempest of sensations further and further towards bliss.

The pressure inside me grew unbearable, especially because I felt him hardening behind me as he watched me in the mirror. His fingers sped up, sliding in and out of me in a deep, steady rhythm, while he moved his thumb to play with my clit.

"Come on," John coaxed. "Eyes on me, gorgeous. Watch me make you come."

I met his gaze in the mirror, hard and commanding, and a rush of intense euphoria filled my body. A hoarse cry escaped me, then another, and another, as the pleasure worked its way through every muscle. When it passed, I went limp against him.

"That was a nice one," he said as he pressed kisses against my shoulder, but his reflection had a wicked glint in its eye. "But I think you can give me more."

My eyes narrowed. "You're awfully smug for a guy that's so hard his dick is like a brand against my back."

He arched an eyebrow. "Getting mouthy, hmm? Maybe this will help."

Without warning, he lifted my hips and pulled me backward, pressing the tip of his erection at my entrance. I gasped as gravity aided me in taking his full length, my buttocks braced against his thighs, and John gave a deep, throaty groan. He kissed my hair, and his gaze moved to our reflection. He lowered his hand between my thighs to touch the point of our joining, and I trembled.

"There's my sweet girl," John murmured. "Taking me so well."

Watching him make love to me added another intimate dimension; I loved seeing him revel in our pleasure. His fingers drifted up from our connection to stroke me, knowing instinctively how to work my clit, still sensitive from orgasm. His rhythm inside me was slow, deep, and deliciously sensual. I gave a low moan, which quickly turned into a high-pitched sob as I shattered again. Pleasure exploded again in my body, spreading all the way to the tips of my fingers and toes, curling them.

"Fucking hell, that hot little cunt pulsing around me," John growled, his voice uneven. "You feel so damn good, baby. You're holding me so tight."

"I need more," I whimpered. "I don't know how, but I do."

His reflection smirked at me. "Good girl. Keep coming on your husband's cock."

I didn't even know if I could, but I was a woman possessed, addicted to the way John made me feel, and he was determined to push me to my absolute limit. I let my hand fall between my thighs, massaging my clit as I lifted and dropped my hips, riding up and down his shaft. He cursed again and grasped my hips tightly, guiding me.

I came apart once more, unable to stop myself, and yet I was insatiable. Stimulated past the point of reason, I needed even more. I increased the pace until I was bouncing eagerly on his lap, my breasts jiggling lewdly in the mirror. I was beyond caring as the tension broke inside me, and I came hard again, enveloping him with my climax. As the pleasure ebbed, I fell back against him.

"I can't take any more," I gasped out, pleading. "Please let me stop."

"Thank Christ," John panted. "I deserve a medal for lasting through that."

I giggled breathlessly, feeling loose and free in a way I only felt in these intimate moments with the man I loved. *My husband.*

"Turn around, beautiful," he murmured after we'd caught our breath. "I want to look at my wife while I make love to her."

My heart felt fit to burst as I maneuvered into position, straddling his lap and taking him inside again. He looked up at me with pure adoration, and a lump rose unexpectedly in my throat. I tilted his head back and rested my forehead against his, cradling his cheek in my hand.

John sighed, his eyelids falling shut, and I copied him. We breathed as one, in sync, as I circled my hips over his. I held his face in my hands and kissed him with languid sweetness, eager to savour him. He tangled his tongue with mine, one hand twisted in my hair, the other cupping my bottom and urging me on.

A kind of trace overtook us, and we temporarily stepped out of time and space. Only we existed—only the tender need in our kisses, the gentle rhythm of our bodies, and the breath we shared. *We who are two would be one.*

"Ah, my love," John whispered, and the spell broke.

He shuddered deeply as he came in hard surges inside me, his arms around me in a death grip. Low, guttural groans came from deep in his chest, and I trailed kisses up his jaw as I watched him unravel. When he finally relaxed, he buried his face in my shoulder.

When he'd recovered, John looked back up at me. Concern touched his eyes as he caressed my wet cheek, slick with tears.

"You okay, baby?" he said, so tenderly that another tear escaped.

"Yes," I replied, a tremor in my voice. "Just...a little overwhelmed."

"I know," he soothed as he wiped away tears with his thumb. "It's alright, sweetheart. Come with me."

He led me to the bathroom, and we took another brief shower. He rubbed my shoulders under the warm water, easing tension with his strong farmhand fingers and murmuring endearments meant only for me.

We settled back in bed, and I propped myself up on my elbow at his side, smoothing his hair before stroking the contours of his face with my fingertips. He gazed up at me, his eyelids growing heavy under my patient attention, and I smiled. It was rare that he fell asleep first, and I savoured the quiet trust he gave me by letting himself drift.

I sang softly, a French lullaby taught to me by my father so many years before, and his eyes closed.

"What's it mean?" John mumbled, his words slurred by drowsiness.

I translated roughly, tracing his bottom lip with my thumb.

"If I am the night, you are the stars."

CHAPTER 45

Claire

Sunlight streamed in through a crack in the curtains, searing my eyes, and I groaned and rolled over onto John's side of the bed. Even though I was always up early nowadays, I didn't think I'd ever be a morning person like John was. He actually *enjoyed* getting up at daybreak every day, the maniac.

I smiled. He'd woken me at dawn and made love to me again, slow and tender, before tucking me back into bed with a kiss, telling me to sleep in. The Claire that had just met the gruff man on the rooftop could never have imagined he'd turn out to be so sweet.

Then again, she'd have a heart attack if she knew he was now her husband.

So would most of the people I grew up with, I thought, and my mind drifted to Asha. I wondered where she was, or if she was even still alive. I doubted it, and somehow—even though she'd betrayed me so completely—I mourned her. I should've hated her, but I couldn't find it in me to do it. She was the last piece of my old life, and she'd died trying to get back to that life we'd lost. Not so different to how I'd been when I first entered the Wasteland—ignorant, insolent, and pitiable.

It was unfathomable how much of a difference simple kindness could make, how it could change the course of a life. It was the reason I'd survived—the reason that everyone in the Valley survived. Kindness was the root of love, and created bonds that could not break, even when tested.

Whatever had happened to Asha in the Wasteland, she never found kindness...and it had broken her in a way that couldn't be repaired. It didn't excuse her actions, but it made me understand them. I'd been saved from the Wasteland and from myself; she had not, and by the time I'd found her again, it was too late. She'd never stopped thinking of herself as an outsider, never accepted her new place in this ever-changing world.

But I had. And someday, I'd forgive myself for not being able to save her.

I let out a long breath, trying to return to the present. The last couple days had been so joyful. I threw my legs over the side of bed just as the bedroom door opened and John appeared.

"Morning," he said with a sweet smile. He held a plate of eggs and toast, and my stomach grumbled audibly, making him chuckle. "Brought you breakfast."

He sat down on the bed next to me, handing me the plate. I gave him a quick kiss, then proceeded to demolish my food.

"You're a saint," I said between bites, and he laughed.

"Figured you'd be hungry after last night. And early this morning."

A faint flush rose to my cheek, and he caressed it, grinning wolfishly. I finished eating, then set the plate aside and climbed onto his lap to kiss him properly.

"And late this morning?" I murmured, pushing him onto his back as I straddled him.

"Round three will have to wait," John said, amused, looking up at me. "I'm taking you on our honeymoon today, remember?"

Truthfully, I'd nearly forgotten in the flurry of activity yesterday, but I beamed.

"Where are you taking me?"

"It wouldn't be a surprise, then, would it?" John replied with a grin. "Pack your things, and bring something to swim in. We'll be gone a few days."

***

After packing supplies, we hiked for most of the morning to get out of the Valley. Thankfully, it was another beautiful day under the warm June sun. We walked arm-in-arm as much as we could over the rough terrain, chatting and enjoying one another's company. With everything that'd happened in the last few months, it was nice to be alone together in the peace of the forest. It felt like our first days together, when we were getting to know each other for the first time.

"Still no clues on where we're going?" I asked for the third time since we'd left. "Come on. You have to give me a hint."

"No hints. And besides, it's noon now—only a couple more hours till we're there."

I groaned, and John grinned.

"You've gone soft on me after these months at home, huh? Have you already forgotten what it's like to walk all day?"

"Forgive me for not wanting to relive that joyous period of our lives," I replied dryly. "I like being a homebody."

His smile softened into something tender. "I like it, too. A lot easier to get through the day knowing that I get to come home to you."

"You're just trying to sweet-talk me so that I'll forget that my honeymoon thus far has involved a six-hour hike."

He chuckled. "Maybe."

I backed up against a wide oak tree, pulling him with me. "You'll have to make it up to me. Somehow."

He caged me in, resting his hands against the bark on either side of my head.

"Is that right?" he said, his voice lower and huskier as he leaned in, his lips inches from mine. "Maybe I will."

His lips brushed mine lightly, tempting me. I fisted my hands in the fabric of his shirt and pulled him in, slipping my tongue into his mouth. He groaned and pressed me hard against the tree, stroking his tongue over mine and kissing me deeper. His knee pressed between my thighs, and his hands came up to hold my face. He kissed me until I was hot and breathless and eagerly rubbing myself against him, and then...it all suddenly stopped.

John backed away, a small, teasing smile on his handsome face.

"We're making good time," he said. "Let's keep going."

I shot him an outraged look. "You did that on purpose."

He laughed. "Obviously. I like seeing you all hot and bothered. Now come on."

"Tease," I grumbled.

The rest of the hike was mostly uphill, and by the end of it, I was covered in a thin, unpleasant coat of sweat. Finally, we reached the summit of a cliff, where a small log cabin was mostly concealed amongst the brush. It blended into the scenery, with ivy snaking over its worn walls and trees looming overhead.

John went ahead and unlocked the door with a key he'd brought. Inside was a simple, one-room cabin with a stone fireplace, a wood-stove, a small kitchenette, a dining table and two chairs, a sagging sofa, and a big, comfortable-looking bed that dominated the space. It was sparse but had a homey feel to it, with a few framed photos on the walls of places I'd never seen: a leaning tower; a large, red canyon; and a massive, horseshoe-shaped waterfall.

"Granny and Granddad built it, back during Old World times," John explained. "A place for them to get away from Summerhurst every now and then. We visited in the summers as kids. They eventually started letting anyone in the Valley use it, and over time, it became tradition for new married couples to come here for their honeymoons. I thought it'd be nice for us to do that, too."

He gave me a somewhat apprehensive look, as though he somehow thought I might not like holing up alone with him in a beautiful, isolated spot for a few days.

"That's a great tradition," I said with a smile, touching his arm. "If it's empty most of the time, how's it so clean?"

He chuckled. "Danny and I rode here a couple days ago to give it a good clean-out while you were at school. Put clean sheets on the bed, chopped some firewood. I wanted to make it nice for you."

My heart squeezed, and I kissed him.

"Thank you, darling. I love it."

He beamed. "And you haven't even seen the best part yet."

We dropped off our bags before John led me back outside and through a small copse of trees, to the edge of the cliff. My breath caught as a large lake came into view, forest sloping all around it, crisp blue sky against greenery. The cliff jutted out over the pristine blue water, and in the distance, I could see a narrow swath of sand that met the water's edge. It was breathtaking.

John grinned at my awestruck expression. "Pretty great view, huh?"

"You can say that again," I replied, blinking. "Might be even prettier than the Valley."

"With the lake here, we can go fishing and swimming if you like. You've never been to a beach, have you?"

I shook my head.

"It's a small one here, but we can hike down and picnic there tomorrow."

I smiled at him. "Sounds perfect."

We stared out over the water for a moment, enjoying the afternoon sun.

"And now," John continued, "we can get back to what's really important."

Without warning, he hauled me up over his shoulder just like the night before and carried me back toward the cabin as I squeaked and laughed.

"You can't just throw me over your shoulder anytime you want!"

"Oh, really? Because it seems like I just did, princess."

He gave my backside a swat, and I laughed as he walked through the door of the cabin.

"Put me down!"

He flopped me onto the bed with a big, goofy smile, then covered my body with his.

"Should I make it up to you now?" he murmured.

"Nothing to make up for," I replied breathlessly, and the world fell away as he kissed me senseless and slid his warm hands into my shirt.

❄

I stood at the edge of the cliff the next day, staring out over the lake as I waited for John to finish packing for our hike down to the beach. The steady chorus of birdsong and the gentle swooshing of the breeze made me feel more peaceful than I'd felt in a long time, erasing the chaos of the last few months. I closed my eyes and breathed deeply.

For the first time in a long time, I felt safe. I'd escaped the cult's clutches, and with Asha gone, they had no way to find me again. Even if Asha's betrayal had been a setback in the Valley's acceptance of outsiders, I'd proven myself to them. I'd earned my place there, and now I was finally home. I had friends. I had a family. I had everything I'd been looking for my whole life.

The sorrow of losing my sister was still there, still aching, especially since she'd protected me one last time, even when she was in so deep with the Order that it endangered her. But Holly, like Asha, had made her choice, and I'd made mine.

Even after my world had ended, I kept going. Hope grew out of strange places, blooming through the cracks and crevices of despair. It was what had brought John to me. It was why I'd survived a winter in the wilderness. It was why even after I'd been literally thrown off the horse, I got back on.

"You gonna jump?"

I whirled around. "What?"

John grinned. "You heard me. Are you?"

"How do you know it's safe?" I asked, frowning. "It's not a small drop."

"I've done it loads of times," he replied with a shrug. "No rocks, and it's deep enough. But I understand if you're scared."

I shot him a mutinous look. "Is that a challenge, Wastelander?"

He raised an eyebrow, and his grin widened.

"Call it whatever you want...compound girl."

It's on. I could hardly back down now that he'd called me out so blatantly.

"Prepare to eat your words," I said primly as I stripped down.

I'd prepared a little surprise of my own. I'd commissioned Nimkii to make me a new swimsuit. It was a deep blue one-piece, with an open back and pretty ribbon ties at the shoulders. I'd intended on wearing it this summer at Glacier Lake and hopefully dazzling him.

I shed the rest of my clothes, revealing the swimsuit. I felt John's gaze lingering on my body, and I stopped to bask in his attention for a moment.

"Christ, that's not fair," he said with a chuckle, then pulled me against him for a kiss. "Let's forget the picnic."

"No way," I said, amused. "You challenged my honour, and I intend to prove myself."

He held up his hands. "Go ahead, then."

I walked to the edge of the cliff, and one look down at the water made me feel a little less brave. It did seem awfully far down. I bit my lip, hesitating.

"You don't have to do it, baby," John said kindly. "I won't judge."

But I didn't want to give in to my fear. If the past year and a half had taught me anything, it was that sometimes, there was no other way forward: I just had to jump.

"You're sure it's safe?" I glanced back at him.

His expression turned serious. "Of course."

I took a deep breath, backed up a couple steps, and took it at a run. I didn't give myself time to chicken out. One moment, the soft grass was beneath my feet; the next, I was airborne.

I screamed—part-fear, part-exhilaration—as I fell. I hit the water feet-first with a big splash and was enveloped greedily by the lake. The water was cool and refreshing on my skin. I savoured those brief seconds underwater, when everything was quiet and still. The jump was cathartic, and as I swam upward, I imagined leaving the pain of the last few months there, slumbering forever at the bottom of the lake. When I surfaced, I came out clean.

"I did it!" I yelled at the cliff, and John's loud laughter carried to me.

"So you did," he called back, standing at the edge. "My little daredevil. Meet me at the beach, okay?"

Sweet adrenaline still alive in my veins, I turned in the direction of the beach and swam toward the shore. It'd been a long time since I'd gone swimming, and I'd missed it. The lengthy paddle to the beach was welcome.

When I reached the shore, beautiful, untouched wilderness expanded before me in all directions. The beach was small, as John had said: a strip of sand no more than ten feet wide, following the shoreline until it dissipated into soft, tall grass. The grass was mostly clear for several metres before giving way to the lush, green forest that encircled everything. On the left, a natural rock wall rose three feet from the ground, just high enough to conceal a shallow gulley behind it. The low ditch stretched back toward the forest, like a secret pathway.

We spread out our blankets and had a picnic on the beach, watching the lake gently lap at the shore. I stretched my legs out in front of me, wiggling my toes in the sand as I bit into a bright red strawberry. The texture was strange to me; I'd never felt anything so soft, yet abrasive.

"You happy, baby?"

I looked over to see John watching me, a small smile on his face.

"Yes," I said sincerely. "More than I ever thought I could be again."

His smile broadened before he put an arm around my shoulders.

"We should try the honey cakes," I said after a moment. "Kimmy was raving about Sarah's recipe at the wedding."

"They are pretty great," John said as he unwrapped them and offered me one. "Lots of labour goes into them, so savour it."

Eagerly, I bit into the centre of the palm-sized cake. The honey burst out unexpectedly, covering my tongue and half my face. I made a small sound of alarm and tried desperately to swipe away the sticky, golden mess with my hand, but it only stuck to my skin instead.

John burst into laughter. "Little overfilled there, sweetheart?"

I continued to swipe at the honey but only succeeded in making a bigger mess.

"You could help me instead of laughing," I chided, but giggled in spite of myself.

"You're right," he said with a mischievous grin. "Where are my manners?"

Before I knew what was happening, he'd pushed me onto my back and started kissing my face, licking and sucking a little honey off each time.

"John!" I squealed, giggling wildly as he pinned me.

"What?" he teased as he licked honey from the corner of my mouth. "I'm helping."

"Yeah, helping yourself!"

He laughed and kept going, only granting a reprieve when any traces of honey were long gone, and I was gasping for breath from laughter. He chuckled at my exhausted expression. His amber eyes bore into mine, and with his sun-browned skin and sweet smile, he was incredibly handsome.

"Christ, do I love you," he murmured, his thumb stroking my bottom lip. Sunlight glinted off his wedding band. "My Claire. My wife."

My throat tightened. My heart was so full after the last couple days.

"I never thought I'd have this," I said softly, smoothing a lock of hair away from his face above mine. "Someone who taught me to be brave, and strong, and loved me so well that I'd begin to learn how to love myself. I never thought I'd be joyful, or that I'd know any true freedom."

John's eyes shone brightly in the sun, and he lay his head against my breast, wrapping his arms around my middle. I pressed a kiss to his temple.

"I never thought there'd be you."

CHAPTER 46

Claire

T wo days of sun, swimming, and sex passed in a blissful haze that I never wanted to end. The honeymoon felt like a protective cocoon, shielding me from the horror of the last couple of months. Only sunshine, orgasms, and my handsome Wastelander existed here, and I was content to keep it that way indefinitely.

The fourth day was warm, and we took a hike through the woods before spending the rest of the day on the beach. I even jumped from the cliff again, much to John's amusement.

"Horseback riding and now cliff diving?" he said with a chuckle as he watched me swim from his spot on the beach. "Never guessed my Claire would turn out to be so adventurous."

I laughed and waded up onto the sand to plop down beside him. "I'm full of surprises."

He wrapped a towel around my shoulders before pulling me against him. I lay my head against his sun-warmed shoulder, my wet hair spilling over his bare chest. I picked up his t-shirt, which he'd left lying beside him, and pulled it over my head, letting it fall to my thighs before resting my head against him again. He smiled affectionately at me, then reached next to him to pick up a large white flower.

"Found it growing in the grass near the boulders," he said, nodding to our left. "Made me think of you."

I smiled. "And why's that?"

John nestled the flower in my hair, behind my ear. "Because it's beautiful and delicate. Like you."

I snorted in protest. "I am not delicate!"

He chuckled. "You are. In the way you look, talk, and move. I like it."

Mollified, I nuzzled against his shoulder, and we sat in silence like that for a few moments, gazing across the sparkling water and enjoying the sunshine.

I was about to ask John if he'd swim with me again when I felt him tense next to me, suddenly on alert. When I raised my head to look at him, he was frowning, clearly listening carefully.

"What—" I began, but he put a finger to his lips, and I fell silent.

It had gotten oddly quiet. No bird calls, no rustling leaves. There was only the soft whistle of a light breeze that somehow felt ominous. John looked over his shoulder towards the dirt road that led out to the old highway. A faint mechanical whine hummed in the distance. Though I couldn't precisely identify it, I knew I'd heard it before. My heart started pounding.

"We're not alone," John said. "Stay quiet and follow me."

He spoke rapidly in that low, authoritative tone that told me he'd switched into survival mode. Something was deeply wrong.

We grabbed our bags and weapons. I followed John to the rocky wall of boulders he'd gestured to. Beyond them, the terrain dipped into a shallow, mostly concealed gulley. He led me into the ditch, and we crouched behind the boulders.

"Take out the rabbit gun," John instructed as he laid his rifle across his lap. "Be ready."

The whine grew louder, and I suddenly understood that it was a combustion engine. The kind that only military vehicles at the Cave had used. My heart thumped clumsily against my ribs. My only thought was that it had to be the cult. No one else would've had access. And they were here for me.

John's expression was grim and focused as multiple vehicles approached. The engine sounds died some distance away, and vehicle doors opened and banged shut. My hands were clammy around the rabbit gun.

"You're sure the signal came from here?" a man's voice said skeptically. "We're in the middle of buttfuck nowhere, Sergeant."

"Yes," another man insisted. "The tracker says Ainley's within 500 metres of here. She only just popped up again a couple days ago. We verified with IT that it's working properly. So, either she ripped it out—unlikely—or she's here somewhere."

Panic flooded my senses. Somehow, they'd tracked me again. We were hidden, but not for long.

"They have rifles, and some are armoured," John muttered. "Shit."

"They're going to find me," I whispered.

Already, more voices joined the previous two. By my count, there were at least five of them out there, searching for me. One look at John told me that he knew it too: we were vastly outnumbered and outgunned. His jaw tightened, and I could almost see the wheels spinning in his head.

"Run," John said in a low voice.

"What?" I shot back. "No!"

"Yes," he replied, his expression hardened. "Crawl along the gulley until you reach the edge of the woods. I'll buy you time to get there. The forest will give you cover. Then you run like hell, you understand?"

He fished in the pocket of his pants, produced his compass, and pressed it into my hand.

"Follow it northwest back home."

"I can't leave you," I whispered, my throat constricting.

"I'll be fine. Send outriders back."

To clean up what's left of you? Tears welled in my eyes as John pulled me close and kissed my lips, equal parts tender and desperate. The truth it contained tore me open: it was a goodbye kiss.

"I love you," he murmured. He wrapped a hand around the back of my head and brought my forehead to his lips, pressing a quick, hard kiss there. "Go."

For a half-second, I was frozen, my pulse pounding in my ears.

A million images of John came into my mind all at once. The first time I saw him, up on that rooftop at the abandoned factory. My first fishing lesson and his pride when I caught one. His stunned expression the first time I kissed him. His sweet, uninhibited laughter when he was messing around with Kimmy or Danny. His sleepy, satisfied smile as he held me after we made love. The tears he shed at his grandparents' grave. The way he looked at me at our wedding, just days ago, as if I was the most precious thing in his entire world.

As I watched him shift into a more comfortable shooting position, my stomach flipped. They didn't want him—only me.

I knew what I had to do, and it was either completely crazy or moronic. Likely both. But there were no other options left, and no time to come up with a better plan. I would do anything to save my Wastelander.

"Hey, Sergeant!" a man's voice called, uncomfortably close to our hiding spot. "Looks like somebody's camped here recently."

Heart in my mouth, I took my pistol and tucked a pocketknife into the ribbons of my swimsuit at the shoulder. I crawled deeper into the gulley as John instructed, until I was far enough away that I was no longer in arm's reach. I looked over my shoulder, watching John carefully. He was waiting in position, watching to see what they'd do before he made himself known.

I had seconds before the first shot would be fired.

I sprang to my feet and ran up the slope, towards the voices, screaming as loud as I could.

"What the fuck—?" another male voice shouted.

I reached the top of the slope and briefly caught a glimpse of my pursuers—men in military uniforms like the ones they'd worn back at the Cave. No black Order uniforms. No Eye masks. No markings of the cult anywhere.

Who are these people? I had no time to contemplate. Instead, I put my plan into action.

"Bear!" I screeched like a ninny, pointing behind me in the opposite direction from where John was still hidden.

I sprinted like a marathon runner for the woods, suddenly very aware of the fact that I was barefoot and wearing nothing but a bikini and John's oversized t-shirt. I pulled on my braid, loosing my long, red hair. Instantly recognizable, easy to spot in almost any landscape—a beacon to my pursuers.

"I've got eyes on her!" someone yelled stupidly, as though that wasn't exactly what I wanted.

That same someone gave chase. He was closer than I'd anticipated and gained ground on me quickly. We were still on the beach—flat and open, no trees to conceal me. Only a few feet from the treeline, I cried out as a hand closed around my hair and yanked me backwards, toppling me onto the sand. I dropped my pistol.

No, I need to keep running, I thought frantically. I need to draw them farther away.

"Sir—" the soldier holding my hair began calling, just as a deafening bang split the air. I yelped as I was splattered with hot, sticky blood. The right side of the soldier's head was now a gushing, gory mess of tissue. Blood spurted out, and he let go of my hair, collapsing like a marionette with its strings abruptly severed.

As always, John's aim was impeccable.

The soldiers scattered, yelling to one another and struggling to find cover. I sprang up and retrieved my pistol from the ground. *Deep breath, Claire.* I screamed again, louder and longer, and bolted for the trees.

I heard a cacophony of cursing behind me, and more men pursued me. I couldn't be sure it was all of them, but I hoped it would be enough. It had to be enough.

I ran through the woods, wincing as my feet scraped over sharp rocks and tree roots. I got caught momentarily on a branch and pine needles rained down on me, but I used the surge of adrenaline to keep going.

The soldiers weren't used to the rough terrain of the forest, and though their apparent inexperience slowed them down, I had been running for far longer and was beginning to tire. I darted behind a large tree trunk for cover, gasping for air, then peeked around the side.

"You see where she went?"

He was only twenty feet away, his grey tactical uniform practically a flashing red light in the green of the forest, and I didn't give myself time to overthink. I aimed my pistol around the tree trunk and fired, hitting him square in the chest. John would've been proud of that shot.

He fell backwards, and there was immediately answering gunfire. I stayed with my back pressed against the tree until it stopped, and mercifully, I wasn't hit. I took off again and we repeated the pattern: I hid in the thick brush and fired on them when I could.

I took out two more soldiers, but there were still at least three following me. I didn't know how long I could keep this up. I only had a handful of bullets left, and I hadn't planned this far ahead. My single-minded goal had been to draw them away from John.

"There!"

They'd spotted me again, and I started running once more. I burst into a large clearing. Without the cover of trees, there was nowhere to hide, and my lungs were screaming in protest.

A soldier entered the clearing and let out a feral yell as he caught sight of me. My whole body ached with exertion, begging me to rest, and I could hardly breathe. He was gaining on me. Ten paces away, then five, then two, then...

Pain exploded in my head as I was slammed into a tree trunk on the opposite side of the clearing, face first.

"Drop your weapon," a furious male voice growled in my ear. "Now."

I panted helplessly, my strength gone, and released my grip on the pistol. It clattered to the ground.

"Don't fucking move." Cold steel pressed against the nape of my neck—the barrel of a gun. "Or I swear I'll blow your fucking head off your shoulders."

I couldn't do much besides what I was told.

"You think you can take out my guys, bitch?" he continued, rage imbued in every syllable. "What gives you the right?"

He abruptly flipped me to face him, slamming me against the tree trunk again. I whimpered at the splitting pain that went through my head in response, but the movement jostled the pocketknife I'd tucked into the ribbons at my shoulder, reminding me of its presence.

In one motion, I grabbed it and flipped it open. In the next, I stabbed my attacker, aiming for his throat. However, he jostled me violently, and I slipped, sinking my blade in the crook of his neck, just left of his tactical vest.

"You little bitch!" he screamed, his hand automatically grasping at his neck. He didn't pull it out like I hoped; instead, his gloved black hand closed around my throat, squeezing, crushing my windpipe against the tree.

I choked, reaching instinctively for my neck, uselessly trying to pry his hand away. He tightened his hold, and no air was coming into my lungs. Spots appeared in my vision as I writhed desperately, flopping like a fish that knew it was dying.

These were to be my last moments. I knew it. I could only hope that my little stunt had saved John from this same fate. Either way, I'd never see him again.

I love you, Wastelander.

The world went dark, and the next thing I knew, I was lying in the grass at the base of the tree. Two soldiers were in a physical altercation a few feet away, where one man appeared to be trying to restrain the other. Too weak to move, I lay there blinking rapidly, trying to ascertain if I was still among the living.

"What part of *alive* is hard for you to understand, Sergeant?" the taller soldier was shouting. "You were ordered not to harm the target. Now I find you choking the life out of her?"

"She wounded three of my guys!" the other man yelled back. "And she fucking stabbed me! I want that little cunt wiped off the map, Major!"

The Major shoved him hard, toppling him onto the ground.

"That's enough," he growled, panting. "When we get back to base, we'll deal with your insubordination. For now, gather your squad. *I* will handle the target."

Though his face was obscured by his helmet, the Sergeant looked ready to explode with rage. To my surprise, however, he stalked off, leaving the clearing behind.

The Major walked over to me, lying in the grass, and knelt by my side.

"Are you hurt?" he asked, his voice surprisingly level.

"Besides passing out from being choked half to death?" I croaked. "And being chased into the woods by strange men? I'm doing great."

"My apologies for my subordinate's behaviour," he replied curtly. "However, I advise you to end this. You won't win, and you'll make it harder on yourself if you continue to fight. Come with us willingly, and I'll see to it that no one lays a hand on you again."

"Come with you where, exactly?" I asked, bewildered. "You're not the Order."

"So, you've heard of them," he said quietly. "Good. You'll know what's at stake when we reach the Delta, then."

He offered me a gloved hand and hauled me to my feet. My head was still swimming.

"The Delta?"

"A compound a couple hundred kilometres from here. That's where we're bringing you."

I stared at him. "Why?"

"That's as much as I'm authorized to share at this time. I had one of my guys drive the vehicle back out to the highway, so we'll meet him there. Now, you can walk out of here with me willingly, or I can tase you and carry you out. What'll it be?"

I automatically glanced in the direction of the beach. I couldn't go. I couldn't leave John. But what choice did I have?

"You don't need to worry," the Major said, clearly seeing my reaction. "No Wastelanders will pursue us. I left a crew behind to deal with the one who was chasing you."

The air left my lungs all over again. "What?"

"The Wastelander," he said, more slowly, as though I was stupid. "He's been dealt with. He won't hurt you again."

I fell back on the ground and buried my face in the grass as raw screams ripped through my throat, echoing through the forest in a demented choir of anguish.

CHAPTER 47

John

I love you.

Those were the last words I said to her, begging her to run. I didn't have any illusions that I'd survive this fight. There was one of me and at least a dozen of them—soldiers, too, from the look of it. But I could give her time, and I could give these bastards a taste of what they deserved.

When Claire screamed and ran, I wanted to shake her. At the same time, I was terrified. They had a clear shot at her, and she was barely armed. The opposite of everything I'd taught her.

What the fuck were you thinking?

But when the soldiers chased after her, I understood. She was trying to protect me. To lead them away from where I was still hidden. Hoping they would never know I was there.

Too bad for them that they were dead the second they said they were looking for her.

I silently tracked the soldiers chasing after Claire through my scope. My finger itched over the trigger. They were far enough behind, but when one grabbed her by the hair, I fired. Blew his head off without a second thought.

Chaos broke out. Men yelled at each other, seeming confused about what the hell just happened. After a beat, they split up. The ones in tactical gear chased after Claire. Fuck. The regular uniformed ones stayed behind to investigate.

Claire bolted for the woods. At least she'd have cover there…for a while, anyway.

The makings of a plan formed. If I stayed behind the boulders, I might have a shot against them. Not a great one, but better than nothing. I could stay low in the ditch behind the rocks and try to use that to get to the woods, where I'd have the upper hand.

I peeked over the top of the rocks and let out a breath. Most of them were fumbling with suppressors, except for one that advanced toward my hiding spot. Perfect. I aimed at where he'd be with my pistol and listened to his footsteps. When the lone soldier rounded the corner, I damn near emptied it into him. He let out a wet gasp, staggered, and collapsed.

More shouting, more confusion. I took advantage of their surprise and popped up, snapped a sight picture, and fired. I didn't stay to watch, but knew he was down. A barrage of return fire whizzed over my head. It looked like maybe four men and one body. I hunted bears with this rifle, so it was going to be two bodies pretty soon.

After unloading at me, they all stopped to reload. Idiots.

I shot another one as he fumbled with his magazine. They paused again after returning fire, as if trying to decide what to do. There was more shouting back and forth, and I heard them moving toward me. I palmed a rock and tossed it in a high arc over the boulder as hard as I could to buy me precious seconds of distraction. Staying low in the gulley, I dashed up the hill toward the treeline.

Shots followed me, but with the cover of the ditch, they only hit dirt or trees. Distance and terrain were my only advantages.

I'd intended to follow Claire, but having to cover myself meant that I was off-course, and I didn't know the exact way she'd gone. I heard gunshots in the distance and had to force myself to take a breath. One problem at a time. The sooner I dealt with these bastards, the sooner I could find her.

They followed me into the brush, but they were clearly out of their element on the rough terrain. I hunted them silently. The trees provided decent cover, and I could tell by the way they spoke to one another that not having eyes on me spooked them. Good.

We danced around each other through the trees, and I stayed out of sight. Waited for the right moment. Two of the three finally broke away to search, and I picked them off before they knew what was happening. As soon as he realized he was alone, the last guy broke away and ran.

I had one last shot. I let him run, watching him through the scope. Just when he was about to reach the beach—just when the dumbass thought he was safe, putting distance between us—I gently caressed the trigger and put a bullet through his head.

□I reloaded my guns and waited just long enough to be sure no one was left, that reinforcements weren't coming. The forest was eerily quiet. The distant gunshots I'd heard earlier were silent now. There was no rustling, no sounds of anyone running through the brush. Silent as a grave.

My breath caught. *Don't think like that.*

I ached to call her name, but I couldn't risk giving away my position to the surviving soldiers. If I had to fight them, surprise and stealth would be the only things on my side.

Instead, I'd have to track her, the way I would on a hunt. I made myself go back out to the beach and find my pack. I only stopped to fish out a few cartridges of ammunition before running back toward the woods.

I retraced Claire's steps, following the impressions in the sand and then the trail of disturbed soil and broken branches she'd left behind in the woods. Her small footprints in the dirt reminded me that she was barefoot, and somehow, that made my blood boil all over again. Attacking a woman so defenceless that she wasn't even wearing shoes when she fled—what brave soldiers these men were. The kind of guys I wouldn't piss on if they were on fire.

There were bullet holes in the trees as I silently followed her trail, and nausea crept up on me. A sputtering noise came from up ahead, and a low moan of pain. Lying up against a tree, clutching a uniformed leg soaked with blood, was one of the tactical soldiers. I waited a beat to see if anyone was with him, but no one appeared.

I walked over to him and before he could react, held the barrel of my rifle against his forehead, under the tactical helmet.

"Where is she?" My voice was deadly quiet.

"Who the fuck are you?"

I kicked his wounded leg, and he screamed in pain. A small, dark part of me enjoyed it.

"You heard me."

"Gone," he gasped out. "Little bitch shot me. She ran that way."

He pointed east, and I moved my finger over the trigger.

"Hey, man, that's the truth!" he sputtered.

"I believe you," I answered, and executed him.

I headed east and discovered another soldier bleeding in the dirt, but he was dead, a bullet through his neck. *Good girl. Just like I taught you.*

I finally made it to a large clearing, where it became obvious that something had gone down. I followed the impressions in the grass to a spot right in front of a big oak tree. My stomach twisted as I spotted drying blood on the bark. It was about Claire's height, and though there was no blood anywhere else, I had to push down another swell of nausea.

Her pistol was on the ground by the tree, and that didn't help.

I kept pushing until I reached the edge of the forest, where it met the Old World highway. There were boot prints and drag marks in the dirt, and then fresh tire tracks on the crumbling asphalt. They'd had multiple vehicles. Any hope of catching them was gone...just like her.

I threw my rifle down and slammed my fist against the nearest tree, a shout of rage and horrible emptiness escaping from me. My knuckles came away bloody, but I didn't care. My chest heaved with every breath as I tried to calm down. Think rationally. Not fall into the trap of despair.

I headed back to the lake to investigate. I collected everything I could from the corpses I'd left behind, desperate for anything that might hint at where they were going.

Several of them had printed maps crumpled up in their packs, along with identical mission briefings from somewhere called the Delta. I didn't know where that was, and the maps didn't mark its location, but the area it highlighted was small enough that Kimmy and I could figure out where it was most likely to be based on where resources were—fresh water, hunting grounds, and the like.

They had working vehicles—something I'd never seen anyone besides the Valley have before. Except the cult...who had access to them because they came from a compound.

It stood to reason that this Delta was probably another one. That meant it'd be fortified and guarded better than anything I was used to. And no Claire to get me in this time.

I didn't want to go home. I wanted to follow their trail until I found my wife. The reality was, though, that I wouldn't catch them before they got to this Delta. I needed to prepare.

As I got ready to leave, I spotted something crumpled in the grass. The big white flower I'd put in Claire's hair, torn and crushed by the chaos. I knelt next to it and cradled it in my palm. I saw the flash of her sweet smile in my mind, and something inside me suddenly broke—just like that.

My hand clapped over my mouth. I tried to stop the ragged sounds of pain that broke through, but it was useless. For a long moment, I just stared at that stupid flower, lying broken in the palm of my hand. It was everything I'd been afraid of—the loss that was going to destroy me. In an instant, everything good in my world...gone.

My hand closed into a fist around the flower. *Get a grip.* I wasn't going to grieve her as if she was already dead. I had work to do. I stood and walked in the direction of the highway, hardened now by determination.

I'd get my girl back, or I wasn't coming back.

CHAPTER 48

John

H aunted.

That was what Summerhurst felt like that night. I couldn't sleep in my bed, where Claire and I had cuddled, slept, and made love. I couldn't stand to look around the room—*our* room—and see her things, lying exactly where she'd left them just a few days before. The closet was full of her clothes and her scent. The desk was covered with books she was reading, and lesson plans she was making, all in her neat, pretty handwriting.

The rest of the house was no better. The study was home to her art studio; her paintings hung on every wall; and the kitchen and living room were full of things she'd made and loved. When I told her that this was her home now, too, she'd taken me seriously. Every inch of this house held memories of her now.

At the same time, I didn't want to be anywhere else.

I sat on the floor at the foot of our bed, leaning back against the frame. Only the bedside lamp on Claire's side provided light. A half-empty whiskey bottle sat next to me. I stared blankly at the floor, twisting my wedding band around my finger, waiting for daybreak. I needed to rest for the long day ahead of me, but if drinking hadn't helped, I didn't think there was much hope.

A soft knock on the door made me look up. When I didn't answer, it opened, and Kimmy poked her head in. Her expression softened when she saw me.

"How you holding up?" she asked, gentler than I may've ever heard her sound.

I took a swig from the whiskey bottle. "Awesome. Thanks."

"Mind if I join?"

I shook my head and moved over so she could sit next to me. She took the bottle from me and took a swig of her own. Neither of us talked for a while.

"We'll find her," Kimmy finally said. "No matter what it takes."

"I know."

"It doesn't matter what they said at the council meeting, you know. Nearly three years ago, we left on our own and look what we accomplished. We can do it again."

I grunted and took another drink. I'd called an emergency council meeting when I got back. It hadn't gone well.

Even after everything I'd done—after everything Claire had done—nobody wanted to go with me to find her. Except Danny, but he was still in no shape to go anywhere. As soon as I told them that a compound was involved, everyone cowered. They were scared—for themselves and their families.

Some part of me totally understood. If someone had asked me to leave Claire behind and go on what might be a wild goose chase, I'd hesitate, too. But another part of me was angry. Angry because I'd risked everything—*everything*—for this place and its people, and when push came to shove, most of them wouldn't do the same for me when I needed it most.

Kimmy, of course, stuck by me the way she always did. She'd been the only person who always had my back...until I met Claire.

Oh, they'd all promised supplies. Food, clothing, ammunition, and survival gear had started arriving at the house as soon as the meeting ended. The Armstrongs, McNeils, and Hardings had promised to look after Summerhurst again while we were gone, which was no small amount of work, especially with the farm now running. I'd dropped Poppy off at the McNeils', who'd be caring for her while we were gone.

I sighed. *They're supportive in the ways they can be, I guess.*

"Last time," I said, "we weren't up against a fortified giant with way more resources and technology than us. Even I have to admit...it doesn't look good for us, Kim."

I took yet another drink. "But I have to try."

Kimmy squeezed my hand. "Of course you do—*we* do. We love her."

Her voice shook, and I squeezed my eyes shut.

"She did it to protect me," I croaked. "That's why she got taken. Every time I think about that, I feel sick. I failed her."

"Do you think you could've taken all of them on by yourself?"

I blew out a breath. "No."

Kimmy smiled sadly. "Then I think Claire was just doing what you would've done for her."

My chest ached, but I couldn't let the pain in. If I did, I'd be useless.

"Are you ready?" she asked after a moment.

"Yeah," I replied. "Everything's packed."

"Me too," she said. "First light, we can leave. But we both need sleep."

I snorted. "Good luck. What do you think I've been trying to do for the last hour?"

She squeezed my hand again. "I'll be right back, okay?"

I nodded. She disappeared for a few minutes, then came back with our sleeping bags in her arms. She spread them out next to each other on the floor by mine and Claire's bed.

"Let's try this," Kimmy said softly. "So you can feel close to her...but you don't have to sleep in the bed."

I swallowed hard. It was a rare gift to have two people in my life who always seemed to know what I needed.

I got into my sleeping bag, and Kimmy turned out the lamp before doing the same.

"Thank you," I whispered into the darkness.

"Anytime. I love you, John. I know I don't say it enough, but I do."

I didn't have it in me to respond, but she seemed to understand, because she kissed my cheek and turned over to sleep. And when I closed my eyes, sleep finally found me.

By the time dawn broke, I was already up. I'd made the last preparations for leaving, checked and double-checked everything, and Kimmy and I had saddled up Ghost and Bella for the long ride ahead. Now, we waited on the front porch for Danny and Jenna, who'd promised to see us off. We'd already said our goodbyes to everyone else after the council meeting.

When the wagon pulled up, though, it wasn't just Danny and Jenna in it. Noah and Isla were there, too, with baby Ely strapped to Isla's chest.

Isla pulled me into a one-armed hug, and the baby cooed in his wrap at her breast. I forced a painful smile.

"This is one of those times," I said, clearing my throat, "when I really hate you for cursing me, all those years ago."

She gave a watery laugh, stroking Ely's blonde head. "I'm sorry. But I gotta say, seeing you two at your wedding...I think it was worth it."

As I moved back, Noah gave me a nod of acknowledgement, which I figured was all I'd get from him. He'd always been a man of few words. So, it surprised me when he said, "Sorry I can't go with you. It's just—"

"It's okay, man," I interrupted, clapping him on the shoulder. "I get it. You've got a family to think about. Just...take care of them for me, alright?"

He nodded, putting an arm around Isla's shoulders. "Always."

I turned to Danny, who gave me a smile that looked as painful as my own.

"You still sure you don't want my help?" he asked with a forced chuckle. "Pretty sure I could take a few of them out with these." He made a swishing motion with his crutches, and I snorted.

"Absolutely not," Kimmy interrupted, folding her arms. "I did not set that leg just so that you could go and fuck it up again."

He shrugged, unbothered, in that typical Danny way. Jenna had been mostly quiet, but as we turned toward the horses, she caught my hand. Her bottom lip trembled as she looked at me. She suddenly looked so young—the way I always remembered her in my head, as a twelve-year-old girl.

"Just bring her back, okay?" she said in a near-whisper.

My throat tightened. "I will."

For the second time in my life, I left home behind without knowing when, or if, I'd ever be back.

❄

The forest was quiet.

We'd broken for lunch around noon, sitting by a small creek to eat and let the horses have a drink. The whole ride had been silent other than occasional navigation talks. We knew the general area we were headed, but not much more. We were loosely following an old logging road on our maps to get there, but it'd probably take a day or two on horseback.

When we set out again, I stared up at the grey sky. It'd been overcast all morning. Hopefully the sky wasn't about to open up and drench us.

The thought of rain triggered the memory of the first time Claire came to my bed. It'd been storming that night, the first time she kissed me. The first time I thought there was more between us than just basic attraction. The first time I thought maybe I could love her, if she let me.

Sunlight peeked through the clouds a moment later, and I was hit with the sound of her voice, singing to me in the flickering lantern light at my grandparents' grave.

I am the sun that shines.

I urged Ghost into a gallop, speeding ahead. I heard Kimmy's call of confusion, but I could hardly breathe. The forest felt like it was closing in on me.

I am the wind that sings.

I weaved Ghost through the trees, as though trying to outrun the haunting song in my head. I finally stopped in a clearing, panting heavily, as though I'd just run a mile.

I am everywhere and nowhere at all.

I waited for my heartbeat to slow down. Breathed through the pain that sliced through my chest every time I heard her voice in my head. Slowly, the sounds of the woods came back, and leaves rustled in the breeze.

Fate was a cold bitch, though, because at that moment, a bluebird landed on a nearby branch, tilting its head and twittering like the world hadn't already ended. Like there was reason to hope, when she'd taken all of them with her.

The agony of loss rose again, but alongside it, something else took root inside me: cold, calculated fury.

They'd stolen her from me. They would pay in blood. I'd set their whole world on fire and gladly watch it burn. They would suffer—from now until I had her back in my arms. I'd end all of them without a thought, without a regret. I smiled grimly.

I'd become their worst fucking nightmare: a Wastelander, a brutal and savage outsider, with no mercy and nothing left to lose.

***

END OF BOOK TWO

Acknowledgements

As always, my first acknowledgement must be my fantastic husband, Steven, who has always supported me 100% no matter what ridiculous thing I decide to do next, including treating being an indie author as a real job. Imagining amazing fictional men is much easier when I have one IRL. I love you!

I also have to thank my editor, Logan, and my group of incredible beta readers: Erin, Madi, Katelyn, Bethany, Mackenzee, and LaBrie James. Your care, attention, and feedback make me a better writer and your love of my characters and my world motivates me to create. Thank you.

I also have to thank my lovely friends—Emily, Erin, and Kate—for keeping me sane when I'm not writing (no easy feat). Thanks for sharing in the joys and sorrows of indie publishing with me, even when you undoubtedly wish I'd talk about something else for a change.

Thank you to everyone on my street team, who work hard to spread the word about my work to the world. You make marketing somewhat bearable for an introvert who's intimidated by social media.

And finally, to you, if you're reading this: none of this would be possible without you, whether you loudly shout about my books from the rooftops or quietly read them for your own enjoyment. Thank you for taking a chance on this unknown indie author, and for following John and Claire's story. I hope we'll both be here for the long haul.

About the Author

E.S. Luck is a copywriter by day and an author when no one is watching. When she's not writing post-apocalyptic romance that'll make you believe in love at the end of the world, she's reading all the books, petting her dog, drinking Coke Zero, or staring at her blinking cursor and having an existential crisis. She lives in Ontario, Canada with her husband and their adorable golden retriever, Rosie.

Visit her website at esluckauthor.com, or follow her on Instagram, Facebook, or TikTok.

Also by E.S. Luck

The Wastelander Series
Island (prequel)
The Wastelander
The Outsider
Third Wastelander Novel (Upcoming)